Up
&
Out

Ariella Papa

Up & Out

**RED
DRESS
INK**
™

First edition December 2003

UP & OUT

A Red Dress Ink novel

ISBN 0-373-25042-8

Visit Red Dress Ink at www.reddressink.com

Printed in U.S.A.

To Mr. Rogers for encouraging make-believe
and Mr. G. for encouraging me

Oh my goodness! I want to thank everybody that read and supported *On the Verge* and gave me the opportunity to do this again. I have the best bunch of friends and family ever and I am always in and down with them. So I would like to rethank all my last book's thank-yous for still being a part of my life and making sure all the people in your life knew about *On the Verge.* You rock.

I would like to thank Anthony and Daryl for opening up their apartment to workshops and laughter. Thanks to Joel and Kelly for tarts and faces. *Grazie* to Katie, my ceci princess. Thanks to Jason Hackermann for pulp in his juice and choosing a wife who is good with book titles. Thanks to the Greaney and Hackett families. To Jim for always making me sound good and learning my fave ukelele songs. Thanks to Alan for learning about makeup with me. Thanks to Appalachia, the best monkey ever. Thanks to Amy Lyn for working so hard and reading into characters the right way. Thanks to Meredith for sticking signing stickers like nobody's business. Thanks to Kim Leebowee for coffee breaks. Thanks to Kathy for shypoke stealing of sweet potato fries. Thanks to Lauryn for setting her alarm early and lite fm concerts. Thanks to Robin for providing North America with OTV. Thanks to Asabi, Erin, Jessica, Kelly, Rebecca and Roxy for closing the door and talking to me when I needed it. Thanks to Margaret Marbury for introducing me to the best part of having an editor: the lunches. Thanks to Irene Goodman for future endeavors.

I would really like to thank my caribou photographer for going to all Boston signings and doing the photo shoot. And *merci* to my prenatal editor for always helping me get where I need to be and knowing the best thing to do when you get fired, *franchement,* is go to France.

Mo' Money, Mo' Problems

I like to think of money in terms of the rock shrimp tempura at Nobu Next Door. When I take a cab, I think *that's about a third of a plate of tempura.* So I prefer the subway. Sometimes, I don't buy clothes because that's usually two to four plates' worth. I try not to think about my rent in those terms. That might make a girl lose her appetite.

New York City is filled with food. Everything from the beef-cheek ravioli at Babbo to the handmade hand-glazed all nat-ural doughnuts at Doughnut Plant. Don't even get me started on the loads of possibilities opening up to me every week in the "Dining In/Dining Out" section of the *New York Times.* It's almost too overwhelming for this foodie to bear.

So every two weeks I invite a friend out for rock shrimp tempura, always with the spicy, creamy sauce. It just sort of keeps things in perspective. In a city full of savory, tempting sub-stances, there's got to be one thing that's familiar.

But let me back up a bit. I was your typical working girl struggling to make ends meet and pay off my credit card and student loans. Next thing I knew, *On the Verge* magazine named

Esme, the character I had created and animated, a feminist icon for the tween generation.

Esme's Enlightenments was just a bunch of "interstitials," which were like short films that advertised Explore! Family, the channel where I worked. It is an upstart channel trying to make its way in the tough world of kids' TV. Unfortunately, the channel had no animated series at the time, but as soon as Esme got on the radar (and who would think anyone even read *On the Verge* magazine?), Hackett, the head of Programming, called me into his office and set unbelievable deadlines for me to get a legit episode produced. He wanted me to turn my sixty-second shorts into an actual TV show!

I loved my character, Esme. She may have been a bespectacled smart-aleck twelve-year-old, a glorified imaginary friend, but she was my baby. She was comfortable with herself and her smarts.

So, while I adored her, I couldn't believe other people liked Esme so much. And then I began to like her for more than what she represented. I liked her for fast-forwarding my career. Overnight I got a staff, a promotion, a fat raise and a haircut. I busted my ass to get the first twenty-two-minute episode of *Esme's Enlightenments* ready for the Upfront, where all the advertisers gathered for a presentation in the ballroom of the Waldorf Astoria. It was pomp and circumstance thinly disguising sales pitches. This is where the ad execs would lay their money down for the following season.

And boy did they lay their money down! Esme was a huge success. The network ordered a full season. The licensing department worked up all these plush Esme dolls and created an Esme board game and the advertisers spent their money as if there was no tomorrow. Hackett gave an inspiring speech about how Esme was going to help shape the future of the network. Even though she was a girl, she had tested well with boys, who thought she was a techhead. I felt tears coming to my contacts when he talked about how Esme had tons of possibilities, and it was all thanks to one young woman who believed. Me.

I stood up at my front table when Hackett pointed to me.

The spotlight shone on me and the camera plastered my smiling face on all the screens for even the back tables to see. I prayed I didn't have spinach in my teeth from the so-so chicken Florentine they had served at the luncheon. I got a huge round of applause. If my life were the movie I often wish it were, the credits could have rolled right then. Well, maybe after Tommy, my recently exed boyfriend (whom I still find time to have stress-relieving fantastic sex with), would have run down the aisle through the balloons and lifted me up into a freeze-frame, just like in *Dirty Dancing.* Then my movie audience could have left with the feel-good smiles that commercial blockbusters aim for. (Like many people who work in TV, I'm obsessed with movies.)

But Tommy didn't come and the credits didn't roll…even though it was a really great feeling. I still had to produce thirteen episodes of *Esme's Enlightenments* in a matter of months and I barely had time to breathe, much less properly blow out my new haircut.

The first few episodes of the series got exceptional ratings and press, but my work wasn't done. Another season was ordered. Now we are constantly rolling out new episodes, and that means late nights and ignoring some of the people I care about the most. And believe me, all the delivery food I can order in to my office doesn't exactly satisfy this food addict's jones.

But I am an adult and these are adult responsibilities and I have to deal, right?

So, I'm out for an every-other-week dinner at Nobu with my roommate, Lauryn. I barely see Lauryn with the hours I keep. When I arrive, she has already ordered a mango martini for me. We kiss hello and I take a bite of the dried piece of mango that comes with the drink.

"You seem very happy," I say. Since Lauryn realized her marriage to Jordan was really only a starter marriage and his ideas about commitment involved spending her money and sleeping with other women, she had become very bitter. It was nice to see her smile and not mention that I was twenty-five minutes late.

"Well, Rebecca, it's finally over."

"What?"

"My D-I-V-O-R-C-E became final today," she sings.

"Wow! That's great," I say. I'm not sure I really think so. I mean, we're barely twenty-seven and she is divorced, but I guess it's cool because she is happy and Jordan is a dick. I hold up my martini glass and clink it into hers and a little bit of our drinks spills.

We order our meals—we each get shiitake mushroom salads, and I order my usual rock shrimp tempura and she gets yellowtail sashimi with jalapeño. I approve, knowing I will be able to sneak a bite. I try not to associate with anyone who doesn't believe in sharing foods.

We get more drinks. I'm exhausted, but kind of enjoying just listening to Lauryn chatter about her day after going to her lawyer. She is telling me about all the birds in Central Park and how she had always been a closet birder.

Suddenly, I realize that Lauryn is telling me something big.

"Wait a second! What?"

"I'm quitting my job and going to study the feeding habits of piping plovers on Martha's Vineyard this summer. I'm also applying to get a Ph.D. in ecology in Boston."

"But, what about our apartment? Your apartment?"

"You can have it, if you want. I just figured you're never there and the lease is up in June, and you're probably moving back in with Tommy soon, anyway."

"Why? I'm not dating him anymore."

"But you're still sleeping with him."

"Three times!" I say, holding up my fingers. "Three times in five months. And they were all after extremely stressful days!"

"This city is full of stress," Lauryn says suddenly, strangely seeming at complete peace with herself. "That's why I'm moving out. Anyway, I think you're forgetting a few drunk dials."

"They were stressed-out drunk dials." She smiles at me. She has been more cheerful since starting therapy.

"You can keep it if you want. I bet you can afford it now with your promotion." The waitress sets my tempura down in front of me. For the first time ever, I'm not hungry for it. There is no way I can afford $2,100 a month and ever expect to see this plate in front of me again.

The next sip of my drink tastes more like vodka than mango and only one thought occurs to me: What if this were my last plate of rock shrimp tempura ever?

1

Debaser

Lauryn refused to say much more about what she planned to do. Back home, I questioned her about it as we were brushing our teeth in the bathroom, but she shook her head and said, "Listen, Rebecca. I know what you're going to say. I talked about it all with my therapist. We knew you'd have issues with me doing what's healthiest."

"What?"

"I don't want to have a conflict after we've both been drinking. I've come to a resolution that I feel is healthy and we can dialogue about it at a later date. Good night." She kissed me on the forehead and left the bathroom.

I liked her much better before she had started seeing her therapist. It was easier to deal with the bitter Lauryn than the Lauryn who started every sentence with "My therapist says…"

Lauryn's therapist lets her get away with a lot. She did seem happier tonight, though. Weird and slightly off the deep end, but happier.

She and I have known each other since first grade. We went to college within an hour of each other in Massachusetts. Jordan went to my college and was Tommy's best friend.

I had introduced the now ex Mr. and Mrs. at a kegger. At their wedding, I reminded everyone of that in a drunken toast. Of course, when things went sour, I hoped Lauryn would forget that I was responsible.

Lauryn used to be this incredibly funny girl before the marriage. She is tall and extremely thin. She could be a graceful Audrey Hepburn type, yet she has a way of scrunching up her face and using her body in hysterical ways. I haven't seen that side of her in a long time. Throughout her whole separation from Jordan, I never could tell what mood Lauryn was going to be in, but it was rarely a good mood. I missed her. I missed laughing so hard that my stomach hurt hours later.

It's midnight. I want to call Kathy or Beth to tell them Lauryn's moving out, but I'm exhausted from the week. It's only Wednesday. Kathy's probably already in bed with her fiancé, Ron. They've had five-minute sex and conked out. Beth is most likely with some of her music-industry friends dancing at a spot I haven't even heard of yet. She's got her cell phone on vibrate, so she won't miss the call from other VIPs. I'm not sure if I rank as a person she would answer a call for.

On the other hand, if I reach everyone, I'll be on the phone for hours. I need sleep. I decide to leave them what we like to call "a caffeine greeting" on their work voice mails: "You are not going to believe what the shrink has Lauryn doing this time. Call me in the a.m. and I'll give you the dirt."

I get into bed and try to imagine tomorrow. With all this production going on, I am starting to lose touch with Esme. I created her, but now my staff has had to take over. Janice and John are animating her and Jen has asked if she could write a couple of scripts. Tomorrow, I want to spend the day coming up with the concepts for the last five episodes of the season.

I think teen girls rule the world. When you think about it, they create all the trends. When you're a teenage girl, you're just forming, mentally and physically, and *everything* makes you who you are. I really want Esme to be the kind of girl you'd want to have for a best friend. The kind who's tough enough not to give a shit about the dumb things guys say and the kind you can trust with anything.

I wish I were more like Esme and not desperate to bust on Lauryn with my pals. I just need to get their take on it. I won't psychoanalyze too much.

Tomorrow I will spend some time with you, Esme. I will strive to be like you, I promise.

Two hours later I wish I had called the girls. Insomnia is something that started right around the time *Esme's Enlightenments* was made into a show. Now I spend my nights wondering about Esme's ratings and how to keep her plots interesting. I also rehash what the critics have to say when they pick apart my program. I don't get a lot of beauty sleep.

This whole year (since I found out last April that I had to produce episodes for the show) has flown by. I barely got a chance to lift my head up from my computer terminal.

When I finally pulled my nose up from the grindstone, there was the slightest change in my relationship with my friends. Sometimes everything was normal and I couldn't feel it, but other times it seemed we were all moving in different directions. When we moved to New York after college, we spent all this time together. We didn't really have any family around. The fact that we wound up in our group was one of those things that was either fate or an amazing and fortunate coincidence. I think friendship works like that—people just get pulled in.

Beth was my roommate in college. Thanks to Beth, I met Tommy, her brother and my ex-boyfriend. I introduced Beth to Lauryn. Kathy was Beth's cousin's roommate who looked up Lauryn when she moved to the city. We all just clicked and felt like we discovered this city together after college.

We each brought something to the group. Lauryn brought her funny physicality, Beth motivated the group to try new things—to go forth into the city as if we owned it—and Kathy was the practical one, the stylish one and the one who seemed to believe all of us were going somewhere.

I can't pinpoint the exact moment things changed and I can't say it was all because of how much time I spent at work. Maybe it was Lauryn, who had held us together all along. When she started spending days in her pajamas, crying over Jordan, we started hanging out less. Or maybe it was Kathy, going completely crazy over her fiancé, Ron. She kind of settled in with him, moved to the suburbs and decided her reason for being was to be the most beautiful bride in the tri-state area. None of us could have predicted that the girl who got all the best clothes at sample sales would be asking us to try on pewter bridesmaid dresses. But maybe we stopped hanging out as much when we stopped being able to keep up with Beth.

Beth didn't have to worry about insomnia. Most nights she passed out drunk, unless she had taken something to keep her up and partying all night. She had plenty of people to go with her to the hottest clubs now that she worked at the music studio. I found her new friends wild and intimidating. Although I think the changes in my relationship with Beth had a lot to do with Tommy and me breaking up.

We should have broken up a lot sooner. Part of the reason we stayed together so long was that we lived together. It's a sick joke that couples stay together in New York a lot longer than they should because of apartments. It sucks to find an apartment here. You overpay for spaces the size of closets.

The other part of the reason I stayed with Tommy so long was that I loved him. And I still kind of do. As hard as it is to find an apartment in New York, for me it's even harder to find a guy who gets me. Tommy got me. All my quirks and all my food addictions he enjoyed. He even managed to indulge me and talk about Esme like she was a real twelve-year-old.

But Tommy is also very immature. Dating an overgrown boy can be fun when you want to brainstorm about kids' TV but difficult when you want him to stop planning his life around sporting events and video games and start spending quality time with you.

In the end Tommy and I agreed to be friends and I moved

in with Lauryn, and now I was going to have to either find a new roommate or start the search again. Part of me can't quite give up on Tommy and me getting back together. And as soon as we agreed to be just friends we started having the sex we had stopped having in our relationship. Something about not really being together made it better. Is that sick? We always said each time would be the last time, but did it again anyway. It's as if neither of us can truly cut the cord. I still rely on him so much. I wish that moving back in with him wasn't one of the first things that came to mind when Lauryn said she was moving to Massachusetts.

I also wish Beth could be as okay about our breakup as Tommy and I pretend to be. I know she is protective of her brother, but I care about him, too, and she would never understand that.

Ugh. I hate insomnia. It forces you to think about all the things you try to avoid during the day. I don't want to put work into my relationships; I just want them to be normal.

I can't do this. It's almost 4:00 a.m. I need sleep. I will count sheep backward until it comes.

The radio is on. My favorite way to get up—listening to 1010 WINS. I can rely on them for weather and news and a slight (very slight) cynicism. No matter how loud I turn it up I always sleep right through it. It's 9:35. Not too bad. Most people in the business roll in way after ten. But, I am trying to go in early and set an example for my team. I don't want them to think that we can slack off now that the ratings are high. But at this rate, there is no way I am going to make it in early, much less take a shower.

I brush my teeth really quick, put my hair in a clip and pull on a comfy pair of jeans and a thin black sweater. There are dark circles under my eyes as usual, but I don't have time to do anything about it.

On the way to the subway, I stop at a quilted truck (the stainless steel panels are quilted). I always make time for coffee. The guy in the cart has my coffee and change ready when I get up to him. I come here every day for a cup of coffee with lots of milk and sugar, which will usually sustain me for a good two hours (depending on whether or not I went out the night before).

People always complain about how expensive things are in this city, but coffee off the street proves it all wrong. Does any other city have coffee this good for a mere fifty cents? And, if it's a really bad morning, I can throw in a buttered roll for fifty more cents. A steal.

I don't get a seat on the subway. There is a bit of humidity in the air. The city is about to cross the line from the crisp coolness of spring to the smelly oppression of summer. In a matter of weeks everyone on this train can count on being stinky and disgusting and we'll all just have to hold our noses and accept that it is summertime.

I stare up at an ad for the New York City Teaching Fellows. That's the program where they pay for your master's in education if you become a teacher in a tough inner-city school. The campaign is tight. Someone is obviously getting paid well to come up with these great inspiring slogans. This ad says, *"You remember your first-grade teacher's name. Who will remember yours?"*

Mrs. Gordon was my first-grade teacher. I think she was the first person to appreciate the essays I wrote on small pieces of yellow lined paper. I remember how she smelled like Fig Newtons and perfume when she leaned over my desk and said, "Rebecca, you're very creative."

I should give Esme more scenes at school. I'm always trying to think of ways of making her more real to kids. Maybe she can figure out who stole the class hamster. No, I've got to come up with something better.

Luckily, I don't have a long trip. The subway brings me a block from the Explore! offices in Midtown East. I hate this neighborhood. ARCADE, my last job—the first one I had out of college—was over on the far west side. I felt more comfortable around the truckers and transsexuals there than I do around the finance suits, who are ubiquitous in this neighborhood.

I go through a lengthy but halfhearted security check from one of the guards in the lobby. Once he's assured that I'm not carrying any explosives in my knockoff purse, I head up to our floor. I pass the giant poster of a spacecraft in the lobby. As I pass the kitchen, I realize I forgot to bring lunch, leftovers from two nights ago. Damn! Coffee may be cheap in this city, but lunch in Midtown is another story.

As I expected, Jen was in early. She is Hackett's niece and also the production coordinator for my team, the group that works on Esme. Jen is going places in this business and I'm not sure I'm the right person to be managing her.

"Good morning, Rebecca."

"What's up, Jen?" I expected (hoped) to hear "nothing," but Jen is a woman on top of things.

"Well, we have to go over the title test for episode seven with my un-Hackett at eleven. We've got a script meeting at twelve. There's a programming waste of time at one. Before you get any ideas we are required to be there. We really have to figure out the second segment of episode nine this afternoon. Oh yeah, a budget thing at four-thirty. And Janice has a dentist appointment she forgot about and John is running late because his electricity is out."

We smirk at each other. We strongly believe that our two animators, Janice and John, are an item. In a group of four it creates an interesting dynamic.

"Well, with any luck their morning will put them in an agreeable mood." Jen and I keep tabs on their relationship by observing how well they are able to work together. There were times it got downright ugly. "Did they say how late they would be?"

"They were both curiously evasive."

"Well, I'd like to have them around for the title test. Shit!" Already my day was sounding crappy.

"I'll call Meg and try and push it back." Meg is Hackett's assistant and I swear she runs the company.

"Thanks, Jen. I mean, I could do that if you want."

"No, it's fine. I think you should take a look at the scripts."

"Okay." I go to my office and shut the door.

I'm not really comfortable being in charge of a team. I have a hard enough time being responsible for myself, and now I control the livelihood of three people under me. I always feel strange when Jen does stuff for me. She keeps offering to fax things for me and do my expense reports, but I just can't handle that. It makes me feel helpless and worse, it makes me feel like a boss, which I guess I am.

I take a deep breath and stretch. I can do that because of my door. I always worked in a cube—and it was fine with me—but now I have an office, which means I have a door. A door is a very big deal. If I close it, I have my own little space. I can surf the Net for porn, listen to loud music, sniff my armpits or scratch my ass. I can do anything—if I can just find the time.

I also have a window. Granted, it's small and it looks right out at a brick wall, but it is a window. It's silly, but I'm proud of it. My mom cut hair in Pennsylvania and my dad worked in a factory. All their lives, they worked at the same place. They never seemed to believe that I made a living at what they thought was drawing. It seemed like no matter what I did, they didn't get it. And they still don't, even with Esme on TV. But, I bet if they saw my office, they would be proud.

Jen's number comes up on the display of my phone. "Hey."

"I pushed it back," she says. "Everything else is moved, too."

"So, I'll be a half hour behind all day."

"Right. Janice just walked in."

"So we can expect John in a respectable five minutes?"

"I'm sure he's circling the block as we speak," Jen comments. "Oh yeah, and you're going to the affiliate party tonight, right?"

"Shit, I forgot about it."

"I keep telling you to get a PalmPilot, but you insist on Luddite living."

"I'm not even sure what that means. Where's it at?"

"Party space at the Seaport. A trek and a half. I'll e-mail you."

"Seriously. I guess I have to go and schmooze with bald fatties from the Midwest." Pause. "Sorry." Jen was from Minnesota. "And I'm never going to have a chance to get home. I have nothing to wear."

"This is why we have H&M. I've got to go, Meg's on the other line. I'll see you in about twenty."

She has a point, but when would I find time to get to H&M? My phone rings again. Outside line. Should I pick up? Caller ID makes me scared of the phone. It could be someone I didn't want to talk to or it could be a solicitor. I take a chance.

"Rebecca Cole."

"Re, it's Beth."

"And Kathy." They are conference-calling me. They want details.

"Guys, I'm going to have a crazy day. I just found out I have a meeting in like fifteen minutes."

"We just need the broad strokes," Beth says a bit testily.

"Yeah, don't be such a corporate whore. Everything with Rebecca is urgent these days, have you noticed, Beth?"

"Yeah," Beth says. I can understand their interest, I just feel like I am playing beat the clock and won't have time to hash it out.

"Okay, the basics, and I got to be quick for real. Divorce is final." I start to hear them cut in with their opinions, but I have no time to analyze. "And the whammy, she is moving out of the city and up to Martha's Vineyard."

I can't resist pausing for effect. It is too unbelievable.

"Has she lost her mind?" Kathy asks.

"She's on antidepressants, I'm certain now," Beth says. Beth prefers dabbling in nonprescription drugs, but enjoys knowing that other people have similar needs.

"I know," I say. "I know."

I allow myself one more moment with them and then I have to be a productive bee and get off the phone. They want to know what I am going to do about the apartment, but I haven't decided yet.

"Don't forget we have to look at bridesmaids dresses this weekend," Kathy says. "Try not to plan a meeting."

I hang up as they laugh. I am certain they will stay on the

phone and talk about it. Kathy is an accountant and this is her slow time, and Beth works at a music studio, hence the trendy crowd. I long for the days when I spoke to my friends three times a day and tried not to laugh too loud in my cube.

I am too young to be nostalgic, but it seems to me that I was much happier when my day was filled with hushed gossip with my friends rather than bullshit meetings on the half hour.

My first meeting of the day doesn't go as well as I planned. Hackett claims to love what we did with the titles, yet he doesn't like the font size. This is something he could have told us three meetings ago. But, because he's the boss, he's allowed to interject opinions whenever it suits him. And we have to deal. Now we are going to have to re-render everything. Janice's smile fades, but I'm glad she is here to hear Hackett's comments. I don't want her to think these changes had been my oversight.

Janice and John go to work on fixing the problem. I hope their morning interlude was good so they don't mind working very hard—but not so good that they get distracted with details. Jen and I start on the scripts. I thought we were meeting with Hackett again, but he decided he had another, more important, meeting. That can only mean he is going to decide he doesn't like the scripts a few weeks from now when it will almost be too late to rewrite.

If only I could do everything, I could insure this shit didn't happen. It is hard to have a tiny bit of control, which in the end amounts to nothing.

"Rebecca Cole." I answer the phone while Jen is still in my office.

"Hey. It's Tommy." He must have talked to Jordan about Lauryn and wanted to see if I was okay about losing a roommate at my overpriced apartment.

"I'm fine." I don't want to stay on the phone long. Plus, I hate talking to him in front of people—it only leads to questions. "I'm not sure what I'm going to do about it yet."

"Right," he says. He doesn't really seem that concerned, after all. "I was wondering if you had my *Matrix* DVD."

I moved out almost a year ago, yet he constantly finds reasons to call me. At times, I am happily convinced he is still into me. At other times, I'm annoyed by it and want him to just leave me alone. Right now, I'm getting pissed that he's calling about his stuff and not my feelings.

"No. I don't. I would have found it by now. Check the hall closet. I bet it's in there." Jen looks up at me and then turns a page as if she's really intently reading the script copy. I lower my voice. "Did Jordan tell you about the divorce?"

"Yep."

"Well, did he tell you about Lauryn moving up to the Vineyard?"

"Uh-huh."

"Were you a little bit curious as to what I was going to do with the giant rent?"

"Well, I guess so." Herein lay the problem in our relationship. Sometimes we clicked and other times we needed a translator to communicate. I hear an electronic sound in the background. Tommy tries to cover it up by speaking really loud and fast. "So what *are* you going to do?"

"Are you playing Grand Theft Auto III right now?" I yell so loud Jen jumps. I can't believe him. You'd think he could focus for a five-minute phone call.

"Uh, yeah." I hang up on him. When we were dating, we promised never to hang up on each other, but now that we've broken up there are no rules. I smile at Jen. Her eyebrows rise over the pages she is reading.

"So, getting back to the scripts…" I say.

We are in a meeting actually called the War Room. I don't know who thought of that name, but it pretty much sets the tone for bloodshed. It happens every Thursday and it almost always lasts too long and accomplishes very little. Production and Programming duke it out about their priorities and resents one another and wastes the time that everyone needs.

Even the seating in the meeting is combative. The round table has too many chairs around it, so everyone bumps armrests and apologizes constantly. Programming stakes their claim early. I am always running late, but once I managed to show up fifteen minutes early and they were already there, plotting their means of attack.

This week the programming department has decided to be sour at me for not having all the scripts I was supposed to have. As punishment, they decide they need to preempt episodes of Esme for sporting events they seem to be making up on the spot. How can they know that the candlepin bowling championship is going to happen on the day the episode airs where Esme figures out who vandalized the library? Jen tries to argue with them, but I shake my head. They are Programming, they can do anything. They confidently sip their coffees knowing they have people at *TV Guide* on speed dial.

Eventually, the programmers grow tired of toying with us and decide to attack Don Beckford, the producer of another new show, *Gus and the Gopher.*

"Yeah, we're completely on schedule," Don says. "There's no way we won't have thirteen eps ready to roll out in September. There was an article on the type of animation we'll be using in *Tyke TV* magazine. Did anyone see it?"

Don is handsome in a way that is not completely trustworthy. He is in a constant frenetic state. He practically bounces when he talks and he always has a way of selling his show. (I kind of admire him.) He also refers to the trade rags a lot. Who has time to read the latest issue of whatever stupid magazine the industry puts out to pat itself on the back? Not me.

But the programmers did and they loved to brag about it—but today they aren't taking it. Cheryl, who has some position of imagined power and a haircut to go with it, clears her throat.

"You may have the animated aspects intact, but you don't have a live action host yet. The show is called *Gus and the Gopher.* Without Gus, it's just a gopher."

"Right," Don says. He is preparing to use a lot of words to say nothing. "Well, we are in the process of casting at this point. The animation is going to be a lot harder to deal with than the host."

"Can we see who you've narrowed it down to?" Cheryl asks. She definitely has an attitude.

"I really don't feel comfortable sharing that with you yet, but I can assure you we've narrowed it down to three terrific personalities. They are going to be like nothing kids have ever seen." They are doing a complicated dance. Don was hired away from the Cranium Network to create a kids' show that looked like all the ones he had already produced for Cranium. No one seemed to notice or want to admit that *Gus and the Gopher* sounded a lot like *Bob in the Barn* and *Amy's Animal Adventures.*

"Well, get us a tape as soon as you can," Cheryl says. Programming always wants a tape.

"Well, I have a three o'clock," Sarah says. She is another programming henchman. "I think that's all for today."

We file out of the conference room. I race to the bathroom on my floor. All the programmers will be in theirs. The problem with seeing them in the bathroom is that they try to talk about work and get you to agree to do things for them when you just want to pee in peace.

It's almost three o'clock and I still haven't had lunch. I have a four-thirty meeting and I was supposed to complete segment two of episode ten so Janice and John could work on it. We have a process of getting episodes in and approved, so we can start doing the voice-over. I don't want to be the one to get us off schedule. I also have to get something to wear tonight.

I grab some free coffee in the kitchen and add a ton of sugar. I open one of my drawers looking for a snack or a fabulous outfit I forgot about. I find some microwave popcorn and the spare pair of underwear I keep in my desk, just in case. (There haven't really been any "cases" lately.)

I bring the popcorn into the kitchen and start making notes on the script while it heats up. Jen wrote this script and I'm impressed. I like getting a fresh perspective on Esme. It was hard for me to accept that other people were giving her a voice, or a look, like Janice and John have been doing with their animations of her.

"Hey, you." I look up to see Claire Wylini, Director of Production Budgets, smiling at me. She is so flaky; Miss Nice-Nice—until you go a dollar over budget. Then she stops smiling.

"Hi." She points to the clock.

"It's almost time for our meeting." She speaks in the singsong voice you might use to talk to a preschooler. She has a four-year-old and a two-year-old and each of them has their *own* nanny. Her children give her a certain amount of credibility.

People who work for kids' TV are always trying to figure out ways into the minds of children. It's kind of sick. Of course the further up the ladder you move the less in touch you are with kids. People tout that childlike creativity, but basically we're adults trying to sell a product. Anyone in children's television who has kids likes to reference them constantly. It's some sort of badge of honor. They feel that their opinion is always correct and defend it with things like, "Well, my five-year-old would love that." I suspect that some people have kids as a type of business insurance.

"Oh, yeah. I'll be there. Just finishing up a script. Popcorn?" I hold the bag out to her and shake it.

"No, thanks. You're sweet. Okay. I'll see you in the meeting."

"Okay, see you. Bye-bye." *Bye fucking bye?* I'm even talking like her. Who am I turning into? The day is mostly over and I haven't done anything but go to meetings and comment on other people's work. I've created nothing. I've done nothing.

Jen pokes her head in. "Mmm, that smells good." She grabs a handful of popcorn. "Oh, you're reading my script. How is it?"

"Really good. You did a terrific job. I only have a few more notes to make." She grimaces. "Not big things, just continuity. We got to get to the meeting."

After two more unproductive meetings I leave work to get something to wear. The crowd at H&M is horrendous, as usual. I weave through the tourists and club kids and find a see-through shirt with flower designs. I grab a tank and black pants. It's a good thing I wore black shoes today.

The pants are too tight, even though they should be my size. I have to go back to the floor where hip-hop is blasting. It's getting more and more crowded as people get out of work. Of course, the only other sizes of the pants I want are four and six. A preteen grabs a pair of the fours. Another reason teen girls rule the world—slim hips.

I bypass the skirts. I can't deal with tights and my legs are stubbly (hey, I'm not dating anyone). I find more pants. These look like they would be even tighter. They don't have any pockets in back, my butt is going to be huge. I take my size and the sizes one and two up from mine. I don't want to think about how high into the double digits I am getting. I have no time to go to the gym, and besides, I hate going to the gym.

Now there is a line for the dressing room. I look at my watch. I'm never going to make it. I split the difference and grab the pants that were a size above mine. If they don't fit I might as well just call it quits, anyway. I also grab a sweater, just because it's cheap and I continuously laugh in the face of my increasing debt. The more I make, the more I spend. I still have college loans.

I take a cab down to the Seaport to save time. With traffic, it costs me an outrageous sixteen bucks—one whole plate of tempura. I'll expense it. There is a pizza shop nearby. I smile at the guy behind the counter and ask if I can use the bathroom.

"It's supposed to be for customers only." I can tell he is going to let me, anyway, but I am quite hungry and it smells good in here. I haven't eaten all day except for a couple of handfuls of popcorn.

"Okay, maybe I'll grab a couple of garlic knots."

I go to the bathroom while he heats them up. It's not the best place to change, but I have no choice. The mirror is tiny, so I don't get the full impact of my butt.

The guy behind the counter whistles when I come out of the bathroom. I smile, because he doesn't seem too lecherous. I pay for the knots and eat them quickly at the counter.

"Well?" pizza man says.

"Delicious," I say, licking my fingers. I notice the way he is watching me and I grab a napkin.

"You like that, you should try our pizza." It smells good, but hors d'oeuvres will be passed at the party. Nobody skimps on the affiliates.

"Some other time," I say.

"Have fun," he calls after me. "Don't party too hard."

When I get to the Seaport space, I check my bag of clothes immediately. The room is big and swanky. Someone has gone a bit crazy draping white fabric and rose petals over every solid surface. There are waiters with tall flutes of champagne on trays. I grab one and take a quick peek at my watch. Only twenty-two minutes late. Not too bad. I spot Hackett across the room. He waves me over. I down the champagne and get a vodka gimlet from the bar before making my way through the crowd. I need to take the edge off. On the way I eat two small potatoes with cream cheese and caviar and baby beef Wellington. God, I love food.

"There she is. Here's Becky," Hackett says. He puts his arm around me. (Did I mention I hate to be called Becky? Hackett's the only one who does it.) "She's the girl behind Esme."

I wish he'd said "woman," but who am I to split hairs? I stand in the same place for the rest of the night and meet people and eat whatever appetizer comes my way. There is great food, but I can't even enjoy it because I'm too busy being nice to everyone. Every time I'm introduced to someone new, I only really hear the wait staff introduce the appetizers.

"Rebecca, this is Mike Jasse from Boston."

"Salmon and cream cheese on black bread."

"Let me introduce you to Louisa Siciliano from Baltimore."

"Olive tapenade on toast."

"You have to meet Cindy Betti from the Des Moines office."

"Some coconut shrimp."

I have the same conversation with everyone and because I am standing with Hackett, people come and bring us drinks. I want to go over and talk to Janice, John or Jen, but every time I finish talking to one person there is someone else to meet. Everyone says complimentary things to me about Esme. I smile and blush a lot.

Do you ever have the feeling like you don't belong somewhere? Like no matter how nice people are being, they're eventually going to find out that you are in way over your head? That's what I kept feeling when people said how much they liked Esme and how happy I must be. The more I drank and ate the more I felt like a big faker. What the hell was I doing? Was Esme or I worth all this praise? I couldn't help feeling that any minute it was all going to end.

I keep looking over my shoulder. I keep waiting for that person to come over and escort me out and say, "Rebecca Cole, you big faker, you don't really think you're the star of the show, do you?"

"Who are you looking for, Becky?" Hackett asks. "Why, here's Ellie Egher all the way from Denver…."

By the end of the night, I think I have met and attempted to charm every affiliate in the entire country. Hackett finally ran off for a moment and I look around for my team but can't find anyone. Then, I feel a hand on my shoulder. The "they" I'd been dreading has finally caught up with me. This is it. I am out.

I take a deep breath and turn around. I knew it all had to end eventually. What I see is the biggest, most beautiful woman I have ever seen.

"Hi. I'm Tabitha Milton," she says. "I heard you were the girl to meet."

2

Raspberry Swirl

"Hi," I say, shaking her extended hand. She is balancing a plateful of cheese and bread in her other hand. She has a firm grip and that intimidates me. "Your name sounds familiar."

"Yeah, I founded *On the Verge* magazine."

"Oh, my goodness, hey. Thanks for the great article on Esme."

"Congrats on the series."

"Thanks. It's a little overwhelming."

"Oh, you should never admit to being overwhelmed. That's how they get you. You should always be closing."

"Isn't that a sales term?"

"Yeah, but we're all in sales one way or another." A waiter comes over with another tray of champagne. Tabitha takes a glass, so I do, too.

"I guess you're right."

"Believe me, I am."

"So what are you selling?"

"Well, I'm not actually here to sell. I came with a date. He's the affiliate from L.A." She gestures over to a big muscular guy standing in a crowd.

"Wow."

"Yeah," she says. "He's Samoan. We met on the Internet. It's just a fling."

I'm not sure why she is telling me this, but I'm thinking that maybe I should look into one of those Internet dating services. It was getting harder to find decent single (straight) men in the city.

"I have a new venture in addition to the magazine. Underwear."

"Underwear? Like skivvies?"

"Yeah. Would you wear my underwear?"

"Um." She doesn't wait for me to answer. She hands me her plate, sets her empty glass down on a passing tray and fishes a pair of lace panties out of her bag. They are packaged quite nicely.

"Tabitha's Taboos," I say, reading the ribbon.

"That's right. I find it makes a great gift for your man, too. I encourage you to regift them. Thank you." She grabs another glass of champagne off another tray. She moves fast, but gracefully.

"Well, thanks."

"No problem." She takes a big bite of bread and cheese. "Ugh. Fats and carbos. Nothing makes me feel more alive, except of course…"

I know what she means. I have to laugh. I am beginning to feel drunk and I'm not sure if it is all the champagne or her.

"It's almost time for me to go." She is still eyeing her man and it looks like he is looking at her, too. "It's been very nice meeting you. Good luck with everything."

"Thanks—and thanks for the underwear. Good luck with all your stuff, too."

I say my goodbyes to Hackett and Jen. Janice and John have already left. I get a cab right away. It's twelve-thirty. I keep thinking of Tabitha. She didn't seem like many other women I meet. I envy her confidence. She is one of those people who just believes what they say and doesn't care whether or not you do. I have to start being more confident. Maybe I will give Esme a friend named Tabitha.

I creep into my apartment quietly. There is a note on my bedroom door saying that Tommy has called. Lauryn made one of those winking happy faces that people do over e-mail. Fuck Tommy. He'll be sorry when I meet my Samoan over the Net. Then he can have his Grand Theft Auto III all to himself.

In the morning I got to the office early. Not even Jen was there yet. The phone rang before I had a chance to hang up my jacket.

"Rebecca Cole."

"Rebecca, hi. It's Paul Perry. How are you?" Paul was one of the freelance designers who used to work for the kids' block on ARCADE when I was the production assistant there. There could be only one reason he is calling: he wants work.

"Hi, Paul. How are things?" I wonder how long he will make small talk before getting to the point. He isn't a bad guy, but we aren't friends and I know he just wants a connection at Explore!

"Oh, terrific. Things are wonderful." He begins to list a bunch of projects he's been working on. I think about interrupting him and just asking him to send me his résumé reel instead of giving me this laundry list. He compliments me on Esme and drops some trade rag references.

"Is it absolutely insane over there?" This is a trick question. I have to answer carefully.

"Sometimes." Does he think I don't know where he is going with this?

"Well, I was thinking maybe I could help alleviate some of that stress. You know I'm freelance now? Cranium TV had all those layoffs. Par for the course in this business." He does a little fake chuckle. It seems odd to me that he is acting like we were equals when I used to be so junior compared to him.

"I guess so."

"So is there any work over at Explore!?" Finally.

"Well, Paul. Why don't you send me your reel?" It is kind of a brush-off, but, as he must have expected, "par for the course in this business." He could send me his video résumé and feel like something was happening. "We're not really hiring right now."

He is disappointed, but I take all his information. He makes me promise to call him if anything comes up. Kids' TV is cutthroat, he explains, and we have to look out for each other. Then he says something really strange.

"Any truth to the rumor Explore! is for sale?"

"Um," I am caught completely off guard. I should read the trades more, but I am in my own little Esme world. "I don't know anything about that."

"Well, be careful, Rebecca, ride the wave."

"Thanks, Paul. Good luck." People are so melodramatic about things in business. It's obnoxious, but you have to placate them.

I began work trying to plot out a segment with Esme's new chubby friend, Tabitha. Janice stops in my office when she gets in, the aroma of her coffee filling my office.

"Who's that?" she asks.

"I thought it was time we gave Esme a little friend. You ducked out of the party early last night." I can tell by the way she looks at me she thinks I'm playing boss. I'm not, so I try to joke. "You're lucky. It was really stuffy and Hackett made me talk to all these suits."

"You *are* the It Girl of Explore! Network." We laugh.

"So did John leave early, too?" I raise my eyebrows. I wish she would just come clean about the two of them, but I guess she's trying to be professional.

"Um, I guess so. Do we have anything big happening today?"

"As opposed to the usual grind? I just have the music people calling with the score for ep eight."

"Cool. I'll stop in later to see how it went." She leaves, still revealing nothing. The phone rings again. It's Lauryn. She sounds pissed.

"Rebecca, are you hiring Jordan for something?"

"What? No."

"He called me to tell me that he was making big changes and that he was going to be on your channel. He always has to one-up me. What's this about?"

"Well, as you know, he's full of shit. I have no idea what he's talking about."

"You sure he's not one of your voices or something?" Jordan, her ex, is a waiter who wants to be an actor and who's constantly bugging me for an in. Unfortunately, I don't work with live action.

"No, Lauryn, relax. I thought you were cool about all of this."

"I was, but I don't need Jordan rubbing shit in my face. And by the way, Beth called and I don't appreciate you guys discussing my life."

"Lauryn, calm down. How many times have you discussed my life or Beth's or anyone's?"

"Whatever." I look up to see Don Beckford standing in my doorway.

"Listen," I change my voice to make it seem as though I'm a nice person and not an exasperated friend. "I'll call you back."

"Whatever." She hangs up. (If she were on antidepressants, like Beth is convinced, you'd think she'd be a lot nicer.)

"Okay, bye. Thanks." I say to the dial tone. I don't want Don Beckford to think people hang up on me. "Hello, Don."

"Hey, Rebecca." Don was so damn jolly all the time. "Is this a bad time? I can come back."

"No, what's up?"

"I wanted to get your feedback on something." Really? Don wants my feedback on something, one seasoned producer to another? Nice.

"Sure."

"Jordan Barsotti." I open my mouth and shut it.

"What about him?"

"Of course you know he's one of our finals for the live actor who will interact with Gus." So that's what Lauryn meant, "Gus the Gopher."

"Of course." Shit! What? Does he want my feedback on him? Does he want to hear what a dick he is? How he has a gambling problem, uses drugs more than recreationally and treated his wife like shit? Maybe I should tell Don that one time Jordan grabbed my ass at a party (I never told Lauryn or Tommy) and how it still makes me sick whenever I think about him.

"I figured you'd be happy to hear about it. He said you guys were good friends."

"Well, the thing is, I feel like I never get to see my friends anymore with this show." Not a lie exactly. What a position to be in.

"Tell me about it. What friends?" He laughs like Paul Perry had earlier. "But, can you see him as Gus?"

Before the divorce I had seen Jordan play everything from *Hamlet* to Stanley Kowalski to the guy inside a sandwich board. Now he would be acting with a blue screen that would later be a gopher.

"Absolutely," I say. Playing second fiddle to an imaginary gopher might be enough revenge for Lauryn. "He *is* Gus."

"Terrific. See you later, Becky." Now that I've helped him he thinks it's okay to call me Becky. I hate that. "Hey, great coverage on the premiere episodes."

"Thanks." He probably knows all about the fact that we are up for sale. I need another coffee.

At four o'clock Tommy calls me with "great" news. Jordan is Gus. He acts like I hadn't hung up on him yesterday or like Jordan isn't an asshole as far as I am concerned. I hear Tommy talking to a woman in the background. He comes back on the phone.

"Who was that?" I ask, trying not to sound as interested as I am.

"I'm at the store."

"What store?"

"Didn't I tell you? I got a job."

"A job. You already have a job." When Tommy was laid off from his dot.com gig, it was still early enough for him to get a sweet severance deal. He used his money to start a Web site that appeals to guys like him who buy and sell comic books, video games and the paraphernalia that went with it. It is small and independent, but has a cult following.

"That's not really bringing the money in. I'm almost through my savings. Rent's a little more expensive these days." I'm not sure if I should be pissed about the dig or feel sorry for him that his dream isn't exactly going as planned.

"So where are you working?"

"The video store on Ninth, you know, where we used to go." Oh, that one. "It's not bad at all. I get to watch movies all day. I get a deal on game rentals and when it's slow I do a little writing."

"I see."

"Anyway, I should go. So you okay about Lauryn going to the Vineyard?" Finally some concern.

"What can I do? If she's happy, I'm happy."

"Right, well if you—" He stopped. I waited. "Tell her I said…congrats. Maybe she and Jordan can finally move on with things now."

"Maybe," I say, and wait again. I'm not giving in to this today. If he has something to say, I'm not going to extract it. "Okay, well I'll talk to you."

"Yeah, take care." And we hang up. No definite plans made. No nothing. That's the way it is now. It has been a month since we last slept together and now we are just getting off the phone like two acquaintances. I don't know when this is going to get easier.

Today turned out to be another wash. I barely got started on the segment I was working on and the people who were composing our score had gone slapstick instead of zany. Now we had to wait another week at least for music. Nobody listened. Instead of meetings, I spent the day on the phone.

It's now five o'clock, and it looks like it's going to be another late night if I hope to accomplish anything. Friday of all nights. I'm to meet the girls for dinner and drinks. My computer dings and I open an e-mail about a meeting in our large theater at five-thirty. Does it ever stop? The meeting is to be global, which means that the entire company, including the L.A. office, is going to attend. My phone rings again—Janice.

"Is it true? Have we been bought?"

"I don't know. This e-mail is so cryptic."

"I bet Jen knows."

"You think?"

"Well, I know she's not going to tell me." That is my cue. I go out to their workstations. Janice and John are already standing up and peeking out over their cubes at Jen, who is whispering on the phone.

"I got to go," she says when she sees me. I am relieved to see that she makes personal calls at work, although maybe this signifies how serious this meeting is going to be. "What's up, Rebecca?"

"You tell us," John says. It must sort of suck for Jen to be related to a big shot like Hackett. Everyone kind of resents you, no matter how well you do your job.

"Do you know anything about what we're meeting about?" I ask. Jen looks a little nervous. That's the other sucky thing. No one really wants to give you any dirt, but they expect it from you.

"The meeting's in fifteen minutes," she says, gesturing toward her computer.

"So, that means you know," Janice says.

"Okay, if you can't tell us you can't tell us." I look at Janice. I want to know, too. Bad. But I have to be the good cop. "We'll find out soon."

We all head to the meeting together. Most of our floor seems empty. Jen doesn't say a word throughout our odyssey to the elevator banks. When we get to the theater (which is like a small stadium), it is packed. They hand us chocolate chip cookies as we go in. Janice, John and I look at one another. Only John says what we are all thinking.

"This means it's bad," he says, holding up the cookie. "I'm getting another one."

Hackett is up on stage with the rest of the honchos, including Kristina Amos. She is the VP of the whole shebang and the head of the New York office. She's one of those women who always looks put together. She is at least fifty. But we love the sight of her. We love to dish about her.

"Hello, everyone," Amos says after a little microphone feedback. "We're going to keep this short because we know it's the end of the day."

"Not for us," Janice says.

"We hope everyone's enjoying their cookies." Now they expect us to be grateful that they are leading us to slaughter. She starts talking the typical shit they talk at these meetings and I can tell it isn't going to be quick. If it is good news, they wouldn't have waited until the end of the day. Of course, they are trying to act like it is. Amos blabs about how hard everyone has been working, how ad sales are doing as well as they can in this economy, blah, blah, blah…

"Of course we know that often the best way to get revenue up is to partner with someone who already has capital and whose brand initiatives are parallel to your own."

"Do you think she really means parallel?" Janice whispers to me. "Don't you think that would be bad?"

I shake my head. Amos is still working up the benefits of having what she is calling an industry giant.

"I hope the industry giant is Prescott Nelson Inc.," John whispers. "They're getting into TV, and have you ever been to the Nook, their cafeteria? It's great."

"So, we've decided—and I think you'll all agree that it was the wisest decision—" as if we had any kind of choice "—to align ourselves with Indiana Mutual. You can rest assured that this move will be beneficial to everyone's future and fiscally responsible for the brand. Have a good night."

That was it. They got off the stage. They didn't take questions. They didn't say who was going to get fired or what the hell they were thinking. They just announced the merger and ran. Nobody in the audience moved. We were all in shock. I took a deep breath and looked at my team. Janice shook her head, John was picking and eating the cookie crumbs off his pants, and Jen looked like she was going to cry.

"Did I hear what I think I heard?" someone in front of me asks. "You mean to tell me that we are a television company and we just got bought by a bank?"

3

32 Flavors

I was late to meet the girls, as usual. And it didn't help that the directions Beth left on my voice mail didn't make any sense to me. I wandered my way around the West Village, which can be the most confusing place on earth and finally found the restaurant they were at, Poor Man.

"She made it in under an hour, this time," Beth says. "That's quite an improvement, isn't it, ladies?"

All my friends were convinced that Esme was based on them. Kathy knew Esme was her because of the glasses. She never fell for the "men don't make passes at women with glasses" bullshit and more than once convinced me to spend far too much money in Selima. Selima is the funkiest eyeglasses shop in the city. One look behind their glass cases and I was hooked. Beth thought it was her because she was sure that Esme was Portuguese like her and Tommy. And of course, Lauryn was certain that Esme's detective skills were derivative of her discoveries of Jordan's money troubles and infidelities.

The girls are already sloshed. They've been filling up on bread and booze. Kathy is dressed up the most. Her nights away from the fiancé are becoming more of an event, and she is more put together than she used to be. Beth looks like a hip, cold New Yorker, and Lauryn seems to be working some New Age thing with an Indian-print shirt and no makeup.

"I'm sorry. We got bought today—I mean, Explore! did." I sit down and order a gimlet from the waiter.

"By who?" Lauryn asks. I tell them the whole story and explain how I had to stay at work late, not working but rehashing with my co-workers, except Jen, who left as soon as she could. I tell them all the theories people had, and Kathy gives me some anecdotes about corporate takeovers that depress me. The waiter comes over, his presence admonishing me for being late and not looking at the menu.

"You guys order, I'll be last." I like menus. I like to travel around the city and look in restaurant windows to see what they offer and decide what I would get if I ever went there. I like to be prepared. Lately, I'm always rushing to order something, so my friends could be a little less mad at me for always being late. I'm doing that now, trying to hurry up and figure out what to get.

I had, of course, read the review of Poor Man online at Zagats and Citysearch. I also saw the write-up a week and a half ago in the *Times*'s "Dining In/Dining Out." I had done some research, but looking at a complete menu was a different story.

"And for you?" the waiter asks. My time is up. This restaurant is supposed to celebrate the food of the poor in various countries yet with an "upscale twist." That twist is apparently the price.

"I'll take…" I am still scanning the menu, desperate. Fuck! I need more time. "Um…"

"Oh, boy," Kathy says, giggling.

"I'm thinking about…" What do I want?

"Here we go," Beth says, sounding bitter.

"Okay, I think I'll have…" Wait! Should I get a starter? Of course I should. But, what?

"She does this all the time," Lauryn explains to the waiter. She might have been flirting.

"Okay, I just have a question," I say. They all groan. "No, seriously. I want to ask you, sir. What do you recommend? The *puttanesca* or the mutton pie?"

"The mutton pie."

"Really." I look back at the menu. I'm still not sure.

"Rebecca!" they shout.

"Okay, okay. I'll get the dandelion salad and the mutton pie." I hope I am making the right decision. I hate commitment.

"Good choice," the waiter comments. He reaches for my menu and it takes me a second to let go. Lauryn orders another round.

"You're ridiculous," Beth says to me when he's gone.

"So, okay," Kathy leans into the table, gesturing us all to do so. "How hot is the waiter?"

Ever since Kathy got engaged she feels she has to prove she is still one of us. She constantly punctuates our outings with cries of "girls' night out!" and she is always checking out guys. She is more obvious than Beth, who is the single one. No wait, so are Lauryn and I. I keep forgetting that we are also unattached. I'm still not used to it. When will I be? Kathy talks tough, but when we are out and any of these men approaches us, she holds up her giant ring and sings, "I'm taken, I'm taken."

"He's okay," Beth says.

"Not really my type," Lauryn adds. The next round arrives and we get another look at our waiter.

"He's cute," I tell Kathy, and wink. She winks back through her glasses.

"So are you ladies ready for Sunday?" She claps her hands. Our starters come just as she does this, so we are momentarily rescued from indulging in wedding talk. But Kathy is tenacious and goes right back to it after we each have a few bites.

"So you guys have to remember to bring your strapless bras to the store on Sunday." After six excruciating trips to bridal shops around the city and two in Connecticut with Kathy's pregnant, domineering sister, we have narrowed it down to five bridesmaid looks. Kathy swore she would make a decision this Sunday.

"You got it," Beth says, curtly. Something has definitely made its home in her ass. Kathy looks hurt. She sees us so rarely and hardly ever in nonwedding-related occasions. She needs to feel she is still a respected part of the group. Of course she is, but she is very sensitive about it.

"It'll be fine," Lauryn says, sensing this. She smiles at Kathy. It is the most positive thing she has ever said about the wedding. Kathy had the luck to get engaged just as Lauryn left Jordan.

I take a piece of the rustic bread and mop up my dressing. I know Kathy is concerned about my belly, but I don't care. I was voting for the strapless empire-waist dress. I might soon be answering to a bank teller. Bread might be my only joy. I ask the waiter for more when he clears our starters. Lauryn orders another round.

"So, do you still have that date this weekend?" Kathy asks me. I put my piece of bread back on the dish.

"Oh," I say, remembering what day it is. "I guess I do. I mean, he said he would call when he got back from Napa."

"Yeah, I told them. I forgot to tell you," Lauryn says. "He left you a message."

"Lauryn said he sounded sexy," Kathy says.

"He is. I can't believe he called."

"How did you meet this guy again?" Beth asks, nonplussed. She's from southeastern Massachusetts and she's taking this cold New Yorker act a little bit too seriously.

"I met him at jury duty." I had spent twenty grueling days as a Supreme Court juror for New York State. (Okay seventeen days. I had two excused absences and one religious—ha!—observance.) I was juror number three, he was juror number nine. His name was Seamus and we had done a lot of flirting before the end of our session. From what I remember, he has nice teeth and had some job relating to food. It sounded too good to be true.

"What are you guys going to do?" Kathy asks. I look at Lauryn.

"He just said he hoped you were still on, he didn't say for what."

"I know for what," Kathy says, and does an awkward little shake at the table. She is beginning to remind me of the way I felt about my mom when I was a teenager. Is that what happens when you get engaged?

"She's not even sure he's straight," Beth says. I'm about to fling my leftover bread at her, but our food comes.

We stuff ourselves for a while on mediocre food. (At least my meal was mediocre.) The pie dough and lamb fat would have been delicious if someone had bothered to warm it up. It was greasy, and since this place has been contrived by someone who had no idea what poor people are like, I only had thin paper napkins to wipe off my face.

Kathy's French peasant sausage dish was just plain bad, but she acted like she didn't notice. Beth's perogies were good, but twice the price they would be in the East Village. Lauryn's jerk goat was the best. We opt out of dessert.

When the check comes, it's outrageous. As usual, we doubled the price of our meals with our bar tab. I knew then why they called this place Poor Man. Lauryn wobbles a little when she stands up. I grab her arm.

"Thanks, I think it's the antibiotics I'm on." I look over at Beth. She doesn't meet my eye. "I think I might pass on another bar, guys."

"I'm definitely going to pass," Beth says. "I'm meeting up with this guy from work."

"Rebecca?" Kathy says.

"Um, maybe I should go back with Lauryn."

"Don't worry about me," Lauryn says. She looks a little flushed.

"Do you want to sleep over?" I ask Kathy.

"How nice, a slumber party," Beth says. She pushes her chair out. "I'll see you guys on Sunday. Have fun on your date, Rebecca."

I'm certain she didn't mean it. She leaves the restaurant. I sort of shrug at Kathy.

"No, thanks, Rebecca. I told Ron I wouldn't stay out too late." I picture her going back and cuddling with him, and feel a pang of jealousy. My night of intimacy will be checking on Lauryn at regular intervals.

We share a cab. Kathy drops us at our apartment near the Flatiron Building and continues on to Grand Central Station.

"Are you okay, Lauryn?" I ask from outside the bathroom. There are some bad sounds coming from in there.

"I'm fine, Re. Just need to wash up and have some water. Have a good night." My bladder is set to burst, but I don't think I want to go in there. I hold it, and go to my empty bed. I've had just enough to drink to pass out and not think about being in bed alone.

The phone is ringing. It is Saturday and someone is calling at ten o'clock. I am not one of those people who seize the day. Not on the weekend. Who the hell is calling? If it's a telemarketer, she's going to get a piece of my mind.

"Hello," I say to the devil on the phone.

"Is that Rebecca?" The voice is vaguely recognizable. Male. Strange.

"Yes."

"It's Seamus. Hello. Did I wake you?"

"No." I sit up in bed. "Not at all. I've been up for…hours."

"Oh, yeah. It's a great day, isn't it? It's really spring."

"Yes, great." I like the sound of his voice.

"So are we still on for today?"

"Absolutely." Uh-oh. That might have been a little too I-haven't-had-a-date-in-three-years eager. I clear my throat. "Yes, if you're free."

"Yep. I was thinking of a few ideas. I just had my run, but I was thinking since it's so lovely out we could meet up and bike around Manhattan and then maybe head over the bridge and go to Grimaldi's."

Pizza good. Exercise bad. Is he serious? Does he realize it is Saturday? I may be getting desperate, yes, but not that desperate. I don't even own a bike.

"Or we could go to Esca for dinner," he says. Sweat or fish? The choice seems obvious. I'm not even sure I understand the question. I'm too tired to be thinking about this. I have to just be honest with him. I don't want to start a relationship based on dishonesty.

"I've been having trouble with my…" I don't even know what parts are in a bicycle. Gear? Seat? In one of Lauryn's manic moments a telemarketer had preyed upon her. She had a mini breakdown and because he was so kind to her, she agreed to subscribe to magazines like *Field & Stream* and *Bicycle Boy*. If only I had read them, instead of ridiculing her when the mailbox was stuffed. "…tire. And I have a lot of work to do."

"Oh, yeah, your TV series. How's that going?" He remembers. How sweet. He is wonderful and I am a low-down, lying ho.

"It's terrific. Actually, it's been really busy. I have a lot of work to do today, unfortunately. I'll have to take a rain check on that bike ride." Let's get through an evening together first, bud, then we'll see where we go from there.

"That's too bad. I took the liberty of making reservations at Esca." Bless this man. He might just see me sweat before he could say *fresh sardine*.

"Cool." We make plans to meet at the restaurant. Kathy would tell me never to meet at a restaurant, to always be picked up, but I didn't necessarily want to land a guy like Kathy's fiancé, Ron.

I finally go to the bathroom, then go back to bed for another two hours of blissful sleep. It is my Saturday. I earned it.

When I finally wake up, Lauryn has bagels and coffee. She's feeling better. I ask her what medicine she was taking to make her have such a bad reaction to alcohol. I am expecting her to tell me something about allergy medicine. I'm wrong.

"Well, Rebecca, my doctor prescribed some antidepressants." I can't believe it. She's being honest, coming clean. She is just admitting it. "I don't know if you realized, but I've been feeling a little, well, bummed about the whole Jordan thing, and my therapist thought I should see someone who could help me with medication."

"Oh. Well, how come you never told me?"

"I don't know. I guess I was worried you guys would all be worried about me. Maybe I didn't want you all to talk."

"We wouldn't have done that." I am the worst friend ever. We *were* doing that. Now that Lauryn is being so honest, I feel guilty.

"I know," she says. "If you ever want to know about anything, you could just ask. I'm still getting used to this stuff, so I should probably take a break from drinking for a while. Not to be lame, but I think it's the right idea. It's part of the reason I'm moving out of New York. I need a break from this lifestyle."

"I can see that."

"Thanks, Rebecca. I'm sorry about the way I've been to everyone since this whole crazy thing." She looks like she might start crying. I hug her. "Honestly, I'm feeling better and I appreciate your concern."

I decide to tell her about Jordan becoming Gus of *Gus and the Gopher.* Instead of being pissy about it she just laughs and insinuates that he'd be hitting on the gopher by the first episode.

"Honestly, I think I'm coming to a place where I'll wish him well. Today at least. But keep your eye on him." It's amazing she can be so okay about it. I guess the medicine is working. I feel kind of weird talking about this with her. I worry that her mood will turn dark any minute. "So, do you want to go get pedicures? Sandal season is upon us and you have a date tonight."

I sure do, and I have to admit I'm relieved not to be talking about Jordan with her anymore.

I make it to the restaurant on time. I hate my hair. It seems to have grown out of the cut I spent too much money on. Now it is too long for short hair and too unhealthy for long hair. Plus, the red highlights I added when I got my promotion have grown out, revealing my nothing brown underneath. My clothes have failed me, too. The outfit I bought for the affiliate party smelled like an ashtray and my old standby black "sex shirt" stretched unflatteringly across my chest. So I'm wearing this loose deep red silk button-down that I borrowed from Lauryn who borrowed it from Beth. I doubt it fits me as well as either of them.

I have some things on my side. My nails, toes and fingers look damn good and I have recently shaved my armpits. I'm not saying Seamus is going to see them—but it's sort of an insurance policy.

I don't think I've conveyed how much I like food. You know I like restaurants, but did you know I read recipes for fun and watch the Food Network when I can't sleep? I love that there is a network of mostly men cooking for insomniacs like me. I have a huge crush on one of the British chefs with a show, Jamie Oliver, but it's really Mario Batali, *Molto Mario,* who gets me salivating with his fresh Italian dishes. Esca is his restaurant.

I can't say what I am more excited about—a possible glimpse of Mario, or of Seamus, who I remember as being a little sexpot. Then I see Seamus sitting at the bar, by the crabs. He is a *big* sexpot. He gives me a look that says, in spite of my bad hair, I might still have it.

He gets off his stool and kisses me on the cheek.

"Hi." He gestures to the glass case and smirks. "Crabs?"

I laugh. He's confident enough to make a bad joke and trust that I'll get it.

"I know," he says, "never on the first date. They're setting up our table. Do you want something at the bar?"

"Yeah." I'm about to tell him I want a gimlet, but he's already ordered something from the bar. It's a dark drink. It tastes different, but good.

"You like it?"

"Yes, it's weird."

"It's liquor made out of artichokes. It's one of my favorites. This bartender does it really well." I am enjoying this already. We're at the bar, having a drink, and soon we'll have a delicious meal. He acts as into the food as I am. This is what it is to date in New York. Tommy thought going out like this was a waste of time and money. His idea of romance was going to the movies or trying to get me to play strip PlayStation. I am pioneering new territory: an adult man, with an adult job.

"What do you do again?" I ask when we're sitting at our table. It's clear that the maître d' knows him by name.

"I'm a wine distributor to restaurants. Mostly Italian wine, occasionally Californian."

"So, you must eat a lot of good meals."

"I do." He smiles. I forgot how nice his teeth are. "Do you like to eat out?"

I'm not sure if this is a trick question, or innuendo or what. "I like to go out to eat."

"Cool."

He encourages me to get a *primo* and a *secondo*. He doesn't seem to want to accept that I wouldn't be able to eat a first and second course. I order the spaghetti with tuna belly followed by the grilled octopus. It's a lot of food, but I can't resist the chickpea *crostini* that comes to the table. Because they know Seamus, we also get an appetizer of soft shell crab.

I can't help making comparisons in my head. With Tommy, there was this kind of shorthand between us, where we could just hang out and not talk. Seamus has an intense, well-crafted opinion on everything. I am a little intimidated about expressing myself. I nod at him and try to figure out what the hell he is talking about. He keeps throwing matter-of-fact statements at me.

"I think you're going to appreciate this wine. It is, dare I say, rousing."

"That movie had merit, but at times, didn't you find the music a bit too invasive?"

"Loved the CD, but his whole string obsession was downright jarring, don't you think?"

I'm not sure if I should agree or disagree. I'm not sure how I feel. I haven't thought about a lot of these things. Not having an opinion seems worse than either possibility. If I am going to get into this dating thing, I guess I have to start having opinions. I'm not going to find a guy like Tommy, who has experienced everything with me already. It is "dare I say," daunting.

"Do you like your spaghetti?" he asks.

"I think so." He grins. I feel more confident. "Yes, absolutely."

"You know I forgot your eyes were green."

"Thank you. I mean, you did?" I'm not an asshole, really I'm not.

"Yeah, they're lovely. You're welcome. Do you want to try my pasta?" Yes! Yes! Yes! I nod. I think I am really attracted to him. I can stand behind that opinion. "Can I try yours?"

We switch. I watch him taste my pasta, paranoid he'll hate it and declare my palate "downright immature." He chews, closing his eyes.

"Pepperoncino," he says. "You can really taste it."

He is one of those. Kathy's fiancé, Ron, is one of those. It must be indigenous to the New York male. They like to identify every ingredient in what they think is a good meal. He opens his eyes. They weren't so bad, either.

"I like you," he says. "I can't wait to try your fish." Of course. The place is called Esca, after all. That means bait.

4

Moon Child

We are back at Seamus's place. We are drinking wine—one of his favorites. He is telling me something about tannins. I think. He is saying things like "jumps in your mouth," and I'm not quite sure what we are talking about. I am beginning to feel like he doesn't need me to be a part of the discussion, like he has already determined how the whole conversation should go and I'm his audience.

I like wine, but I don't think I ever drank wine to this extent. My chest feels hot and I know my cheeks are red. He keeps stopping to rub my cheeks. I'm not sure what to say and I think if I stand too close to him, we might end up making out. In spite of the wine and my clean armpits, I'm not sure that's what I want.

"You've got cute feet," he says. Finally, I am clear on what he's saying. The new sandals are killing me, and I've taken my shoes off. If the room wasn't lit by candlelight, he would see the red welts that were forming on my feet.

"Thanks," I say. I get up off the couch and go to look at the pictures on the mantel of his nonworking fireplace. He has a nice place. My apartment still looks like a college pad, with all the hand-me-downs that I have had for years. He has new furniture that he picked out himself. His decorating has a theme.

"Those are my grandparents," he says, coming behind me, close. I am holding an old-fashioned black-and-white picture of a couple. "In Ireland."

"Oh. Is this Ireland?" I point to one of his many landscape pictures.

"No," he laughs. "That's Chianti, from last spring. You would love it there this time of year."

"Oh." I move a bit away from him to the window, which looks out onto Barrow Street. Jen lives on Barrow. "You know, I think this woman I work with lives on this block. She might even live in this building."

"Amazing." He follows me to the window and rubs my back. It feels good, but I'm still not sure what I want. I shouldn't have come back with him. I stiffen. He senses it and takes my glass. "I'll get you more wine."

"Are you trying to get me drunk?" I ask when he is far enough away.

"A little." He sits back on the couch and holds my glass out. I join him, leaving some space between us. "So what are your plans for tomorrow?"

"I have to go bridesmaid shopping with my friends."

"Oh," he raises his eyebrow. "Are you all up and getting married?"

"It seems that way. I mean, I don't want to get married. My roommate is actually already divorced. This is for my friend Kathy. I'm dreading it—we've looked at so many dresses already. It's such a racket. And my friend Beth is going and she's been such a pain in the ass lately. I used to date her brother and now—" I am babbling. Why am I bringing Tommy into this? I'm going to ruin everything.

"Weird," he adds.

"Yeah. Everything's been weird."

"What do you mean?" The wine was definitely affecting me. I feel something, stoned, I don't know. I'm not sure I want to even think about this, much less talk about it, but now it is too late. If I don't talk, I'll probably do something stupid, like give him a blow job.

"My friends, it's just like we can't connect." I stare at my hands. Lauryn and I did have fun getting our nails done today, but when was the last time that happened? "We were so close and now it's like, Lauryn's moving away, Beth's got an attitude and Kathy—I swear it's like she's trying so hard at what should be natural. It's fucked."

"Well, what are you, twenty-five?"

"Twenty-seven, thanks."

"I think things get weird with friends when everyone starts getting married. Then you wind up having less and less in common and the people you see more are the ones you work with. You've still got your good friends, but you find it's harder to plan shit with them, but you get used to it."

"I'm not sure I want to. I like them. They're my girls."

"Your backup."

"Yeah, they got my back." We smile at each other. For the first time, I feel like he is listening. "So, how did you get to be so wise? What are you, twenty-eight?"

"Thirty-one, thanks. So this guy, this brother of the friend, when did that end?" I shake my head. I can hear Kathy telling me that whatever I do, I am *not* to talk about an ex.

"It ended a while ago. I would say a year, but officially six months." He doesn't need to know about all the relapses.

"So, you're over him?"

"Yeah." Granted, I thought I was many times before, but he doesn't need to know about that, either. Does he?

"Good." He takes the wineglass out of my hand and sets it on the coffee table. I see the kiss coming, but it still feels strange when it happens.

"So how was your date last night?" Kathy asks when we're on the subway to Queens. We had to hit the outer boroughs to get the best deal on dresses. Kathy claims she is thinking of us, but, honestly, time is also money. We are all looking pretty tired and I'm still a bit off. "Did you already give Lauryn the details?"

"Not yet," Lauryn says. Beth is supposed to meet us there, she made this last-minute change by leaving a message on Kathy's cell.

"Well, it was interesting." The train is pretty crowded and only Kathy has a seat. I dread telling tales on the train, I feel like I'm going to get caught. I give them the dirt on dinner, which they tolerate politely.

"I heard you come in late, though," Lauryn says. "What happened next?" I fill them in on his amazing place, leaving out my musings on them, of course. By the last stop in Manhattan we get to sit together. Kathy moves over so I can be in the center.

"So, did you kiss him?" she asks. She is getting really excited.

"I did," I say, looking up at a sign in Spanish for help with STDs.

"Did you fuck him?" Lauryn asks, following my eyes.

"Oh, I hope you used a condom," Kathy says, like a health teacher.

"Relax, all. The box stayed closed."

"Really?" Lauryn asks.

"Was he a good kisser?" Kathy asks.

"You guys, it was strange. He is a good kisser, but I haven't kissed anyone else in so long it feels weird. I kept opening my eyes to make sure it was really happening. Kissing is a strange thing, and kissing someone new is downright scary." Lauryn shakes her head and Kathy makes a little "humph" sound and smiles in a way that I interpret to mean, *thank God, I'll never have to kiss anyone else. I have found my soul mate unlike my pathetic friends.*

"Did he kiss you anywhere else?" Lauryn asks.

"Laur—" Kathy yells. Then she lowers her voice and her eyes. "Well, did he?"

"Um, yeah. Somehow, he maneuvered me down on the couch and his hands were everywhere. He opened up the buttons on my shirt. My chest was so hot, I think from the wine. It felt good. Except his nibbling—I'm used to biting. Tommy used to play this game, too. Tease me until I would scream 'Bite me!' Of course, I couldn't do this with a new guy because he might think I am a freak."

"That is pretty freaky," Kathy says. "I didn't know you were into that. It's almost like S and M."

"A light bite never hurt anyone," Lauryn says, coming to my defense. "No judgments. Continue."

"And he is talking a lot. He's moaning and saying 'yes.' I'm used to making all the noise. It's sort of funny, although I don't want to laugh. You can't laugh—that would be the worst."

"You definitely can't laugh," Lauryn says.

"They're very sensitive about that stuff," Kathy adds, from what I gather is experience. "Then what happened?"

What do I tell them? I pulled his face up to me and he smiled. His cheeks were flushed, too. He kissed me again. *Okay, this is good,* I remember thinking. *I can do this. I can do this. I am single. I am not dating Tommy anymore. It's not weird that my boobies are all over the place or that I've had too much wine.* I know what I'll tell them. They want the good stuff.

"'All the protein makes me so hot for you,' he says." My friends are howling. "Okay, that's weird. But in the heat of the moment, people say weird things. He likes food, I like food. Protein is in food. That's fine.

"Then he starts working his way down. Okay, this is good, I think. I like this. He looked pretty expert with those crab legs, I'm sure it's going to be fine," I reason.

"I'll say," Lauryn says, elbowing me. It's almost our stop.

"Wait! He started grabbing my ass. I don't think Tommy ever—"

"Oh, fuck! I can't believe you," Kathy says.

"Tell me about it. I'm retarded. 'I can't do this,' I say, sitting up. He looks up at me. My lipstick is all over his face. I shouldn't see him like this yet. I barely know him."

"What did he say?" Lauryn asks.

"'What? Wait. Relax. Are you okay?' 'I'm fine,' I say. 'I'm just—I need to go. I can't stay.' At this point I'm buttoning up my shirt. 'I'm sorry. I'll call you.'"

"You can't call him," Kathy says.

"Shh!" says Lauryn. We are getting off the subway.

"I know. I couldn't find my sandals. My bra was all twisted because he didn't take it off. It's impossible to get a cab at that time of night on Barrow Street."

"Barrow Street's nice," Kathy says.

"Shh! What did he say?"

"Well, he ran out of the room and I thought maybe he was going to get psycho or something."

"Did he?" Kathy is horrified.

"No, he came back with the leftover pasta I got from Esca."

"That's funny," Lauryn says.

"And thoughtful," Kathy adds.

"I know. I felt like a big loser. I kept saying I was going to call him, but I can't."

"Sure you can," Lauryn says.

"No, you can't," Kathy counters.

"Do you have any idea where we are going?" Lauryn says to Kathy, who shoots her a look. "I can't believe you're still so into Tommy."

"I know," Kathy says.

"I'm not. I mean. I didn't think I was. It's just I sort of forgot, you know, what it's like. I mean, I can't believe I'm going to have to be with a guy you know, like that, again. It seems so weird. You know, all the sounds, the messiness, the general awkwardness."

"The fucking, the fun," Kathy says.

"The orgasms," Lauryn adds.

"The cuddling," Kathy says cutely. Lauryn and I roll our eyes.

"I miss all that stuff, I do. I want it. But the getting to it is just so strange. What if I can't?"

"You can," Lauryn insists.

"You have to," Kathy adds.

"I wish I could go out and just pull like we used to, you know?" Lauryn nods, Kathy makes that stupid settled-down face again.

We are finally at the bridal shop. No sign of Beth. There are women waiting to assist us, to pin us and maneuver us and stand in the room while we change. There was no more talk of my disastrous date and there was no sign of Beth.

"Where the hell is she?" Kathy says for the third time. She is obsessively looking at her cell phone. "This isn't like her."

Finally, Lauryn checks her cell and there is a message from Beth saying she isn't feeling well and can't make it. It was calculated. What the hell was her problem?

"I can't believe she would do this. How could she? Now we have to come back," Kathy says, on the verge of tears. Lauryn and I exchange looks. We are not doing another bridesmaid day. We have to draw the line.

"Look, Kathy. She can't help being sick." What she could help was playing cell phone games. "She said we should just pick whatever dress we like and she'll go with it."

"But then, we'll never know how it looks on her." Kathy is usually so confident in her style and decisions, but when it comes to the wedding, she is a wreck. I can't take it anymore. I have tried on every dress in every color. I've had more seamstresses see my tits than I choose to remember. I am not leaving this store without a decision. I will boycott the wedding if necessary.

"Listen, Kathy." I decide to be calm. "We know how all these dresses look on her in various colors and styles. I really don't think we should wait any longer."

"Yeah," Lauryn says. She's going to work with me. "We don't want to get to a point where we wait too long and the dresses can't be ready for the wedding."

Nice job, Lauryn. She's playing on Kathy's constant fears.

"Exactly," I say. "Let's just get this one."

Kathy finally agrees to get the red dress with spaghetti straps and a low-back empire waist. I know Beth was against thin straps, but that is her problem. She likes red the best, so she will have to deal. Besides, Kathy's sister, Dina, was going to pick out thin jackets or wraps for us to wear in the church.

"Crisis averted," Lauryn whispers while Kathy harasses the salespeople about when the dresses will be done.

"I just couldn't, Lauryn," I say. "I could not."

"I know. Just think, we'll only have to come here a minimum of two more times for fittings."

"Yippee."

I have no idea how I'm going to get through the rest of this wedding planning, let alone the wedding itself.

Since we are already in Queens, I figure it's only natural to take advantage of some of the indigenous cuisine.

"Are either of you guys in the mood for some Greek in Astoria or Indian in Jackson Heights?"

"Actually, I'm supposed to be having dinner with Ron tonight. I promised I'd make him lasagna." As if she didn't see him every night. I think about trying to rally her with a "girls' night," but I'm sure she is anxious to gush to him about the color of the dresses. I doubt Ron can really keep up her level of enthusiasm.

"How about you, Lauryn?"

But, no, Lauryn has decided to spend her Sunday night at Barnes & Noble to do some research on her bird stuff. Our cable is out, so I'm destined for a night of reheated leftovers and lying on the couch with Esme scripts.

At home, I'm lonely. I realize we never got to finish our conversation on the train. Back in the day, we used to spend Sundays together rehashing the weekend, no matter what we did. Sometimes we met up late Saturday night and got dirty sandwiches from a bodega and crashed at whoever's house.

None of us cared about work. None of us had serious issues. There was no drama. We didn't hope to get each other's voice mail. We wanted to talk. We didn't even have cell phones.

Tomorrow, I have to go in and deal with everyone else's shit about the takeover. Who knows if I'll even have a job? I can't call Tommy. I'm scared to call Seamus. I laid enough shit on him last night and then ran out with no shoes on. He must think I'm the biggest freak. Fuck!

I am going to bed early. That's how I'll forget it all. I remember the vibrator the girls bought me as a joke when I moved out of Tommy's place. It's nine-thirty. The bookstore closes at eleven. No, I shouldn't. I'll feel even lonelier. If only the *X-Files* was still on. I am going to call Tommy. Damn it, I'm not even drunk. There is no good reason to call him. It would be an obvious booty call. I pick up the phone. I dial the first few numbers. I can't. I won't.

But we used to have such great Sundays. We were both closet *X-Files* geeks. We had a routine: sex, bong hits and *X-Files*. We would watch the new episode and then one classic from Tommy's DVD collection. Afterward, I'd make us ice-cream sundaes. *That* was the perfect Sunday. Now I'm reduced to the hot-pink wonder wand and leftover pasta. With any luck, I'll find some NyQuil in the bathroom cabinet. I suck.

Whenever I feel this low, I comfort myself with something Tommy said on one of those nights. It's become bittersweet, but at this point, I'll try anything. We watched the *X-Files*— the one about the androgynous guy who is a sexual dynamo. He seems to be part of a religious cult, but then it turns out they're all aliens and they leave the planet. Oh, the *X-Files* had some knockout writing in the early days. Anyway, in my special little memory we were eating our ice cream.

"So," I said. "What if I were from another planet?"

"You are from another planet."

"No, Tommy, seriously."

"Oh, are you being serious now?" He leaned over and kissed me with cold lips. I didn't budge. "Okay, what if you were from another planet?"

"What would you do?" He shrugged. "Come on, you feed me weed—this is what you get!"

"Okay, okay. I'd be like, 'Cool, my girlfriend's an alien.' What could I do?"

"What if I wanted you to come back with me?"

"To your planet?" I nodded. "Is it safe for Earthlings?"

"If you're with me."

"If you really were an alien and you really wanted me to come back to your planet, then I would. That's good enough for me."

"Even if there was no ice cream?" He shrugged. "Or no *X-Files?* Or no weed?"

"There would be you. I'd think, 'This girl is cool, top-notch. She's an alien, but as long as I can survive on the planet and she's not already betrothed to a Klingon, what more do I need?'"

That was a very good night. And even though we aren't together anymore, it's nice to think that at some point in my life there was someone who would have come to my planet, just for me. I know I'm getting past my prime. I have blown my shot with Tommy...and now Seamus.

I get up and go to my bureau. I dig deep into the bottom of my underwear drawer and find it. It practically glows. I turn it on and shut my bedroom door. I pray Lauryn stays at the bookstore until eleven. I'll hear her come in. I hope.

I just want to feel something good. Desperate times call for desperate measures.

5

Shitloads of Money

I get to work at nine-thirty. There are signs all over our floor redirecting us to the theater. Didn't we already go through this Friday afternoon?

We aren't allowed into the theater, but in the lobby of the theater they have set up breakfast stations. Now, it isn't the usual cold bagels and quasi-molding cream cheese. Somebody actually went to some trouble. There are French pastries, giant doughnuts and bagels in all flavors. Wait a minute! Do I see lox? I do. If they are trying to buy me, it's beginning to work. The only thing that could have sealed the deal was an omelet station. And maybe some bacon or French toast. Okay, it could always be better, but this was a start.

I look around for my teammates or anyone I know, but seeing mostly the type of people that came in early (and therefore not the people who work on creating the programs), I go to work on fixing the most amazing bagel with lox and cream cheese ever. There are even fresh lemons to squeeze on top. I smell decent coffee brewing. Of course, I have to get a doughnut. How will I balance it all?

"Rebecca." It is Janice and John, making their way to me. I

have the coffee, but I will have to sacrifice the doughnut. I hope there will be pastries left over when we get out of whatever harm is going to befall us.

"Hi, guys." I try to avoid looking at the quiche that someone is just putting out. "You guys are here early."

"We decided it would be a good idea to get in early today," John says.

"Yeah, funny how we both came to that conclusion and ran into each other on the subway," Janice says, obviously correcting him. If only they keep talking, I'll be able to eat my way around the table. If the powers that be are going to do a mass termination, at least they could offer Tupperware.

"Well, it was smart you guys got here early—you know what they say about banker's hours." If anyone dares to leave at six, we accuse them of keeping banker's hours, a set day that has an end. I take a quick, desperate bite of my bagel masterpiece.

"How can you even eat at a time like this?" Janice asks. I thought she knew me better by now. The truth is I can always eat. Luckily, John comes to my defense, so I get another bite in.

"We might as well take advantage while we can, hon." I pretend not to hear the "hon" and bite the overhanging salmon off my bagel.

"I'm thinking Zabar's," I say to John, who is getting the evil eye from Janice for the term of endearment. "Have either of you seen Jen?"

They shake their heads. At that very moment the doors to the theater open. John curses.

"Now I won't have time for breakfast." Out of the corner of my eye, I see him stare at the other half of my bagel. Now, I'll do a lot for my team, but there is no way I am sharing smoked salmon of this quality—Zabar's smoked salmon—with him. To be sure, I lick a little of the cream cheese off that half.

"We can save you a seat, John," Janice says. I nod.

"Do you guys want anything?" Janice, the iron-willed, shakes her head.

"Maybe just one of those baby brioches," I say. "If you don't mind."

We herd in with the rest. The big screen is down. Now we are going to be watching movies?

"How long do you think this is going to last?" Janice asks.

"I don't know, but I have deadlines." A graphic for Indiana Mutual came up on the screen. John returns and hands me a big brioche.

"Sorry, Rebecca, this is all they had left." He winks at me. There is the usual sound of feedback. This time, instead of being as horrified as we usually are, everyone gets quiet. A middle-aged man with a beer belly and a nice suit is standing at the podium.

"Hello, everyone, my name is Cobb Michaels." Did he say Cobb? "I am the president of Indiana Mutual Worldwide. We are so excited about this partnership and thought it would be great if we all took a day to get to know the company we're all going to be working for." A day? A whole day? I look at Janice and John and they shrug.

For the next three hours, we watch tape after poorly produced tape of propaganda about the diverse and profitable ventures that fall under the Indiana Mutual umbrella. Their motto is something dumb, as in, "Saving for you." I can't believe this is really necessary.

"The graphics are horrible," Janice whispers.

"Quiet, infidels," John says, smiling. I swear they are going to kiss. I'm not sure if I have more of a problem with being brainwashed or being seated next to the top-secret-but-not-really couple.

Various heads of various departments come up to the podium to introduce themselves and discuss how much they love working for Indiana Mutual. I wonder if they realize that Explore! is an entertainment company. That we wear jeans and read *Entertainment Weekly*. I wonder whose awful idea this is.

"Hey, guys," I hear someone whisper behind us. Don Beckford. "I got pulled out of a production shoot for this."

Now there is another snooze at the podium—a woman. She is talking about what a great fit our brands will be.

"We've got a really fantastic afternoon planned for you after lunch, and to give you a little idea, take a look at this. I think you'll recognize the client."

The lights go dim. It starts as a commercial in a bank. When the bank teller calls "next" she has trouble seeing the customer. Then we all see the customer and my mouth drops open. I turn to look at Janice and John and they are also in shock. My eyes must be deceiving me, I can't, I just can't believe this is happening. The red onions I lovingly placed on my bagel start to repeat on me. It is Esme, with a different voice, poorly animated, asking a teller to open a banking account. It is a strange thirty seconds. During the spot, I think time is standing still, and afterward I can't believe it has really happened. My only proof of what I might have seen is the way Janice reaches out her hand to squeeze my shoulder. My tongue feels thick. *My Esme* is being prostituted to promote a bank. *What?*

"They must have stolen the animation test we did when she goes to get ice cream." I appreciate that Janice has tried to crack how they did it. It is very Esme of her to play detective. But my real concern is why? And how often will it happen?

"They've got an awful voice-over, that's for sure," John says. "Rebecca, are you all right?"

I don't know what to say. The lights come up and the media guru who benignly ruined my creation comes back to the podium.

"Okay, everyone, enjoy your lunch, but save your energy, we've got a big afternoon ahead of us." That is our cue to leave the theater. I can't move.

"Rebecca, come on, let's get lunch," John says.

"Hey, Becky, great job—way to get in with the big guys." Don Beckford again. I finally speak.

"If you think I had anything to do with that travesty, you're mistaken." I don't mean to sound so snotty. It is one thing to lose a little control of Esme, but this is beyond that. She is hawking savings accounts. Is nothing sacred?

"Why not?" Don Beckford asks. "I can only dream they'd like the Gopher that much."

"I wish they would, too. Let the Gopher open a bank account." I say this really loud, I am sure of it, but I am pissed. I don't want Esme to be overexposed. I don't want people to make decisions about her without me.

"Lunch, Rebecca, *let's get lunch,*" Janice says, leading me out of the theater. "Calm down."

"How can I?"

"It was just a mock-up, they would never air that."

"Maybe not that one, but how do you even think they got the animation?" I look at her and John.

"We have no idea, but you need to relax."

Our lunch is a far cry from breakfast. It is all a sick joke. We get soggy sandwiches and an apple. I don't say a word the entire time. I'm certain that Janice and John would have preferred to eat alone, but they are stuck with me.

After lunch, I try to get up to my office, to check e-mail, voice mail and scream, but there are human resources reps at the doors. We are a captive audience. They say things that they've obviously been trained to say, like "This is a day of transitioning. It's important to have this time."

Where the hell is Hackett? Where is Jen? We go back into the auditorium after being ushered to the bathrooms in shifts. The stage dims and then the lights come up and some guy is singing a song that sounds familiar. There are dancers.

"What is this?" John asks.

"It's that song from the early seventies. I think it was a one-hit wonder," the woman in front of us says. "I forget what it's called. I think I've seen the guy selling memorabilia on QVC."

"Are we supposed to be impressed by this?" John asks. The guy onstage is a cheeseball. I doubt there is even a "Where Are They Now?" segment about him on VH1. I can't believe it. I feel gassy from the soggy turkey sandwich.

The rest of the afternoon is something I never want to think about again. It was like someone's idea of a pep rally. It made no sense. We were expected to do call and response. There were people—cheerleaders—who came onstage and encouraged us to answer their cries of "Indy" with "MU." They kept saying, "I can't hear you!" You could tell they tried to get a real diverse group, but no one seemed to have any sense of rhythm. This was abundantly clear because they insisted on blasting a lame version of hip-hop.

There were some traitors who were getting into the call and response. I had to believe that it was all for show. I had to believe that they were so desperate to save their jobs that they would resort to screaming "MU!" like a cow whose udders were getting pulled too hard.

For their enthusiasm, they received bank teller dolls or sparkly calculators that were hurled at them by the rhythmless dancers. Needless to say, no one threw anything back to my row. I had been duped. No response was my response.

We got released at five-thirty. Again, banker's hours. They encourage us to go home and think of all we can bring to the company. Balloons come down from the ceiling. I imagine how much money this day cost. I am going to be sick.

On the way out of the theater, I notice they put the leftover breakfast pastries back in the lobby. There is something shiny over the top of some of them. I feel nauseous in the elevator up to my floor.

Hackett's office door is closed. I go back to my office but I come out every ten minutes to check on Hackett so I can give him a piece of my mind, despite the warnings I got from both Janice and John. It doesn't take long to realize he is gone for the day.

"People in his position lose out big when these things happen," John says, suddenly a sage. Claire Wylini walked around the floor saying "hey, you" in her ditzy way, as if it was any other day and we hadn't just been bought by a bank.

I have no new e-mails, which is unheard of. I can understand the lack of business-related messages, but none of my friends has even bothered to send me a dumb jpeg or a chain. It was like I'd fallen off the face of the earth or got caught in a time warp. I have two voice mails, both from the brother-and-sister Sousa team. The first was from Beth.

"Rebecca, call me. Sorry about yesterday. I just couldn't take another day of bridesmaid torture. I know, I know I'm an awful friend. How pissed is Kathy?" I certainly wasn't absolving her, not after the way she had been acting. It was between her and Kathy, but it sounded like she didn't even have a good excuse. Of course it sucks, but it's all part of the bridesmaid job, no one liked it, you just went along. I listen to the message from Tommy.

"Hey, Rebecca. How's it going? Wanted to see what you were up to this week."

Was he asking me out? Had he decided he was going to woo me again? Was he going to grow up and be normal again? I could say goodbye to the wonder wand forever. I liked being in a relationship. I didn't want to ever get naked in front of anyone new ever again. I didn't want to worry about going through the formalities. I pick up the phone. I put it down. This is my ritual with Tommy, I could never figure it out.

There is a knock at my door. It's Don Beckford.

"Hey. I wanted to know if you wanted to grab a drink. A bunch of us are going, we don't feel like working. Janice and John are in if you are."

I am touched that they wouldn't play hooky from working late without my okay. My amount of work hasn't changed, but my motivation has. It's Monday night, but I feel like tying one on. I deserve it.

We got a big table at the back of the bar. Although Don comes off slimy sometimes, he has the right idea and there is a pitcher of beer on the table before we even have our jackets off. I never do this. I had been at Explore! for a year and a half and I never just went out with the crew after work. Tonight, I meet the young PAs and the producers of the other shows and everyone just chugs beer and talks shop.

We start playing the name game and talking about where we have all worked before. Everyone has a story. Everyone has been in a tough situation. Even the few representatives from Programming are letting loose with their war stories.

I am getting drunk, but fuck it. I tell Don Beckford never to call me Becky again. Janice and John hold hands openly.

"Just come clean, I don't care," I yell at them. I grab Janice by the shoulders and shake her. She laughs. "I'm glad that someone is getting some."

I put songs on the jukebox. Don Beckford comes and stands too close to me. We dance to some Biggie. It is fun.

Three hours later, we are doing shots. We are toasting mutual funds. Cheryl from Programming and one of the PAs from *Let's Go,* the game show, are making out. They might regret it in the morning. We all might.

"We need to get some food," I say, and everyone cheers.

"Let's split this," Don whispers in my ear.

"What?" I am leaning too close to him, a result of drinking. I am beer-goggling. Maybe his leather jacket isn't so bad.

"Production expense. You get Janice to put half on her card, I'll get my AP to put half on his. Then, they'll expense it and we sign it. Regime change, they'll question, but they won't kick it back."

"Can I do that?"

"Rebecca, you are the executive producer. You've got signing power."

"Another round of shots! I've got signing power!" I beat a drum on the table and knock over everyone's drink. They groan, I laugh. I yell over the music, "Another round for everyone!"

I might as well enjoy it while I can....

The next morning, my head is pounding. I don't want to push my luck, but there was no way I could get in before ten-fifteen. There is a scribbled sticky note on my computer from Hackett. It reads:

B, TTM Re: al—M

It was Hackett code. Translation. Becky, Talk to Me Regarding Everything, Matt. Great. I check my hair in my computer monitor and grab a breath mint. I sniff a strand of hair on the way to his office. So I might not be able to keep up the new hair, but it was still too short to absorb much smoke.

"Hi," I say to Hackett when I knock. I notice he's on the phone. "Oh, sorry."

He shakes his head and motions for me to come in and shut the door. I hate closed doors. This is bad. He finishes up his call.

"Becky, I'm sorry about all this getting off track."

"You mean with production. Yeah, well, all these meetings might affect our deadlines for season two."

"Rebecca, I know you were tight already, but you're going to have to make it." He is calling me Rebecca; that is more serious than a closed door. "I'm going to be taking a position of greater importance in the company. I'm meeting with all the EPs to let them know. My replacement starts tomorrow. I would like to stay for your transition, but unfortunately Kristina Amos has left the company."

How typical they get her to deliver the news and then they shitcan her. Great for morale. It is as if Hackett can read my mind.

"She got quite a nice package."

"Where is Jen?" I ask.

"She hasn't been feeling well. She's young—you know how it is. She doesn't understand that this is just business. In our industry these changes happen all the time." Do they? Was I suddenly ancient?

"If you have anything you want me to approve before I go, please get it to me before five. I'm on the red-eye to London tonight."

"Do you have to relocate?"

"It hasn't been determined yet." I realize that Hackett is a survivor. For all the gruffness and loyalty he may or may not have had, he was in it to get by.

I pass Don in the hall. We smile at each other. I remember him putting me in the cab last night; I think I held on a little too long when we hugged goodbye. But, we aren't attracted to each other, we just had a lot to drink. He looks sheepish. He holds his fist out to me. It is a cheesy gesture, but I punch his fist with mine, just to say everything is cool.

"You were fun last night," he says.

"Yeah, it was nice to blow off some steam."

"I think we all needed it." He nods solemnly. I liked him better five shots in. "You have your face time with Hackett yet?"

"Yeah."

"Get that expense report signed before he's gone." He was right, of course. Who knew what we had to expect?

Back in my office, I take a look at the calendar on my wall. My deadlines are unbelievable and now I am going to have to negotiate them with some unknown person.

I leave Janice and John a message: "We are going out to lunch."

6

Devil's Pie

Tommy and I meet for a late dinner at the Greek place near our old (now his) apartment. I had this constant feeling of nausea, and only the avgolemono soup at Uncle Nick's could cure me. I had been denied in Astoria, but Tommy was willing to go wherever I wanted.

I'm making it seem as though we are suddenly complete adults about the breakup, aren't I? Don't be fooled. I find myself wondering what boxers he is wearing and how drunk I can get him. Very, very bad.

We order a bottle of white wine and the four-dip sampler to start. Tommy requested the fish-roe dip, *taramosalata,* be on a separate plate. I wait on the soup order to give Tommy a chance to look over the menu again. We have been to this restaurant quite a few times, but he isn't as familiar with Greek food as I am.

I'm not sure if I want the swordfish kabob or the moussaka. The swordfish is healthier, but how often could I get authentic moussaka? Never.

"Do you want to split an order of the potatoes?"

"Rebecca, I'm not that hungry and I'm trying not to spend too much."

"Right." Damn! He was going to be difficult. "Okay, we'll skip the potatoes, but I'll get the tab."

"Rebecca, you don't have to do that."

"It's no problem. Don't forget I make the big bucks, and I suggested this place." The dips and wine come. Tommy goes through the ceremony of tasting it. He prefers me to do it, but the waiter has poured it in his glass before we can say otherwise. Whenever Tommy tastes wine, he shrugs.

"I guess it's okay." The waiter pours some wine in my glass and more into Tommy's. He holds up his wineglass to me. "To Indiana Mutual."

"Please, Tommy."

"Okay, to Grand Theft Auto Vice City." I raise my eyebrows, but smile because he is in a good mood. "Do you want to make the toast?"

"Yes, to your new job." He rolls his eyes. "We should celebrate."

"Yeah." We drink. He looks down at the little dishes of dip. He turns the plate so the eggplant dip faces me and the tzatziki and potato dips face him. He hands me the smaller plate of the fish-roe dip. "You can eat that stuff."

I was hoping he would say that. I rip off some toasted pita and start to dig in. Tommy watches me eat.

"It really is good."

"Right," he says. Something is on his mind, but I am done trying to guess what is it. He is an adult, it's time he learned to communicate. Besides, there is dip to eat and the waiter is back to get our orders. I feel a bit piggy when Tommy decides against another starter and gets a lamb kabob. I also order soup and moussaka (the moussaka here is so good, I couldn't resist. I'm only human!).

They bring out my soup, and I start to slurp. It is chicken soup with lemon, egg and rice. Say what you will about matzo ball, that's great, too, but this is the stuff.

"You really like it, huh? You're, like, groaning."

"Mmm."

"So when is Lauryn leaving?"

"She said she will be gone by Memorial Day."

"Wow! Are you going to get a roommate?"

"I don't think I have the time to look for one. I should be working right now. I am so behind."

"But can you afford it on your own?"

"I told you I make the big bucks."

"Even with the changes at work?"

"Are you trying to rain on my lemon soup?"

"No, just asking." He is infuriating. Why can't he get at his own issues? I decide to try a different approach.

"You know, Lauryn's therapist thinks it's a good idea for you to get to the point." He laughs, then quickly grows serious.

"Lauryn doesn't really…talk about me to her therapist." I really enjoy Tommy's rare moments of paranoia.

"Yeah, she blames you for the breakup of her marriage."

"Jordan and I did play a lot of PlayStation," he says, laughing.

"Tell me about it."

"Okay, I was wondering if you wanted to move back in." I almost do Tommy's favorite comedy move, the spit take. I don't have to because his big statement was punctuated by one of the waiters lighting a plate on fire at the next table. We feel the heat.

"When you get to the point, you really get to the point, huh."

"I'm not saying move in, move in."

"What are you saying?"

"I am really short on funds these days."

"Okay, and…"

"And you need to support your problem." He gestures to my empty soup bowl. "You're going to have less disposable dollars when Lauryn moves out. And we're supposed to be friends."

"Thanks."

"And when Indiana Mutual took over CBB Federal they laid off like seventy percent of the workforce." I was surprised that he had done his research. The waiter clears my soup bowl and sets down my moussaka. I close my eyes and inhale. I hear the laugh in Tommy's voice. "You know, you're crazy."

"It smells delicious," I say. I pour more wine. He wants me to move back in, maybe he wants other things. Maybe I do, too. We broke up because he was the kind of guy who didn't want to grow up at all. Maybe he is beyond that and this is the first step. He seems to guess what I am thinking.

"Of course, we'll have separate rooms." Of course? This isn't going to be any fun. *Of course* it is the way it should be, but it isn't any fun.

"You don't live in a palace." I take my first bite. I was a fool to believe I could have been satisfied by the swordfish kabob. It is a good meal, yes, but this is eggplant, ground beef and béchamel all in one delicious pasta shell. I wonder how you say *heaven* in Greek.

"No, but I would move into the computer room."

"It's the size of a closet. And then I would have to walk through your room if I wanted to pee."

"I'll move the computer into the living room. We'll put up the screen."

"I don't know, Tommy. I think it's weird if you don't want to start dating again—not that I do." I'm not sure what I want. Why does he have to be clueless on the things I need to know and decisive on what I don't think matters?

"Of course you don't. Well, just think about it."

"I will," I say. He has a point about money.

"Thanks for not saying no right away." He pours the remainder of the wine in our glasses.

He begins to tell me about ideas he has for his Web site. He's not giving up on it, he just isn't going to devote as much time to it. The economy is shit and no one wants to know all his thoughts on comics, collectibles and video games. I tune out what he is saying and just keep repeating a mantra to myself. *You will not sleep with him. You will not sleep with him. It would be so simple and fun. No, no you must not sleep with him.*

The moussaka is good, but filling. I have half of it wrapped up for leftovers that I will eat tomorrow when they introduce me to my new boss. I coax Tommy into ordering some rice pudding so I'll be able to have a few bites, and we get strong Greek coffee. I need the buzz. I have to write two scripts.

After I pay the check, Tommy puts me in a cab. It is just past midnight, which I consider the cutoff of safe subway hours. Our goodbyes are weird now. We just kiss on the cheek.

"Thanks for dinner and for not saying no right away."

"Yeah, I'll let you know. Bye."

And away I go.

In the morning there's a knock at my closed office door. I hurry to slip on my shoes before answering. I am reminded of the evil banker in the awful commercial when I find myself having to adjust my line of sight downward to see a small thin woman extending her hand up to me.

"Delores Wagner. I am your new—" she hesitates, and I bend a little lower to hear what she is going to say. She finally settles on two words. "Creative Director."

She is my new boss. I'm not intimidated because she is about four foot eleven. She has dark brown wavy hair with no particular style. I smile. "Oh, you're the new Hackett."

"Delores Wagner," she says again. I notice she doesn't really open her mouth when she speaks.

"Right, nice to meet you. I'm Rebecca Cole—" I, too, hesitate, then add, "the creator of Esme."

She nods. I hated to be that kind of girl, you know the kind, the wear-my-résumé-on-my-sleeve kind, but somehow I think it is the right thing to do.

"So you work for Indiana Mutual?"

"We all do."

"Right, but I meant—" she is already being condescending, but she is new and I am optimistic "—is that where you came from?"

"In production, yes. I created all the international advertising. I promoted the ads throughout the world. I am quite fluent in production." Talk about wearing your résumé on your sleeve.

"So you came from Indiana?"

"The international headquarters are in Germany." The banking industry is all new for me, but she speaks like I am a fool for not knowing where the headquarters are.

"Do you want to come in?" I ask, realizing our get-to-know-you meeting might be better in my office instead of the hall.

"You'll want to meet with me later to go over the work you've done so far." I will? "Right now I have a meeting with Joe Leissle."

He's one of the new big shots. I'm not sure what exactly he does or where he has come from or what havoc he is certain to wreak in my life, but I notice that Delores said his name with a combination of reverence and name-dropping attitude.

"Okay," I say. "Do you want to grab lunch?"

"Thank you, but no. I have a working lunch with Claire and some others in Programming to go over our plan of attack for the new season."

"Should I be in on that?"

"That's not necessary. It's imperative that I meet them to get buttoned up." Oh, she works the office lingo, too. I am losing patience and I have too much to do to play games.

"So, okay, when do you want to meet?"

"Are you going to be here until six?" I am usually here much later than that.

"Yeah."

"Let's meet at six." Now, one could argue that I said I was going to be here *until* six not *past* six, but I am a mere cog in the wheel.

"Great," I say.

"You'll want to bring me a thorough report of the progress you're making on Esme and a complete production calendar." Is that so?

"Great," I repeat, trying to smile.

I go back into my office and shut the door. It is too soon to make judgments. I have to just work. My phone rings.

"Re, can you meet for lunch today?" Kathy.

"Oh, Kathy, I'm so busy. Can we do it later in the week?"

"Come on, I'll come to you," she says. Kathy works a few avenues over and we always say we are going to have lunch more, but our schedules never seem to coincide.

"I am *so* swamped."

"We can just go to Prêt. It'll be quick. I promise. I really want to talk to you." She sounds desperate. It's almost eleven. If I work for a solid two hours I could meet her for about twenty minutes. I probably should stay to show my new boss what a good worker I am, but I should also set some parameters—like, I won't eat lunch at my desk every day....

"Okay, but I won't have much time. I'll meet you at one."

At 1:12 I show up at Prêt à Manger. It's gourmet fast food; you pick from a variety of fresh sandwiches and salads. Everything is very bright and clean. Kathy is waiting for me on one of the stools, her jacket over another.

"I'm so sorry. I have a new boss." It's a lame excuse, I just lost track of time. "I'm sorry."

"It's okay. I had to fight off some people for this seat. I got you a coronation chicken sandwich and an iced tea." I smile. Fresh iced tea means summer is on the way. It was really sweet of her. I am the worst friend and I feel even worse for being late.

"I'm sorry," I say. I start to pull out my wallet. She swats my hands.

"Don't worry about it, it's on me. You can get the next one." I sit down and start to eat my sandwich. I am still tense from work—it wasn't easy to just pull myself out of it and socialize.

"Have you talked to Beth lately?" Kathy asks.

"Not really, not since we went to that awful restaurant."

"She's been hanging with her too-cool-for-school music crowd."

"Really. I just think she's been weird." I am almost done with my sandwich and haven't tasted a bite. Kathy has barely begun. I need to relax. I still have fifteen more minutes of freedom.

"I just worry that no one is into my wedding," Kathy says. "You're so busy and Lauryn's off to God knows where."

"The Vineyard."

"Right, and Beth is acting so strange."

"Well, I'm into it, and I think everyone else is, too." Sometimes white lies aren't so bad.

"I think I'm going to ask my sister to plan my shower."

"Are you sure?" Beth is the maid of honor. I knew Kathy couldn't have wanted that.

"I don't know. I just can't deal with the drama. I've got drama. This is the biggest day of my life." Kathy is a very cool friend, but when it comes to her wedding, she turns into a prima donna. I can understand Beth not wanting to deal, but she has to. I know what this is about.

"Do you want me to talk to Beth?" I shove the last piece of sandwich in my mouth. Feeling rushed is the worst way to eat.

"Could you, Rebecca? Would you?"

"I can. I will."

"Thank you. It means so much to me." She is gushing. I have seven more minutes.

"Do you want to split one of their cookies?" I watch her silently calculate if she can afford it on her diet. Then, she shrugs, nods and I buy one.

"So how is your new boss?"

"I don't know yet." I'm not going to jinx myself by giving voice to my concerns. "I have a meeting with her tonight."

"Her? It's a she?"

"Yeah, why?"

"How old?"

"Not very. I don't know, maybe early thirties. Why?"

"Oh, girl," Kathy says. "Be careful."

For the rest of the afternoon, I couldn't shake the hiccups I had from eating too fast. And I couldn't stop thinking about what Kathy said. I assured her that our businesses, finance and entertainment divisions were two different animals. She kept saying it didn't matter, women were women.

"But I'm not one of those women. I don't care." Kathy just shook her head and gave me a half of her half of her cookie.

Back at the office, my e-mail double-dings, which means that someone has sent me an urgent e-mail. I've been ignoring the single dings all day to get stuff done. I see that I have ignored twenty-three messages and the newest double-ding is from Delores Wagner.

Rebecca,

I am putting out a lot of the fires Programming started. I hope we can reschedule until seven. I am sure you recognize the importance of dealing with these urgent matters. Thanks.

Delores

It annoys me that she assumed I could just rework my schedule to accommodate her. And who is she, a fire chief? I expel a long breath and vow to not let her get to me. At seven, I print out a document Hackett had used to present to the big guys and grab my scribbled-on production calendar.

I pass Claire on the way to Hackett's old office.

"Hey, you," Claire says. She gestures down the hall to what is now Delores's office. "She's great, isn't she? She's got a ton of ideas."

I nod and say good-night. This ass-kissing is going to have to be par for the course for a while. I knock on Delores's door.

"Hi, there," Delores says. She is perfectly welcoming. Perhaps I was judging her too quickly. She could be the mentor I've been longing for. Everyone always talks about mentors, but nobody ever seems to be one or know one. It is a lot like hermaphrodites; you hear about them, you just aren't sure they exist.

"How's it going?"

"Well it's obviously going to be trial by fire, but that's to be expected." If she is going to be my mentor, I wish she would just talk like a normal person. I listen politely as she gives me a rather involved anecdote about her first days in Germany. She worked in a place called the Black Forest and throughout her story I find myself imagining her as some sort of hermaphrodite fairy, only animated. I need to start getting more sleep.

"So did you bring those documents I asked for?" I hand them to her. She rifles through them and shakes her head a little.

"Do you think you could get a cleaner copy of this calendar? It's very hard to read."

"Okay, the thing is, it gets updated every day." She nods.

"I realize that. I think I would like you to set it up as an Excel file, so I could just look down the list and see when scripts are in, et cetera."

"You want me to set up a whole other document."

"Yes, and this…" She holds up the document Hackett created that we used as a template to work up story ideas about Esme. "I don't understand it."

"Actually, that's something Hackett did."

"Oh." That apparently satisfies her, but I wonder if it is because Hackett was still in the company and pretty high up. "Well, I'll take another look at it tonight. Do you think you can get me that calendar ASAP?"

"Yes, I'll do it tonight."

"Wonderful. I wanted to talk to you about Esme's animation."

"What about it?"

"I think it looks a little pedestrian." I feel a knot rising in my throat. Does she realize that Esme is my baby, that I had initially animated her? Immediately, Delores's itty-bitty hands go up and she starts making big apologetic circles. "I'm not saying I don't like it."

"You're not?" I hear a little fake sarcastic laugh escape my lips. It isn't a sound I usually make.

"Of course not. What I'm saying is that maybe it could be a bit more stylized." We are making this for kids. I thought that was clear.

"Well, that's the style." I feel myself about to say something I never dreamed I would. Eccchhh! I feel dirty already. "They loved it in the focus groups." Have my senses been impaired by saying something so foreign as "focus groups"?

"I'm sure they did, but maybe we should talk about doing our animation in Korea."

"Wait a second, what?"

"I just think they might do a better job."

"But what about Janice and John—and me, for that matter—when I can do a great job."

"But it might be a wiser economic choice to do it in Korea."

"We could bust the budget on FedEx."

"It worked fabulously when I was at International." I want to tell this dwarf that we aren't doing commercials for international mutual funds, this is kids' TV. She is obviously unfamiliar with kids' television. "They do real sexy stuff."

I get what Tommy used to call the douche chills, a shiver that comes from hearing something really gross. For him, the word *douche*. I never understood what he meant until this very minute. Why is she using the word *sexy* to talk about an animated show for girls? It is gross. I take another breath and decide to try another approach.

"I just think the Korean animators might have trouble with Esme's voice."

"We have voice-overs for that," she says condescendingly.

"I'm not talking about audio." I stop and swallow. My voice is getting too loud. "I mean they won't *get* Esme."

"Well, I'm not saying that we have to make these decisions now." You're not? "But you'll want to think about being able to put together a good case for keeping the animation domestic."

I will? Does she ever fully open her elfin mouth? I have no idea what to say.

"Okay," I finally settle on. "I'll get you that calendar."

"Thanks. And have a wonderful night."

And so as if I didn't have enough to do, I created a worthless Excel document. Where the hell is the Black Forest, anyway? Is it in Middle Earth? I think about calling Tommy to vent and tell him I am working for a Hobbit. A mere mention of *Lord of the Rings* would be like talking dirty. Maybe he will take pity on me and give me some oral pleasure.

No, no. I must push these thoughts out of my head. I am never having sex again. Wait, maybe I could move in and molest him in his sleep. That would help me relax. No, fuck, I have to work on making a case for Janice and John to keep their jobs. Who the hell is this chick? I decide to procrastinate even more. I call Lauryn on her cell.

"Hey," she says, recognizing my work number on the caller ID.

"Where are you?"

"At a birding event." It was too bad to be untrue.

"Does Delores mean pain in Spanish?"

"I'm not sure. I kind of have to go."

"Want to grab a late dinner?"

"No, there's food here."

"What?" I ask, giggling. "Chicken?"

"I'm hanging up now." And she does.

I am starting to get hungry. My lunch hiccups have finally subsided. I think my system went into shock when I said "focus group."

I could stay here and work on my scripts and order in or I could go home and work on my scripts and eat something alone. Neither is very enticing, but I am anxious to get into my sweats.

On my way to the subway, I check my cell messages. I stop in the middle of the street when I hear the first one. It is Seamus.

"Hey, Rebecca. I waited a few days, but you still haven't called me. I had a terrific time the other night and I was hoping you did, too. I was hoping we could go to Tabla Bread Bar this week. I don't know if you've ever been there, but their small dishes are all incredible."

He is making my mouth water. I can't believe he called me. It is 9:40 p.m. He left the message at two o'clock. I shouldn't call him back tonight—I'll call him tomorrow. I can't believe it. I forget all about Delores.

I hop on the subway, praying that there aren't any delays. I need to get to Whole Foods before they close at ten o'clock.

I make it just under the wire. The security guard shakes her head at me and they make the final checkout call over the PA. I go straight to the fish department and order a pound of cooked shrimp. The fishmonger gives me all that's left and it's exactly a pound. We both laugh when we see the scale.

"You are a lucky lady," he says.

"Yes, I am," I say, imagining the crispy fried onions at Tabla Bread Bar. Oh, I have been there, all right, but I couldn't wait to go with Mr.-Sophisticated-New-York-Wine-Guy Seamus. I am a lucky lady and I am getting lucky. A straight New York male is interested in me, despite my obvious shortcomings. I will not freak out without my shirt on again.

"You having a party?" the fishmonger asks.

"Sort of," I say.

After I got some parsley and sparkling water, I brought the fish back to my place. I love to eat, but I hate to eat alone. So sometimes I like to add a little ceremony to my solitude.

When I get home, I change into my sweats, put a little D'Angelo on the stereo and take out the silver platter Lauryn got for her wedding and arrange my shrimp cocktail around the center dish of cocktail sauce. I garnish with parsley. I pour my sparkling water into a champagne glass (another gift someone was regretting giving the couple now) and dance my way into the living room. I eat all twenty-three of my shrimp and thoroughly enjoy my cocktail party for one. There is plenty of time for friends and boys. This is me time. I am proud of myself and my work. No one could make me feel otherwise.

When the CD ends, I make myself some cocoa with schnapps and watch the eleven o'clock *Friends* episode.

There really isn't much more I can ask for.

7

We're Going To Be Friends

Life is funny. One night you might be sipping sparkling water and eating shrimp by yourself and the next night you could be getting served crispy, Indian-fusion delicacies while a hot guy rubs his knuckles along your neck and buys you expensive big-girl drinks called Tablatinis.

One night you might be considering a booty call to your recently exed boyfriend and the next you might be worried that all of the West Village might hear you getting down with the new guy.

So yes, my life is full of surprises and some of them are very, very nice. For example, I never expected to be back in Seamus's apartment, but it didn't matter, I was having a good time.

Okay, so it was kind of weird afterward…you know, *afterward*…and I wasn't sure if I should stay. I couldn't really look him in the eye as I rehooked my bra. Seamus suggested I stay but I left. There are things you have to try to hide with someone new as long as possible. Frankly, I was tired of trying to position myself so Seamus would get my best angle.

"Did you?" he said throughout the whole thing. "Did you yet?"

It was a lot of pressure. Now, I certainly appreciated his efforts, but it takes some time for me to relax, you know. The night had gone so well and I guess I thought I might ruin it, by, I don't know, screaming Tommy's name (I swear I didn't think that much about him this time) or making some ugly face, or God knows what. But I didn't. Ruin it, that is. That's why it's better to quit while you're ahead.

All and all I felt I crossed a bridge of sorts. I was now a single woman and back in the saddle. I held my head up high when I crept out of Seamus's building and quickly hailed a cab.

Lauryn is up working on an essay when I get home. She is also smoking in the house.

"Are you taking that up again?" I ask.

"Why not? You want one?"

"I did just have sex," I say. She holds up her hand limply and I smack it five. We smile. I take a cigarette. It makes me feel a little sick, but I work through it. I have just had sex, I am entitled.

"How was it?"

"It was fun." She raises an eyebrow. I know what she wants. "No, I didn't, but it was still fun."

"Working that Tommy out of your system?"

"I'm trying. I know it's over. It's just not easy."

"I know. I heard about his offer. You want a drink? I can't write this stupid essay application crap anymore." I probably shouldn't, I have work tomorrow, but it has been too long since we hung out like this. I can't resist.

"Okay, just one." I watch her pour some Stoli Vanilla into a glass and add some ginger ale. "Nice. Did you talk to Tommy?"

"No," she says. "Beth."

"Really?"

"She's getting into an interesting crowd."

"Those studio people." She nods and taps her nose.

"Is she okay?"

"I guess so—you know Beth." I do. Everyone thinks Beth is Italian, but she is first-generation Portuguese. In Beth's family, her brother Tommy is the star. Their parents are straight off the boat from the Azores, and the only reason Beth was able to move to New York City was because Tommy was going to be here. Her parents assumed he would keep her out of trouble. They never had a problem with my relationship with Tommy, but Beth could never admit to having a boyfriend. She is expected to date the man she is going to marry. It sucks, but luckily she has a good relationship with Tommy and he helps her out all the time.

"What did Beth have to say about Tommy's offer?" Lauryn shakes her head and rolls her eyes, so I know that Beth believes I was wrong for even entertaining it. Things were cool between us when Tommy and I dated, but as soon as we broke up, Beth took his side. Even though he isn't angry at me, it seems like she is sometimes.

"You know Beth," Lauryn says again. "What are you going to do about it?"

"I don't know. Economically it's a good choice, but emotionally…"

"I'll say. Although Kathy is worried that they are going to do layoffs."

"Who?" I ask as I pour some more vodka in my glass. I was far gone now.

"Indiana Mutual."

"I'm sorry, but aren't you the girl who expressed dissatisfaction with people talking about you behind your back?"

"Rebecca, don't worry about it. I realized today as Kathy was telling me how pissed off she is at Beth for not going to the fitting that we just like to talk about one another. It's part of our friendship. So go ahead, talk about me if you want. My life is an open book."

"How generous," I say. She nods and pours more vodka into her glass. I was never going to get up tomorrow at this rate. "So have you slept with anyone since Jordan?"

"Well, other than the night that I went out and got completely shitfaced and fucked the bartender at Roxy's—Rest in Peace?" We give Roxy's its appropriate moment of silence. We

had to ban Roxy's after that. It was a forgivable sacrifice because Lauryn discovered the extent to which Jordan was cheating on her. "This box is locked. I'm done with men until they
start acting like the rest of the human race."

"Maybe one of those plover lovers in the Vineyard will
open it up for you."

"Birders are old."

"You are a divorcée."

"I know."

"I don't get it. Aren't things supposed to get easier when
you're older? You know, like aren't I supposed to be nearing
my sexual peak?"

"In like another twelve years. You faked, didn't you?" She is
not exactly accusing.

"I kept trying to clear my head and get into it, but it was so
weird to be with someone new. I didn't purposely do anything.
I just let him believe he was on the right track."

"Well, make sure he finds the right track."

"I will, when I feel more comfortable."

"You're going to miss me, aren't you?" She smiles and ex-
hales a smoke ring and I see a flash of one of her old school
funny faces. I am going to miss her. She holds up her glass. I
clink it.

"Of course I am. Without you New York's just a cold,
friendless city."

I regret only getting three hours of sleep after I have to sit
through a two-hour meeting with Licensing and Delores Wagner. Why can't people just do things and make everyone else
deal instead of meeting and pretending to care what everyone
else said and then just doing what they want, anyway? And because Delores was name-dropping about various executives, all
the licensing people felt they had to name-drop, too.

I hate the outfit that Esme was wearing on the sample plush
toy. There is a part of me that is excited that Esme even has a
plush toy, but at the same time she looks hokey. And I was expected to be happy that the Esme sample was created by some-

one who one time cleaned the bathroom for someone who worked on a sample of Snoopy or something.

The Stoli Vanilla hangover was making everything very hazy.

Don Beckford is creating quite a ruckus about the size of Gopher's teeth on his plush toy. Delores continues referencing anecdotes from her old job. She has a tendency to talk a lot without really going anywhere. She reminds me of one of those tops that just goes when you pull the string. She lets it "slip" that she went to Harvard.

Don, who is sitting next to me, elbows me so I would read a note he wrote on his production calendar. "Where's she from?"

I write, "A forest. Germany."

He laughs and I write, "Seriously."

"I think we should lose the glasses," Delores says to the designer. I tune back in.

"We can't lose the glasses," I say. "They're Esme's trademark."

"I just think kids like to see characters' faces." Where is she getting this from? And why does she feel she can speak with authority about what kids want?

"I think the glasses came out fantastic," Carl, the head of Licensing, says.

"Well, I'm not saying that they didn't. I'm just not sure they're working for the brand."

"It's a kids' brand. Kids wear glasses," I say, feeling Don kick me under the table. Here we go again: "And they loved it in the focus groups."

"Well, we'll have to make a decision about this ASAP," Delores says. I think one had been made. "For now, let's talk about the game tie-in."

After the meeting, Don pulls me aside. "That didn't have to be that long. I asked about her and no one knows who she is."

"She's from abroad."

"She's full of shit and she confuses everyone. I've had hit shows. I'm not going to deal." I notice that when someone new comes around, everyone has to justify their jobs. "But watch yourself."

"Why?"

"She asked me about your other show experience when I went in for my meeting with her."

"Why would she ask you?"

"I don't know." I'm not sure I can trust Don. "I told her that everyone thought you did a really great job and Esme was your creation. And it's true."

"Well, thanks. What did she say?"

"Nothing, she went off on some rant about Gopher's curriculum. They expect kids to learn lessons about morality from a talking gopher."

"How's Jordan doing?"

"So far, so good. It's to be expected. He's too much of a nobody to be a prima donna."

"Right."

"No offense." I shrug. I hated Jordan after the way he treated Lauryn, but I felt a little bit protective of him. Kids' TV is tough business. It chews people up and spits them out. "Anyway, make sure you hold your ground."

"Okay, thanks."

That doesn't make me feel confident. Neither does John standing at my office door holding an e-mail in his hands.

"What is this?" I take it from him. It's a long-winded e-mail from Delores with notes from the tenth and eleventh episodes John had been animating.

"When did she even see this?"

"She asked for it. I gave it to her. Notice how every change she wants is ASAP. And the very last one is *very* ASAP."

"I see she put that one in bold." I smile at him, but he isn't having it. I rarely see him get upset, but he certainly is right now.

"Who am I supposed to be listening to? You or her?"

"Well, I'll talk to her about them and get back to you. ASAP." At last, he smiles.

I'm beginning to dread this walk down the hall. I knock. "Come in."

Delores is a flurry of activity. She is giddy (with power?) and speaking in a baby voice. I imagine this is to prove her creativity.

"Hey, I see you made some notes on a couple of the Esme scripts," I say, trying to sound firm but nonthreatening. I keep thinking of what Kathy said. I don't want to believe women can really be so threatened by other women.

"Yeah, I had a couple of very significant concerns that you seemed to have overlooked."

"I haven't had time to check out those scripts." Delores takes her glasses off and rises to her full four-foot-ten frame.

"Rebecca, do you know how dangerous it will be if we let this get away from us?"

"We have plenty of time before we have to animate."

"A week."

"The way things have been moving that seems like a long time," I say.

"I realize we're all very busy. I was here until eleven last night." God, she's one of those. We don't have to punch in a time clock, but every once and a while there's someone who feels the need to justify their job by announcing how late they worked. I hate those people. "But getting these episodes out is an emergency."

"John and Janice work really well under pressure," I say, giving them the props they deserve.

"They need to work better. You need to get them to work better." I am furious. She doesn't seem to know anything about timetables. But she is the boss, so I have to accept.

"Okay. I'll talk to them about it." I start to leave. I can't resist. "ASAP."

"That would be terrific." She's back on the giddy baby voice, but then suddenly switches back to condescending. "I haven't gotten your calendar today."

"There aren't any changes from the last one."

"Send it, anyway. Thanks."

Never in my life was I so glad it was Friday. I am not usually one of those people who "worked for the weekend." Even before Esme, I always kind of liked my job, but now I am turning into someone who can't wait to get home.

Wasn't I the It Girl? Hadn't I been the person who got the affiliates so excited? Doesn't that count for anything anymore?

My phone rings just as I hit Send to e-mail the pixie her unrevised calendar. It is Lauryn, inviting me out for drinks with the girls. It is her attempt at peace between the warring factions of Beth and Kathy.

"Kathy has actually agreed not to go straight home tonight, and Beth can give us some time before some party she was noncommittal about. I'm short on dough so I was thinking maybe Pepe Giallo."

"Do you think the garden's open yet?"

"I dunno. It's warm enough."

"Okay, I'm in." Pepe Giallo is cheap and has reliable pasta and cute Italians running around. If the garden is open, it might be just what we all need to relax. I hear Lauryn sigh on the other end. "What?"

"I've got some bad news. The lease is up and if you want to keep the place, the rent's going up."

"Again? Do they want our blood? How much?"

"Twenty-five."

"Fuck! $2,500! Do they think we are made of money?" (This is why it is good to have an office door.)

"It's two bedrooms and a pretty big kitchen. Only two floors to walk up. They know they can get it. The Flatiron-Chelsea neighborhood is hopping these days and we're right there."

"Fine."

"There *is* Tommy's offer," she says, mocking.

"I'll just see you at Pepe's."

"Okay, bring your smile. And be there in twenty because I don't want Kathy to get antsy or Beth to piss me off."

Thirty-three minutes later, I get to Pepe Giallo. Kathy and Lauryn are there, but Beth is not. They have downed half a carafe of red wine already and who knows how much bread, but luckily the garden is open. Lauryn is smoking and Kathy is waving it away. Her smile looks forced.

"Hey, guys, sorry."

"That's okay," Kathy says, bumping me with her new pink glasses as we kiss hello.

"I was sure you'd be later than Beth," Lauryn adds.

"Is she still coming?" I ask. They both nod.

"Are you ready to order?" the waiter asks. I am starving, but it's only fair to wait for Beth.

"Just more bread, please, and a glass," I ask the waiter, almost pleadingly.

"It feels like summer," Kathy said. She's right. It isn't even really dark yet, and you can feel the warmth in the air.

Beth finally arrives. She kisses us all hello and doesn't apologize for being late.

"I'm starving," Kathy says, and I'm not sure if it's a dig for Beth.

"Have some more bread," Lauryn says. It's pretty strange that she organized this. We used to have to drag her out of the apartment. The waiter brings Beth and me glasses.

"Were you late, too, Rebecca?" Beth asks me.

"A little," Kathy says before I can answer. Is she still bitter about the bridesmaid thing? We pick up our menus. In days gone by we never usually got around to looking at the menus (I, of course, was the exception); we gossiped for a while until the waiter would come over and ask us for the second time if we were ready to order. Now we are thankful to have a prop to cover our faces.

"Well, I know what I want," Kathy says.

"Of course you know," Beth said. "We've been here a zillion times."

"I want to hear the specials," I say. Beth turns to me.

"Honestly, Rebecca, you always get the *pappardelle.*"

"I know, I just want to hear the specials. Is that okay?"

"Of course it is," Kathy says. She is taking my side by default.

"Remember that time we came here before your work party, Beth?" Lauryn asks.

"I do," I say. "I remember Kathy was so shitfaced, she spilled pesto all over her white shirt."

"And she was too shitfaced to care," Beth adds.

"You lent me that cardigan you had in your desk," Kathy says to Beth.

"And afterward you met Ron," Lauryn reminds her. I wink at Lauryn. She is acting like some sort of negotiator. I'm not sure why it's so important to her to make sure Beth and Kathy are getting along. Maybe it's her therapist's idea. The waiter came over.

"'Ave you decided?"

"She would like to hear the specials," Beth said, then stuck out her tongue at me in a playful way. The spinach-and-ricotta ravioli special sounded good, but I decide to stick with what I know.

"I think I'll have the *pappardelle* with spicy *ragu*." The rest of the girls laugh at me and I mock bow.

"You are de star," the waiter says in his hot little Italian way. Kathy got gnocchi with pesto. Beth got the spaghetti with peas and potatoes and Lauryn got penne a la vodka with chicken. And we agreed to split a baby-greens-and-goat-cheese salad and buffalo mozzarella tomato appetizer. The order is the same as always.

When the starters came, we fell right into a normal routine. Kathy started telling us about Ron's mother's annoying dietary demands for the wedding. Beth complained that her mother, who had been opposed to her dating all along, was now asking her if she wanted to be an old maid. I did an impressive impression of Delores Wagner and Lauryn ordered another bottle of wine.

It was perfect and comfortable. When our pasta arrived, we all took bites of one another's dishes and moaned with savory delights. It could have been any other night.

Then Beth's cell phone rang.

Then she answered the call.

Then Kathy excused herself to go to the bathroom.

Then she came back with red eyes.

Then Beth got off the phone and muttered an insincere apology.

Then we ate for a little while in silence.

Then Beth's phone rang again and Kathy slapped her hand on the table.

Then Beth looked at the number, looked at Lauryn and left the table.

Then I ordered another bottle of wine.

Then Kathy said, "Don't even bother. I'm going to go home soon, anyway."

Then Lauryn said, "No, let's have more."

When Beth returned to the table, she didn't say anything for a while. She pushed her food around her plate and ate another potato.

"You know, I'm full, and I told some people I would meet up with them," she finally says.

"Well, have fun with your people," Kathy says.

"Do you want to wrap up the rest of it?" I ask.

"No, that's okay. I won't eat it." She already has her bag on her shoulder. "How much do I owe?"

"Don't worry about it," Lauryn says. "It's on me. My last big night out."

I knew then why she planned this, what she wanted—a normal night out.

"What about next weekend?" Beth asks.

"I'll be busy packing. I'm going to take the ferry up next Monday."

"Oh, okay. Well, I'll call you before you go," Beth says. "See you guys."

"Bye," I say.

"I need your measurements to give to the dress shop," Kathy says without really looking up.

"I'll e-mail you," Beth shouts as she was already almost out of the garden.

The waiter comes over to clear her plate. I rescue one of the potatoes in her pasta before he gets it.

"You can take mine, too," Kathy says. "I should get the train before it becomes too sporadic. I didn't realize this was your last night out, Lauryn. Maybe I'll stop over to help you pack this week."

"Thanks, Kathy." While they hugged goodbye, I stole one of Kathy's gnocchi before the waiter could grab it away. Then I hugged Kathy and told her I hoped to see her this week.

When she's gone, we pick at our food a little more. Lauryn holds her plate out to me and I take a piece of chicken and mop it in more sauce.

"I wish I had known tonight was supposed to be special," I said. "I should have planned it myself."

"It's okay. So, I guess you're going to move in with Tommy?"

"It doesn't seem like I have much of a choice."

"I'm sorry."

"And I'm sorry I was late."

"That was the least of the problems." She looks down at her plate and squeezes a piece of penne between her fingers. "Rebecca…"

"Yeah?"

"Who do you think called Beth? That last time?"

"I dunno," I say. "One of her cooler friends, I guess. Why?"

"I don't know." She squints at me, sizing me up for something. She squinted at me like this many times when she was sleuthing Jordan. I made Esme squint in a similar way when she is questioning school bullies. I hadn't realized that I got the look from Lauryn until right now. "You don't think there's something…funny going on."

"Funny? I don't know." But there is something in my head that I can't quite pinpoint. It was just out of my reach and for some reason, I didn't want to know.

Lauryn stares at me for another few seconds, like she wants to ask me something. Then she says, "I guess you're right. Let's finish the wine."

"Good idea. I know one thing that could turn this night out." She raises her eyebrows.

"Tiramisu?"

"Thatta girl."

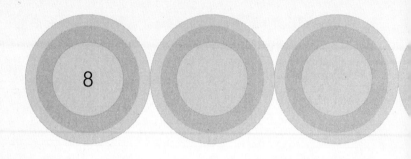

8

Wiser Time

My phone is ringing. Does anyone respect Saturdays any-more? Every Saturday, it's like Déjà Vu. No, more like Ground-hog Day. I squint at the clock. It's ten-thirty. It stops ringing. Bless Lauryn, I think, and fall back to sleep.

When I get up an hour later, I smell cleaning products. Lau-ryn is on one of her crazy housekeeping sprees. I really need to pee, but she is scrubbing the toilet bowl.

"Can't you just wait?"

"It's going to get dirty eventually." She sighs and pulls off her rubber glove. She has her bandanna on, which means she's going to attack the kitchen next.

"Who called?" I yell from the toilet.

"Tommy with questions. You should just move in with him."

"What about Seamus?"

"What about him?"

"I don't know. What if he finds out I'm living with Tommy?" I come out of the bathroom and go into the kitchen. She is pulling cans of soup out of the cabinets.

"Well, he won't know who Tommy is." She turns to me. "Rebecca, you didn't tell him about Tommy, did you?"

"I did a little. I didn't tell about the offer."

"Well, don't. Just have him keep calling you on your cell and never let him come to your place." She learned a few things from Jordan's lies.

"So I should move in with Tommy?"

"Well, it doesn't seem like Beth is going to ask you. Unfortunately, everyone else is pretty much paired off. Unless you want someone's couch. I think it should be a very transitional thing with Tommy. You can't stay there for more than a few months. It just won't be good." It's nice to have a person who has no trouble making your big decisions for you. She's right. I can't afford this rent, not with my credit card debt.

"I don't know why you're cleaning, we're moving out, anyway."

"It puts my mind at ease." She pauses. "So I can tell the landlord we won't need to resign."

"Yes, and while you're at it tell him to fuck himself for rent like this."

"Okay." She pulls out some pasta boxes and smiles. Cleaning makes her strangely giddy; I will never understand it. "What are you up to today?"

"Well, I think I'll go to Madison Square Park and work on the final scripts and some notes for the animators. Then I told Seamus I would take him out for dinner since he's treated me the past couple of times."

"Nice. I'm going to clean out my closets and take stuff to Goodwill."

"Do you want to go to Johnnie's first?" Johnnie's is a small restaurant with a lunch counter and a couple of tables. They make the best BLTs.

"Do you ever think of anything other than food?"

"Is there anything else?" She shakes her head, but closes the cabinet. I begin to salivate.

A mere hour later, I am happily full of bacon and trying not to be distracted by all the cute dogs at the dog run when I look over some final scripts. Some day I want to have a dog in the city. If things don't work out with Seamus, I will get a dog. But things seem like they're working out—it's starting to feel like a relationship. Although, he seems busier than I am.

I am not calling Tommy yet. I don't know why. It's not like I'm going to magically move into Seamus's fabulous apartment in the West Village. Still, it would be nice to have a fireplace (even if it's fake) and a boyfriend with the inside track on New York's restaurants. Okay, I have to stop this food obsession. I am getting out of control.

I think I'm starting to believe in all the work mumbo jumbo. We are in "transition" there—and I feel transitional. My apartment, my job, boyfriends, friends—everything. It's like melancholy, but less clear. I just want to feel normal again. I don't want to keep referring to focus groups where we pump kids full of pizza and soda and try to elicit answers we can use in Power-Point presentations to get more money. I want to feel like myself again.

I can't focus on the scripts. I don't want to think about Esme. When I first started working on her, I got so into it. It was like rewriting history, creating the type of person I wished I could have been.

My friends were all behind me. Tommy totally got it and knew her just as well as I did. Everyone who saw the interstitials said they were totally inspired by those little films. I even brought them home to show my parents over Christmas two years ago, and for once I thought they finally kind of understood what I did. Okay, they still didn't get how I could be paid for doing it, but it was a start.

Now Esme belongs to everyone else. Funny how a promotion can be the fastest way to lose control. Sure, it was hard for me to let Janice and John animate her after I made executive producer, but I believed they got it. I don't think someone in Korea who doesn't get what it's like to be a kid in this country would be able to figure it out. I hate that all these decisions are being made based on money, either, or that they are being made by people who don't know jack about kids.

When I was putting the pilot together, I caved to Hackett's

suggestion about changing Esme's sister to a brother. It was easy enough to change Ellie to Eric, but once I made the first change I essentially made it okay for all the changes. This was all a part of the job. I wasn't doing a solo stand-up act, I was making TV. I couldn't work in a vacuum. People had say. Fuck.

A young black retriever comes up to me and sniffs my leg. "Hey, buddy," I say. I let him put his front paws in my lap and I rub under his chin.

"Vixen," says his owner, a twenty-something blonde in low-rise sweats. She holds his leash in one hand while the other is wrapped around the waist of a guy.

"Cute dog," I say, and the couple smiles at each other proudly. They give Vixen a tug and are on their way. It must be nice to have a boyfriend *and* a dog.

I take a deep breath and focus on the scripts. These doubts about life are only putting me further behind schedule.

I told Seamus that he could pick any restaurant he wanted and make reservations, but he could not offer to pay. I insisted. I want to establish myself as an equal in this relationship. He picked Nobu, not Next Door Nobu. Delicious, but not cheap.

Don't get me wrong, normally I would be thrilled to go, but this time I was paying. I had made that clear. As soon as we sat down at our table, Seamus started talking *omakase*. *Omakase* is the chef's choice. It is prix fixe, but not like a $9.99 all-you-can-eat buffet. No, there's a bunch of courses offered for varying prices, each one more expensive than the next. Seamus assumed we would get the most expensive. I couldn't get out of it by saying I wasn't hungry because at least two people at a table had to do *omakase*. Also, there was no way I could watch Seamus enjoying all the savory Japanese treats without yearning to sample my own.

"Is this okay, Rebecca?" Seamus asks. "I would have picked somewhere a little less popular, but I remembered how you said you loved the rock shrimp tempura."

"I do. This is great and I usually go next door, not to this Nobu." I am flattered he remembers. I decide to forget about the tab and just enjoy. I just got that promotion and I have been paying all the minimums on my credit card bills. It is a mere token. I won't always have to pay.

I order a mango martini and Seamus gets sake. He knows what kind of sake he wants. I have a feeling he's been here a million times, too.

"Do you like it here?" I ask.

"I do. It's lost a bit of its wow! but it's still a fantastic meal for the layperson." Am I a food layperson? "To me, nothing compares to West Coast sushi. I like Nobu, but this place in L.A., Matsuhisa, is far superior. Of course, there are arguably places in Vancouver that can rival that."

"Of course." I don't always choose the restaurants when it comes to going out with my friends, but I am usually the person everyone looks to to choose the wine, even though I was learning from Seamus that my knowledge is limited. I am also the person who generally gets the "good choice" comment from the server when I order. With Seamus, I feel out of my league, yet it turns me on.

"I'd like us to try something," he says. Uh-oh! Is this when things get kinky? "I want you to drink sake with me for dinner tonight."

"Instead of wine?"

"Yes, I know. It's out of the ordinary, but, Rebecca, I know some great sakes that are positively euphoric. I want you to trust me."

"Okay," I downed the rest of my mango martini. I could get used to this. "I'm in. Let's do it."

When the first bottle of sake comes, it tastes strong and gross at first, but I agree to finish my whole cup. Toward the end I could stomach it, so I took another cup. By the time we were on our second bottle, I was no longer tasting the delicious foods that were put in front of me. The cod in black bean could have been a Filet-O-Fish.

By the time dessert comes in its attractive little box, I am no longer sure what Seamus and I are saying to each other. I just know that he has invited me back to his place and I am ready to go. There aren't too many things I like doing when I feel this full of alcohol. I was looking forward to doing one of them in front of Seamus's fake fireplace. All my inhibitions have been cast aside. All systems are go. There was no way Seamus would ask, "Did you, did you yet?"

When the bill comes, it's unbelievable. Despite my alcohol haze, I could still make out the amount was over $400. Not including the tip. I have never spent that much on a meal (for two!) before. Thank God for plastic.

We get a cab right away, and we kiss the entire way home. Seamus pays for the cab—I save six dollars. (Every little bit helps after that dinner.)

Seamus gives me a brand-new toothbrush. He went to the dentist just last week. He also gives me some pajamas, which I don't understand. I brush my teeth in his bathroom, studying my spit to try to remember what I had eaten. In the morning, I will hate myself for getting too drunk to enjoy my food and for spending too much, but tonight I need a little sugar in my bowl.

I strip down to my black bra and Tabitha's Taboos underwear and go into Seamus's bedroom. He is lying on his back on the bed. His eyes are closed and his pants are still on. This doesn't look promising.

"Seamus," I say, letting the "mus" ring out at the end.

"Mmm?" He moves his head to me, squints his eyes open and closes them again. It looks like I'll have to take matters into my own hands. The room is spinning, but if I make it to the bed, I will be fine. I climb up on the bed and straddle him.

"What are you doing?"

"Dunnnoooo."

"You don't." I reach for his belt. "I do."

"Rebecca?" he says with a question in his voice.

"Yes, Seamus?" I lean my face close to his. I start to kiss his chin.

"I think I'm in a food coma." Record scratch. This wasn't supposed to happen. This is the fucking honeymoon period.

When you first go out with someone, it's like television sweeps. You pull out all the stops, guest stars, props, everything. You don't eat too much, drink too much and fall asleep. Not when mama needs a little treat.

"Are you sure?" I kiss his neck this time. I rub the front of his pants. Nothing is happening. "You don't want to…see?"

"Errrrrr." I could get the hint. I am used to being celibate. If only I had kept up with him in the beginning, then our drunkenness might have peaked together. I roll off him.

"Do you want me to stay?" Honestly, I could have fooled around for hours, but there was no way I was getting myself dressed and into a cab. There was only one right answer to that question.

"Yes." He pulls me into him rather clumsily. He might suffocate me. Also, he hasn't had the chance to brush his teeth yet. I wriggle into a more comfortable position. He is spread across the bed, so it isn't easy to get under the sheets, but I manage.

"Okay," I say. I still hope for something. "Set the alarm for the morning."

"Okay," he says, but he doesn't move.

I fall asleep soon after…and wake up first in the morning. I have a raging headache, so I can only presume how bad he must feel. He is snoring. He looks pretty cute. I get up and brush my teeth.

When I crawl back onto the bed, I am wearing his robe for maximum coverage. I have found my inhibitions again this morning. I leave the robe open a little at the top.

As I am positioning myself to go in for the kill, he opens his eyes, which kind of freaks me out.

"Oh," I say, lifting my face up. "Hi."

"Ugh, I feel like shit." Then he smiles. "Good morning."

He pulls me up close and kisses me. I don't even mind the morning breath. I could deal for a little morning nooky.

"You got me very drunk, last night, Rebecca." He slips a hand into the robe. It's warm.

"Me? You are the one who was serious about the sake."

We laugh and kiss. Okay, this is looking good. Then he pulls back. "Do you want me to go get bagels?"

Is it possible that I have found a guy who likes to eat more than I do? Perhaps he just can't perform when he's hung over. Questions are already forming in my head, which will likely preoccupy me if we ever do get round to the act. There is no use doing anything now. The moment has passed.

"I'll go," I say, sitting up. "You just rest and I'll also get you some orange juice and coffee."

"You're wonderful." He reaches out to touch my hair. I feel like we are skipping straight to the comfortable period—without the honeymoon.

I get directions to the local bagel shop, and specific instructions on what kind of cream cheese to get. In the shop, as soon as I smell garlic I am hungry again. Okay, maybe Seamus had a point. We just need fuel and then we can have some afternoon delight. I order my bagels and pick up the paper. This will be great. We'll eat, read and see what else happens. The couples' perfect Sunday in New York.

"Rebecca?" I turn to see Jen behind me in the bagel line. She's been out sick all week but looks fine.

"Hey, Jen, how are you? We missed you this week. Is everything okay?"

"Yeah, I feel much better." She looks nervous.

"It's all going okay, I mean our new boss is…" I shouldn't say what I really think. She is Hackett's niece, and besides she has to make her own impressions. "Well, she's no Hackett."

"Who is?" she says in jest.

"But are you okay?" I ask.

"I think the change of weather really messed with me."

"It has been very warm." I wonder how sick she is or if Hackett has given her some kind of warning about more changes. "Will you be in on Monday?"

"Yeah, everything's fine now. I feel much better. I'll be in tomorrow." That's right, tomorrow is Monday. It just kind of snuck up on me—like the sake. "What are you doing around here? I thought you lived in Hell's Kitchen."

"I did." That was where I had lived with Tommy. "Actually I probably will again, but now I live in Flatiron. I'm just kind of visiting someone. I think he lives on your street. You're on Barrow, right?"

"Yeah."

"Cool. I'll wait for you." I hope that she doesn't feel like I've caught her doing something wrong. It's just a coincidence.

She eyes my outfit. I had thrown on my tight silk black shirt from last night and a pair of Seamus's sweats that are too big.

"Actually, I had a date with the guy I was telling you about."

"Seems like it went well."

"Um, yeah." She gives me a look and I feel like she is Lauryn, trying to gauge whether or not I had success in the sack. You just can't reveal those things to your co-workers. Instead, I tell her about how I confronted Janice about her relationship with John.

"I'm sorry I missed that. This is me." She stops in front of Seamus's building.

"What a coincidence, this is my friend Seamus's building, too. What floor are you on?"

"The second."

"Small world. He's on the fourth. You're lucky you don't have to walk up more. There are what, ten apartments?"

"Yeah." We go inside and say goodbye. I walk up to Seamus's apartment and knock. He answers the door. He's on his cell phone. He's washed up. His curly light brown hair is still a mess. He looks really sexy. He smiles at me and doesn't stop watching me.

"Yeah, I'll call you later, okay. Bye." He hangs up the phone and puts it on the fireplace mantel. "Hi."

"Hey."

"You look good in my sweats."

"Thank you."

"I'll help you take them off."

"Thank you…"

By the time I remember to mention that Jen lives in the same building, I am otherwise occupied.

On Monday morning, I am tired, but I have a much better perspective on things. I did not spend Sunday with *The X-Files* or with Mr. Wizard. Instead, on Sunday night, Seamus and I went to Brite Food Shop, in my neighborhood, because he hadn't been there. He really enjoyed their Asian Latin Fusion and was way into his white-bean-and-wild-mushroom quesadilla.

I am thinking of considering him my boyfriend. It was still a bit strange to have sex with someone new, but there was a point where I just relaxed and it all happened the right way. Once. That's a start.

If we are going to be in a relationship, I think the best thing to do is to keep my living situation a secret. I hint over dinner that I might be moving soon. He has work to do tonight, so he doesn't come over.

Lauryn doesn't say a word when I get in. She just raises an eyebrow. I give her a thumbs-up and she slaps my hand with more fervor.

"What should I do with the TV?"

"Storage?" I suggest.

"Okay, but if you and Tommy aren't living together anymore, you should take it. Have you made your decision yet?"

I have, but I haven't told Tommy. I don't want to think about him today. I just want to enjoy the good day I had with Seamus. I'll call Tommy tomorrow after my meeting with Delores. Then I will surely appreciate the sound of his voice.

Delores is wearing a very long skirt that flared out like a mermaid's tail at the bottom and an oversize dull gray shirt. If I were four-nine, I would have dressed a bit better, but I'm not going to be catty; I have gotten laid.

"How was your weekend?" she asks brightly.

"Oh, it was great." I decide to try a new approach. Maybe we could be friendly. "I had a date. How was yours?"

"What weekend? I worked all weekend. I thought my junior year thesis at Harvard was difficult, but it was nothing compared to this." Perhaps she's bitter because I'm glowing with post-date happiness.

I will not be tricked into friendliness again. If I went to an Ivy League school would I reference it in every conversation? No, I would like to think I would be confident enough to let my capabilities speak for themselves. I try to smile like I understand how tough it is for her.

I listen politely as she starts to go over budgets. I want to tell her that Explore! has more money than any division. It isn't her money, yet for some reason she is explaining to me how she wants us to fill out forms in triplicate and how it's my job to tell Janice and John about it.

"Also, I am curious as to why you signed this expense report for Janice from last week. What was this two hundred dollars used for?"

"It was a business meeting," I say. I knew it was a mistake to listen to Don Beckford. He is able to squirm out of anything. I, on the other hand, agree to anything once I get a few drinks in me. I have a quick flash of Tommy's Facts of Life fantasies. "Anyway, Hackett signed off on it."

"Also, I wanted to talk to you about Kim's attendance."

"Whose?" She is confused and looks down on her desk at some papers. She's vacillating between confusion, giddiness and downright condescension.

"I think you mean Jen." I decide not to tell her that she's Hackett's niece. "She was ill, but I think she's okay."

"Wonderful. I think we're going to have to have a meeting about punctuality with John and Janice."

"They're here until eleven at night sometimes."

"Sometimes," she parrots. "Please set that up. Also, I look forward to getting your calendar today."

"Right," I say. "I'll send it ASAP."

Perhaps I can avoid her. Maybe I can keep her at bay with constant e-mails and forms filled out in triplicate. Triplicate?

We have deadlines! Instead of meetings and excess forms, we should be working.

I call Tommy when I get back to my desk. I wake him up. *Take that* for calling me before eleven o'clock on a Saturday. I tell him that I will begin moving my stuff in next weekend. He sort of grunts when I say it.

"I hope I'm doing the right thing," I say, hoping for some word to indicate that I am.

"Me, too," he says. Very reassuring.

I spend the rest of the day making notes on three episodes. We are going to do all the voice-over next week. I get three e-mails from Delores, each detailing intricately some new policy that she's putting into effect for the sole purpose of wasting my time or creating more piles of paper on her desk. I wonder how the other executive producers feel about all of this. My work keeps me separate from everyone. This makes it nearly impossible to plan a coup.

Seamus calls when I'm in the middle of laughing at the thought of it.

"Rebecca Cole."

"You sound pissed off. I thought this weekend would have put you in a real good mood."

"Hi," I say, and try to put a smile in my voice. "Things are insane at work, but it's nice to hear from you."

"I just wanted to tell you how much fun I had yesterday and Saturday." He laughs. He is acting a bit sure of himself, but it has been a long time since I was in the beginning stages of a relationship. Maybe I don't know what is supposed to happen at this point. I'll have to roll with it.

"Me, too. What are you up to tonight?"

"Oh, I have to meet with a couple of clients tonight and do a bunch of paperwork tomorrow," he says. "I'd really love to take you out for some Moroccan on Wednesday."

"I have a lot of work to do, too." I try to downplay how desperate I am to get away from all this. "Wednesday sounds terrific. I love Middle Eastern."

"I knew you would. I'll call you Wednesday to set things up." Does that mean we aren't going to talk until then? If only I knew the right protocol. We have had sex (while sober)…wasn't I at least entitled to a daily phone call?

"Okay, I'll talk to you, then."

"Okay. Bye."

"Thanks, bye." The problem with working in an office is that you have a tendency to be inappropriately polite. I find myself answering my cell phone as "Rebecca Cole" and thanking my friends when I get off the phone with them. I hope Seamus wasn't really listening. Maybe when I see him on Wednesday I can try to get us onto a daily e-mail schedule.

I get an e-mail from Human Resources. It's for everyone. They are taking the soda fountains out of the kitchen, as well as fresh milk. They cheerfully mention that we would now have nondairy creamer, both regular and flavored, and a pay soda machine. This is big.

"I can't believe this!" I hear Janice yelling from her cube through my closed door. She and John subsist on soda; having to pay for it is going to strain their budget.

I also get an e-mail from Delores. It's shorter than usual, but no less annoying.

Hi Rebecca,

I understand you approved the color (red) of Esme's shoelaces in the large plush toy. As this is the only size plush that will have shoelaces, it is very important that we select a color that accurately represents the brand. If you think about it, I'm sure you'll agree that red seems a bit too whimsical for the character. I think we should stick with traditional white. In the future, you'll want to cc me on any correspondence with licensing. If we aren't on the same page it could be catastrophic. :)

Best,

Delores

Immediately after I read that message, my computer dings again. It's another e-mail from her. I can't believe that she can type another one so fast. Maybe she works on the drafts simultaneously so she can send them rapid fire. Could there be a method to her madness?

Okay, at least I don't actually have to look at her. I take a deep breath and open the next one. Just as short, equally annoying.

Me again.
I think the first four eps of Esme are animated rather sloppily. We are going to want to sit down with Janice and John to discuss technique. I'd like you to come up with a document detailing what you think are the important plot points for each episode and ways that the animation isn't working for you. I'll need this first thing tomorrow at the latest. Then we can take about an hour to brainstorm about the issues together before we meet with them. ;)
Thanks,
Delores

Whoa! A whole hour with her? I don't think I can take it. And how the fuck am I supposed to come up with this document when I didn't have any "issues"? I approved those episodes—so did Hackett. They got solid ratings and terrific press. Shit! I'm going to have to start quoting focus groups. Plus, it's nine o'clock at night. What if I had another date? Of course, I don't, but what if I had a life? She is a sadist. My new boss is a sadist.

And I was beginning to realize that I was something else. I was something much, much worse. I am no longer the It Girl, no longer a creative voice—or even someone with any real say into a character she has created. My office door is closed, but I know I'm going to scream loud, louder than Janice had. I have to. It is either that or call Tommy and have a breakdown.

I look around the office. The only thing that could help was the two-and-a-half-foot plush sample of Esme with the red fucking whimsical shoelaces. I grab her and bury my face in her soft belly.

I scream my new identity into Esme, for she has done this to me. I scream at the top of my lungs, but I'm pretty sure no one hears me.

"I AM A MIDDLE MANAGER!!!!!"

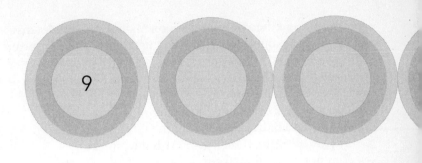

9

Flying Saucer

I did not leave work before 11:00 p.m. for the entire week, except for Wednesday when I went to Chez Es Saada with Seamus. The food was pretty good—I had chicken with almonds and couscous and he ordered a spicy lamb kabob—but the ambience was incredible. There were rose petals on a spiral staircase. Seamus launched into a whole spiel about ambience versus food versus service.

Seamus is always making a case for something. I am getting used to it. His arguments are compelling and organized; in other words I am certain that other people have heard this stuff before he tells me. I wish that he could be a bit more spontaneous…but his good qualities outweigh my minor pet peeves. Although, sometimes I think my attraction to him might blind me a little.

We are constantly drinking wine together, good smooth wine. The only times he doesn't talk is when he is studying the wine list. When he looks up from it this time, he presents me with three possibilities, which means I have to struggle over making the right decision. I'm not sure if he is testing me or if I am paranoid.

I hesitate and then he eliminates one bottle and decides that we should have our starters with the first bottle and our meal with the second.

Every meal with him is a two-bottle ordeal. (We both vowed not to do the sake anymore.)

"Do you ever drink anything other than wine?"

"If I could I'd drink Kool-Aid," he says.

"*If you could?* Why can't you? At home, at least?"

"I'm not going to make it."

"All you do is add water." I can't believe he's serious.

"Yeah, but then you have to buy a pitcher. There are people who do those things. I'm not one of them."

"You mean you don't have a pitcher in your apartment with all those wineglasses?"

"Wine is premade."

"Kool-Aid takes two seconds." This is the first time I've argued with him—about Kool-Aid, no less.

"I have enough disposable income to have other people make the things I consume."

Was I being too picky in wanting a man who could add water to a pitcher? *People who do those things?* I had just seen another side of him I wasn't sure I liked.

On Friday I spent the working day in a voice-over session and returned to my desk to find a boatload of e-mail from Delores. I had to cancel my dinner plans with Seamus when Delores decided she wanted to review the sound design at eight-thirty. We were supposed to go to Vong. It hurt to cancel.

Delores was wearing a T-shirt with Esme on it—it was like a dress on her four-foot-eight body. (No one had told me that we had new T-shirts made.)

At nine-thirty I longed for lemongrass coconut soup as she talked in circles about her views on the noise grass should be making in a scene where Esme was teaching her brother Eric to fly a kite.

I realized then that she just didn't get it; she was underqualified for this job and scared shitless about it. Instead of working *with* me, she had decided to pretend that her way was the only way. The minutiae mattered to her, because if she could nitpick the tiniest detail, it would seem like she knew her stuff.

Oprah would call this an "aha moment," but in spite of my revelation I still worked until 11:30 p.m. on a Friday night.

"Were you out with Seamus?" Lauryn asks when I come home. She is wearing overalls, which swim on her, and a bandanna in her hair. Boxes and papers are strewn everywhere. I have to be out in a week and the sight of this mess traumatizes me.

"No, I had to cancel. I was working with an elf."

"Jesus. You want a mudslide?"

"How very eleventh grade of you."

"They're still good. And I need a little break."

"Why not?"

We sit on the couch with our mudslides. On Sunday movers are coming to move all the big furniture to Lauryn's aunt's house in Framingham. It will stay there until Lauryn finds an apartment in Boston at the end of the summer.

I have been instructed that Jordan will come by sometime next week to pick up the love seat. I wonder how the conversation between the two of them was, but I know from the last eight months of their marriage that if Lauryn wants me to know something she will tell me.

"I'm sorry I haven't been around to help you pack," I say.

"That's okay. I know you've been working late."

"I'm going to have to work from home tomorrow, unless that's going to get in your way. I could go to the library—I just won't go to the office. I have sworn not to do that after the UpFront. Remember how I lived at work scrambling to get the pilot together so the affiliates would approve it?"

"Sounds like Delores might be worse than the UpFront deadline," Lauryn says. "No, stick around tomorrow. It'll be good to have someone else here. Maybe I'll make dinner—one last trip to Whole Foods." She licks her lips in mock seduction.

"Don't go getting sentimental on me." We sip our drinks and look around the cluttered living room floor. "Did you talk to the guys?"

"Kathy came over Wednesday night to help pack. We ordered Indian."

"That's sweet. What's new with her?"

"Same old. She's having a quasicoronary about the wedding. She is worried her diet isn't helping her biceps. You should give her a call. I think she's feeling a little out of touch with the whole Beth thing."

"Is it a 'thing' now?" Lauryn shrugs. "Did she call?"

"Did you think she would?"

"Yes, I still do. What?"

"You're so busy. You don't have the time to realize what little effort she puts in." She has a point. And what's worse, I am almost relieved about Beth's lack of effort because that lets me off the hook.

"She'll call," I say, though not as certain as I was before.

I spend Saturday on my company-issued laptop, listening to the occasional crash sounds coming from Lauryn's room, followed by her yelling, "I'm fine!"

I break only to go get eggplant falafel sandwiches for more energy. I make sure to send Delores several e-mails. I want her to see that, I, too, am working on a weekend. I will never be ambushed into admitting having fun again.

For every e-mail I send her I get two back. She keeps confusing Esme details with those of the other shows. I politely point this out to her. I recognize a commiserating self-important tone in her e-mails. Perhaps I have finally expressed my dedication to the job to her.

But in the next e-mail, she elaborates on how difficult it is to be managing so many shows, and I know she is back on the condescending kick. It doesn't matter that I am working like a dog. I could never justify my job as much as she could or be as busy as she was.

Thank God the gnome didn't have my home number.

★ ★ ★

When I look at the clock it is close to seven. A fucking Saturday down the drain. I go into Lauryn's bedroom. She is sitting on her windowsill, smoking. Her room is incredibly tidy, but also empty.

I feel like a shit. I should have been spending more time with her, but my stupid job is ruining my life. When had I become the person who let that happen? It was time I would never get back.

"Do birders smoke?" I ask.

"Why do you think I'm doing it so much now?"

"Are you excited?"

"Sort of," she says, and rubs her eyes.

"Scared?"

"Sort of."

I flop onto her bed and she flops the other way. We stare up at the ceiling. I turn and lean my cheek on her leg.

"I never realized you had those stars up there."

"Jordan put them up." I don't say anything. "He cried on the phone yesterday. That's his new thing."

I peek up at her. She has her eyes closed. I rest my head again, look back up at the stars, and try to imagine them happy.

"Did he mention his job? Is it going okay?" I tread carefully.

"Yeah, he is scared shitless—you can hear it. That's why he feels like he needs me again."

"Well, it's a little late for that, isn't it?"

"Yeah," she sighs. "You know you're lucky that Tommy and you are okay, you're like adults about your breakup."

"Whatever," I say, lying on my back. "Who knows?"

Lauryn lets out a long sigh. "Let's go to Whole Foods."

I don't want to leave this moment with her. I feel like we should talk more about everything. But my stomach growls and Lauryn laughs and gets off the bed. Once again, I have avoided finding out how she is feeling.

On Sunday, I couldn't get in touch with Seamus. He wasn't home or answering his cell. I didn't expect him to be at my beck and call, but there was no way I was doing any work today.

Lauryn was mostly done with packing. The movers were supposed to arrive at noon. I decided to get out of the house, so I took a book down to the dog run in Madison Square Park. I had started this trashy novel a couple of months ago, but I couldn't find my place.

I decide to start reading my book over again.

When I get home, the house is empty except for my easy chair and coffee table. Lauryn is sitting in it. Her eyes are red; she is staring at the corner where the TV used to be.

"What's up?" I ask, plopping on the floor next to her. I kept looking in the corner where the TV used to be, too.

"I'm all done. I'm exhausted."

"So you don't want to have one last drink in NYC?"

"No, I'm gonna hit the old sack." She punches the air with her fist. "Hey, did you talk to your friend Seamus?"

"No. Did he call?"

"Yeah, he said he hoped you had a good weekend. I told him to try your cell."

"I had it on, but he didn't call. What time are you leaving tomorrow?"

"Early. The train, then the ferry, then who knows." Lauryn stands up and opens her arms. "No big scenes, okay? I can't. I'll call you when I get there."

I start humming "Memories" and she swats me and then meows.

She goes into the bathroom. She's sleeping on the floor in a sleeping bag.

"You can have my bed if you want."

"No thanks," she yells. "I'm fine."

A minute later she peeks her head out of the bathroom. Her toothbrush is stuck inside her foamy mouth.

"Byth the way. Betsh nevah called." She goes back into the bathroom and I hear her spit into the sink.

When I get to work on Monday there is a three-page memo about using music in episodes from Delores. She slipped it under everyone's door. The memo doesn't just say you can use

Library A for music and Library B for effects, but never ever Library C. No, it details the entire process that Delores had gone through to arrive at the four-page form that we have to fill out in triplicate whenever we use our CDs from the stock music library.

There is also a message from Seamus, left on Sunday night. He hopes I had a good weekend and that we can hang out Tuesday night.

If I didn't know better (and I wasn't sure I did), I would think he was trying to avoid actually talking to me.

Maybe I'm just being paranoid. He had mentioned Zarela on the message. A guy who didn't want to see me wouldn't be taking me for upscale Mexican. Would he?

I am distracted by the double ding warning of another "urgent" e-mail from Delores to all of the executive producers.

> Hello all,
> Happy Monday! Hope you all had a terrific and restful weekend. What does that word mean again (ha! ha! LOL). I'm certain you all got my memo about the new procedure for music cues. (What, more forms? Hee! Hee!) Well to make things even more convenient, I am sending you the memo in this nifty attached file. I know you'll all want to fill these out for any future shows, but in addition to that it would be real troubleshooting to fill out forms for all past episodes.
> Thanks, all.
> Best,
> Delores
> P.S. The word of the day is mayhem with a y.

Is she giving us a spelling lesson or trying to be cute? Past episodes? The dwarf is crazy. The word of my day is Dwarf with a capital *D* for fucking Dwarf Dramatic Delores.

And yet another Monday spent with the door closed....

When I get home, Lauryn is gone. The apartment feels

lonely and empty. I feel unsure of everything. The people I care about I can't seem to connect with and the people I'm not sure of or just plain don't like are taking up most of my time.

I remember my dream from last night. I was looking for Esme in her schoolyard. There were kids everywhere, but I couldn't find her. I knew she was around, the way you know things in dreams, but I never found her.

I am so unsettled, nothing feels like it should. I check the messages. There is a message for Lauryn from Beth. It is 10:45 and I haven't eaten dinner. I never called Seamus.

It seemed too late for everything.

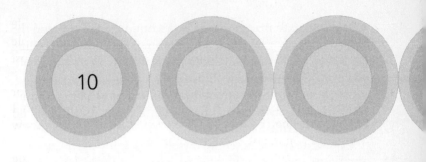

10

Man in a Suitcase

There is nothing like having to move that makes you want to give it all up and become a monk or a nun or whatever you could be that requires no earthly possessions. The only point of earthly possessions is to collect dust. And dust brings you down. Apart from the knowledge that magnified dust is actually a killer-looking mite, it gets into your contacts and into your nose and forces you to sneeze and—simultaneously—curse at your ex-boyfriend.

There have been times in my life when I have considered Tommy the funniest person on earth; however, today is not one of them.

"Was it really necessary to buy all these shoes?"

I find it best to avoid speaking to him. I know he is doing me a favor by letting me move in. I must keep telling myself that. I didn't have any time to pack up during the week, so I had to do it all on Saturday and Sunday and move on Memorial Day. Even though it's only the end of May it's already really hot. Tommy has come over to help me. I thought about asking Seamus, but that might entail explaining why I was moving in with Tommy. I stuck to the story that I had hired movers and wouldn't have a chance to set up my phone for a while.

It isn't easy to maneuver the bed around the corners and the situation is only exacerbated by Tommy's insistence on calling me Mrs. Cole because he thinks my glasses (which I had to put on because of dust) make me look like a librarian or something. I have stopped paying attention to what was cracking him up so much. My arms hurt from carrying boxes and I'm in no mood to be trifled with.

I alternate between telling myself he is doing me a favor and reminding myself that it could be worse—I could have to find my own apartment in New York City. And that would really drive me over the edge.

The thing about moving in Manhattan is that it can be very good for getting rid of stuff; for example, I decided to get rid of my little bookcase so I left it in the street, and by the time Tommy and I made our next trip with a couple of boxes it was gone.

There are a certain amount of groupies who seem to follow moving vans around the city. A crowd has formed around ours. I had to shoo people away from my mother's antique dresser. We left it next to the truck for a second while we got into the back and tried to rearrange our space. A woman and what appeared to be her teenage son pounced, and they were halfway down the block when I caught up with them.

"Hey, that isn't trash."

"Oh, I saw it on the street for a while and I figured I would ask you about it," she says. It was on the street next to the van for all of three minutes and she didn't ask me about it. I shake my head and she puts it down and walks away. Tommy is right beside me.

"Nice job," he says. We high-five goofily and stand looking at each other for a strange minute. I think I should have given a lot more thought to moving back with someone who is still so cute to me.

By the end of the day, we have finally driven the van to my "once and again" apartment. My thighs hurt from stair climbing and all I want is to get a foot massage from Tommy, but he is not my boyfriend anymore. That is not allowed.

Jordan is over, a little surprise I get when we pull up in the rented van. He is waiting outside smoking a cigarette.

"What's Jordan doing here?"

"I called him," Tommy says. "There's no way I'm hauling all that stuff up five flights with a girl."

I know Tommy was only teasing and I know that he was smart to call Jordan, but it isn't easy to hang out with a guy who did your best friend so wrong. I kiss him hello and try to avoid him for the rest of the evening. Not an easy task when you're moving stuff up five flights of a narrow staircase.

I am on the defense at any mention of Lauryn. At one point he asks me if I've had any word from "my friend." Please.

"I have a lot of friends," I say. "If any of them wanted you to get word of them they would give it to you themselves."

I ignore the look I get from Tommy, but later when we're moving in my dresser, he gets pissy.

"He's trying, you know. You're lucky he's here to carry up all your fucking clothes."

"You have a short memory," I say. I wasn't going to forget the way Jordan treated Lauryn. I feel Tommy let up a little on his side. "Okay, we can talk about it later. Next time, I'll hire movers." Although I did that last time I moved out of here and it drove me further into debt. Now I was back, anyway, and it's all the same, except that I'm poorer.

I buy pizza for the three of us. Jordan insists on getting half pepperoni. I hate pepperoni and some of it crept over on the plain slices. This meant I could only have two, which really pissed me off, especially when Jordan is shocked that I could actually eat two. Lauryn must have been a saint!

"You've got quite an appetite," Jordan says. Is this what Tommy meant by trying? I can't wait for him to leave. He tries another approach. "Nice glasses, Rebecca."

"Thanks," I say.

"She looks like a nerd," Tommy says.

"Thanks," I say again, and mouthed *Asshole* at Tommy.

"You want to play some Tony Hawk?" Tommy asks Jordan. Was the purpose of getting me to move in with him so that Tommy could annoy me? What have I got myself into?

"Sure, my call time isn't until ten," Jordan says.

Ten! Now we are going to have an all-night tournament. Soon, Jordan is calling his guy for a pot delivery and Tommy is bringing out the bong.

"Um, I have to get up tomorrow," I whisper to Tommy while Jordan is on the phone placing his order.

"That's why you have your own room."

"Welcome home," I say to myself—and my cell phone rings. It's Seamus. I smirk at Tommy and take it in my room.

Of all the executive producers, only Don has e-mailed Delores back. He has replied from the Hamptons —it is Memorial Day weekend, after all!—and even his e-mail implies that he really doesn't want to be bothered. It seems that Delores has slowly lost her mind, and by mid-Monday, when normal people are enjoying a barbecue and a day off, she is "inviting" us to a mandatory meeting for the entire staff at 10:00 a.m. Tuesday morning.

My body still aches from moving and it is a miracle that I got in at nine o'clock, but I knew that losing the whole weekend of work was going to be a problem. Even though I could barely lift my arms to put a shirt on, the subway arrived just as I went through the turnstile, so I was feeling pretty good.

Of course that all changes when I go into the meeting. The first twenty minutes consist of Delores dressing us all down for not being accessible all weekend. She wonders aloud if we are at all aware of deadlines. All four-seven of her is filled with rage as she demands we submit our revised production bibles by the end of the day.

Revised? The meeting room is a buzz of activity. She is one step ahead of us. She slams a box on the table and pulls items from large stacks of collated pages.

"I spent my Memorial Day putting these packets together." She says *Memorial* as if it was the most insidious word in the English language, and begins to distribute the stuff.

"I expect everyone to make this their priority."

I begin to look through the packet. It was a new format for the production and a lot of rhetoric. Production bibles are giant documents about the show, the characters and storylines. It's basically the who, what, when, why and how of a series. They take forever to put together. Hackett and I had gone back and forth for about two weeks the first time we did it. If we are on production deadlines, how could we possibly stop what we are doing and rewrite a document that already existed?

I look around; everyone is riffling through the sheets of paper. There are a lot of eye rolls and head shakes, but no one looks like they are actually going to say anything. Were we just going to take this lying down? I can't afford to lose more time producing the show. I need to keep creating the episodes—not stop and describe them.

I started to raise my hand—but wait! I don't need permission to talk. I am an executive producer—I had a right to be heard.

"Um." The whole room turns their eyes to me. "Don't you think this is a little…" Shit, shit, what is the word? *Redundant? Excessive?* Which would get me in less trouble? I have opened my mouth and now I am getting fucked. "Much?"

I felt pure evil come through Delores's eyes. I have dared to question her. The word of the day is *retribution* and it will be hers. Up until this point she has toed the line between giddy pretend-a-friend and calculated condescension, but this, this is fire. The mutant is actually a demon.

"It's interesting that you would bring that up, Rebecca, since Esme is the program with the most discrepancies."

"What?" I think I might stutter.

"I don't think this is the forum for all of the issues there are with Esme." What issues? "But I will say to all of you that it's going to be Armageddon if we aren't all buttoned up."

Arma-fucking-geddon? I don't know what to say, but at that moment, Janice slams her hand onto the table and gets up and walks out. I feel myself begin to shake.

"I have one more issue I want to discuss with you," Delores yammers on. "Summer is here, and with it come summer Fridays. I know you were allowed to leave at one o'clock last year, but Indiana Mutual says the weekend starts at three o'clock. Although, I'm sure you are all quite responsible about finishing your work and therefore we probably won't ever get to leave at that time." She giggles, reverting back to giddiness, as if a ruined summer was something to joke about. She manages a sweet "thanks, everybody" and sends us on our way.

I stop by Janice's cube on the way back to my office. John is already there.

"Are you okay?"

"This sucks, Rebecca. Do you know that they are doing layoffs? Have you seen Claire lately? People at the adult networks have been laid off at random. These people have no idea how to run a network, and yet we have to listen to them. How dare she say that shit about Esme? Fuck her! And if I were you, I'd start getting my résumé together. That woman is clearly threatened by you."

I look at John and he is looking down at one of his three computers. I feel a mutiny coming on and I don't know what to do.

"I think you're overreacting," I say to Janice, although I really don't believe it.

"The woman doesn't even know my name. She sent an e-mail to the entire Esme group and put someone else's first name on my last name. John forwarded it to me. You weren't copied. She wants us to lose the glasses." *What?*

"Wait. What?"

"That's right. No more glasses. I thought that was Esme's trademark."

Ten minutes (and one cigarette) later, I make the now-notorious walk down the hall to Delores's office. She has her shoes off and one of the plush gophers on her head. What the hell is going on?

"Rebecca, I was just going to send you an e-mail." She is back on the cheerful, "smile while I screw you" trip.

"Really." I am in no mood for small talk. "I didn't appreciate your comments in the meeting."

"Yes, well, I know it was the forum for my grievances, but you seem to have trouble grasping protocol."

"Protocol? The last thing we need is more forms. This isn't a fucking bank, this is supposed to be a creative environment."

"I'm not sure if you are the right person to be managing a team," she says, obviously trying not to let her mouth turn up in a smile.

"Well, I'm not sure *you* should be managing anything." I have gone too far, but instead of being upset Delores looks smug.

"The outburst from Janice was really unprofessional."

"People are getting emotional."

"Do you know what this channel is about?" Is this a trick question? I think of the slogan we use on-air. We are Explore! Family, after all.

"Family. We Are Family." She seems downright orgasmic at my answer.

"No, money. We are about money, and if you and your team—" she says *team* like she says Memorial Day, with disdain "—can't handle that you might want to think about getting a new job."

"Why, because I disagree with you?" *Because I don't think you have any idea what you're talking about?* I want to say but don't.

"No, because you're wrong." I hold her eye as she says this.

"What is this about Esme losing her glasses?"

"Glasses don't work. They aren't cool. They aren't sexy."

"She's not supposed to be sexy, she's an animated twelve-year-old. And yes, they *are* cool."

"Glasses don't sell advertising space," she says. She is taking a tone with me, as if someone has already authorized her to talk down to me.

"Advertise glasses."

"It's not that easy. This is the decision."

"It's my show." She looks me up and down before answering.

"It's Explore! Family's show. You developed it for us." Us?

Now she is an us. I hate her. She is practically frothing at the mouth. I get up.

"I'll work on that bible."

"You better. I need to see it ASAP."

I almost salute her but I fear if I raise my hand it will slip across her cheek.

11

Four-Eyed Girl

I am sitting in my office with the door closed. I lock it now to avoid anyone busting in. My contacts are bothering me. My jaw is clenched. There is a knock at my door. I get up to answer it and realize I'm not wearing any clothes. I grab the pages of the production bible and try to cover myself.

When I open the door, Esme is standing there. She is very short; I have to look down at her. Her shoelaces are white and she isn't wearing her glasses. She is no longer animated, and as a real girl she looks a lot like me.

"Hi," I say. I am happy to see her. There are a lot of things I want to ask, but she is mad. She starts to yell.

"I can't see anything. You made me not be able to see." She keeps screaming at me and my jaw gets tighter and tighter.

Then I see Seamus and I realize I am in his room.

"Are you okay?" he asks. I'm sweating and wearing nothing beneath the T-shirt he gave me. I fell asleep without taking out my contacts.

"I had a bad dream," I say.

"I see that. Are you okay?"

"I think so." I'm a little embarrassed.

"I'll get you some water." When he leaves, I get up and go to the bathroom. I pull out my contacts and put them in little plastic cups.

He comes back in with the water. He looks pretty cute in his boxers with his hair messed up. Maybe having a bad dream will be another first for us as a couple. I drink some water.

"Let's spoon," he says, and he just cuddles me—no funny stuff. I fall asleep happy and thinking that maybe Seamus really is my boyfriend. It's better than thinking about how much I disappointed Esme.

In the morning I think about asking for a drawer at his apartment. But when I ask if he wants to go to Nobu Next Door tonight, he tells me he is going to be busy for the next couple of evenings. Hmm. Is it possible that both work and my private life are equally messed up?

To top it off, my contacts have dried out in the cups and I don't have my glasses with me. I squint through the day at work as we put the finishing touches on a few episodes. Esme still has glasses in these. Delores's new regime will not begin until the next round. I have a sinking feeling every time I see Esme. She is so happy deducing things in her glasses. They are a part of her. Fuckers!

I think Janice, John and Jen are disappointed in me for losing this battle. Maybe I *am* a sucky manager. This whole thing is making me doubt every aspect of my life.

When I get home, Tommy is on the couch. He has just started watching one of his favorite movies from one of his favorite actors, Tom Hanks.

"*Joe Versus the Volcano* again, huh?" He wasn't up when I left the apartment yesterday morning. I can't tell if he knows that I haven't been home in two days.

"Nice sweater," he says. It is Seamus's. Proof that he knows. *We are not together anymore*—only roommates. This is what I must keep reminding myself.

"Did you eat?" I try to sound friendly.

"Yeah."

"Okay." I order a small mushroom pizza and *straticella* soup from Don Giovanni. I watch a little of the movie as I wait for my food.

I am getting a lot of negative energy from Tommy, but I am too exhausted to get up and go to my room. I don't think that I have ever watched this whole movie, despite Tommy's insistence.

There are a number of movies that Tommy thought I must see, but a lot of times I just sort of humored him and read a book or a magazine while he watched his DVDs. In this one, Tom Hanks is in a dingy-looking office that makes rectal probes when he realizes he has a terminal disease called a brain cloud. He starts ranting that he has suffered all these indignities for $300 a week.

He keeps yelling about $300 a week and the next thing I know I am sobbing. I feel so exhausted and spent. I'm not sure what Tommy thinks is going on, but he kind of starts freaking out. Then he does something he rarely does, he stops the movie.

"Rebecca, what the hell is going on? Are you okay?"

I can't stop crying. Then the bell rings and I know it's my food. I get up to buzz the guy in, but Tommy stops me.

"It's okay, I got it." I try to get my wallet, but Tommy runs to the door. I hear him talking to the delivery guy in the hall and he comes back into the living room. I am trying to pull myself together.

"Um, Rebecca, can you float me five dollars?" I start laughing, the hysterical kind of laughter you have when you've been crying too much. I finally get my wallet and toss it to him.

"Just take the money out of there," I say. "Don't pay for my pizza."

He comes back in and gives me change. I wipe my eyes and open up my soup. I am a little bit out of breath. Tommy stares at me.

"Aren't you going to watch the rest of the movie?"

"Are you going to tell me what happened?"

"It's nothing," I say. I want to forget it ever happened.

"Nothing. One minute you're sitting here normal, as normal as *you* can be, and the next you're crying. What happened? It's like fucking science fiction."

I remember the alien girl he said he would run off with, but I don't mention it. I just shrug.

"I don't know, maybe I'm PMS-ing." Normally any mention of the monthly condition I have would quiet him, but Tom Hanks must have given him some bizarre courage. It was terrifying in a way, as if someone had replaced my ignorant gym teacher with a bizarre female teacher who knew that having my period wasn't an excuse not to play volleyball.

"If I ever tried to suggest something like that you would tear me a new one." I hate that expression and he knows it. "What's going on?"

"Esme lost her glasses." He swallows and looks confused.

"Is this the plot or something? You want me to help you figure out how she finds them?" In days of yore, when the ratings were high, before we had to jump the shark in our relationship, Tommy used to help me come up with ideas for the sixty-second Esme shorts I created. He was really tied to her, too. Even though we had already broken up when I found out we were turning her into a show, I knew he was really proud. Sometimes I felt like she was our kid. I got custody, but now I had been a bad parent and social services had come to take her away. Except it was an evil force named Delores who was now going to raise her. I start bawling again.

"Jesus, Rebecca. I'll give you a hand."

"It's not a plot. She lost her glasses."

"I don't get it."

"No more glasses. Maybe she'll get contacts. I don't know."

"What?" He is about to give up.

"The fucking peanut that I work for doesn't want Esme to wear glasses anymore. It's not sexy enough."

"She's what? All of twelve?"

"Yeah. Glasses are not going to sell ad time."

"Jeez." He runs a hand through his hair. There was the reason I could never get pissed and not have Tommy in my life.

Whatever went on between us, somehow he always understood the things that were important to me.

I turn the movie back on, eat a couple of slices of my pizza and give him the other two.

Kathy calls me at work the next day. As soon as I hear her voice, I get anxious about finding a way to get off the phone. That feeling is immediately followed by guilt and then defiance. I am making a lot more than $300 a week, but it's not worth all the stress. If one of my best friends calls, I am damn well going to talk to her.

Kathy is hot by most standards, but the thing that makes her the most striking is the funky-colored glasses she always wears. It's her trademark and it became Esmes's. I am envious that she had an object so tied to her identity. She brought me to Selima for the first time, and it was with her that I finally found a pair of glasses that I liked.

If anyone else was going to feel my pain it was Kathy. I tell her the whole sordid tale. When I finish she waits for a long time before speaking.

"That just sends the worst kind of message. If I was a little girl and feeling dorky enough I would love to see a cool character like Esme wearing glasses."

"What is so obvious to TV watchers is often derived by TV makers only after a series of focus groups and meetings. No one can ever just accept a good thing. When a program is doing well there is this constant need for tweaking. God! I hate my job."

"Do you know what you need?"

"Rock shrimp tempura."

"Rebecca!"

"To get sloshed."

"No, a trip to everyone's favorite optical store."

The secret of people who work in TV is that the majority want to work in film. One of the geekiest things Tommy and I ever used to do back when things were good between us was to film-parody different conversations we would have. For example he would ask me what we should have for dinner and I would say, "spaghetti western," and then he would have to re-ask in a certain way.

I might be telling a story about work or something and he'd say, "But how would you direct that like a film noir?" Sometimes I try to imagine my life as a movie and recast certain aspects of it in different genres. It was a lot easier to do when I had more free time.

If ever I get the chance to direct a big-budget Technicolor musical, I am going to shoot one scene of the heroine (because all my protagonists will be women) shopping for glasses in Selima. In fact, the chorus of dancing salespeople and customers who glide around on glass cases and giant optical instruments will do jazz hands and shout "Selima!"

Kathy's motives for inviting me aren't as selfless as I originally thought. She is picking up the special mother-of-pearl glasses with yellow accents that she ordered to go with her wedding dress. They look great on her, but after I oohed and aahed about how beautiful she will look with the glasses complementing her dress and bouquet of yellow flowers, I figured it was my turn.

Although Kathy is a CPA she really should be a personal shopper. The bespectacled salespeople at Selima are quite helpful, but they don't stand a chance against Kathy. You've barely adjusted the earpiece when she is declaring, "no," "maybe" or "fabulous." She is very sure of herself and of what looks good on her friends. We travel around the cases, followed by the admiring salesperson, and Kathy has me try on various glasses until she is satisfied.

Even though I got a new pair of glasses—black Martine Sitbons that Tommy enjoys ridiculing—last year, Kathy has determined that buying another pair—a funkier pair—is just what the eye doctor ordered to improve my spirits.

We narrow it down to four pairs. I really like a pair of brown glasses that are sort of square. Kathy is having a real quandary over a pair of thick turquoise-and-brown glasses and a red pair.

There are also the titanium frames that the salesperson suggested that I take just to appease her.

Kathy has me try the titanium ones first and then shoos them away with a swipe of her hand.

"I don't know, Kathy, I think these are the way to go," I say, holding up my favorites. I look at the salesperson, who shrugs, afraid to speak unless spoken to by Kathy. Kathy looks at me for a long time.

"I just don't know if they suit the shape of your face." No one has ever spoken so earnestly about glasses before. Then Kathy closes her eyes as if channeling a spirit. "I'm seeing you in a long camel coat with an ecru cashmere turtleneck peeking out. Yes, I like what I see, but it's very conservative, very winter. It's summer now, Rebecca. It's hot, you're hot. Try the turquoise."

I try them. I look in the mirror. They are really nice, but it's a lot of glasses.

"I'm not sure, Kathy. I like them. They seem like a little too much glasses." She closes her eyes, as if wounded. She takes this shit seriously. I see the salesperson shake her head.

"I just mean that they are a little thick." She opens her eyes and nods, giving in a little.

"Okay, if you don't like them, that's valid. I'll defer to you on that." I appreciate the small victory. "But, I think they look hot. Try the red."

I try the red. I look at Kathy. Kathy smiles and nods. I look at the salesperson, she agrees with a nod, cocking her head. I look in the mirror.

"I don't know," I say. They look good, but red? Kathy sighs.

"Those glasses are like a silk robe or a Prada suit. Those glasses say, 'I am a children's television producer, but I give a mean blow job.'"

"Kathy!" I say. I look at the salesperson, who is laughing nervously. "What will they match?"

"They're red. Everything matches red."

"Even pink," offers the salesperson. Now they're a team. Another customer comes over to us. She's a woman in her mid-forties with a nice dress, but a bad haircut.

"That's a great color for you," she says to me. "I wish I could wear that color."

Kathy looks at me with her eyebrow raised over her funky purple vintage frames. She told me so.

"Can you help me decide between these two pairs?" she says to Kathy. I feel for the salesperson. I look at myself again in the mirror. Red glasses, red shoelaces, maybe this is solidarity.

"I'll take them," I say to the salesperson. I do like them. The woman with the bad haircut is telling Kathy about her Internet dating experiences.

"Well, that's why you have to get these." She holds up a pair of midnight-blue frames. "Those tan ones make you look ten years older. I wore a pair of green-and-brown ones that had a similar shape when my fiancé proposed."

"Oh my goodness," says the woman in true awe. Kathy holds up her ring.

"Tiffany's," she says. The woman gushes over it. Kathy is quite smug. "I know."

I hear gasps as Kathy recounts the whole story of Ron's proposal. I rub my temples as I sign the credit card deposit receipt. More debt, yippee!

Kathy turns her attention back to me. "When are they going to be ready?"

"Next week," I say.

"I want to see them on her again," she instructs the salesperson. Then she laughs. "And I want to start getting a discount. I bring enough business here. She got those at my behest. And that other lady is getting the ones I suggested."

The salesperson adjusts the glasses on me and starts writing up a ten-percent-off coupon for Kathy. She changes it to fifteen percent when Kathy clears her throat. I turn to Kathy.

"Those look great on you," she says. She puts her tongue in the corner of her upper lip. "Mmm."

"You wear your glasses during sex, don't you?" I ask.

"Only if he's good."

We leave the store. Kathy wishes the bad haircut lady luck. She is thrilled to have been the fairy glasses mother for so many.

I am further in credit card debt, but I can't think about it. I deserve a little joy.

"Do you want to go to Nobu Next Door?" Kathy asks. "Will that put you in a better mood?"

"I'm in a great mood. I just paid too much for glasses that I don't need."

"Of course you don't need them. But they look hot, so be happy and let's get some tempura."

"Don't you have to go home to the ball and chain?"

"He's at a game tonight." My mouth has already begun to water about the prospect of spicy creamy sauce. I don't care if I *am* Kathy's backup plan.

Kathy and I have a really nice dinner. It's been a long time since we hung out, just the two of us. Occasionally, I like to get my friends one-on-one. We don't talk at all about Beth or Lauryn. And surprisingly, Kathy barely mentions the wedding. I find myself talking shop way too much.

We split a chocolate soufflé for dessert and Kathy tells me about how there are going to be a bunch of layoffs at her job and she knows about it because she had to report all the overages. She's feeling pretty bad about it.

"I see all these people in the elevator or the lobby, and of course to me it's just a bunch of names, but I know that the cuts will include some of these people. I feel awful. I want to scream, 'Start saving your money! Don't make any large purchases! You're all getting up and outed!'"

"What?"

"That's what they call it, on paper. Up and out."

"You're kidding."

"No."

"It sounds almost like a good thing."

"I know. That's how they get you. I have to talk about this and understand the economic benefit, but I can't imagine how much it's going to suck."

"Up and out?"

"I know," she says. "I know."

"Wow, I'm probably getting up and outed, and I just spent four hundred bucks on ruby-red glasses."

"Don't worry about it. They need you. You're the whole show." I shake my head, eat some more chocolate goodness. I don't even like dessert that much, but I want to eat the whole thing.

"Don't you think those people getting up and outed think they are needed, too?" She nods. I can tell she feels like shit about it. That's why there's been no talk of wedding favors.

"Sometimes it sucks being an adult," she says.

Delores spends the rest of the week in a management conference at a company headquarters in Gary, Indiana. I can't imagine she's spending much time in meetings because she sends me e-mails and voice mails every five minutes. Still, I prefer not to have her around. The very sight of her makes my allergies act up.

Seamus rents a car on the first Saturday in June. We're heading all the way out to the tip of Long Island for the day. We hit a ton of traffic, but he's holding my hand and the windows are open. It's just nice to be out of the city, which is beginning to boil.

"I like your sunglasses," he says, looking over at me.

"Prescription," I say. Another shopping trip with Kathy last summer.

"Nice."

We stop at a few of the vineyards. In the sun, the wine hits me a little harder than I expect. Or it could be the allergy pill. The wine is not affecting him, because after every sip he swirls it around in his mouth and then spits. I am kind of embarrassed, but the people doing the tasting act like this is normal.

We stop at a little place called the Country Kitchen for dinner. It's a small, charming place with purple tablecloths and focaccia bread baskets. We have a really good meal of locally caught seafood. He picks the wine and I feel myself getting slightly drunk.

"I always drink a lot of wine around you."

"I like that. I like how your cheeks get red." He reaches across the table. "It matches those glasses."

"They're new," I say. "I just got them this week. I'm giving my eyes a rest from contacts."

"They're cool. You look good in that color."

"Do you think it's going to take us a while to get back to the city?" I am planning on skipping dessert.

"Well, yeah, I was thinking that maybe we could stay around here if you were up for it. I made a reservation at a place a ways down the road."

"Really," I say. I can't believe he did that. "That's a nice surprise. I would love to."

I'm going to leave these glasses on tonight to kick it up a notch....

We have a great night and we drink one of the bottles of wine that he bought. The motel is clean and cute. It's no frills and that makes it more appealing, like we're having an affair or something. The glasses work, too. We have a lot of fun. In the morning we walk along the bay that is right behind the motel. We go back to the Country Kitchen for breakfast. I'm starting to look ahead and imagine this as our place and the Motel on the Bay an escape. It feels like we are finally becoming a couple and that means that sometime in a future, we will have a past.

This weekend has solidified something between Seamus and me. We keep having all these false starts because of our schedules and other commitments, but now things are getting more intense. I can imagine moving in with him. Sure, it might be a little strange to live in the same building as Jen, but we'll manage. I am definitely getting movers this time. Maybe I'll make Seamus Kool-Aid every morning. Perhaps sometime Tommy can come over for dinner and the two of them can talk about...okay they've got to have something in common. Me, they can talk about me. No, that won't work. What can they talk about?

"What's up?" Seamus asks. He squeezes my hand and puts it on his leg. "You all right, you seem a million miles away?"

"Oh, no," I protest. "I'm right here. I'm just thinking about what a good time I had."

I smile all the way to Queens. Then, he tells me that he is going to do a summer share in the Hamptons starting after the Fourth of July. I've never been into the whole idea of the summer share, but I kind of wish that he would ask me if I care or if I'm interested or something, but he doesn't. I know a lot of partying happens at those houses in the Hamptons, and if we are getting closer and becoming boyfriend and girlfriend it might be nice to be included in his plans for the summer weekends.

"So you're not going to be around at all on the weekends?" I try not to sound too desperate or hurt or anything that could be construed badly.

"No, it's only half the time. A half share."

"A half share." It's more of a repeat than a question.

"Yeah, you can even come out sometimes if you're not busy. A couple of my buddies are doing it, too. I think it's going to be a lot of fun. If I can't spend the summer in Nice…" He tries to make a joke and laughs.

What am I supposed to say? Just when I think things are getting better, we're back to square one.

"What? You're not mad, are you?"

"No, of course not," I say, and smile without opening my mouth. If he was Tommy, he would know I was. Not only am I furious, I am also a passive-aggressive doormat of a wanna-be pseudo-girlfriend. And a coward to boot.

"Do you want to come over tonight? We could order some sushi or some Indian?" Of course nothing that he has to make. He can't buy me. I will not be plied with food and sexual favors. Okay, I would if I thought this was actually developing into something. But is it? It's not every date that we spend two nights in a row together? Maybe he needs time. No, fuck it. I have to be strong.

"No, I have to do some work."

"Okay," he says.

We don't say much more until he drops me off at my apartment and he tells me that he'll call. I give him a quick kiss on the cheek and try not to slam the rental car door.

Tommy isn't home. I sit on the couch and try to find something on TV, but nothing is on. What's the point of digital cable if nothing is on?

No boyfriend. No sex. No Tommy. No *X-Files.* No D batteries. Fuck!

And if that wasn't bad enough, tomorrow is Monday.

12

Shattered

I get two disturbing e-mails first thing Monday morning when I am supposed to be reviewing a fine cut of Esme. This Esme will have no glasses, so I'm procrastinating for as long as possible before I watch my little blind creation.

The first e-mail is from Hackett. Oh, what a fine time for him to come back around. It isn't just to me, but to the entire department. We're having an off-site meeting at the Chelsea Piers driving range next Monday. The two words *team building* strike fear into my heart.

The company doesn't have money for fresh milk in the fridge, yet we can afford golf at Chelsea Piers.

The strange thing about Hackett's e-mail is how concise it is. He wants us to meet at Chelsea Piers, so he says it. As much as he drove me crazy, I miss the way he was so up front, unlike the queen of verbal vomit.

The next e-mail is from Delores. It's in sharp contrast to the one from Hackett. From what I gather she wants me to come for a meeting in her office, but she can't seem to tell me that without mentioning how important it is that we get "all buttoned up" about managing Janice and John. I think I'm reading into a subtext about their relationship. Today's word of the day is *incendiary*. There is also a whole justification of her job in the form of how many hours she worked this weekend in her apartment even though she has no air-conditioning. I am not sure if this part is meant to be friendly.

I don't bother to reply. I just can't. I want a new job, but I can't leave Esme. Esme is mine.

Instead of writing back, I just show up at her office at the appointed time.

"Hi," I say, making an attempt to ignore the nausea that fills me every time I see her.

"Hi." She is sitting in kind of a strange position. "Have a seat."

"Did you have a good weekend?" I know the tone of her answer before I get it.

"Busy, but you know it's to be expected. I've got to try and stop working until eleven." I semi-ignore her. "So I realize we are having some human resources issues and hope we'll be able to resolve them at the team-building meeting."

I was surprised that she was owning up to our issues and also fearing the "work" we would have to do in front of the whole company. Ew. She was sort of arching all four feet, six inches of herself away from her desk in a way that didn't look comfortable.

"I want you to take some initiative on the production of *Hannah's Hacienda*." She starts to shuffle papers around her desk without getting too close to it.

"What do you mean?" *Hannah's Hacienda* is a show that we have been talking about for a while. It was originally called *Joanna's Hacienda* and was supposed to promote diversity by taking an American girl from the city and sending her to live in Latin America. It is live action. One time it was on my plate when it was in animation. "Is it back to animation?"

"No." She still strangely isn't sitting close to her desk. Were we being bugged or something? "I just think that if you are going to be the executive producer your title says you are, you need to work on more than one show."

"So this is a test?"

"No, this is experience you need." She was looking at me as if she had already won some sort of battle. "You know that Jack Jones's production company has expressed interest in this. We are already casting. You could oversee their production."

"Whoa! What about Esme?"

"I'm sure you can handle both this and Esme. I have the directive from above, and if I were you I would choose your battles." This is weird. I haven't done live action and I probably could have figured it out if that was all I was executive producing, but not with Esme. It was impossible, and we both knew it. It was her way of getting me out.

Just fucking fire me, I wanted to say. *Up and out, lay off, terminate me, whatever. I can't take it anymore.*

I don't say that. I don't say anything.

Finally I see why she is sitting so weirdly. She's trying to get me to notice the card that she has propped up next to the bouquet on her desk. From Hackett.

Delores,
I know you are working very hard. You are doing a great job.

Matt

How could he? Hackett was supposed to be overseeing the whole department, but he was obviously clueless about what was going on, splitting his time between London and New York. It sucked. And what was worse, Delores knew I saw the card—just what she wanted. She smiles.

"Now, we all know Jack is someone we need to impress." Jack Jones had been a sitcom star in the seventies, and no matter how cheesy celebrities were, Explore! Network liked to be associated with them. The theory being it made us seem cooler when everyone thought of us as a dorky network. Fuck us! I'm not part of the us.

"Sure," I say.

"So he's coming in for a meeting with us and Hackett tomorrow at nine. You'll want to be on time and do a lot of kissing up."

"I'll use my tongue," I say, and walk out.

I really said that. I am so getting fired.

I walk by Don's office and he's on the phone. There is nothing worse than hovering around someone when they are on a call, but Don sees me and gestures me in.

"Does it seem like a problem, Kurt? Okay. Let me know." He hangs up. "Hey, I was actually going to stop by your office after this."

"Why?"

"Does your friend Jordan have a drug problem?"

I smile. "Well, no. I don't think so. No more than anyone else." I knew he smoked pot and there was some talk of cocaine when things went sour with Lauryn. I wasn't sure how much I should trust Don.

"Okay. My producer, Kurt Cressotti, tells me he's been showing up late and is kind of out of it."

"Well, I guess sometimes he could be more responsible." This is the last thing I want to hear. Don sighs.

"You didn't come by to talk about this."

"I just got put on *Hannah's Hacienda*."

"We're actually doing that?"

"Jack Jones's company is into it now."

"You know how we love getting boned by celebrities." I laugh at his crassness. "Talk about drug problems. I've seen the *E! True Hollywood Story*."

"Apparently that's all behind him and now he's a perfect candidate for kids' TV. And I'm executive producing. I've never done live action."

"Are they trying to make you fail?"

"That's what it seems like, doesn't it?" I stare out his window.

"How are you?"

"I feel sick every time I come here."

"You know, the exact same thing happened to me at Playtime." He shakes his head.

"I just don't know what to do. Should I quit?" I ask.

"That's what they want. You can't, or you'll get no severance. It sucks. She's been jealous of you since she got here."

"That's just it. I never was this kind of woman, now I'm turning catty—and I never did anything to her."

"And she's driving everyone crazy. Everyone hates her and
everyone likes you. I'm glad I'm not a woman. Sorry."

"Thanks. If everyone hates her and she sucks as much as we
know she does, how come she's here?"

"They're never going to fire someone they just hired. With
this whole merger thing, they'd do anything to avoid the bad
press. They got to kowtow to the big guys at Indy Mutual, she's
from there. We just have to suck it up. I'll help you with whatever I can. You need advice. Anything."

"Thanks. It's all such political bullshit." I sigh.

"Rebecca, listen to me. No matter what, you can't quit.
They want that. They're hoping you do. They're never going
to fire her. This is a test for you. If you quit you'll get no severance, no unemployment. You cannot do it. You'll lose too
much."

"What about my peace of mind? What about my stress level?"

"Look, it won't be long now. Just hang in there."

It seems like everyone knew I was being set up to fail.
Throughout the day, different people came into my office and
shut the door and told me they thought the situation was
shitty. I didn't believe that Don had let it slip to all these people—at least not this quickly. But things have a way of getting
out. It was bizarre that it seemed so certain.

I appreciated all of the support, but I knew in the end there
was nothing anyone could really do. In the end, all of this support was not going to stop me from getting up and outed.

I wanted to call someone—not Seamus—one of my girlfriends or Tommy. But, I knew that if I called one of them I
would start crying on the phone. I promised myself I would
never cry at work.

I start to look over all the paperwork I had on *Hannah's Hacienda*. Why did everyone love alliteration so damn much?

I couldn't really get that into it. I was going through the motions. It didn't seem to make a difference what I did, so why should I try? The outcome would be the same no matter what.

Toward the end of the day, Delores peeks in my office.

"I'm not leaving," she says. "I'm just going to get lunch."

I know the correct response is to point out that it's almost seven o'clock and isn't she a little trouper for working so hard that she hasn't had time to eat lunch?

But, I just nod. If this was what it was going to take to keep my job I was happy to get fired.

I check my cell phone. There is a message from Seamus apparently "just calling to say hi." He has to work late. He hopes we can go out on Thursday.

I decide to leave early, but I take a bunch of my folders with me. I need to be prepared, just in case.

I think of something as I close the door to my office. I walk down to Delores's office. I look at the bouquet. The card is no longer propped against the vase. That had only been for me, to prove something to me.

She really is threatened, the tacky, petty freak.

It's still light out when I leave my office building. I don't want to go home. I decide to go down to Lupa and sit at the bar and order myself a good fattening dinner. The place is crowded, but the maître d' finds a seat for me at the bar pretty quickly. I order a little carafe of white wine and pasta *cacio e pepe*. It's really a winter meal, but it's comfort food. It's so simple, pasta with pepper and cheese.

The only trouble is, there's this lump in my throat that makes it hard for me to swallow. I push my food around my plate for a half hour when the bartender asks if he should wrap it for me.

"Please." I decide not to get another drink, just the check. I walk home up Sixth Avenue. The summer city sky is turning pink. I walk past Bryant Park. Soon there will be free movies in the park on Monday nights. There are things I love about summers in the city. I must be happier, but I didn't feel my emotions were under my control.

★ ★ ★

At the *Hannah* meeting, I'm completely out of my element. I don't have the first clue about appropriate budgets for a live-action show and that's what this meeting is about. Budgets and casting for a show that seems to have a sucky premise. I can't believe anyone thinks we should actually be doing this show. Did I mention Jack Jones is a washed-up sitcom actor from the seventies who has decided to produce children's television shows? I thought so.

He pitches his gig with a confidence that says he believes he doesn't have to. He thinks it's in the bag, which it is. Explore! is desperate to get the press that goes with partnering with a celebrity no matter how C-list they are. What's worse, he's asking for an exorbitant amount of money.

Delores is running the meeting and is doing her best to impress Hackett with faux efficiency and pedantic words. She manages to slip in one anecdote about Harvard, just in case Jack Jones wasn't aware of her alma mater.

"Okay, we will have to revisit the budget at our next meeting, but it seems quite sound." She is totally doing the "I've dressed up as an executive" act. She turns to Hackett. "Unless there is something else you want to add, Matt?"

Okay, that is offensive. There are only three of us here representing the network, and by not asking me if I have anything to add, she might as well send me out for coffee. Clearly the purpose of this meeting is to demonstrate that I mean nothing to anyone.

"Let's move on to casting." Jack Jones is one of those guys who is half-bald with a big potbelly, but still thinks it's cool to have a long ponytail down his back. He plays with it constantly throughout the meeting.

"Right, well you know we were thinking ethnic for Hannah." He spreads a couple of head shots of young attractive girls on the table. I reach for one of them immediately, ignoring Delores's eye roll. I like to check out what else they've done. I'm slightly amazed by parents who have their kids acting at six months—and a lot of these girls have been in the biz for as long as they could drool.

"That one is a front runner," Jones says, pointing to the photo I have in my hand. "But we think she's part Hawaiian, and you know what they say about Hawaiians. She'll probably fatten up as soon as she sees the craft services table."

I look up at him to be sure he's making a joke, but he isn't. I look at Hackett, who appears equally disturbed. Delores, on the other hand, is nodding.

"I don't think she even really reads Asian enough," she says. What the hell is "Asian enough"? I study her résumé. It says she was born in Japan and is fluent in Japanese. She lives in California.

"Um—" I say, trying to cut in. "I think she's actually Japanese."

I can't wait to hear what they will have to say about Japanese.

"If we are going to go ethnic I think we should go Latin," Delores says, ignoring me. She picks up a head shot. "Latins are very sexy right now. How about this one?"

I am disgusted. Did she read that in *USA TODAY*?

"She's part Indian and she can't act. Of course, if you like her look we could have her play Latin and coach her." Delores nods, considering.

"Excuse me." Why am I talking? Why did I decide to open my mouth? This is the trap. "I think we should get the actress we think will be most accessible to the audience. Putting on weight isn't the biggest detriment. I don't know if the girls need to be a certain ethnicity…."

I could go on, but I realize that Jack Jones is only interested in his ponytail because he already understands that I don't have any say. Hackett is shuffling through papers uncomfortably and Delores has straightened her four-foot-five frame in the chair and is smiling ever so faintly.

I don't say another word. I know I've done exactly what they wanted me to do, given them reasons for things they would have done, anyway. In the end, they go with a blond girl and decide to forget about having an ethnic lead. They'll make one of the teachers black. Maybe. It's no longer that important to them.

After the meeting, I save a lot of my files to disk and plan to bring home a couple of things from my office.

Jen comes into my office, hopping from foot to foot. I assume she is going to offer me her support about what's going on and spend a little time dissing Delores, but she is acting weird.

"Do you want to shut the door?" I ask. I go back and forth between wanting to just sit here all day with the door closed and feeling like I should have the door open and try to fool the world.

"Okay." She shuts it and sits down in one of the chairs. She is fidgety.

"It's going to be okay, Jen. Nothing bad is going to happen to you. You've got Hackett." I try to keep my issues with her uncle out of my voice.

"It's not work," she says. "Are you still seeing that guy who lives in my building?"

"Seamus? Yeah."

"It is Seamus." She looks upset.

"Why? Have you seen him?"

"No."

"What is it, Jen? You're acting funny."

"Well…" She starts to pick at her cuticles. "I keep seeing this girl in my building."

She stops and sort of grimaces. I take a deep breath, not really sure where this is going, but suspicious.

"Today after I got coffee at the bagel store we met at, I saw her on the subway platform."

"Who is she?"

"Her name is Petra."

"Petra?" I don't like the sound of this.

"I was friendly to her and we obviously recognized each other. 'You live in my building,' I said."

"What did she say?"

"No, my boyfriend does." I open my mouth. I close it. I open it again.

"And is her boyfriend's name Seamus?" She nods.

"I'm sorry, Rebecca. I agonized about telling you this. I was hoping maybe you had gotten back with your old boyfriend."

"I didn't."

"I'm sorry."

"It's not your fault. I'm glad you told me." I really am I guess. I just don't know how to feel.

"I'm sorry, Rebecca."

"I know. You said that. It's okay." She acts like she isn't sure what to do next. I really want to be alone. "It's *okay.*"

She takes the cue and leaves my office. I pick up the phone, intending to call Seamus. I could shoot this as a horror film or as a subtle foreign drama. I hang it up. I don't want to deal with this right now. When it rains it pours. I'll see Seamus on Thursday, we'll eat a good meal and then I'll get to the bottom of this. I can't care about it much more right now.

We go to Blue Water Grill, because we can sit outside on the patio. I keep looking for some sort of sign from him. I keep trying to figure it out. Is he going to break up with me?

I've been running through this situation in my head a lot. No, I haven't told any of my friends. No one knows but Jen, who has been hovering around me awkwardly. I guess it sucks to be her, too. It's not easy to give someone such bad news. And yet, I feel responsible to her to get to the bottom of this, to dump his ass before he dumps mine. Jen knows I am seeing him tonight and therefore she is entitled to some sort of story.

Part of the reason I haven't told anyone, I think, is because I want there to be a reason for this. I figure if I don't tell my friends, they won't think he's a dick, and then remind me of it when I don't want to hear it.

In spite of myself, I've played this out in my head in ways that actually absolve him. Like maybe there is another Seamus who lives in his building. Jen didn't know my Seamus, before I told her about him, so maybe when I mention this to him it will all be a happy coincidence. Tomorrow, I'll go into work and explain the silly mistake and we'll laugh, ha-ha-ha.

Or maybe this Petra is a crazy stalker. Maybe they used to date and they broke up and now she just lurks around his apartment building. Seamus is just too kind to get a restraining order. Tomorrow, I'll go into work and describe the girl's tragic life and the honest mistake and we'll laugh, hee-hee-hee.

It's possible that he'll completely deny it and I'll believe him and go and speak to Jen tomorrow and she'll tell me that she has this ear infection that she didn't know about, which made her unable to hear things properly. When she heard Petra (whose name is probably Kendra) tell her she was dating Seamus she was really dating Raymond who lives in 3B. Jen will ask me to put drops in her ear for her, and I will, and then we'll laugh about the crazy mistake, tee-hee-ha.

He is acting normal. During our chopped salads, he tells me about the process they use to make the blueberry vodka that's in the delicious lemonade I'm drinking, which leads to a discussion about basil-infused olive oil. I'm following him and realizing once again that whenever we talk I just kind of listen to what he says. I don't need to participate in the conversation at all for it to happen.

Something in me just can't ask. Our three-tier tray of seafood comes out, full of oysters and shrimp and crab. He smiles and takes an oyster, chewing carefully. I think it might only be the idea of him that I am into. I *like* being with someone who knows so much about everything, dresses well and has buffed fingernails. No, I have to get to the bottom of this. I can't just be cheated on and accept it. I can get over an idea, can't I?

"What's up with you, Rebecca?" This is the perfect time.

"Nothing." I am a coward. No, wait. I have to do this. I can't.

"Are you thinking about work?" For the first time in a while, I'm not. Maybe I should be getting dumped all the time, to take my mind off work.

"No, I was just—" Do it. Oh, I have a better idea—a test. "I was just thinking about our first date."

"You were?" I think he's squirming. I kind of like it. "We didn't come here. Did we?"

"No." The fucker. "Don't you remember?"

"Was it Jewel Bako?"

"You've never taken me to Jewel Bako." Is that where he took Petra?

"Look, kids on a rope." I turn to look over the little bushes that separate us from the street and there is a group of children walking by with their hands on a big white rope.

"Weird." This would be the surrealistic breakup film.

"Must be some kind of rich kids' day camp at night."

"Must be."

"Only in Manhattan." I nod. I want to get back to the business at hand. But he changes the subject. "Try the crab leg."

I try it and it's good and fresh and perfect for a summer day. But I am not going to be distracted by food. Not this time.

"Esca," I say. "Don't you remember?"

"Oh, of course. Sorry, brain freeze. Of course I remember now."

"Really." I know, I know. I'm playing a stupid game, but for some reason I can't help it. "So who did you go to Jewel Bako with?"

"Um, must have been a client."

"Must have been."

"Are you finished with this?" The waiter is back at our table.

"Yes," I say.

"No," Seamus says, and grabs the last shrimp. "Okay, now we are. So, do you want to go up to the Boat Basin for a drink?"

"I know about your other girlfriend." There. I said it, and now he has to confirm or deny. I'm ready. I think.

"What?"

"Yeah, a girl I work with lives in your building. Imagine that." He swallows and picks up his butter knife. He is trying to figure out what to say.

"Look, we never decided we were going to be exclusive." I see the waiter come over with the dessert menu and then pause awkwardly when he hears what Seamus is saying. I'd say that's good service.

"We didn't. We're sleeping together. I didn't think we had to be specific." Seamus sees the waiter.

"Do you want coffee?" Seamus asks.

"Not right now." I am getting angry. "What does she think about this? Have you been up front with her about me?"

"Brianna is very progressive."

"Brianna? I thought her name was Petra." He looks like he's been completely caught. "Who is Brianna? How many are there?"

He sighs and doesn't say anything for a long time. I think he is calculating and trying to decide whether or not to cut his losses.

"Listen, Rebecca, this is New York. I know I'm a catch. There's not a ton of single straight men out there who know how to treat a woman. It would be selfish of you to want to keep me for yourself."

"You're kidding, right?"

"No, I'm just being honest. We're adults."

"You weren't honest from the beginning."

"We never made any kind of commitment. It isn't my fault that you had the wrong idea." He looks me in the eye.

At this point I'm thoroughly ashamed of myself. I realize I was hoping to get a feeble excuse from him I could accept. I can't believe how desperate I was for a cool boyfriend. Apparently I'm not the only one.

"No, it isn't." I push my chair back and fish fifty dollars out of my purse. "Thanks for dinner and good luck with everything."

"Rebecca, it doesn't have to be like this. I don't see why we can't have fun together."

I shake my head. "It's still early, Seamus, you can catch that drink uptown with someone else."

When I get home, Tommy is sitting on the edge of the couch playing World Cup Soccer. "How was your night?"

"Fine," I say, and shut my door.

And, speaking of shut doors…on Friday at 4:00 p.m. the phone rings. I'm reading an e-mail from Kathy's pregnant, domineering sister about a shower. I check the caller display. It's one of the guys from HR that I barely know. I pick it up.

"Rebecca, it's Matt." Hackett is calling me from Human Resources? And I know immediately when they call me down what is happening. I've known it was going to happen. You could say I was expecting it, but I realize now that there is no way I could have imagined how it would feel.

13

Guess I'm Doing Fine

I have an hour to clean out my office and put everything into the box provided. I send out a really quick e-mail with a new e-mail address and that I will no longer be at this number. Then my e-mail is turned off. It's a good thing I have been cleaning out files for the past few days. There is a knock on my closed door. I think about not opening it (they may be coming to rush me out), but when I do, it's Janice.

"What happened?" She sees my face.

"Come in." She looks at the box and turns back to me.

"No!"

"It's really not a surprise."

"When?"

"Five minutes ago."

"They waited until now, when a lot of people have left on their summer hours. Those fuckers! Are you okay?"

"Um, yeah. I'm a little in shock. I have an hour to clear out."

"You're kidding. An hour? Like you're some kind of criminal? What did they say?"

"The word that Dwarf used was *terminated*. Hackett tried to soften it by saying 'let go,' but she insisted on saying 'terminated.' Twice."

"That fucking bitch. I am going to make her life miserable."

"Well," I say, throwing a few of Esme's press clippings into a box. "Be careful."

"Let them fire us. Let them fucking fire us all. That'll be great press. Do you need to be alone or can I go get John?"

"No, get him. I'm just going to be packing up for the next half hour until they send the guards."

"You think they'll send guards?"

"Who knows?"

Janice leaves and comes back with John. He stares at me and shakes his head.

"Did you punch her? You could probably get away with it. Temporary insanity."

"No, I didn't say a word. I didn't want her to be happier than she already was."

"I didn't tell Jen," Janice says. "Should I? She knows that something is up."

"Go ahead. It can't hurt now."

John starts helping me get my posters off the walls. The phone rings. It's Don. One of his PAs saw me carrying a box into my office.

"What's going on?"

"I have an hour to get out. I've been let go—" I correct myself "—terminated."

He lets out a sigh. Up until this very minute I thought Don and I were only colleagues but now I realize that we are friends, and I'm glad because at this very minute I appreciate having someone who has been through this advise me.

"Okay, I won't even waste your time telling you how fucked up it is. There are nights at bars for that. First thing is, did you get severance?"

"Yes. They gave me an offer and I have till Friday to sign it."

"Good. Are you happy with it? You don't have to tell me what it is, but I know a lawyer or two."

"Of course you do." I laugh. "I don't mind telling you. Two months. Is that good or bad?"

"It's fair. And what was the cause of it? I mean, we know what the real cause was, but what did they say on the papers?" John lets Janice and Jen in. I wave at Jen, who looks like she is about to cry.

"Performance. I guess the whole Jack Jones meeting. Or something."

"Jesus. Okay, we are about to start shooting again, but listen, I'll call you this weekend. This isn't so bad. You were miserable and now you get two months off. Do you have savings?"

"Not really." He gives me the number of an attorney who helped him negotiate a deal two networks ago. It's worth a shot, I guess.

"Okay, well I'll figure something out. Hang in, okay."

"Okay, bye." I hang up and Jen rushes over to give me a hug.

"I can't believe this."

"It was your uncle that did it," Janice says, and I shake my head at her.

"Hackett was just going along with it." I start to print things out that I hadn't taken, while listening to Janice, John and Jen talk about how much this sucks. I am glad to be leaving with so many people thinking it's wrong. I just want to be done with everything and never see this place again.

"Do you want to go out for a drink?" Janice asks.

"Or five," John adds.

"No, I think I just need to get home."

"Do you need us to help you?" Janice asks. I have this feeling they think I'm going to slit my wrists or something.

"Yeah, I can carry whatever you need home," John says.

"Honestly, I'm fine. I'll grab a cab. It's all good."

"I can send stuff to you on Monday," Jen says.

"Okay," I say. "That's good. I'll give you whatever I can't take now."

"We should let her be alone for a while," Janice says.

"But call us if you need us," John adds.

They leave my office and I worry that they need more comforting than I do. Maybe I'm not seeing the whole picture, but I just need to get through this hour and then I will let myself react however I need to.

I say goodbye to them on the way out. They still seem upset and keep trying to get me to go out for a drink. I give Jen a bag of tapes and scripts and give everyone a hug. I fear Jen is the one who is handling it the worst, because Hackett was involved.

I get into the elevator and two of Don's team members are in there talking about me and looking upset.

"Are you all right?" one of them asks.

"Yes, thanks."

"Don told us. It really sucks."

There are a ton of people I will never get to know and these two guys are two of them. How will I ever meet anyone if I don't have a job? Will I wind up on the street? No, I just need to get out of here.

I stop on the human resources floor in order to drop off my ID card so I can't break into the building.

I am certain you will do this all with the dignity I have always known you to exhibit, the human resources guy said when he told me I had an hour to clear out. I don't think we had ever had a conversation before that except when I wanted to find out if my dentist was covered in my insurance plan.

I could take a cab, but then realize I should start saving money. Although I deserve a cab, I take the subway and regret it instantly because it is so muggy down there that I get a headache. I get dirty looks from people because of my big box. In New York, big boxes and bags on the subway rank with golf umbrellas on the sidewalks. You just shouldn't go there.

I look up at an ad for the NYC Teaching Fellows that says, "Nobody ever goes back ten years to thank a middle manager." No, they certainly don't.

My shirt is drenched in sweat by the time I get outside again. I am panting as I walk up the five flights to my apartment, but all the while grateful that I moved in here when I had the chance. I might have slit my wrists if I had to worry about $2,500 a month on my own.

Tommy is—can you guess?—on the couch playing the Spider-Man game. Last night he opened another level, so now he has the fever. He shouts hello. I drop my box in the hall. We need an air conditioner. We will not last the summer at home together without it.

"It's hot out, huh?" he asks, glancing up at me. "What did you do, walk home?"

"I got fired." He actually stops (not pauses) the game and stands up.

"Are you okay?"

"I don't know," I say. Then I sit on the floor and start to cry.

Tommy buys an air conditioner first thing Saturday morning. It's there when I wake up. He is off for the weekend and I hear him calling all the guys he was going to have over for some kind of PlayStation tournament to cancel. I appreciate that. I make him stuffed banana French toast out of challah bread. I'm unemployed now. I will cook.

We sit on the couch for the entire weekend watching movies, ordering takeout and playing the boxing video game. We do not talk about my job. I do not check my cell phone. And, in case you're wondering, we do not have sex.

Monday is my first official day as an unemployed person. Tommy has to work at the store. He promises to bring home some movies. I make a pot of coffee and watch *The View.* I don't even want to think about getting another job. Ever. I can live like this; relaxing in the air-conditioning, watching *The View.* We've got cable. I can start icing my coffee. It will be great.

There are several messages from people I work(ed) with. Everyone recaps the Monday morning meeting that Hackett attended and how the news was announced as if I decided to leave on my own, even though he knows very well that everyone knows that isn't true. Each person has a different choice word for Hackett and Delores and everyone reiterates how low morale is and how they will never look either of those two in the eye or help them if they see them lying in the street. I think about taping all of these messages and doing some kind of experimental art project. Maybe that is how I will earn my living.

Each message ends with "we have to get together soon." And I count my blessings that I work(ed) with such amazing people. In retrospect I feel like a gladiator who was cheered as I went into battle to get decapitated. I guess that counts for something, right?

I have yet to inform anyone other than Tommy or people I work with about the news. I give myself one more day of sloth and watch all three *Back to the Future* DVDs with Tommy.

On Tuesday, I reorganize the kitchen cabinets and clean the toilet. I return all of my work phone calls. The latest news is that Claire Wylini is on temporary disability for some suspicious back problem, but everyone knows she is getting fired. I return the calls from Kathy and Lauryn who each left me confused messages after I sent the e-mail about my change of contact info. I also tell them about the Seamus situation—or lack of one.

"It sucks about your job, but that Seamus sounded kind of like a dick, anyway. I think you were just transitioning," Lauryn says, using that funny businesslike word. "Why don't you come up here in a couple of weeks?"

"It's tempting, but I should probably start looking for a job."

"Are you kidding? Just enjoy yourself. It's like free money. I wish I had a job to get laid off from." This from a girl who is spending the summer on a vacation island looking at birds. I assure her that I'll consider it. I'm still kind of reluctant to make any plans, although if I did get a job my severance would stop. And I intend to make Explore! pay for every last bit of my termination fee.

Lauryn sounds happier than she has in years. She fills me in on her days of sun, birds and seafood. I promise to go visit.

"I got canned," I tell Kathy. She gasps.

"Oh, honey, are you okay? You kind of knew it, though. You were kind of prepared, right?"

"Well, I guess so, but it still felt weird to have only an hour to clean out my stuff."

"I know," she says. I think this is sort of par for the course in her industry. "Now you can be a lady who lunches for a while."

That does sound sort of intriguing, although in this town it takes money to lunch. Kathy is full of self-serving ideas.

"Now you can be one of those people who go to Bryant Park at like three o'clock with a big blanket to stake out a good spot for the Monday-night movies."

"Great."

"Maybe you can even run some wedding errands for me!" Kathy sounds like she is getting ahead of herself.

"Um, we'll see about that." I tell her about Seamus and she seems a little distracted. I think I hear her lightly tapping her computer keys in the background.

"Well, I'm sorry to hear that, honey." I know that she is sorry for me, that is, because she thinks that at twenty-seven, we are bordering on being old maids. "Let's try to get together next week, okay? I want to talk to you about the rehearsal dinner."

"Okay, sure."

"Did you call a lawyer? You should call a lawyer, just to make sure you can't do something to the company you gave some of your best ideas to. You created Esme, for God's sake!"

I get Beth's voice mail, which doesn't surprise me.

"Hey, it's me. I'm just calling to give you the details about my layoff. I'm okay, but if you want to reach me, call me at home or on my cell." I don't mention anything about Seamus because I haven't really told her anything about Seamus since I felt weird with the whole Tommy thing. I wish Tommy and my breakup could be a nonissue between Beth and me—in the same way that our dating didn't matter to her.

I call the lawyer, Kraig Hitchcock. He's a friend of Don's. I've never had to call a lawyer before. I've never gotten arrested or divorced. I'm starting to think I should have worked out some legal recourse when they decided to make Esme into a series, but I was just so excited about the fact that my idea was going to be a show. I was naive, and now I'm paying for it by not getting paid.

I explain the whole story to the lawyer, who listens kindly and sighs at the appropriate times. I tell him I have until Friday to sign the severance agreement, which stipulates I can never sue.

"It's unfortunate that you didn't consult an entertainment lawyer when this series of yours got picked up."

"I know."

"Basically, you believe you got fired because your new supervisor is an incompetent drama queen with a Napoleon complex…" He's quick, but I guess I didn't mention that she probably made a deal with the devil in the dark forest or wherever the hell she came from, but it seems pointless now.

"Yeah, basically, yes."

"Unfortunately, Rebecca, I'm going to urge you to sign. Two months is fair. Unless you feel you were sexually harassed or discriminated against, there is not much you can do."

"Um, can I be discriminated against for being tall, efficient and hard-working?" He laughs.

"Unfortunately, that isn't how the law works in wrongful termination." I notice he uses the word *unfortunate* or some form of it a lot. I think that's a lawyer trick to make the situation more benign than it is.

"So, I'm basically out of luck."

"I know your pride is hurt, but you're in a better position than most. And you know what? You can still walk down the block to another kids' network. You sound pretty young. I would advise you not to burn any bridges. You may wind up working with these people again at some point."

"No, thank you." I immediately regret being so insolent. "Thanks for the advice."

"No problem."

"Can I send you a check or something?" I'm always awkward when it comes to money for things I don't normally purchase. I wonder how many plates of tempura he bills an hour….

"For a ten-minute conversation? For a friend of Don's? No, that's okay. But, listen, give me a call when you develop your next series. I can help you negotiate a better deal from the get-go."

"Thank you," I say. I have a new respect for lawyers.

When I hang up with him, I take a deep breath and exhale. I don't want to think about how much I screwed myself by not working some kind of deal for the rights to Esme. How could I have been so stupid?

Okay, I won't think about it. My one recourse will be that I will not send my signed severance in until the very last day it has to be postmarked. This is a small victory, but it's mine.

Finally I call my parents in Pennsylvania. I have been dreading this because I know to them getting fired is devastating. In their world things like severance don't matter. Firing means a ruined reputation and failure. This isn't too far from the way I'm feeling, but I have to put on a brave face.

As I suspect, my mother is home and my dad is at work. My dad and I don't have much of a phone rapport, so I'm glad that I can tell my mother and she can break the news to my father and I'll be spared the awkwardness of having to tell him myself.

"Oh, sweetheart, that's horrible. Was it because you were always so late?"

"No, Mom, it was because we got taken over by a bank." So this is a lie—but it's sure to be more palatable to my mother. I made the mistake once of telling my mom that my day started at ten o'clock; I don't think she ever believed me, but rather tried to justify my irresponsibility.

"Remember when you worked at the bank, sweetie?"

"Yes." What was she getting at? I worked there in high school and the summer after my freshman year. I was a teller. The only benefits of that job were that I was able to make car payments and that I realized I didn't want to ever do anything that involved money. Ever.

"Well, maybe you should think about getting into a field like that. You know, one that's more secure."

I count to ten before I speak again. I stare down at my painted toenails, remembering that the first pedicure my mother ever had was last summer when she came to visit me. She giggled the entire time.

She is never going to change. She thinks of working in a bank as a "good job." On the other hand, whatever she imagines I do is flaky—and therefore always cause for concern. I haven't told her that I moved back in with Tommy.

"Mother, I'm not going to change careers. And I don't want you to worry or to make Dad worry. I'm going to be fine. I have two months' severance. It's as if I'm working but I'm not. Get it? I'll be getting money, but I won't have to work." Saying this to her makes me feel slightly better about the whole thing. If I keep having to convince people that it isn't so bad, I might be able to convince myself.

"Okay, honey. So, when are you going to start looking for another job?" I haven't developed a plan, but the one I come up with on the spot sounds pretty good.

"I'm going to enjoy two weeks doing stuff that I never get to do, like errands and hanging out in the city. Then, I'm going to visit Lauryn in Martha's Vineyard, then—"

"Is she still separated from her husband?"

"Actually, they're divorced. It was final a couple of weeks ago."

"Oh." Victory. I may be twenty-seven and washed-up career-wise, but I'm sure my mom is grateful that I haven't gotten a divorce. I've got some things working on my side. "So what is happening with the apartment?"

"Nothing, I'm still here." More lies, but I think sometimes you have to lie to your parents to keep them calm.

"Well, I tried calling your apartment and the line was disconnected." Now I have Sherlock Mommy all of a sudden. Next thing I know, she'll be telling me that Esme is based on her. Luckily, I am ready.

"That's because I figured I could save some money by just using my cell phone. I get free nights and weekends and cheap long distance. In this day and age there's little need for a land line." I'll confuse her by talking technology.

"Oh, okay. Well, let us know if you need anything or if you want to visit at all now that you have time."

"Okay, I will. Bye, Mom."

"Take care, honey."

I love my parents and I miss them, but at times like this I'm glad I don't live near home anymore. I think their concern would make me crazy.

On Wednesday, I actually go out of the house and walk down to the Union Square farmer's market. I usually go on the weekends when it's packed, so it's cool to get there when I can actually move around and sample cheese and bread. I get a bunch of chili peppers and decide to make Tommy some white bean chili when he gets home.

Foolishly I touch my eyes after I cut up the chili. I am trying to flush my eyes out under the sink when my cell phone rings. For some reason I answer it even though my eye is stinging out of control.

"Rebecca, it's your father." He is screaming into the phone.

"Hey, Dad, what's up?" I try to wipe my eye with the back of my hand.

"Your mother told me to call you on this phone because you don't have a real one."

"This is a real one."

"I heard you got fired."

"That's right—um, laid off." Why, why, why did I forget not to touch my eye?

"Well, I just want you to know that if you need anything, your mother and I are here to help. We can help you with your phone bill, groceries, whatever."

"Well, thanks, Dad. I think I'll be okay. Like I told Mom, I got a severance package."

"Yeah, okay. Your mother says hello. Let us know. We're here. Bye." I'm certain my dad is glad to be done with this conversation. My father, who has been in debt forever and who drives a twelve-year-old car, is offering me help. They took out a second loan on their house when I got into college, and now I can't even hold down a job.

★ ★ ★

"Have you been crying again?" Tommy asks when he comes home. He holds up a DVD. "I got *Mad Max*."

"No," I lie, sniffling. "It's just the chili."

I don't go out on Thursday, just watch *The View*, cable and eat leftover chili. Veg-ing with TV and food is becoming a dangerous pattern.

On Friday, I sign my severance package and put it in the mailbox. I consider spitting on the mailbox, but that wouldn't be ladylike, now would it? I call for unemployment. I'll have to call every week to collect about $415. That's about twenty-five rock shrimp tempura dishes and almost a third of what I used to make every week.

On Saturday Tommy and I go to the movies and it distracts me for a little while. Maybe I'll spend the summer going to all the blockbusters....

I can't fall asleep Saturday wondering if Tommy and I should just get back together and what that would mean exactly because we already live together and have been hanging out nonstop. He hasn't had any of his friends over lately and I'm not sure if that's out of respect for me and my constantly changing mood or if maybe he is thinking that we should get back together, too.

As far as I know, he hasn't seen any other girls. Maybe I've ruined him for other women. Of course, I didn't exactly tell him about Seamus, so maybe there are things I don't know. But I *did* spend nights at Seamus's apartment. Tommy hasn't spent nights anywhere else. He is always around when I need him.

Maybe, I'm just a needy person. I know I'm not in any condition to be making decisions about our relationship and I'm thankful that Tommy is a decent-enough guy that he doesn't manipulate the situation to get fabulous and confusing sex for himself.

I dream of Esme when I sleep. She doesn't have glasses on and her eyes are red. She walks over to me and her sneakers fall off. I keep saying hi to her, but she doesn't answer. John and Janice are behind her, shaking their heads, and Jen is hopping on one foot.

When Esme gets to me, she throws a bunch of money at me. I wake up.

What is she trying to tell me? That I shouldn't have signed my severance agreement? That I should have initially gotten a better deal? What did I know? Back then, I would have paid to have my show on television. Maybe Esme thinks I only care about money.

I created her and now she was confusing me.

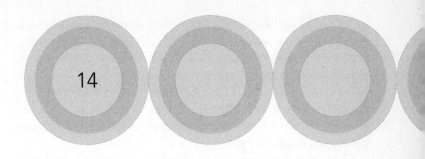

14

These Days

Restaurant Week comes to the city twice a year. I think of it like the first day of school. (Exciting, with an opportunity to wear some new clothes.) In theory, I am supposed to be able to go to many of the top restaurants in the city and pay a fraction of the price to sample the food and enjoy the ambience. It should be the best time of my life.

I think it's all a conspiracy.

First of all, now that I'm unemployed, I can call to book a reservation often and immediately. At like nine o'clock on the day the listings come out I'm on the phone trying to procure lunch and dinner reservations that I can hand out to my friends like favors. They shouldn't be booked so soon, but they are.

Second of all, I wind up spending more money on lunches and dinners for a week than I ever would if I just went out for a couple of nice dinners during the week at regular prices. I realize I can't blame Restaurant Week for this, rather my own lack of self-control.

Third of all, many of the restaurants I want to go to for dinner only have lunch options.

"Actually, we are booked for the whole week," says the hostess at Felidia when I ask to book lunch there on Wednesday.

"Sorry, I'm booked that night and to be quite honest for the whole week," says the woman at One If by Land Two If by Sea. I know I shouldn't even be trying to get a reservation at what is supposed to be the most romantic restaurant in the city without having a date, but the prospect of their beef Wellington makes me act a little crazy.

"I can only get you into the dining room for lunch at two-thirty," says the woman at Acquavit, trying to call my bluff.

"What about the day before?"

"All of my seats for two at lunch are at two-thirty." Oh, right, because that is an obvious time for the Western world to eat lunch. I will not be defeated, though. I am determined to get into that place. My money is good and I plan on spending twenty bucks for a superb experience.

"I'll take it." Now, if I could just find a date it would be perfect. I fear I will have to sacrifice my reservation because all of my friends have jobs.

It's pretty much the same sad story at the next few places I call. No reservations, dinner at eleven o'clock. I even wind up getting the fax number for one of the places. This city wants to thwart me.

The only place I don't call is Nobu. They only offer a Restaurant Week lunch and I'm still having flashbacks to my dinner there with Seamus. I hope he hasn't spoiled it for me. I am going to have to go to exorcise my demons soon, but I swear I will never, under any circumstances, forgive Jewel Bako for being the place he took one of the myriad of his other girlfriends.

I imagine the hostess at Nobu mocking me for trying to make a restaurant reservation at a time when it is certain to be packed. *We are booked for the entire week and the entire week after that and, oh yeah, way into August. And you know what? Those people are willing to pay full price because they have actual paying jobs. And by the way, they also have boyfriends who don't have handfuls of other girlfriends. Those people are good friends with Nobu. They call* him *"No." And, by the way, I eat rock shrimp tempura whenever I want it and sometimes I even leave some on my plate, because I get to gorge on it all the time. Of course I don't gorge because I'm a tall, thin, beautiful person—the only kind who is supposed to come to this place. Buh-bye.*

I don't think I could handle it.

My phone rings. I think about screening it, but quickly rule that out. Everyone knows I'm unemployed and what else would I be doing on this beautiful summer day but sitting in my apartment imagining that the hosts at the major restaurants are out to get me? I take a deep breath and answer the phone.

"Hey, it's Kathy. You're home." She did just call me.

"Yeah."

"Are you sitting on your couch?"

"Um." I look around for a camera. I think I might be getting paranoid-contact highs from Tommy. "Yeah."

"I am so jealous—I would give anything to get out of here. I hate work. You are so lucky." It's all about perspective.

"Thanks."

"Did you check your e-mail?"

"Um, no."

"Well, I sent you some ideas for the flower arrangements and I wanted to know what you think."

"For what?"

"For the tables." Oh, *right.* The wedding. How could I forget?

"Okay, I'll check it out."

"Are you okay? You sound down." Because I'm not squealing with joy about the chance to decide between lilacs and Easter lilies?

"No, no. I'm fine."

"Have you talked to Beth lately? She hasn't returned my calls."

"Join the club."

"She's getting just as bad as you were when you were working on your pilot." I'm not sure what to say to that. Is she trying to remind me that I used to have a life? I suspect she regrets it from the little noise she makes in her throat. "So next week is Restaurant Week."

"Really?" Duh.

"Yeah, and I know that money is tight right now and that you and Tommy really aren't together or anything." She is tripping all over her words and I feel bad for being bitter at her. "Anyway, Ron and I were thinking maybe you two would like to go out to dinner. Ron got reservations at some Italian place downtown."

"Thank you, Kathy." She means well, even though she'll probably force me to talk about seating arrangements all night.

"Let me talk to Tommy. This feels suspiciously like the double dates we used to go on in the past."

"Well, you could bring someone else...."

"I know, but Ron wants me to get back together with Tommy."

"Just let me know. It's Thursday night."

"Okay."

I have to admit, I'm not one of Ron's biggest fans. I think he used to be a frat brother, the kind that usually wears a white baseball hat—a "white hatter," and while there isn't anything explicitly wrong with that, I worry that he has jerk tendencies he's waiting to reveal. Kathy seems to be happy that she is settled down. I guess I expected Kathy to go for a long-haired, artistic type, the kind she always seemed to go for when we first moved to the city. Ron can be a little obnoxious to wait staff and I think that is a sure sign of a closet asshole.

Another thing about Ron is that he likes to talk during movies. He is also one of those people who announces what they think is going to happen, like they want everyone else in the living room or movie theater to be amazed at their deductive skills. I've watched enough videos at their place to know it's a chronic thing. I don't understand how Kathy can spend the rest of her life with a man who doesn't take the moviegoing experience seriously. Luckily, I've only gone to the movies with him once.

In spite of what I think are shortcomings, Tommy and Ron always got along. They found common ground talking about sports and Batman. While I don't think they would have chosen each other as friends if not for Kathy and me, they didn't mind spending time together on double dates.

It's important that friends' boyfriends get along. I could tell that Kathy was secretly relieved when Lauryn and Jordan broke up because Ron and Jordan didn't get along. Conversely, she was bummed when Tommy and I broke up because now she and Ron would have to invest their time getting to know someone else. I'm sure Seamus and Ron never would have liked each other. They both would have been trying to talk louder than the other. I can imagine them fighting over something like what ingredients were in the stew. So maybe in some ways it is for the best that it didn't work out.

Tommy brings up the mail when he gets home. My mail has only just started to get forwarded and somehow that means that I have double bills. I've just missed the payment on my credit card. I stare at the bill from May, which includes all of my Nobu splurges, including the time I treated Seamus. He was so not worth it.

I am also going to pay for my stylish new glasses. I am never ever going to be out of debt. Now, more than ever, would be a good time to start job hunting. I know I should be placing those phone calls, but I just can't motivate. This is not like me. I am (was!) a hardworking person, but I just feel exhausted. I just want some space, some something.

I write a check for the minimum payment on my credit card, knowing that I will see a late fee on my next statement. I feel completely helpless when it comes to paying my bills. If I could just put them in a drawer and forget them, I would. It almost seems like there's nothing I can do to get out of debt. It seems insurmountable. It's as if I've accepted debt and just continue to live the way I enjoy. But now I wonder if there will come a time when I will not even be able to afford the minimum payment. I suppose when the severance runs out.

Maybe I should get a sugar daddy....

★ ★ ★

"I thought you were unemployed," Tommy says when I tell him about dinner. "It's time to give up your vices."

"Um, severance," I say defiantly and a little bit snottily, but then realize I'm going to have to change my tactics if I want him to go with me. "I need to eat, you know."

"Last time I checked there was plenty of food in the fridge."

"It's Restaurant Week. Dinner will be like thirty bucks."

"Make it sixty at least with the wine Ron is going to insist on ordering. She's your friend, why don't you just go?"

"C'mon, you like Ron."

"Rebecca," he smiles. "I'm not your boyfriend anymore. I'm not required to like your friends' boyfriends. I'm not required to spend time doing things I don't want to do. I'm liberated."

He thrusts his arms in the air and continues to shout "liberated" around the rooms of the apartment and into the bathroom, where he shuts the door and locks it. I crack up in spite of myself.

I know he's got a point. If I want this to be over I can't expect him to be my backup date. I keep wishing I could be one of those people who just cuts off their exes, but I can't. I would like to tell myself that the only reason I'm here is financial, but as fucked up as our relationship can be, Tommy is the only one of my friends that I still feel I can truly relate to. I go and wait outside the bathroom for him.

"Jesus," he says, when he comes out. "Give a brother a break. Did you make any dinner?"

"Oh, I'm good for cooking, but not dinners out?"

"You're good for a lot of things," he says, raising his eyebrows. He's not really flirting with me, just teasing.

"All right, a hand job." I call his bluff. He isn't ready to deal with certain aspects of our relationship, either.

"What is with you girls?" he asks, shaking his head and pulling a block of cheese out of the fridge.

"What do you mean?" I know I'm defensive and I'm not sure I want to hear what he is going to say.

"Do you ever, like, just chill anymore?" I hate to be analyzed, especially by the likes of Tommy.

"What do you mean?"

"Okay, calm down." He cuts a hunk of cheese. "You never hang out anymore, you know, you girls."

"Did Beth say something?"

"No." He finally looks annoyed. "She hasn't really talked to me lately. It just seems like there is something funky going on."

"Well—" I take a piece of cheese "—Lauryn's gone and we went through all this weirdness with her last year and now it's almost like we sort of turned kind of catty about her problems. Not like, you know, malicious, but she gave us a lot to talk about. Now she's gone and I don't know what we have in common anymore. Any of us. I mean, I still really like hanging out with them, but there's all this stuff that goes with it. I'm not sure if we hang because we feel like we owe one another or because we still want to find the good times we used to have. I think when we made the switch from all-night ragers in bars to calm little dinners in restaurants, we lost something."

"I know what you mean," he says. "I've been wondering lately what Jordan and I actually talk about. It's like he's always trying to impress me, but there's nothing beneath the surface. It's like he studies me to try to figure out who he should be, what he should like to do."

I nod. I haven't let myself articulate anything like that before and I'm glad to hear that Tommy has had these confusing feelings, too.

"Do you think Beth is okay?" I ask, and he shrugs.

"Do you think Jordan is?" he asks, and I shrug.

"How much do we get involved? And how shitty of a thing is that to ask?"

"I don't know, but I wonder about the same kinds of things."

"Will you please come with me to dinner? It's only thirty bucks! I know your sister doesn't want to go and I know I don't want to be the lone witness to what is Kathy and Ron's relationship."

"Fine," he says. "Just don't sign me up for anything else."

★ ★ ★

The restaurant is in SoHo. Osteria del something. I block it out as soon as the hostess insists on checking my light summer jacket.

"Your party has already checked in. They're up having drinks." We climb up a circular staircase to a bar area that looks down on the diners. The restaurant is dim with lots of dark curtains and high-backed chairs. I see Ron looking down at everyone with a smug expression. This is his kind of place. Kathy is talking to him, but he doesn't really seem to be paying attention.

"Hey, guys," Tommy says, and Kathy turns as soon as she hears him.

"Hello, you two. Isn't this nice?" She pulls the both of us into a big hug and kisses us.

"Why don't you get a drink?" Ron suggests, then summons over the waiter.

"I could just wait until we have dinner," Tommy says, but the waiter is already there. "Okay what do you have for beer?"

"Peroni and Morretti," the waiter says.

"No Bud Lite at this place," Tommy comments.

"They have terrific bellinis," Kathy says. Maybe she noticed me rolling my eyes.

"Do you want a bellini?" the waiter asks, looking at me.

"Um, sure," I say. This is more pressure than I like to have at restaurants.

"I'll get a Peroni," Tommy adds. I smile at him, trying to convey my gratitude for what I fear is going to be an intense night, but he doesn't meet my eyes.

Ron is a pharmaceutical salesman. He makes a lot of money and enjoys talking about everything that has to do with money. I once told him how I viewed money in terms of rock shrimp tempura and he didn't get it.

"How's the Web site, Tommy?" Tommy hasn't even gotten his drink yet and already he has to defend his failed dreams.

"You know, like most other dot.coms. I'm working part-time and trying to figure out what to do."

I tune out as Ron launches into why the dot.coms failed and how stupid everyone was to believe in them. He keeps saying, "I'm just saying you need to be selling something."

I feel like Ron has said these things many times to many people and maybe even to me. I look at Kathy. She is smiling at Ron as if he is running for office. This was a girl who liked long-haired guys who played guitar. What is she doing with him? Is this the best potential father for the children she wants to have by thirty?

I excuse myself to go to the bathroom. I am greeted by the bathroom attendant. I hate when normal restaurants have bathroom attendants. It's just so uncomfortable. I don't have my wallet, but even if I did I think it sucks to be expected to tip when you are just using the bathroom. I have no money so I have to suffer the guilt I feel as the attendant stares at me when I wash my hands. Leave it to Ron to pick a place with a bathroom attendant. This guy loves to be catered to.

He's not a bad guy. But why does Kathy even have to get married now? We're twenty-seven. We've got plenty of time. Lauryn got married early, but look where it got her. Her marriage always seemed like a fun thing to do after we got out of college. It didn't faze me when it happened, because they fought just as much as ever. I look again at Ron when I find the table we're sitting at. I just don't see it.

We get a booth. Kathy, determining it's safe to stop giving her full attention to Ron, momentarily starts talking to me about the table centerpieces. Ironically, as soon as she stops listening to him, he starts listening to her and interrupts her about what *he* thinks would make a better centerpiece. They start to argue about the price of Ron's preferred centerpiece, but it isn't a full-out argument, it's like they still have a semblance of politeness, which makes it even worse.

I glance at Tommy for a sign, but he is looking intently at the menu. I open it up. There is no sign of a prix fixe or "Restaurant Week" menu. I peer over Tommy's shoulder to see if he has some kind of special insert. He looks up at me and shakes his head. I'm in trouble.

"I just think four thousand is too much to spend on centerpieces," Kathy says.

"I think you're right, Kathy," I say. "Where is the Restaurant Week menu?"

Ron and Kathy finally pick up their menus and look inside. It isn't there.

"Maybe we had to sit up in the bar to get it," Ron says.

"We can ask," Kathy says. I think she is trying to quiet me. She looks back at Ron to get him to finish the centerpiece "discussion," but he's distracted by the wine list.

"How does everyone feel about red?" I look at Tommy. I'm willing to say that I am fine with water, but Tommy shrugs, and when the waiter comes back, Ron orders a bottle of something Italian that I've never heard of. He doesn't ask about the prix fixe menu and neither does Tommy.

"Kathy wants to have a budget wedding," Ron says. He reaches over to rub her cheek with his rather hairy hand. "I want her to have the special day she deserves."

I feel a little uncomfortable with being so involved in their relationship issues. I think maybe Kathy wants the father of her children to have lots of money. Maybe that's what makes the relationship tick. Long-haired guitar players aren't usually financially stable and, heck, somebody's got to keep her in the glasses she's accustomed to.

"I just think we have to draw the line somewhere," Kathy says.

"You're right, Kathy," Tommy says with a poker face. He's acting like none of this fazes him, like he wouldn't be much happier at home watching *Star Wars* again. I fear that inside he's calculating the cost of this in his head. "You have to draw the line somewhere."

The waiter comes back with the wine. Ron asks Kathy to taste it.

"No, Ron, you know better," Kathy protests.

"C'mon, I showed you how to do it." The waiter knows who is calling the shots and pours the wine in Kathy's glass. Ron watches her sip it and nod.

"Excuse me," I say to the waiter. "Is there a menu for Restaurant Week?"

"It's at the bar," he says haughtily. "I'll get it for you."

I smile at Tommy, who has perfected the art of showing no emotion. It's something Ron could learn from. He is currently reprimanding Kathy for not tasting the wine properly.

"You just swallowed, you didn't even taste it."

"Ron, I wasn't going to go through that whole rigmarole in the restaurant."

"Why not? That's how you taste it." The waiter hands me a menu with the lunch fixed price on it—they aren't doing dinner. I hate him and his attitude. I guess we have no choice but to order a plate of twenty-eight-dollar pasta. I point the word *lunch* out to Tommy and mouth, "I'm sorry." He picks up his wineglass and holds it up and out to the arguing lovebirds.

"Here's to just swallowing," Tommy says.

We all clink his glass.

Sixty-five dollars apiece later, we climb up the five flights to our apartment. Ron and Kathy were kind enough to give us a ride back in their cab. Kathy insisted on paying. Tommy volunteered to sit in the front so as not to suffer through Ron's stock trading ideas.

"I'm sorry," I say in a heartfelt way.

"About what?"

"The cost of the night, Ron's incessant talking, asking you to go."

"What about the lack of beer selection and the fact that the waiter gave us an attitude for serving us food we were paying for?"

"I'll never ask you to do anything like that again."

"Oh, you can ask, I'll just never go."

"I'm sorry. This proves what I've always suspected about Restaurant Week. That it's a scourge on innocent diners. I can't believe Kathy is marrying him."

"Why?"

"Did you see how he kept cutting her off?"

"She seems happy."

"I think she just wants to get married." Tommy shrugs, as he has been doing all night. Even though he is one of my only friends that I can still feel comfortable around, what I really need now is a girl to rehash this with.

I change my mind about how I feel about being unemployed from day to day. Some days I really can't get motivated to do anything. Other days I find myself walking around the city or being really social, calling old college friends I haven't talked to in a while and e-mailing Lauryn. Sometimes I start making lists of things I'll have to do when my two months are up. One thing is constant; I am not going to get a job before I absolutely have to.

I often walk over to the air-conditioned twenty-five-screen movie theater on Forty-second Street. I hop from cool movie to cool movie, smiling at the ushers if they suspect me. Most day screenings don't have a big audience and I feel like (especially with surround sound) I am momentarily in other people's lives.

At times I feel so guilty. I know there are people out there who work a lot harder than I did. Not everyone gets a cushy thing like severance and that makes me feel worse and less motivated. From minute to minute my feelings and moods change. Someone has pulled the rug out from under who I was. I have no idea how to navigate my life.

My inertia is totally against the work ethic of my parents, but I feel so let down. No one owed me anything, but at one time I believed that the stuff I created was really for kids and now I know that it was for a network to try to sell to advertisers who wanted to brainwash kids. How could I have been so naive for so long?

So when I'm not feeling too bad about myself I tell myself that I deserve this for the time I spent on the front of the corporate world. This is my life, no one else's, and I can't feel guilty for what I have that other people don't. "I'm regrouping" will be my party line when people start to ask me what my plans are. Of course, no one does. Everyone expects that I'll just hang out till my severance sentence is up, so I don't have to explain myself.

Some days I miss Esme so much. It's hard to think that something that was once in your head—such a big part of you—is now a part of some corporation. I think about the way she looked when she discovered why her neighbor's cat was getting sick or how she solved the mystery of where the school flag was. These were simple stories, but I made them and I fear for what is in store for her.

Maybe what I lack is a routine, so I start to make dinner for Tommy and me every night. I still want to eat well, even though I can't afford to go out to a restaurant. I prepare very light things because it's summer, orzo feta salad, steamers, grilled mixed seafood. I start walking down to Union Square every other day when the farmer's market is there to buy fresh produce, artisan breads, seafood and cheese. Every Friday I buy fresh flowers.

Tommy appreciates my efforts, but I feel him trying to maintain a bit of distance sometimes and I totally understand that. He is as confused about what to do as I am.

I meet Janice out for lunch. It's been almost three weeks since I've seen her. She's called me pretty much every day with whispered updates on the fate of my sweet little Esme, but I finally agreed to meet her in person. I have a little anxiety about it because I've been spending so much time alone. And then there's the lunch bill to worry about.

We go to Baluchi's for some Indian food. Janice is studying me and I'm not sure why. Since I haven't been up on things too much, I wonder what I'm going to talk about. Not having a job makes me feel like less of a functioning member of society, but it's okay, because after Janice inquires as to how I am, she has plenty to say.

"Jen is taking it really hard."

"She's so young," I say. It's not unusual to get so disillusioned on your first job out of college.

"She wore a black lace doily on her head for the whole first week you were gone." I laugh.

Our meals come, chicken *tikka masala* for her and *chana saag* for me.

"She can get away with it," I say.

"Yeah, but it's got to be embarrassing for Hackett. I would hate to be at that table for Thanksgiving." She hesitates. "Do you mind talking about this?"

"No, not at all. I guess I'm curious."

"No one is even looking at Delores. Apparently Cheryl from Programming went on and on about how creative you were in War Room."

"Really? I never thought she liked me."

"I don't know if she did or if it was some kind of tactic against Delores."

"Jeez, the politics!"

"Everyone misses you. We want to take you out for drinks for a proper goodbye. Are you ready to see everyone?"

"Sure, I mean I don't think I have anything to be ashamed of. Do I?"

"No, you're innocent." She laughs. "Do you want to go out next week? I've been elected to organize it."

"Sounds good to me." I am curious about one other thing. "How are things with you and John?"

"Well," she smiles. I guess she's realized it's finally okay to come clean with me. "Great, actually. We're thinking of moving in together."

"Wow! That's big."

"You lived with your boyfriend, right?"

"Yeah, that's what did us in." All the while we worked together, I never really talked to her about Tommy.

"But you still live with him, don't you?" She looks confused, and I realize how weird it must be if you don't know the whole history.

"Um, yeah, that is sort of a financial thing." She rolls her eyes. I appreciate that we are close enough now to rib each other.

"Do you still…?" she asks, leaving the end hanging.

"No, not for a while." It's true! It's been like over four months since we had sex.

"Do you want to?"

"God knows." I shake my head. "Things can be so compli-cated. We are such good friends. There's a lot between us, you know. Baggage." She nods, and I realize how weird it sounds even when you do know the whole history.

"I'm sure you'll figure it out. You seem to know what to do."

"I'm glad I give that impression."

"You have no idea how on your side everyone is."

"I think I have an idea." The check comes and Janice insists on paying.

"It's really not necessary."

"C'mon," she says. "It's only right. When I was unemployed, people always paid my way. Just enjoy it."

I let her pay.

15

Like a Feather

M_y "Already Gone" party happens on Thursday. I know I've
gained a lot of weight, because none of my "going out" summer
clothes fit me. The black capri pants that looked so good last
summer when Esme was only a bunch of interstitials and I
couldn't afford to eat so much now stretch across my stomach
and give me an icky camel toe. One of the mixed blessings of
unemployment is that I will no longer be able to eat so much. I
guess.

I should start working out, but gyms also cost money. Maybe
I'll get a Taebo tape. Maybe after this, I'll never leave the house
again.

But tonight I'm headed over to a commuter-friendly bar
near Grand Central Station. It was picked because about half
the people working at Explore! live in Connecticut and up-
state. I settle on a drawstring peasant skirt and a sexy pair of
sandals. They are higher than I would usually wear, so I'm certain that I will have blisters by the end of the night, and if given
enough to drink, will perhaps fall flat on my face. (I hope my
former colleagues will be kind enough to pick me up.)

I get a great turnout if I do say so myself—even some of the

Programming hired guns show up. Everyone tells me how wonderful I look and I almost feel like I've just been cured of a terminal illness. Janice, John, and Jen smile benevolently as if they are bringing my goodness to the people. I know they have been providing little tidbits about my progress to the rest of the office.

Everyone is drinking and dissing the company with stories of how their budgets have been slashed, mean things Delores has said, and how much working for a television station that's owned by a bank sucks.

Thanks to me, they are being forced to go to all these team-building human resources seminars. They start throwing out catchphrases in execuspeak. "Parking lot" seems to be a big one, as in, "We can't talk about this right now, so let's put this issue in the parking lot."

According to Sarah from Programming, talking about "the hiring and firing policies" of the company is something that keeps getting put in the parking lot. "And the thing I hate about those human resources people is the way they always say your name," Sarah goes on. "They can't just say, 'good idea,' they have to say, 'Sarah, that's a great and pertinent comment, Sarah.' They use your name constantly to fool you into thinking they're actually listening."

"Sarah, what an astute observation—you really got it, Sarah," I say, getting the hang of it. She laughs. In all of the War Room meetings I went to with her, I never knew she had a sense of humor.

"I miss having people like you around. We are just going to turn into a dry company with people like Delores running the show."

"Tell her what you found out," Janice says when she comes up to us. She looks at me. "You're going to love this."

"Yeah, you're never going to believe it." I can tell Sarah is getting drunk because she grabs on to my sleeve. "So Delores is what, thirty-four?"

"I think so," I say. I shrug at Janice, and she makes a face at the mention of Delores's name.

"Well, my stepsister is about that age and went to Harvard. Since Delores finds it necessary to bring up her alleged alma mater in her every breath—"

"All the time," Janice says, nodding emphatically. She is also getting drunk.

"Alleged?" I ask.

"Just listen," says Janice, reveling in the knowledge I will soon get.

"So I start asking her if she knows my sister. For once she doesn't go off on one of her long tangents."

"Finally she decides to be curt," Janice adds, growing even more excited.

"You don't mind talking about her, do you?" Sarah asks, suddenly self-conscious.

"C'mon, you have to tell her the rest," Cheryl pipes in. She looks at me. "If it's okay?"

"I think I can handle it," I say.

"Okay, so I sense she's hiding something, so I keep asking her questions. Did she live in this dorm? What kind of media clubs was she in?"

"Sarah's stepsister is an EVP at Disney," Cheryl says, clearly impressed. "You should have seen Sarah, she gave new meaning to the words War Room Attack."

I look at Janice, confused about whether or not they should be revealing their tactics. Janice shrugs.

"So, I sense she's getting freaked, you know how she gets that look when she claims she's stressed like she's vibrating, and I wanna know. I mean she brings this up all the time and I'm just curious."

"She brings it up all the time," Cheryl agrees. "And she vibrates."

"So?" I ask. I am really curious where this is going.

"Well..." Sarah looks around at Janice and Cheryl. "It turns out she just went to some kind of summer animation camp at Harvard. Not exactly alma mater worthy."

"You're kidding." I really can't believe it.

"No," Sarah says, starting to laugh hysterically.

"Can you believe it?" Janice says.

"You are lying," I say. "No way."

"No." I am really amazed.

"So why does she bring it up so much? It's like she calls attention to it," I say.

"Because she is full of shit," John says, joining the conversation. "And because she's so full of shit, you don't have a job."

The group gets serious for a minute, and then I see Don come in. He smiles and makes his way over. Even in the heat, he is wearing his black leather jacket. And even though it's dark in the bar, he is wearing sunglasses.

"Here she is," he says, and kisses both my cheeks. "Sorry I'm late. We had a day from hell. Let me get you a drink. Gimlet, right?"

I nod, and he goes to the bar.

"He is so cute," Sarah says. I look at her and smile. I have a new respect for her after drinking with her, but I can tell she is someone who worries that she'll still be a failure if she isn't married by thirty.

Don comes back and we chat for a while. By day I'm not attracted to Don at all, but after a few drinks he does seem quite smooth. I think, hey, we no longer work together, we could have a meaningless hookup, but I look over at Sarah. Maybe I should lay off.

"We miss you," Don says. "What have you been doing with yourself?"

"You know, a lot of nothing." He smiles.

"I got to get you some names, and I'll also tell some people about you. In the meantime, enjoy it while you got it." He is always on. He makes being unemployed seem like another cycle of life. I appreciate feeling normal for a change.

"I called that lawyer. He said I should take the deal. I realize how stupid I was not to negotiate something better—or something at all for Esme."

"Yeah, it's tough to know that the first time around. I got totally bent over a chair on my first series. You'll figure it out by the time you get the next one. And there *will* be another one."

"Thank you. How's Gus?"

"Well, not so good." I start to worry that he is going to say something about Jordan.

"Why?" He looks at me as if he isn't sure he wants to continue. "Why?"

"Your friend seems to have some emotional problems, and maybe some other problems—substance related."

"He's actually an ex of a friend," I say. "And a friend of an ex. Is he going to lose his job?"

"Well…" Don takes a big sip of his drink. "We've already got a lot in the can and it would be a waste to scrap it all. I think we might have to phase him out with a little cousin or something, you know, a new actor to take over. I think we'll be okay. I doubt the show will pick up that fast, so I don't think anyone will get too used to him. I'm just not looking forward to casting again."

"Shit, I'm sorry to hear that." I wonder if I should tell Tommy or Lauryn.

"Hey, he had us fooled, too. Don't worry about it." He smiles at me. "You want another drink?"

"Sure, I'll get this one."

"Don't insult me," he says, and rubs my cheek. "It's your party."

While he's at the bar, he looks over and smiles. It's do-or-die time. If I have any interest in him, tonight could be the night. I look over at Sarah and am still holding back because of her remarks. I am so confused that it doesn't seem worth it. I'm not drunk enough to hobble into his lap. I am sober enough to realize that I'm just a little lonely and feel a little bit guilty for being at all interested after Sarah kind of staked her claim.

I call Sarah over and start asking her some lame programming questions. When Don returns with my drink I thank him and mention that Sarah is interested in moving to the East Village (she actually said downtown, but I need something to help them connect). Don lives in the East Village and Sarah asks him if he's been to a bar she likes. Don looks at me, but keeps talking to her. I excuse myself to talk to Kim from Licensing. She relishes telling me how ridiculous Delores's expectations are.

"I mean, she decides to make all these changes, but then I'm like 'If it's not in the style guide, I don't have a color palate.'"

"Unbelievable," I say. I am completely supportive.

"And you heard about the Harvard thing?"

"Unbelievable," I repeat again. Kim gets a call on her cell and I look over toward Sarah and Don, trying to gauge if I should go back over. I decide to chat with Jen, who is sitting at the bar smoking a cigarette.

"How's it going, kiddo?" I ask as I sit on a stool. I feel like she is my little sister.

"It's all right."

"I didn't think you smoked."

"Just when I drink."

"While we can," I say. She offers me her pack. "Are you sure? It's tacky with the price of cigarettes being what they are."

"No, take one."

"Listen, are you having fun?"

"Well, everyone is celebrating and I don't think we should be."

"You can't be incensed all the time."

"I know, but you don't have a job."

"I know, but look on the bright side, I get a summer vacation." When I'm around other people I think I need to put on this front, regardless of how I feel.

"You heard about the Harvard thing?"

"Yeah, unbelievable."

"You know, I was so excited to work here because I loved the idea that I could reach kids. You know I bought into all the shit. And now all anyone ever talks about is money. It sucks."

"I know. I think that's what I started for, too. Can I buy you a drink?"

"Let me get you one."

"Please, Jen, I've been getting spoiled all night. Don't get me wrong, I love it, but I'd really like to get you a drink."

"Okay."

"A gimlet for me and—"

"Cuervo Gold margarita on the rocks," she says. I smile.

"Now, that's a drink." I pay the tab. I hold up my glass to her and we clink. "To loving what you do."

"And tween girls," she says.

"And tween girls."

Beth invites Tommy to a Fourth of July party. The owner of the studio she works for has a summer house on Long Island. I get a pity invite. I would like to stand by my principles and not go. I think I want to punish Beth somehow for not really being that involved in my life these days, but I don't want to stay home. Besides, we've been shorting out the electricity a lot and the only thing worse than sitting home alone is sitting home alone in a virtual oven.

"She said to bring your bathing suit," Tommy says to me over dinner. "This guy has a giant pool. I think he's loaded."

We are eating bread with a salad of tomatoes, basil and fresh mozzarella cheese. We ate this two nights ago, but I really like the fresh cheese. Perhaps I've been eating a little too much of it. None of my clothes fit me anymore.

After dinner I dig out my bathing suits. I have a brown bikini and a black one-piece. For laughs, I try on the bikini and stare at myself in the mirror. Now, I've always been one to enjoy my curves—but this is too much. My belly looks paunchy, my thighs are thick, and I'm certain my boobs have begun to sag. None of this is aided by the fact that my whole body is pasty white.

I have to start eating less cheese. I have to start working out. I have to do *something*.

Even the black one-piece looks bad. I bought it when we went on a cruise with Tommy's parents and it's really conservative. My belly seems to stick out even more. The color really makes me look like Casper the Friendly Ghost.

I sit on my bed and wrap myself in a blanket. The party is tomorrow and stores will be closed. I don't think I could stand to try on bathing suits in the dressing room light with a three-way mirror accentuating my every stretch mark. I long for the days of living with Lauryn. I would be able to vent and, if I re-call, she had some really cute wraps.

I call Beth.

"Hey," she says. "Are you going tomorrow?"

"Yeah, thanks." I don't know if she even wants me there or if I will ruin her too-cool image with my quasi-pregnant belly.

"What are you wearing?"

"I got a new bathing suit and summer dress. This is an up-scale crowd." Gee, thanks for the warning.

"Do you have any wraps?"

"What?"

"You know, sarongs—to wear over my bathing suit." I need help. "I'm feeling a little bloated."

"Too much tempura?" There is an actual joke to her tone. I appreciate it.

"Don't I wish. No, I'm just a gluttonous, unemployed fat-tie."

"I'll see what I can do. I've got to go—it's my other line. I'll see you tomorrow. Jordan's driving."

"Jordan's going?"

"Yeah, Tommy invited him. He's got a car."

"Since when?"

"Rebecca, I don't know. I have to get my other line." Her tone becomes testy.

"Okay, bye."

Esme and I are holding hands. We are walking around a pool. She is bigger than she usually is, but still not a real girl. She is wearing one of Lauryn's sarongs. I am wearing my bikini and my stomach hangs down to my thighs. This doesn't really bother me. We are looking for something and it seems that no matter how much we walk the pool keeps getting bigger.

"What are we looking for?" I ask over and over. "Where is the panda?"

The panda is this sort of imaginary friend that Esme has that helps her solve things. I have a feeling we might be looking for him, so I ask her again.

"What are we looking for?" She stops and points into the pool. When she speaks, her voice sounds different.

"Your friends."

I wake up, sweating. My clock says 6:32. I think about getting up, but I lie in bed until I fall asleep.

Jordan and Beth pick us up together in Jordan's new SUV. They are both dressed like they stepped straight out of a Ralph Lauren ad. And they are both wearing expensive supermodel sunglasses. How did they get to be so tanned? Beth gets in the back with me, and Tommy, in the front seat, is really impressed with Jordan's new toy. I wonder if Jordan will be able to keep this car when he gets replaced. Also, how will they explain that Gus is no longer there even though the show is called *Gus and the Gopher?* Why didn't I ask Don that? And what happened with Don and Sarah, anyway?

Jordan is in a really good mood and I wonder if he has been helped in any way by controlled substances. Beth is being really quiet and stares out the window as we go through the Midtown Tunnel.

"Did I show you the coolest thing, man?"

"What?" Tommy asks. He seems to be catching Jordan's enthusiasm. Jordan grabs a remote control and hands it to Tommy.

"It's for the radio." I lean up to the front seat.

"You mean to tell me that you have a remote control so you won't have to reach over and press buttons," I ask in disbelief.

"Yeah," Jordan says, nodding. "Yeah."

"Man, that's awesome," Tommy says.

"Can you believe them?" I ask Beth, who smiles weakly at me.

Jordan insists on leaving all the windows open and pumping some hip-hop all the way there. Beth gets Tommy to roll his window up in a nagging little sister way and that's about all she says for the ride.

Jordan and Tommy are screaming things over the music and they miss the exit.

"I can't fucking believe you, Jordan!" Beth yells, pushing herself up between the seats. Her outburst startles me. "You know this is important."

"Just chill, Beth. I'll turn around." He lowers the volume on the stereo and glares at her in the rearview mirror. I'm surprised at the anger in Jordan's voice and confused at the familiarity between him and Beth. I reach out and touch Beth's shoulder. I can feel the bone. She ignores me.

"She's so fucking moody," Jordan says to Tommy before turning the stereo back up.

"Yeah," Tommy says quietly. I can sense he's confused, too. Beth takes off her glasses and sort of smacks Tommy on the back of the head.

"You know, you could have dressed better, too. This isn't some fucking backyard barbecue." I can't believe she is talking to him like that. They haven't fought like this in a while. Tommy turns around in his seat.

"What the hell is wrong with you?" Tommy asks.

Beth says something in Portuguese, a language neither of them speak except with their parents. Then no one says anything and it's my turn to look out the window.

It takes us another half hour to find the house. We drive in silence, listening to the music and feeling tense.

"I think you need to turn here, man," Tommy finally says. And he's right. We turn onto the private road and go up a hill. We pass tennis courts, a cottage and a really big pool before getting to the main house. There are a lot of cars.

"You see, Beth," Jordan says. "I don't think they are going to miss us."

The party is a pretty swanky affair, but it also seems very contrived. It's a place I would have been impressed by five years ago, but now that I don't have any money, it seems excessive. It certainly isn't someone's backyard barbecue. There are servers in white carrying around appetizers and a buffet-style grill set up that includes a pig. The host comes over to Beth and informs us of all this. He kisses Beth on both cheeks and shakes all of our hands vigorously.

"My house is yours," he says, waving to the air around him.

"Make sure you check out the pool and eat some pig. It's been roasting since dawn."

Beth's mood brightens immediately. I get the distinct impression that Beth doesn't want me around. Tommy must feel the same way, because he storms down the grounds to the pool. That leaves me to wander aimlessly around the crowd of revelers sipping beers. In spite of feeling out of place and having no one to talk to, I like being here. The grounds are beautiful and there aren't any horns blaring or sirens or tall hot buildings that keep the heat in. I'm glad to be out of the city, if only for a day.

Eventually I head down to Tommy in the pool, playing water volleyball with a buff older woman against a buff gay couple. In spite of all these toned bodies, I take off my tank top and hike up my drawstring skirt and hang out in my bathing suit (sort of) and resume reading my trashy novel. The sun feels good on my skin and I laugh when Tommy shows off his volleyball skills.

His skills don't help him, and he and his partner, Jill, get their asses handed to them by Jonathan and Owen. We all head up to the main house to investigate the pig. It's more crowded now. There are deejays and some people are dancing. I can't find Jordan or Beth anywhere.

We grab some grub and sit around a big table, drinking and telling stories. The biceps woman, Jill, is the head of sales for the studio. Jonathan is one of the engineers, and his boyfriend, Owen, is a professional musician who is thinking about going to cooking school.

Jonathan and Owen are sleeping over in one of the guest rooms. They wrangle a bottle of tequila and we do a shot. Our conversation flows even better. I smell the distinct odor of marijuana and smile at Tommy, certain he wants to locate the source.

"Have you seen Beth?" he asks. I shake my head. "I haven't seen Jordan, either."

"Do you think we are ever getting home tonight?"

"You want to leave so soon?" Owen asks.

"No, just wondering about our ride," I say.

"Don't worry," Tommy says. "I'm pretty sober and I won't drink any more. I'll be okay if I need to drive."

"If worse comes to worst, you can stay in our room. Jill's going to," Jonathan says.

"Thanks," Tommy says, genuinely.

"Just keep it quiet, you two," Owen says. He assumes we're together, and neither one of us corrects him.

After a couple of hours and a couple of second helpings, it starts to get dark and people are scattered all over the property, as are torches. Beth and Jordan come over to our table.

"There you are," Beth shrieks. "I've been looking all over for you guys."

"We were down by the pool," I say. "But we've been back here for a while. Where have you guys been?"

"We've been around." She is acting much friendlier, almost too friendly. She keeps patting my hair. "Oh, I brought you the sarong. I forgot."

Although it's too late for me to strip completely to my bathing suit, I am touched she remembers. I look across at Jordan, who is talking to Tommy and Jill. I can see from Tommy's expression that Jordan isn't making much sense. He's embarrassing himself in front of Owen and Jonathan. Jill gets up and leaves the table. I suspect it's because Jordan is yelling in her ear.

I continue my conversation with Owen and Jonathan while Tommy tries to understand Jordan. Beth keeps loudly interrupting the conversation and not really making much sense. But I'm getting drunk, too, so maybe it's my fault that I can't understand her.

Someone sets up an ice-cream sundae bar and we all gather around and make sundaes. Beth makes a really impressive one with three scoops, all the toppings and a ton of whipped cream, but she doesn't eat it, except to lick whipped cream off her fingers.

Tommy and Owen want to take another swim, so we head

back to the pool. Instinctively, I hold on tight to Beth, who re-
fuses to sit in one of the lounge chairs.

Jordan does cannonballs into the water and screams. He
splashes everyone and Beth laughs hysterically. Jonathan says he
is going to bed and Owen joins him. Owen repeats his offer,
but we decline.

"I want to go in the pool, too," Beth says, making her way
to the edge. She and Jordan don't seem to be slowing down at
all.

"C'mon in!" Jordan yells. I'm still holding on to her. I just
don't think it's a good idea.

"No, Beth, we're leaving," Tommy says. "C'mon, we're tired
and it's going to take a couple of hours to get home."

"Okay, Tommy." We go back up to the house and wait
while Beth says affectionate goodbyes to everyone.

Finally at the car, Tommy and Jordan fight over who is
going to drive home. There is no way I'm getting in a car with
Jordan driving and I know that Tommy hasn't had a drink in
five hours. I stay out of it, because he can make a better case
for it than I could.

"C'mon, J., you said I could drive it."

"I know, man, but I'm okay."

"Yeah, you are," Tommy lies. "But when else am I going to
get a chance to drive it? You can work the remote."

Jordan agrees as I pat Tommy's shoulder before we take off.
Then, in spite of the music, I pass out. I wake up when we are
going back through the Midtown Tunnel. Beth is still talking
really loud, but Jordan seems to have calmed down. I'm the only
one who fell asleep. Tommy turns to drop off Beth.

"I can drop her," Jordan says. "I'm okay to drive and I can
drop you guys off Uptown."

"No, it's fine—it's on the way," Tommy says. It really isn't,
but he is very firm. I see Jordan turn and glance at Beth, then
address me.

"Did you have a good sleep?" I think it's the first time he's
looked at me all day.

"You have a very comfortable car," I say.

"I know," he says. I suspect he wants me to tell Lauryn how well he's doing. For some reason, the way Beth slams the door when we get to her building makes me think she suspects that, too.

16

Lie in Our Graves

Kathy calls me during *Port Charles* on Monday. I was never one for soap operas, but I think they set up summer storylines for kids on break and unemployed women to get sucked right in and I do. I mute it because Kathy sounds like she's been crying.

"What's wrong?" I ask.

"Nothing. Is this a bad time?" A couple is having sex on screen. I think this is crucial, but I thought they were brother and sister. I'm never going to figure this all out.

"No, not at all." I switch the TV off. What am I becoming? "Are you at work?"

"No."

"Oh, my God. Did you get up and outed?"

"No, I called in sick."

"What's wrong?"

"I don't know." Her voice shakes.

"Shit, Kathy, is it Ron?"

"No, well, sort of."

"What?" Is the wedding off? Do I dare ask?

"I don't know. I don't know." She stops and it sounds like she's crying a little. I feel awful for her.

"Do you want me to come over there?"

"No, no. I don't know."

"What's going on? Is it the wedding?"

"It's everything. There are too many choices."

"What do you mean? Like favors?" I am so clueless.

"Nooo!" she sobs. "Everything. I can't stand waking up in the morning. I feel so weird. It's not my period. It's everything. I wish it was fifty years ago and I could just not have to decide. My mother thinks I need counseling."

"How long has this been going on?"

"For a couple of months."

"Months, wow. Why didn't you say something?"

"I don't know, I can't understand it. It's supposed to be the happiest time of my life." Although I want to help Kathy, I just can't get into this whole mind-set. Maybe I'll change my mind when I'm engaged, but honestly, where my great-aunt Phyllis should sit is not something that turns me on.

"Well, is Ron helping you plan the wedding?"

"Sort of, he's trying. It's not just that. It's everything. I'm up for this big promotion at work and they want me to get my MBA and there is so much. You know? So much." She sniffles, and then starts crying again.

"Kathy, you sound overwhelmed." I'm treading carefully, because I don't want to seem anything less than supportive about any of it. "Maybe you are trying to do too much, you know, with the wedding, work, everything."

"Oh, I shouldn't have called you." Great, I've done it, I'll be X'd off the bridesmaid list before I even get to check out the ushers. "You've got your own problems."

"Oh, those," I say, not bothering to censor myself. "I'm fine, really."

"Everyone has their own life. We never even *see* each other anymore."

She kind of has a point. "That doesn't mean we aren't here for each other. It doesn't mean we're not excited, you know, about the wedding. It's just that no one knew you were feeling this way."

"Because, we don't, you know, hang out." She appears to have stopped crying, but her voice is teetering on hysterics. I am not sure I'm equipped to deal with this. Maybe I should call in the big guns, Lauryn and Beth. And I realize as I think that, that I'm not sure the big guns would call back.

"You've got to take it easy."

"I don't think I know how anymore. All Ron talks about is buying a house. My job is putting so much pressure on me. My mother thinks this is her wedding. My sister is on kid number two and acts like I'm a prima donna."

"Well, you just got to get rid."

"What?" She laughs for the first time. "Get rid of what?"

"I don't know. It's just something to say." I don't want to lose the laughter. "Maybe get rid of all the shit."

"No one responded to my sister about the bachelorette party. And now she is being induced next week. Dina acts like my wedding is the reason her water won't break or whatever the hell is supposed to happen."

"Shit!" I forgot all about the e-mail. "She sent the e-mail the day I got shitcanned and I never wrote back. I'm sorry."

"No," she sighs. "At least you had a reason. Lauryn and Beth didn't respond, either—neither did my college roommate. I don't want you to think this is just about that. It's everything. Sometimes, I don't want to get out of the shower because it means I'll have to stop crying."

"Boy. There's a lot going on."

"I know. I feel so abnormal."

"You're going to have a great wedding and a great career." She laughs. "And a wonderful, happy life."

"Thank you, Rebecca. Thanks. I just feel so, I don't know. I'm not even twenty-eight and I feel so old."

"I'm sure you're not the only one. I bet a lot of people feel this way before their wedding. Just because you're getting married doesn't mean your whole life stops. It seems like it's a lot of pressure." This is still tricky, her guard is down, but criticizing the wedding can still be construed as blasphemous.

"I know you're right. I wish we could just elope."

"Are you kidding? After I tried on a rainbow of fucking dresses all over the tristate area?" She laughs really hard, the kind of laugh you have when you could start crying any minute. "Oh, I see, it was just for your amusement. I hope you think about that when you are fucking your new husband in the south of fucking France."

"Stop, stop. I can't imagine your tits in that backless number."

"Yeah, saggy, thanks, you like that? You think I need that?" I'm starting to feel like we might be in the clear. "Listen, what are you up to tonight?"

"I don't know." She sighs. It's possible I moved too quickly. "Ron is going to a game. I should start researching MBA programs. I've been putting it off."

"This is the problem, Kath. Why don't you just take a night off? No wedding plans or working from home or looking up grad schools."

"What else is there?"

"Some of the Explore! folks and I are meeting over at Bryant Park for the Monday-night movie. I'm actually going early to reserve the spot. Do you want to go?"

"Will anyone I know be there?"

"No, just me." This could be a deal breaker.

"Great, what time?"

"How's four o'clock?"

"Okay, do you think it's bad that I'm doing this when I called in sick?"

"That's the beauty of it."

"You're right. What should I bring?"

"Booze, and lots of it." Kathy's sigh of relief is way worth missing the incestuous love scene on the soap I shouldn't be following. "That's what the doctor ordered."

I plan on walking down to the Union Square Market, but once I get out of the apartment, I am smacked with oppressive heat. It's so hot my head starts to hurt. I decide to take the subway, even though I know it's certain to stink of all the millions of people who pass through Times Square every day. I walk over to the Times Square station, cutting through all the alleys and hotel parking lots to avoid the tourists. This is the worst time for crowds, but this is when everyone seems to want to visit New York City.

I get the N downtown to Union Square. There is still a bit of a lunch crowd at the market. I promised Janice and John I would make food and hold a spot if they brought wine and beer. Now I have to figure out what to make.

I've been watching a lot of *Molto Mario* on the Food Network. He stresses buying what looks fresh each day instead of having a set idea in mind when you shop. I'm trying to practice this when I got to farmer's market.

I do my usual once-over of the market. I can't get anything that takes too long to prepare. It's already one-thirty and I need to make whatever the hell it is I'm making and get to Bryant Park by four. I'm getting to know what the different stands have to offer and where I prefer to buy tomatoes as opposed to greens and herbs. My preferences are only slightly influenced by how hot the guys are behind the stand.

I decide on a rustic loaf of multigrain walnut bread, some beautiful red tomatoes, arugula and Parmesan. I walk down Fourteenth and stop in Garden of Eden, a gourmet market I used to go to with Lauryn sometimes. I pick up a container of pesto. There is no way I have time to make my own.

I hop on the 1 train back up to Times Square. I walk through the long tunnel to the Port Authority exit and get out on Eighth Avenue closer to my apartment. I am sweating by the time I climb up to my fifth-floor walk-up with my bags. I pour myself some coffee I've been icing and hop in for a quick shower.

It's three o'clock by the time I'm out of the shower. I've almost forgotten what it's like to have a schedule. I'm not going to rush, though. It's too damn hot. Tommy is working until seven o'clock, so I leave my towel wrapped around me and let my hair air dry.

I slice the loaf of bread horizontally and coat both sides with pesto. I cut the tomatoes really thin, layer on arugula and the Parmesan. I add some salt and pepper—and I can't resist a little drizzle of Croatian olive oil I splurged on in a moment of weakness.

I press the bread together and slice the loaf in eleven slices. I wrap it all in aluminum foil and napkins and put them in a plastic bag.

I throw on a tank top and my ubiquitous drawstring skirt. I pile on deodorant, then it's back out into the oven that is Manhattan.

Bryant Park is already starting to fill up. I love going to movies in the summer, but there are times when people take things a little too seriously. There are single people and couples who have already spread out two or three blankets to wait for their friends. Doesn't anyone have a job anymore? I slip off my shoes and weave through the jungle of blanket corners.

Now, the movie isn't going to start for another four and a half hours at least, when the sun goes down. By the time it does there will not be an available inch of grass and there will be people in chairs and standing en masse around the periphery of Bryant Park. However, these early birds get very pissy if you slightly encroach on their territory. I can tolerate some dirty looks, because vengeance will be mine when their friends don't show up. I try to take up as little space as possible with my sheet. I'm not sure how many people I should expect, but hopefully we will all be able to fit on the full sheet I brought. I let my feet hang over the sheet onto the grass.

I start reading my trashy novel, looking up occasionally as people pass. My cell phone rings and it's Kathy.

"Hey where are you?" I ask, standing up to scan the park for her.

"To the left of the screen." I spot her blond hair.

"Okay, you see the guy with the red Happy Birthday balloons?" I watch her turn and spot the balloons. I start waving.

"Oh," she says. She almost starts to skip. "I see you."

She makes her way over to my sheet. She is wearing a great big pair of dark sunglasses, perhaps to cover her red eyes. We kiss hello. Luckily, she brought water. We spread out on the sheet and talk about nothing serious.

"Your biceps look great," I say. I know she's been working them to look good in her strapless dress.

"Thanks." I tell her about the party I went to with Beth, but I don't talk about how weird it was between Beth and Jordan.

"How is Tommy?"

"Cool," I say. "The same."

She raises her eyebrows over her sunglasses, but thankfully, passes no judgment. My cell rings and it's Janice. She and Jen are on the side of the park, trying to find us. I wave and they spot us. (What did we do before cell phones?)

I make introductions and Janice tells me John is coming later. It's only six-thirty, but the park is filling up with people out of work.

"People are so snotty," Janice says, recounting all the dirty looks and comments they got as they walked through.

"It's going to suck when we have to pee," Jen says. There are public bathrooms on the corners of the park, but getting there is going to be tough. I'm certain to be there soon, though, because everyone brought six-packs and we've started drinking.

I think the sun affects how fast you get drunk and I'm starting to feel a bit tipsy. I can tell that my friends are as well. Janice and Kathy are laughing really loud together.

"I got to go pee," I say.

"Surprise," says Kathy, obviously recovered enough from her afternoon's trauma to ridicule me to my former colleagues. "Her bladder is the size of a pea."

"So I guess you won't be coming," I say as everyone giggles. I make my way through the sea of blankets and sourpusses, no longer caring where I step.

There is a long line for the bathrooms and I can't wait. I'm not going to make it. I go into Bryant Park Grill. I head right downstairs to the bathrooms, ignoring the hostess calling after me. Relief, at last! As I wash my hands and reapply my lip gloss, I notice how red my cheeks have gotten from either alcohol or sun, or both. They almost match my glasses.

I thank the scowling hostess. I don't care about her attitude; the crowd of bitter moviegoers has made me resilient. The summer sky is getting purple and the chairs and tables on the periphery of the grassy square are filling.

Again, I'm weaving through the crowd, relishing the fact that a lot of those early birds have been dissed by their friends and are now stuck fighting to keep people off their blankets. As it gets later, people are definitely encroaching on space. I hear someone say "hey!" I'm set to ignore it as usual, but I hear my name. I look up and see Sarah from Programming.

"Oh, hey, what's up?" She introduces me to a few of her former sorority sisters. I tell her that I'm with Janice and Jen. She says she'll call me on my cell after the movie if she isn't too beat.

"I love *Father of the Bride*. I can't wait to see the original," she says.

"What?"

"The movie."

"I thought it was *Double Indemnity*." That's one of my favorites. "I drink from a bottle, too." I quote the movie. Sarah doesn't catch the reference and her sorority sisters give me funny looks.

"No, that's next week. This week is *Father of the Bride*. You know, Liz Taylor?"

Oh shit, I hope it isn't going to be too much for Kathy. Sarah cocks her head. "Oh, hey, how did it go with Don?" I ask.

I catch a look between her and one of her sorority sisters. She manages to keep her face blank for me. I realize that she doesn't remember hinting at a crush or the fact that I kind of left her and Don alone.

"Okay, why? Did he say something?"

"No," I say. One of her friends makes a face. I'm not sure I believe her. Maybe she'll think Don was talking about her and that will boost her confidence with him. "I was just wondering."

"Nothing happened." She is still suspicious. "Say hi to those guys."

When I get back to the blanket, John is there.

"I had to get out of there," he says, referring to Explore! "I could have stayed all night and it would have sucked the life out of me."

I try not to be jealous that he was just working on *Esme's Enlightenments.* I bend to kiss him hello and I tell them I saw Sarah, but don't mention anything about Don. According to them, relations between Production and Programming are at an all-time high now that they all share a hatred of Delores. Still standing, I take a low bow and camp it up.

"I'm just glad my livelihood was sacrificed for the good of network relations."

"When do we get to eat this yummy-smelling thing?" John asks, holding up my party-size sandwich. I'm pretty hungry and I open it up, passing everyone a piece along with a napkin.

The pesto and olive oil have soaked into the bread and tomato, and all the flavors are working really well together. I look around to see if it's just because I'm hungry. Apparently not, everyone is scarfing up their sandwiches.

"This is delicious," Kathy says between bites.

"Mmm, perfect," Jen says.

"You can really make a sandwich," Janice says.

"Is there more?" John asks, eyeing the bag behind me. We all have seconds and John has thirds.

"Maybe Rebecca will do the race," Janice says, looking at Kathy. Have my friends been making plans behind my back? People with jobs have things to say. It must be nice to be employed and have things to say to people.

"What?"

"That's a good idea," Kathy says.

"What?" I repeat. Now they have secrets and good ideas. Wasn't I the one who pulled Kathy out of her funk?

"There's a 10-K at the end of the summer over Labor Day," Kathy explains. "I've been running a lot. I'm going to do it and so is Janice. It'll be wonderful, two weeks before the wedding."

"I don't run," I say.

"It's only 10-K. That's like six miles. It's nothing," says Janice.

"That's six more miles than I run," I say.

"That's what I said at first, Rebecca. Fight the power," Jen says.

"You've got almost two months," Kathy says. "I thought you might want to start training." I think I see her eye my stomach. Okay, I *am* a little bloated from the sandwich.

"Is this about a race or how I'm going to look in my bridesmaid dress?" I can tell my question makes everyone feel awkward. It wasn't what I intended.

"She wants you to *run it* in your bridesmaid dress," John says, trying to break the ice. Jen changes the subject to her weekend visit to her sister's timeshare on the Jersey shore. I don't look at Kathy for a little while.

After what has been hours, the sun is finally down. Someone announces the movie is going to start and people cheer. I think we must all be drunk on beer or sun or long, hot summer days. I glance at Kathy to see if she minds that the movie is wedding-related, but she smiles at me. I think she is worried that I'm upset that she thinks I'm chubby.

A promo for the sponsors of the movie comes on the big screen. All the people who come here every Monday night get up and do a funny hand-clapping dance at the opener. Kathy, who has never been to a Monday-night movie, gets up and sways as Janice and John get goofy. Jen and I look at each other and laugh.

"Nice job," I say to them when they sit down. I realize it isn't so hot anymore. The movie opens with an old *Bugs Bunny* cartoon. Everyone cheers about this, also. There is all this pent-up energy from waiting around so long.

I try to get as comfortable as possible on the blanket that I'm sharing with four other people. I notice the way my stomach sort of bulges out more than usual.

"Maybe I will start running," I whisper to Kathy. She smiles and nods.

I wake up in the morning feeling hot and fat. I take a long look at myself in the full-length mirror and try to decide if

Kathy was hinting that I'd gained weight. I have certainly been going out less since I lost my job, but I think the damage was done from the past year of expensive meals, eating at my desk and being office bound.

I belonged to a gym once. I have the expensive sneakers to prove it. I'm more of a spinning-class girl. Okay, so it's been a long time since I sat on a bike. It's been a long time since I exerted *any* energy.

I'm not a small girl, and I never expect to be. I usually like my butt, but staring into this mirror, I think I'm a lot rounder than is healthy.

I eat a container of yogurt and turn the TV on. I'm going to get out and do something, but first I'll watch a little TV. The prospect of going out into the heat is not very appealing and I certainly can't go joining another gym, so I'm just going to eat my yogurt one spoonful at a time.

I'm flipping through the channels when I see it. Esme—the new Esme—episode number eleven. This is animation that I worked on, but I was obviously gone when they did the sound design. Esme has no glasses and a completely different voice. She sounds like a dimwit. My voice-over talent—the voice I gave her—was husky with a constant edge of sarcasm; this voice is saccharine sweet.

I pick up the phone to kvetch at Janice, but then I hang it up. Of course she knew, she just didn't tell me. I don't blame her. At this point, what could I have done except get as upset as I'm getting now?

I consider calling Tommy, but I've got to try to stop running to him with everything that goes wrong. I have to wean myself off relying on him if I'm really sure I don't want to be his girlfriend anymore. And I'm positive I don't. Okay, almost positive.

I watch the entire episode of *Esme's Enlightenments* with a sinking feeling in my stomach. It's clear that Esme really isn't mine anymore. If only I had been smarter when I developed the series, maybe I would still have some control. If only everything…

I watch the credits roll. I see mine, "Based on a character and story concept by Rebecca Cole." At least that will be there for as long as the show airs, but without my vision for her, I'm not sure I want the credit.

I dig my sneakers out of the closet and find some bike shorts and try on a variety of T-shirts. None of the ones in my drawers cover enough of my butt. I go into Tommy's room. This is a total violation, but I'm not going to go out into the steamy city with my butt on display for every construction worker and delivery guy to critique.

Tommy has an extra-large Incredible Hulk T-shirt and I put it on and put my hair up. I've been neglecting to have my hair cut and I have to bobby-pin some of the longer layers back up into my ponytail. I also take my Walkman. The batteries are dead, but if I am going to get the catcalls that increase ten-fold during the summer, I want to give the impression that I can't hear them. I'm not saying I'm hot, mind you, the New York machismo factor is strong no matter what you look like or what you wear.

I walk fast over to the Hudson River. It's hot, but not as hot as it has been, and once I get over to the pier, I feel a slight breeze. Then I just start jogging.

I run really slow, but it is kind of nice. I look up at the Intrepid and pass the Circle Line Depot. A few other people are out and they kind of smile when they run or bike past me. We are a community of people trying to attain better health.

I am startled each time a biker whizzes by and even more jumpy when they ring their little bells. It's hot and the rest of the runners appear to be okay with this. Of course, they are mostly wearing less clothes than I am—men run by shirtless and most of the women have color-coordinated Nike outfits with half tank tops and tight shorts that show off their flabless asses. I'm never going to look like this.

Everyone is going faster than me, even though I am starting to get a stomach cramp. I try to just breathe. In and out. It should be easy, but I can't seem to regulate it. No one else is having these problems. Everyone is able to pick up their feet in a way I can't. Everyone who goes by has a different way of doing it. Some people look like they're running hard, like it's a struggle they are battling against, and some people kind of glide. I shuffle.

I take a walking break when I get down to Chelsea Piers, but then I start running again and jog to Chelsea Market. It's a lot cooler inside and instead of buying a bunch of delicious cheeses from the Italian market, I get a juice from the juice stand. It hits the spot. I'm refreshed and energized and I manage to run and walk back up to my apartment.

I can't believe that I've probably jogged about two and a half miles! Yes, I'm dripping with sweat, but I have a sense of accomplishment. Maybe I actually will do the race. What else am I going to do with all of this free time? I sit on the stoop of my building and take many labored breaths. I didn't think about Esme or Tommy or my friends or food or anything the entire time I was running. I just looked around me and tried not to hyperventilate.

I can't believe how clear my mind is. Although when I stand up from the stoop, my knees buckle a little, but I grab hold of the railing in time to greet the postman coming out of the building.

"Stay cool," he says.

"You, too," I whisper, unable to raise my voice over a pant.

I check the mail. I got my unemployment check, my severance payment and my credit card bill. I only open up the checks when I stop on the third-floor landing.

Back in the apartment I take a shower but still feel overheated when I get out. I lie down on the couch in a towel and turn on the Food Network. I deserve a little reward, and now that I'm here I don't ever want to move.

Lauryn calls during *The Naked Chef,* just as I am getting slightly excited as Jamie Oliver stuffs a chicken.

"Did somebody say sweat?" she asks.

"How's it going? Is it that hot up there, too?" I flex and unflex my sore legs.

"Hotter, and this town is full of hot men in the summer. The only problem is I'm living in the dry part so I always have to drive to the alcohol. Then I can't drive back."

"Be careful," I warn.

"Oh, I am—they don't fuck around with drunk driving here, which is good."

"They are protecting and serving. It sounds like you are back in the saddle again."

"Kinda."

"Anything newsworthy?"

"Well, I kissed this bartender the other night. There's nothing like a first kiss."

"I wouldn't know. What's with you and bartenders?"

"They've got what I need, plus I have to talk to them. It helps me get over my shyness."

"Because you're really quite shy."

"Yes." Right.

"Did anything else happen?"

"Well he brought me back to his place and all his roommates checked me out. Then he told me all about the girl he was in the process of breaking up with."

"Did you tell him about Jordan?"

"Of course not. We weren't on a talk show. I just wanted some fun—some good clean no-strings-attached sex."

"You're back!"

"A girl's gotta eat."

"Tell me about it," I say, feeling a bit peckish as Jamie, the Naked Chef, pours olive oil over some potatoes. "So what happened?"

"Nothing."

"Not a thing?"

"He had issues. All this talk of his dead relationship stifled him."

"Wow!"

"I know. What happened to guys who just want to get laid? All of a sudden they've grown up and decided to have feelings?"

I started laughing and felt better. It's amazing how a friend can do that for you.

I tell her about my jog and she is truly shocked. I feel like she called at the perfect time. There is nothing I would rather be doing than lying on the couch talking to Lauryn. She's listening to everything I say and it's like we're talking the way we used to in high school.

It's been a long time since we were able to communicate and laugh like this and I've missed it. I tell her that I'm going to come up and visit from Thursday to Monday. She has to do some fieldwork in the early mornings, but she is really happy for me to visit.

"I just need some girl time," she says. "And wait till you see the beach."

"I can't wait," I say. "It's going to be fun."

17

UR

Lauryn is waving to me from the dock when the ferry pulls into the harbor on Martha's Vineyard. It's been a long train, bus and ferry ride to get here, but it's all worth it when I smell the sea and see Lauryn.

I file off the boat and hurry over to her. We hug. She looks so happy and tanned. She takes my duffel bag.

"Did somebody say long weekend?" she asks in her old happy-Lauryn way.

"Did somebody say tan?"

"Oh, look," she says, pointing to some birds skimming along the surface of the water. "Piping plovers. Aren't they beautiful?"

"Did somebody say crunchy bird girl?" She elbows me and looks at them for a minute, shielding her eyes from the strong sun. I can tell by the way she looks at them that it is more than a hobby.

"We ought to get going," she says. "Traffic gets brutal and I want to stop at the Net Result and pick up some lobsters."

I scoffed at the idea of traffic on the tiny island, but at almost six o'clock in the evening the one-lane highway around the island is packed with Jeeps. We are one of them since Lauryn has rented a Jeep for the summer. Her whole mood is brighter; she beats her tanned hands on the steering wheel along with the radio. Her laid-back chill is contagious.

"Beach crowd," she says, by way of explanation. "I figured you might be tired so we could hang in tonight and see if we felt like going out. It's a bit of a walk to the bars, or we can take a cab. Whatever you are in the mood for."

"I don't mind just catching up and seeing how we feel." In truth, I'm kind of tired and just chilling with Lauryn is all I feel like doing after my six-hour journey.

We park at a shack and get two two-pound lobsters that Lauryn called in for earlier. They have steamed them for us. The place smells of fish. My stomach groans and Lauryn laughs.

"Within a half hour you will be eating the best lobster of your life."

Back at Lauryn's rented condo, she makes a salad and I open a bottle of white wine. She heats up some butter for the lobsters. We set the table outside on her balcony. She is alone in a two-bedroom apartment. The two floors beneath her are full of college kids.

"Are they loud?" I ask as we sit down for dinner. I watch her expertly crack open her lobster.

"No, I hang out with them sometimes. I know, I feel so old, but everyone is pretty friendly on the island. I keep such weird hours. I mean, I get up so early and then at like one o'clock I'm back taking a nap until dinner." She is already getting a stipend for her studies.

"This seems like a nice little scam you've got going," I say as I delicately dip some lobster tail into the butter. It's delicious.

"I know," Lauryn says, smiling, "I feel so lucky. Wait till you see the beach tomorrow. I'm gonna go into the field pretty early, but then I figure we can go to South Beach for some sun and swimming."

"Sounds good. I've only been to the beach once this year." I don't mention it was the beach party I went to with Jordan. She hasn't brought him up in a while and I'm not going to. I am getting less dainty with my lobster as I crack the claws. It's so damn good, I hardly want to be sidetracked by salad.

"Remember when we used to go to Jones Beach every weekend?" I nod. "That seems like forever ago."

"I know. Is it real crowded here?"

"Sometimes. Tomorrow will be a great day. This weekend will be touristy, but I figure Friday we'll go out."

"Yeah, I've got no problem hanging in tonight," I say.

"And getting crazy tomorrow night," she says.

"Are you getting crazy, bird girl?"

"Just a bit. You're not done with that, are you?" She gestures toward my lobster carcass.

"What? Should I suck the bones?" She shakes her head at me as if I am some sort of amateur eater. She proceeds to scrape another quarter pound out of my lobster through some kind of strange lobster surgery she must have learned on this island.

"Who would have thunk a girl from PA…" I say.

"Ms. Gordon would be so proud."

We watch the sun go down and open another bottle of wine. For dessert we eat Ben & Jerry's Cherry Garcia and listen to music. We stay up until midnight talking with our legs folded up close to us on the chaise longues and I tell her in detail about everything that happened with work and Seamus. She tells me all about her fieldwork. I can't really understand it all, but I know enough to see that it fascinates her. She has smiled more tonight than in the entire past year. I yawn involuntarily and Lauryn goes inside to set up the AeroBed.

"Sorry I'm so lame tonight," I say.

"Don't worry about it, I have to get up in like four hours. I'm glad you're here. We have plenty of time."

I wake up around ten-thirty. I vaguely remember Lauryn coming in here to grab her laptop early this morning and relishing the fact that I could still sleep. And it's nice and cool in the guest room. I never do this, but I brought my sneakers. I've been running pretty consistently all week and I know that if I don't keep at it, I'll never get stronger.

I throw on my shorts and a T-shirt and grab my Walkman and go outside. I have no idea where I'm going, but I figure that I can stay off the main roads and keep turning left. I run about fifteen minutes and then turn around and start heading back. It's much cooler on the island than in muggy Manhattan and I think I feel stronger because I'm not fighting the oppressive heat. I run by lots of little houses, and realize how much I would enjoy a more quiet summer off. If I ever work again, maybe I'll get a summer house…but then I'll have less time to spend there. There is more than one downside of working.

I see Lauryn's Jeep in the driveway and jog around back and up the stairs to the deck. She is sitting out on a lounge chair in shorts and a bikini top and drinking an iced coffee. She smiles at me.

"Look at you, marathon runner. I never thought I'd see the day when you ran for anything but your supper." She pulls her sunglasses down her nose.

"I'm still running short distances. I foolishly agreed to do a 10-K with Kathy. I think it's a ploy so she can have a more attractive bridal party." Lauryn rolls her eyes.

"There's an iced coffee for you in the fridge. Do you need to take a shower? I figured we would just go to the beach and get sweaty, anyway."

"That's cool, lemme just change."

The beach is not crowded like Jones Beach on Long Island but there are plenty of people on it, mostly families and college kids. Lauryn and I set up our blankets and break out the giant sandwiches we bought. I bought this mile-high veggie sandwich called the Tree Hugger and Lauryn got a Cuban with meat and pickles. It's big enough to rival the Carnegie Deli's. I only get through half of mine and then wrap up the rest.

We put sunscreen on each other and lay back on the blankets with books and magazines. Lauryn says she canceled all her subscriptions, finally. She looks a lot better in her bikini than I do, even with my week of running. Will these giant thighs ever be lean? After about forty-five minutes I'm really hot, so I get up to go in the water.

"Are you sure you don't want to digest a little longer?" Lauryn says like a mom. She takes out a cigarette and lights it. She holds the pack out to me and I shake my head.

"I'll wait until you are done and then we'll go."

"Here, why don't you read this." She tosses me a magazine article about getting over your ex by changing your hair.

"Thanks, I tried this already."

"With amazing results," she says, exhaling smoke.

"Tell me, guru, how you did it," I shoot back at her. It's a testament to how far she has come that she can laugh at that.

"I'm ready," she says. She stubs her cigarette out in the sand and puts it in her empty water bottle. She is certainly concerned for her environment, if not her lungs.

I follow her down to the water. The waves are huge. We stand for a minute, letting the water lap our toes. It's cold. It's now or never, so I run and dive in. Lauryn follows me in, screaming. My body freezes, then numbs, then starts to feel okay. We play and body surf in the waves.

After almost an hour we get out and I start to shiver. Lauryn hands me a towel and we wrap ourselves up and huddle close together on the blanket. My feet are covered in sand, but I don't mind.

"I could stay here all day," Lauryn says.

"I know, you must be psyched to have the summer off."

"It's sort of cool. Are you happy to be out of the city?"

"Yeah, I really am. How are you doing?" I ask tentatively. "You know, with everything?"

"I'm doing good," she smiles. "With everything."

"Are you still taking the pills?"

"Yeah. They help. You know, they really help. Do you want to talk about this?"

"Only if you do."

"I actually do, I mean I wish people would ask me more. I don't mind talking about it. The more I can talk about being depressed I think the better I am. I remember the day when I told you I was taking them. I felt like you were really uncomfortable."

"I guess I was."

"I know I wasn't easy to put up with during the whole Jordan thing."

"I guess I just never knew what to expect." I can't believe I am saying this to her.

"Things were pretty intense for a while. You know, did you ever just not feel like yourself or even know what that meant? It's like I couldn't get out of my own way. I used to be happy, you know. I used to be funny."

"You *are* funny," I say, touching her arm. "You seem back to the way you used to be. Even the last time we talked."

"I know, but like, why did I have to go through all that shit? Why did I take it? Was I that scared of being without him? Was I that scared of being alone?"

"It's where we come from. I mean, back home we would be married with kids. You know, my mother thinks I'm an old maid at twenty-seven."

"But there's got to be some resentment in that. I mean, here you are with all these things going for you."

"What? Unemployment?"

"You're unemployed now, but you had a show. Your thing, you know—not everyone gets to do that."

"But, in the end, did it help anything? Was it meaningful?"

"Yeah, I think it was. There are a ton of little girls out there who don't mind wearing glasses now."

"Um, now they *do*. She isn't wearing them anymore. Now she's just like all the other girls on shows. Glasses weren't sexy."

"It's bullshit. I wish there was a way you could still be in charge of Esme. With the next show, you have to be in charge."

"What next show?" I shake my head and bury my feet in the sand. I tell her about Kathy calling me during her mini breakdown, saying she felt like there were too many choices.

"She's going to be so let down after the wedding. When all the gifts are opened and the dress is shrink-wrapped it will just be them. Alone together and in debt."

"Well, Ron's got money."

"But what does she see in him?"

"I don't know. I have to think when they're alone together something happens."

"What's Beth up to?"

"I don't know. She's the one I worry about the most. She is still partying as much as we ever did."

"With who?" I shrug. I know Lauryn well enough to see her study me, but also well enough to lie.

"I guess, work people. I don't know how she does it." I decide to change the subject. "I can't party like I used to—the body just doesn't recover. But I will tonight."

After showers and a nap, we walk to a pub in town. We sit in one of the high booths and order pints and mussels and a small pizza with fig, roasted tomatoes and feta. I smoke cigarettes with Lauryn and we chat.

On the way to the next bar, we stop in an upscale beach shop and I buy a toe ring and a sarong. I may be working out, but I still need the coverage. At the next bar, peanut shells cover the floor and we order pints of their home brew. We find two bar stools and drink and smoke until a few college kids come to sit with us and all their names go by me in a blur, but I'm drunk enough to revel in the fact that they think we're their age.

I wind up talking to two beefy nameless guys about college basketball. Yesterday, I would have said I knew nothing about this subject, but the home brew has given me a lot of knowledge on the subject.

I smile over at Lauryn. She is standing particularly close to another guy who is wearing a Block Island sweatshirt. Perhaps he is an island Lothario who hops from island to island wooing young divorced women. His biggest dilemma is trying to decide between going to Nantucket or Shelter Island next. I am smiling to myself and feeling carefree.

"I want you to know that I really did love Jordan," I hear Lauryn say to me as one of the boys tells me he's premed. By the time I turn around to talk to her she is making out with sweatshirt guy.

I don't bring up what she said about Jordan during our walk back home. We slipped away from the college kids. It was clear that Lauryn's Casanova liked her and wanted more, but she gave him her number and firmly told him we were going home. This is the benefit of being a little bit older; we no longer behave like floozies, we are firm. (Truth be told, I missed out on some floozy time by starting to date Tommy junior year, so maybe I have one minor indiscretion left before becoming absolutely firm....)

We sing one of the songs from the bar, "Come on Eileen," all the way home. Lauryn raises her voice high and holds my hand as we cut through alleys and walk along the road single file.

On Saturday, we go back to the beach. The water is calmer today, and for some reason, I decide to wear less sunscreen. I feel a tightness around my eyes at the end of the day. We decide the best remedy would be to hit one of the pubs along the pier. We sit out on the open wood patio and drink frozen drinks and eat steamers.

"These are delicious," I say as butter rolls down my chin.

We watch the sun dip down along the sea and feel the faintest wind. To think some people are able to live like this. The corporate world seems a million miles away.

"Are you spacing out?" Lauryn asks.

"I should have come up here with you as soon as I got laid off."

"You like it, huh?"

"Yeah."

"Well, remember you're on vacation."

"I know. I should have spent my time and severance up here."

"I think you'd get bored eventually."

"Maybe I could work in a store off the books or something. I guess I couldn't collect unemployment, though."

"I can't see you working in a store forever."

"What can you see me doing?" Lauryn shrugs, and makes a slurp sound with her straw against the bottom of her glass.

"Another round?" says the perfectly tanned waitress. We nod.

"And more steamers, thanks," I say. I look back at Lauryn. "Well?"

"Aren't you just going to go work at another network?"

"My phone hasn't been ringing off the hook."

"Aren't you supposed to network? No pun intended."

"I guess so. It's tough times, though. Lots of networks are cutting back."

"And you know this because you've done all this research." She is being a smart-ass. "You're going to run out of severance soon, right?"

"Soon." I sigh. "It's such a beautiful thing, that severance."

"So, what are you going to do?"

"I don't know."

"Well, never mind if you don't want to talk about it."

"I don't think I want to deal with it, but I guess I have to. Maybe I'll change careers just like you."

"You should follow your bliss."

"What does that mean exactly? Does following your bliss allow you to pay your credit card bill and eat an occasional meal at a decent restaurant?"

"Occasionally," Lauryn says, raising an eyebrow in a Lauryn way.

"Hey, I'm cutting down on my food obsessing. I'm serious, how can we follow our bliss when we've got to make ends meet? Or what if we think we're following our bliss but we realize that our bliss is controlled by ad revenue and Internet critics?"

"What is it that you want to do, Rebecca?"

"Who the hell knows? I thought it was creating shows for kids."

"So you believe children are our future?" She is doing a good job of keeping this conversation light. Our roles have flip-flopped. All last year, I tried to cheer her up and help her figure out her life. Now she is doing the same for me.

"Something like that. When I think about it, I wonder what the point is." Our next round comes. We hold up our glasses, clink and sip. "These kids are just going to watch my show and see Esme start out cool and outspoken and then turn out high-pitched and wearing a half shirt. Honestly, that's a lesson they'll learn, anyway. Growing up sucks. What do you get?"

"Divorce," Lauryn offers thoughtfully.

"And cellulite."

"Ulcers."

"Debt."

"Prescription medication."

"Sexual dysfunction."

"Men who can't commit."

"No men, period."

"Maybe an STD."

"If you are lucky enough to be getting laid," I say. "Speaking of which. What are you going to do if the guy from last night calls?"

"Fuck him," Lauryn says, and uses her mouth to eat a steamer as no one ever has. The combination of her contorted face and the effects of the frozen daiquiri cause me to rush to the bathroom, giggling.

On Sunday, it's kind of overcast and I have a sunburn. Lauryn suggests we go birding on the island, and before I can say no, I am crouching next to her in high grass.

It's all worth it, though, because we go out to a fancy restaurant Sunday night and eat delicious green salad and thick, wonderful steaks.

Lauryn insists on paying. I try and convince her to let me because she put me up, but she won't hear of it.

"Ever since I got here, I've wanted to take you to this place. Just indulge me."

"Okay," I say. "Thank you."

Monday comes too soon. I would like to extend my trip, but I know that Lauryn has been shirking her research to spend time with me. I have to go back to the hot city and figure out what to do with the rest of my life.

Lauryn and I grab iced coffee and Portuguese rolls and sit by the dock, watching the piping plovers circle and dive for fish. The ferry comes in. It's overcast today, which makes it only slightly easier to leave.

"I had a lot of fun," I say. "I got a little taste of summer, and I saw how the other half lives."

"Yes, you certainly did," Lauryn says, adapting a formal tone. "And I bid you well on your voyage."

"Thank you," I say, trying to do my best sea captain voice. "I trust I leave you in the capable hands of the strapping lad we encountered the other night at the ale house."

"Yes, I pray his hands are good."

"And so it shall be." We smile at each other and walk toward the ferry. She walks me up the ramp to the man who takes my ticket.

"Thank you," I say. We hug for a little while.

"Thank you for coming. Say hi to everyone for me."

"I will." I climb up to the top deck and wave to Lauryn on the pier. I'm bummed to be leaving, but anxious to get on the road. The horn sounds and Lauryn animatedly pretends it hurts her ears.

We continue to wave at each other until she becomes very small and then I can't see her anymore.

18

Pitseleh

I walk to my apartment from the Port Authority, stopping in one of the fish stores along the way to buy some salt cod. When I get on my block, Tommy is sitting on the stoop talking on a cell phone.

"Hey," I say. "New phone?"

"New phone *and* new job."

"What?"

"I'm still going to be working in the DVD store, but I started watching two little boys three times a week."

"What? Where did you get these boys? What are you watching them do?"

"Their parents come into the store all the time. Apparently they had a nanny, but she had to go back to Estonia. Now they need someone to baby-sit and they said they always wanted a guy to hang out with their kids. When school starts I'll only hang out with them after school. Their mom works part-time and their dad works a lot. He rents good movies, though. Lots of cult horror and sci-fi. He knows almost as much as I do about the Evil Dead trilogy."

"Wow," I say, momentarily impressed, but then, "I go out of town and you become a manny."

"What?"

"A male nanny. I read about this in the Styles section of the *New York Times*." It's how I find out about a lot of trends. Lauryn didn't even know she was in a starter marriage until I identified it as such.

"I guess so, though the Greaneys didn't call it that. That's the name of the family."

"I got that."

"The pay is sweet."

"I bet."

"And it's fun to hang out with a bunch of boys, throw a ball around, go to the park, watch movies, eat hamburgers and, of course, play video games."

"Of course." Leave it to Tommy to get paid for doing the things he loves to do. I am jealous that he actually gets to hang out with kids. Real live ones, not the kind you watch behind a glass partition while they get prodded for answers about your television show.

"So you want to celebrate?"

"What do you mean?"

"You know, go out to eat."

"For real?" I'm shocked.

"Yeah, I mean nothing too outrageous. What about the Half King?" I look at my watch. It's Monday, but it's also summer, but work hasn't let out yet.

"If we hurry maybe we could get a sweet spot outside."

The Half King is a great bar/pub in Chelsea. In the winter, there is a warm, welcoming feeling and in the summer they open up the backyard. In the winter, you feel like there is no need to ever step out into the cold again. In the summer, you can just sort of get swept up in all the people talking at once and the outdoor private-party feel.

Tommy and I snag a seat outside and order pints of cold beer.

Slowly, the place starts to fill up and we decide to order Mexican burgers for dinner. I get mine veggie.

"So are you on a diet or something?" Tommy says accusingly.

"No, I'm just trying to eat healthier. I'm not as young as I used to be. I don't like not being able to fit into my clothes."

"You're running—I never thought I'd see the day."

"That's Kathy for you. She kind of convinced me to do it."

"Right."

"C'mon, *you* should talk. Those kids are going to wind you in seconds." I gesture to his burger.

"Listen, Greta Waitz, I could still run the capri pants off you."

"You think, huh?"

"Yeah, without training."

"Oh, really."

"Yeah, I'll do it for all the couch potatoes like me." He is talking trash.

"When are we going to race?"

"Let's do it at the actual race."

"Deal," I say.

"If I win, what do I get?"

"I don't know, a video game, what?"

"No, I can get those at the store. How about a case of Guinness?"

"Okay, and if I win?"

"A night at Nobu."

"For real?" I am very excited.

"Calm down. The place next door." Wow! This is great. Nobu Next Door. I am totally running hard core tomorrow. Tonight I am getting drunk. We shake on our bet.

Tommy is so excited about his new job it's contagious. We're talking, really talking, about all the things we used to talk about. I think he's on sort of an upswing. Things have gone back to normal with Lauryn and are starting to plateau with Tommy. We are adults and we can be friends. It's all good.

They close down the garden for nighttime noise control, but

we move into the pub and keep drinking. Tommy tells me that he is really concerned about Beth. I feel like he is angry with her and just doesn't want to admit it.

"How many times has she not returned your calls?"

"A lot," I say. "I don't expect her to return them anymore."

"Who are these assholes she's been hanging out with?"

"I don't know, but she and Jordan seem to be playing the same dangerous games."

"What does that mean?" For the first time tonight, he looks upset with me. I retreat, not quite sure what I'm getting at. Instead I tell him about Jordan.

"Wait, you mean he could lose his job?"

"Yep, up and out."

"Since when?"

"They have been unsatisfied the whole time he's been there."

"Why didn't you tell me?"

"I assumed you knew, besides, you never want to talk about Jordan. You always get defensive."

"I've heard you and Lauryn tear him a new one. I don't want to be a part of the gossip."

"Well now you see why. He's irresponsible. I can't believe you didn't know he was getting so fucked."

"He's always sort of pushed the limit. He said work was fine." Tommy's eyes narrow and he stares off at his shoes. I didn't mean to ruin the vibe.

"Hey, let's get one more beer. We're celebrating."

One more was actually two because our bartender bought us a round. We are drunk when we get back home. I am having trouble getting up the five flights of stairs. Tommy keeps shushing me. It is 3:00 a.m. and I am certainly never going to be able to run tomorrow.

"I love not having a job." I start to sing. Tommy is trying to quiet me, but laughing really hard, too. "You can play with your kids, but I will be asleep."

"Don't give up your day job," he says, trying to put the key in the door. "Oh, right, you don't have one."

"I can dance, too." I moonwalk on the landing and almost trip down the stairs. He pulls me into the apartment.

"Calm down."

"I can't calm down. Why don't you take out your guitar? I'll play you a song."

"Stay away, will you?" Tommy has a real strange attachment to his guitar. He never really learned to play, but he likes to sit around strumming it. I sit on the armrest on the couch.

"Okay." I remember Tommy playing his guitar for me, the first time we had sex. Then I start laughing thinking about it. Tommy laughs, also, for no apparent reason.

"What's so funny?" he finally asks.

"I know," I say, working myself up into hysterics. "I know."

"What do you know?"

"I know why you played the guitar that time." I am having trouble getting through the sentence without laughing. "The first time we did it. I know why you played the guitar."

"What do you mean?" he asks, looking sober. I know he is guilty. The first time we had sex was in his dorm room. His roommate was at his girlfriend's and I got up and went to the bathroom down the hall. When I came back into the room, he picked up his guitar and started playing.

"You farted!" I scream. I flop over onto the couch, letting my legs stay over the armrest. I am holding my nose and laughing at the same time. "You may have covered up the sound, but there was still the smell."

"Shut up!" Tommy says with mock annoyance. Then he starts laughing again. "You know you're no delicate flower, either. I've been amazed at what the bathroom's like when you come out of it."

"You shut up! You shut up!" For the first year of our relationship, I was constipated whenever we were together, but that had end when we moved to New York and I began eating my way through the borough. I throw a pillow at Tommy and he picks another cushion off the easy chair and wails me with it.

We have an all-out pillow fight for about five minutes and then collapse onto the floor huffing and puffing.

"Aaarrggh!" moans Tommy. "How do I keep up with an eight- and a ten-year-old?"

"God," I say. "I think you're gonna be great as a manny."

"You're such a weirdo," Tommy says, shaking his head. Then he looks me in the eye. "I'm sorry about Esme. You know everyone else is a bit player, but you are the real deal."

"Thank you," I say.

"I mean it. You can't forget what she was when you created her." He looks up at the stereo for a minute. I think he is getting emotional. "I'll always be proud of you for that."

Wow! I know I've lost a lot of confidence, but hearing Tommy say that reminds me of all the things I've been missing. A piece of me was tied into what I was doing. I liked telling people that I worked in kids' TV, but more importantly, I actually *enjoyed* working in it, creating something that I thought kids would see and enjoy.

I reach out and touch Tommy's hand. And then I want more. I want to kiss him and I do. I know that sex in movies is awesome and passionate, and Tommy and I have definitely tried to keep straight faces as we did it porn-star style in the past, but what I want now is comfort. I want to know what I am getting into and what to expect when.

We slept together thousands of times. There aren't any surprises this time and that's what I need. I don't think about whether or not I'm making a mistake.

All of it happens on the couch. When we're done, Tommy sits up and looks at me. We are both sober now.

"Was that okay?"

"Yeah," I say. He seems very confused about what to do next.

"Do you want to…come and sleep with me?"

"Um, no, I think I should go to my own bed."

"Okay," he says, and touches my cheek.

More questions, fewer answers.

I get up at ten. Tommy is already gone, thankfully. I don't feel as hungover as I anticipated. I sit on the couch, having flashbacks of last night. It all just kind of happened before I could consider if I was being stupid or not. We were doing so well at being friends and then I went and fucked it up again.

I feel pretty selfish and I have no idea how Tommy feels. I wish he could just communicate with me. No, it's me—I send him mixed signals.

I decide the best thing to do to take my mind off it is to go for a run. It's only about eighty degrees today, which is quite cool for August. By the time I get to the river, I am sweating profusely, but I appreciate the breeze. Okay, I match my steps and my breath and clear my mind of everything but this minute, the traffic on one side of me, the Hudson and Jersey on the other. There can only be this now, my feet beneath me. I run until I feel like I absolutely must turn around, and when I do, I find some more energy. If there is a Zen of running I experience it and it brings me peace.

When I get home, I look at the clock. I've been out forty-five minutes. It's my longest run ever. If I can run that long, I may actually be able to do the 10-K. I can't believe it.

I call Lauryn who, to my delight, is home. I tell her about my long run and then I casually mention that I slept with Tommy.

"Did somebody say ex-sex?" she says.

"I know. Am I awful? I was doing so well."

"Rebecca, you moved back in with him," she scolds. "It's not like you were doing that well to begin with."

"Well, I was trying."

"Did somebody say denial?"

"I *know,*" I whine. "It just seemed like the right thing to do at the time. Maybe I should start living my life minute to minute."

"Is that like paycheck to paycheck?"

"Sort of."

"But you're unemployed."

"Planning Kathy's bachelorette dinner is going to be a full-time job for the week." I don't appreciate the reminder of my employment status, so I catch a bit of an attitude, then I change my tune. "You're coming down for it, right?"

"This sounds vaguely like a conversation we had five times yesterday."

"Come on, I need you. Her sister put her trust in me and I hate when people do that. I got to get a place for this. And Beth's no help."

"Restaurants are your thing."

"I know," I admit. "So has anything else changed in the past twenty-four hours?"

"Actually, I got lucky, too." I gasp.

"With the coed?"

"The very same."

"That was fast. Was it satisfying?"

"Why, yes it was."

"Cool."

"I guess so." She sounds a little sad.

"Are you okay?"

"Yeah, it's just that it kind of showed me how empty sex can be when you don't really know or care for the person that much."

"I rest my case," I say to excuse my behavior but then remember about her medicine. "But are you okay?"

"Sure."

"Okay, hang in. It's only a week and a half until you come down."

"Okay, bye."

Tommy calls to say that he and Jordan are going to hang out tonight. I think he wants to let me know his plans so that I won't think he is just avoiding me. But, I think he's avoiding me, anyway.

I make a salad out of the cod I bought. I use new potatoes and tomatoes and lots of oil and fresh lemon juice. There is no good TV on in the summer—even the digital cable kind of sucks.

I decide to read *Zagats* from cover to cover and find a place to have Kathy's bachelorette dinner. It's got to be sort of cool and New York enough for the people who are coming in from out of town, but it also can't be one of those places that rushes you out, since we have a big group.

There is a lot to consider when planning a dinner for so many. You have to take into account that not everyone is an adventurous eater, which rules out a bunch of places. Also, some people don't make a distinction between types of Italian food. They are shocked—yes, shocked—when they don't see manicotti or baked ziti on the menu. Of course these things have their place, but not everyone can accept that spaghetti and meatballs isn't on every menu.

The last time Kathy's sister came to the city she was very apprehensive about traveling by subway. The list I have for the dinner totals fifteen people. Some of these women work with Kathy and some are cousins coming in from out of town. It is a sort of girls' weekend in the city for them. I think it's probably best to keep the activities in Midtown, where the lights are bright and no one will have to travel very far from the safety of their Times Square hotels.

I like the control of planning the party and I'm probably the only one who has the time for it, but it's a lot of pressure. I decide to just relax and go through the book until something pops out at me or inspires me.

I am almost done with the *R* section and carefully considering Ruby Foo's when the phone rings. It's Tommy. He's very upset.

"Can you come to the hospital? St. Vincent's. Jordan's had an accident."

The emergency room is hopping. There is no sign of Jordan, but Tommy is sitting with his head in hands. I sit down next to him and tap him on the knee.

"Hey." He looks up at me. "Thanks for coming. Did you call Lauryn?"

"Not yet. I had to figure out what the hell was going on."

"He was fucked up, punched his hand through a window. It isn't pretty. Needed like twenty stitches. They got him in quick, because he's losing all this blood. Also, they need to see if he got a concussion when he fell over. He chipped a tooth."

"What a mess."

"Why don't you call Lauryn?" Tommy asks me.

"To confirm the fact that Jordan is a complete waste of life?"

"Fuck, Rebecca, just call her and quit your judgments."

"Tommy, I don't care what Jordan does with himself, but I hate the fact that I'm here so I can break the news to Lauryn." He doesn't say anything, so I get up and go outside to use the phone. Paramedics are bringing someone else in. It's loud. I decide to walk down Greenwich Ave and cross over to Perry Street. I sit down on somebody's stoop, lean my head against the banister, sigh and dial the number. She answers, sleepily, on the third ring.

"Laur, it's me."

"Shit, it's late. I got to be up at five."

"Are you alone?"

"Yeah, but not for long." She starts telling me about her phone call with the coed. I interrupt.

"Jordan's in the hospital."

"Is he okay?" I hear concern in her voice. "Is he alive?"

"Yeah, he punched out a window, has a concussion, broke a tooth."

"And I'm supposed to do what?" She starts to get emotional. "Haven't I had enough of his shit?"

"Yes, Lauryn, yes you have. It's just Tommy asked me to call you."

"Yeah, well, Rebecca, maybe one of these days you'll learn not to do what the assholes want." I don't deserve that and we both know it, but she is hurting.

"I also thought you would want to know. I didn't mean to wake you up." Neither of us say anything for so long that I think I lost her. "Hello?"

"I'm here, Rebecca, and I'm sorry. I just don't know what I'm supposed to do from here. I don't know what to say."

"I know. Do you want me to call you with an update?" She

lets out a sigh. I can hear her switching on the light, by her bed. I know I have condemned her to a sleepless night.

"Yeah."

"Okay, I will."

"Thank you. I mean it, Rebecca. I—" I hear a little sob that I know I won't forget.

"I'll call you," I promise. There is a knot in my throat. I hang up.

Moments of clarity come at the weirdest times. It's like being pregnant, you can't just be a little pregnant and once you start to realize what's been happening, you almost wish you didn't. Jordan was sinking into a deep depression and he was trying to help himself out of it with various substances.

I thought of how he and Beth were MIA at the Fourth of July party. Maybe they'd been fucking, maybe they'd been doing other stuff. Shit! Any way you cut it, it kind of sucked.

Beth is in the waiting room with Tommy when I get back. She looks like shit. Her mascara is a mess and she is too thin. Her nose is red. When was the last time I really looked at her? She is talking really loud. Tommy is oblivious to everything.

"I can't believe he did this. What an asshole," Beth kept saying, over and over. I wanted to be anywhere but in this room, with these people.

"What did Lauryn say?" Tommy asks.

"To keep her updated."

"She isn't coming down?"

"What do you think, Tommy?" Beth says, with a tone I never could have used.

We wait three more hours, taking turns getting weak, cheap coffee at the deli nearby. Beth is wired, I am anxious and Tommy is quiet. A Dr. Shinners comes out to talk to Tommy about what is going on. He looks at me, and I know that he needs me to listen in, too. While the doctor is talking, Tommy holds my hand. Beth notices and shakes her head.

"We stitched him up, but we still have to do an X ray. I know there were a lot of drugs in his system and the cuts were positioned in a way that might imply intention."

"What's that in English?" Tommy asks.

"Do you think your friend was trying to hurt himself?"

"No," Tommy says. He looks at me. "You don't think?"

"No, not really," I say. But the possibility was there, like my moment of clarity. It was more knowledge I didn't want.

"Okay, well we definitely want to keep him for observation. I'd say at least twenty-four hours."

"Okay, can we see him?"

"Yeah, but don't stay too long. He's in C."

"Beth, you want to come?" Tommy asks.

"That's okay, I'll wait."

"Beth," he says.

"Let her, Tom," I say.

"Yeah, Tom," Beth says, mocking, "'let her.'"

Jordan was still in the E.R., in a room with a lot of beds. He is staring up at the ceiling. He looks pale. He smiles when he sees us. His smile is vacant.

"How you doing, man?" Tommy asks.

"Oh, okay." He looks at me. "I guess I can't be Gus anymore."

"No," I say. "Now you'll have to act with people."

I wasn't sure if that was the right thing to say. I meant it as a joke. Where was the handbook?

"Did you call Lauryn?"

"We couldn't get hold of her," Tommy says before I can react. Jordan turns away from us. He puts the arm that isn't cut up over his face. I touch his hair. For once, I feel bad for him. Maybe he doesn't know how not to be a fuckup.

"She isn't going to come down," Jordan says. He shakes his head. "I thought I could do anything."

"I'll stay tonight, man," Tommy says. "I'll stay with you." He looks at me. "You should go home."

"Are you sure?"

"Yeah." Tommy lowers his voice. "See about Beth, okay?"

"Yeah. Bye, Jordan. Feel better."

The sun is coming up as Beth and I catch a cab. We are sharing it up to my place and then Beth will go on to her apartment or to whatever trouble she can get herself into. The quilted carts are on the street. They are going to the corners where people will sleepily start their days. I feel like there is coffee coursing through my veins instead of blood and I wonder what is coursing through Beth.

"This is it," I say to the driver. "Take care, Beth."

I get out of the car. Beth tells the driver to keep the meter on and gets out, too. "Why the attitude, Rebecca?"

"No attitude. I just need sleep."

"For the long day of unemployment you've got tomorrow," Beth says.

"Beth, just go home."

"Say what you want to say, Rebecca."

"There's nothing to say, Beth. I'm going to bed."

"It wasn't anything, you know." I shake my head—I don't want to know. "It was just fun, you know, one of the things we did when we were having fun. It doesn't always have to be this big deal."

"He's Lauryn's ex." She shrugs. I turn my head and look down the street. I don't want to see her in this light. "Lauryn is your friend."

"It wasn't a big deal."

"Okay," I say. "Okay, I won't make it one. Bye."

Back in my apartment, I crank the AC, put on the Food Network and wrap myself in a blanket on the couch.

Esme is tugging my sleeve again. Ever since I saw her on TV, she hasn't talked to me, she just keeps coming into my dreams and running along next to me. Sometimes she dives into the Hudson River and I hear her laughing when I wake up, but today we are in a classroom.

"Do you want to go for a run?" I ask. She shakes her head.

"What do you want?" I'm not sure if I ask her or think it to her, but I know she understands. She speaks to me and her voice is husky, as I remember it. I listened to a million CDs until I found the voice-over actress with the perfect tween husky voice.

"I want you to meet my friend." She points to a desk where a pale girl with red hair and a ton of freckles is sitting.

"What's her name?"

"Kim."

Esme's friend smiles, revealing a mouth full of braces. "I like to cook."

"Hi," I say as I start to wake up. "It's very nice to meet you—"

Tommy comes in and I sit up, startled. I mute the blasting TV. He hands me a white paper bag. I smell bacon inside it. I open it to find two bacon, egg and cheese rolls.

"Bless you," I say. I smile, and make room for him on the couch. "How is he?"

"Okay. You know, there was no real reason for me to be there and I've got to go to work."

"Yeah."

"I started asking him about what was going on with work," Tommy explains. "I told him he couldn't fuck this up, but he just kept drinking. You don't think he…"

"I don't know," I say really fast. "I don't think so. It doesn't make sense, but what do I know?"

We eat our sandwiches, watching the soundless chef, Sarah Moulton, make enchiladas. There is traffic outside. People are going places; we are here.

"I wish I knew what was going on with everyone lately," Tommy says.

"Yeah, I know." I put the last bit of my sandwich back in the bag. "Me, too."

"What's up with Beth?" She's Tommy's sister, and, in spite of appearances, still my friend.

"I don't know."

"It just seems like everybody's making it up as they go along."

"I think they are. Nobody seems to know what the hell they're doing anymore."

"What are we doing? What was that about?"

"Tommy…" It was too much. It was all too much. "I don't know."

He looks at me. We are sitting so close to each other. Anything could happen, but nothing is going to. "I feel so fucked up lately."

"I know, I feel like for every one step forward there are two steps back. I just can't figure out what it is I'm supposed to be doing with my life, with anything, with you," I say. Then I tell him about how I rely on the memory of him coming to my planet when I am feeling down. I'm not sure why I tell him. I just feel like coming clean.

"I remember that. God, I miss the *X-Files*," he jokes. "Come on, it's true. You know what I remember? I remember driving back from Matt Miller's wedding." Matt was a friend of his and Jordan's from school. "Lauryn and Jordan were asleep in the back seat. You were driving and 'Pressure' came on the radio. I said, 'What must it have been like for Queen and David Bowie, both total nuts, to do that song together?' And you said, 'Yeah. God, they bring so much to the table, it's insane.'"

"I remember that," I say.

"Yeah, but then I said, 'They are even better together.' And you said, 'Just like us.' And then I kissed your hand and put my head on your shoulder and we just drove. And I was sure of everything then. I was sure of you and sure of my friends."

What do you say to that? We don't say anything. Tommy goes into his room and I stay on the couch for a while, but then I go into my room.

I don't think we will ever get back together. I think I'm just going to have to accept that fact.

19

Love Ridden

I am flipping from Food Network to Sundance Channel, as usual, when I go past Explore! Family. Just to torture myself, I keep it on and watch some of the ads. I'm hoping they don't show any promos for Esme, but at the same time, I kind of want to see if they will.

Instead I see a teaser for the launch of *Hannah's Hacienda,* except now it's called *A Home for Hannah* and the star is a very skinny blond girl. Apparently she is able to avoid the lure of the craft service table. Then there's a promo that talks about Gus's surprise family member. Jordan is smiling and dancing like nothing is wrong, like he is really psyched to be introducing all the viewers to his replacement. Don tells me that they haven't cast it yet, so they are making it a mystery.

I shouldn't be affected by this anymore. I have to learn to separate myself. Every time someone from Explore! calls me they always ask me if I mind hearing the gossip before they tell me. I never do, but maybe I should start minding. We'll always be linked by those experiences, but maybe I should stop having them pull me back into the thick of it.

I accomplished a lot for an unemployed person. I have

planned Kathy's bachelorette dinner to the satisfaction of her sister. I have a feeling that this weekend is more about her sister who just had a baby getting a "ladies' night" than it is Kathy.

First, we are going to the Royalton. It's a great white swanky space with strong, overpriced drinks. Then I made reservations at Blue Fin for nine-thirty. From there, I think I will take whoever is still standing (because I have a feeling these ladies are going to do a lot of early damage) to O'Flaherty's Ale House. After all the chichi, I am going to need a bit of the laid-back pub.

But I haven't just been planning social engagements, I also looked at a couple of trade Web sites on kids' TV. The only articles are about violent boys' shows. I hope that isn't becoming a trend. Although, maybe I can pump Tommy's new charges with info.

It's almost eleven o'clock and I'm watching an Iron Chef marathon when Tommy comes in. He looks a little funny. For the past week he's been spending a lot of time with the recovering Jordan trying to cheer him up, I guess.

"What's going on?"

"Nothing," he says. I go back to watching my show. He is antsy. He keeps getting up off the couch and going into his room and coming back out.

"What's tonight's ingredient?" he asks.

"Pig intestine."

"Ugh."

"Yeah, and the competition is trying to make a dessert out of it. Apparently it lends itself well to pastry crust."

"Ugh."

"Did you see Jordan?" I ask, not taking my eyes away from the screen.

"No, not tonight."

"Wow, you were mannying late. Don't those parents ever come home to their kids?"

"I wasn't there, either." I look at him. He looks sort of weird.

"What's wrong? Where were you? Why are you acting so funny?"

"Nothing. On a date. Because I don't know what you are going to say."

I don't say anything. I listen to him tell me all about this nanny that he met in the park. Her name is Nancy and she is from California and she most likely has no hips (although he doesn't say that). According to Tommy, she has no pop culture references, hates TV, never goes to the movies and only listens to classical music. She is a live-in nanny for twin toddlers on the Upper West Side. She's also a music student studying the cello. She is twenty-three.

"I didn't think we would have anything to talk about, but every day I see her in the park and we do."

"How nice," I say.

"We had lunch the other day and now we had dinner."

"I guess breakfast is next," I say, trying unsuccessfully not to sound bitter.

"I guess I shouldn't talk to you about this, should I?" I shrug. This is kind of like those questions my old colleagues ask me. I don't really want to know, but then of course I kind of do.

"We're friends, right?" I say. Friends who slept together last week. "We should be able to tell each other things, right?"

"I'm glad you said that, Rebecca. No matter what happens, you're my best friend." He kisses my forehead and gets up and goes into his room.

I shouldn't be surprised, right? I have no right to be upset, I know. I mean, he can't be celibate for the rest of his life, can he? Could he?

I look back at the TV. The pig intestine pastry was not palatable to the judges. The Iron Chef is not defeated. Iron Chef—1. Rebecca—0.

I can't resist stopping at Antropologie after going to the Union Square Market on Wednesday. I've been running for almost four weeks and I think it has shocked my body into changing. There is nothing drastic, but I feel a bit more solid. I am on a budget, but I have been so good and it's been months since I saw the inside of Nobu. I need something, maybe just a shirt that I can wear when I go out to Kathy's bachelorette dinner.

I go right downstairs to where they have the sale stuff. I won't be thwarted by the beautiful pink silk kimono dress I see in my periphery. I will only buy something that is marked down. I find a great red tank top with delicate beading at the neck, a deep blue shirt with sheer cap sleeves that is cut in an Asian style. I splurge on a regular priced pair of capri pants that someone put downstairs to trick girls like me into buying them.

I can't try any of it on, because I am still super sweaty from running, but I am confident enough to buy the pants in my original size of ten and will myself into wearing them.

I go to the cashier and put all the clothes on the counter. When I look up at him, he looks like someone I know. Sometimes walking around the city, you see people that look like they may have gone to college with you or that you have worked with before, but you aren't sure. This guy looks at least five years older than me, but he is so recognizable I say hi.

"Hey," he says, as if he recognizes me, too. "How did that dress work out at the wedding?"

"No," I say, "I think you're thinking of someone else, but you look familiar to me, too. I'm Rebecca Cole."

"Oh, Rebecca, hey," the guy says, smiling. "I didn't recognize you. It's Paul Perry."

"Oh, Paul! Hey." I hadn't thought about him since he called me at the beginning of the summer looking for a job, and I haven't seen him since we worked together at ARCADE. We awkwardly kiss hello. I hope he doesn't notice how bad I smell.

"How are you, Rebecca? What do you have, the day off?"

"I'm permanently off," I say, laughing. His eyes narrow. "It's okay. I got fired."

"Oh, Rebecca, how awful. Were there a bunch of layoffs?"

"There were some," I say, still smiling. "But I was the only one in production. I think I was a bit of a problem."

"You? I can't believe it."

"Well, neither could I, but I guess I'm getting used to it."

"Have you found anything else?"

"Um, no, not yet. I've still got another couple of weeks of severance." Actually it runs out at the end of next week, but there is no need to alarm Paul Perry or work myself up into a frenzy when there is a possibility I might fit back into a size ten.

"Well, I'm sure you have a lot of connections," Paul says. Then I know he is going to start fishing for some of those connections.

"So, you work at Antropologie," I say. "You must get a great discount."

"Oh, yes, the ladies love it." Paul smiles a nervous smile. "And you know, it pays the bills. It gives me a chance to concentrate on my writing. I'm pitching a couple of shows...."

Paul starts talking and I sort of tune out as he rapidly recites his résumé. Is this what I am going to become? At the end of next week, CRAP!!! I'm not going to have any money except for the four hundred dollars I get every week from Unemployment and SHIT!!! Eventually that is going to run out.

Sure, I'm so sure I could work in retail, and wouldn't it be great if I could get that silk kimono dress I ignored for a bazillion percent off? But FUCK!!! What the hell am I going to do with the rest of my life? I tune back into Paul at just the right time.

"...So, I'm certain that one of those ideas will sell. I would love to have you read it for some input. You know how great feedback can be. Maybe, now that you are unemployed, we could work on something together." I know Paul would never be saying this to me if I hadn't had a show on a network, but eventually people will forget that I had a show, and then what? Then no one will care about my opinion. Then people will be stepping over me on the street.

I've been living in a dream world. I've been a lady who lunches, runs, watches TV and doesn't realize that it's all about to end. What am I going to do?

"Um, Paul, you know what, I think I'm just going to get the shirts on sale and not the full-priced pants."

Last year's black capri pants size ten are going to have to be good enough for me. I was going to have to get to work on getting to work.

Thursday, I make a list of all the people I know in the industry that are at various networks. I organize them by who I suspect has the most powerful job and, thus, the most clout to help me. I have lost track of a lot of them, but maybe someone else will know where they are. I am not a good networker—I hate selling myself—but this is the way it has to go.

I call my first boss at ARCADE. He's big at a women's network now. I actually get put through by his assistant when I say who I am. I think my heart would break if I didn't have any clout.

As a boss, he was okay. He definitely had some control issues, and now, when he hears my voice, he chuckles.

"Rebecky Cole…" He thought it was funny to call me Rebecky?!

"Hi, Jake." When I got out of school and had my first job, I started out by calling him Mr. Sullivan and learned that didn't fly.

"How are you?"

"I'm doing okay."

"I read great things about Esme and I thought I taught that girl everything she knows." I swallow, not able to mention that at twenty-seven, I'm actually a woman and I've taken responsibility for my own career up until now. So, I sort of laugh myself.

"Well, I was actually calling because I was wondering if you were hiring at all."

"You're not with Explore! anymore? I can't believe Matt Hackett would let you leave."

"Yeah, I got laid off." Let him think whatever he wants about why. I hate pitching myself. "So I just thought I would give it a try."

"Oh, Rebecky, it's a tough time." I think that even if he did offer me a job flat out I would have a "no Rebecky clause" written into my contract.

"Yeah, I know."

"Well, we don't have anything right now. Of course, you can send me your reel." This is karma payback for the way I treated Paul Perry. I know that the reel is the kiss of never being called back. "Of course, if you wanted to pitch us some show ideas, I would love to take a look. Have you been developing anything?"

"Yes," I lie. "But, nothing for your audience. Mostly kids' stuff."

"Well, if you can rework something or come up with a new concept, I'm always on the lookout. And I would do anything for my former PA."

I love being reminded of my humble beginnings, but I guess this is the shit that's par for the course when you are pounding the proverbial pavement.

"Thanks," I say.

"Why don't you give me a call in a couple of weeks or when you've fleshed out some ideas or even if you want to pitch your kids' concepts. Maybe we can have lunch."

"Okay, I will, thanks."

Next I call Jennifer Juliano at Playtime Kids Network. She was on a list that Don gave me. I get her voice mail and I leave a stupid introductory message. I'm sure I sound like an asshole and all I really want to say is, "Please hire me, my severance runs out next week…please hire me."

I work my way down the rest of the list, leaving either pathetic voice mails or making small talk with the live ones. No one knows of any jobs, but I wind up confirming "We should hang out soon" with a number of people who will probably never be able to hang out.

For the most part, no one gives me much hope about other jobs, although I do get more names of people to call who I have similar bleak conversations with.

Jennifer Juliano calls me back. I'm amazed that she would because she is the creative director at Playtime and you'd think she would get one of her people to do it. She sounds really young and nice.

"I have to admit, I'm a big fan of Esme. The market needed a character like her."

"Thanks."

"I wish she didn't lose the glasses."

"Me, too—that's part of the reason I'm looking for a job." Why did I say that? I know that means I sound like I'm not a team player. I listen to see if Jennifer picked up on my subversive tendencies, but she seems unfazed.

"I will definitely consider you for any jobs that come up over here. I would love to get your reel. Also, if you have any show ideas, send them over."

"Yes, I've been working on a few things." What have I been doing with my summer? Why haven't I been writing the next show?

"Well, we skew very boy heavy. And, don't quote me, but the more aggressive and gory and gross the better." I was afraid of that.

"It sounds wonderful," I say. I'm sure she knows I'm full of shit. "I'll send you my reel and then when I get my pitch concepts together, I'll get those to you."

We hang up. I plan to dig up an old Esme shirt (with glasses) and send it to her. I'm sure I'll never be able to come up with a script that is violent enough. But, I can try. (Although I'm not sure I want to.)

I decide to go for a run. It is my favorite form of stress relief these days. It's a hot August day, though, and I am huffing and puffing by the time I get to Thirty-fourth. I don't stay out that long.

After I shower I turn on some music and sit at the desk in my room. I've got to just brainstorm about possible pitches. What the hell else am I going to do? Of course, I get distracted and start imagining scenarios where I do develop another popular show and wind up back in an office waiting for the next time I get stuck with a shitty jealous manager.

It makes my head hurt. I want to check the Food Network. I want some rock shrimp tempura.

There is a dearth of cooking shows for kids. How cool would it be to have a cooking show where kids get their hands dirty and make things? I could pitch it to lifestyle channels and to kids' networks. This is awesome! It could be kid-hosted by a girl. Would that be implying that only girls could cook? Maybe she could have boys on as guest hosts. Would that be implying that she is a slut?

She has to have braces just like Esme's friend, Kim. I start getting carried away and before I know it an hour and a half has passed and I have filled up three pages with scribbles and show concepts.

Lauryn calls. She wants info on Jordan, which I don't have, and to tell me that she is coming down tomorrow afternoon. She plans on seeing Jordan Saturday morning.

"Do you want me to come with you?"

"No, I think it's best to go alone. It could get ugly."

"Don't let it."

"I'll try not to. But I would like you to make a good plan for Friday night. I wouldn't mind a little rock shrimp tempura myself." I love when I convert people.

"That sounds great. Maybe we can see if Kathy wants to come. I don't think the delegation gets down until Saturday morning."

"And Beth."

"Right, Beth." I'm not exactly sure how she feels about me. We haven't talked since the hospital. I cowardly left Beth a message at her home number during the workday so as not to deal. None of this I feel like I can tell Lauryn.

"I would really like to see her. It's been a while."

"I know," I say. Then I start to tell her about my ideas for the show just to get initial feedback. I don't get very far before the door opens and I hear Tommy's voice and an unrecognizable female voice. Okay, we're friends, and friends don't mind when you bring girls home, but we're also exes and exes do. And I do. In the middle of the afternoon.

"Lauryn, I'll call you back."

I go out into our living room. There is a stranger here; a very young pretty stranger in a sweater set and pearls.

"Oh, hey, Rebecca, I didn't know you were home." I am unemployed, where else would I be?

"I am." I look at the intruder. I will not be a typical ex. I will be kind. I extend my hand. "Rebecca."

"Hi, I'm Nancy." A nanny named Nancy. I can't believe Tommy isn't opposed to this for obvious reasons.

"Oh, sorry, I guess I should have done that," Tommy says awkwardly. "We were just going to go to the movies. I came to change."

"Oh, great."

"You can come with us, if you want," Nanny Nancy says. I think she really means it. She is remarkably unsweaty in the sweater set. I can't believe I am in this position.

"Oh, actually, I'm doing some writing." That's right, I'm creative. So there.

"Oh, Tommy told me you were a writer."

"Yes," I say. "For television."

That's something Tommy watches and she doesn't.

"I'm not a big fan of TV, of course, now that I have to watch with the twins. Tommy said he would give me a tape of your show. He said it was brilliant." I can't believe he said that. Okay, I can believe he said that—just not to her.

Tommy comes back in. His shirt is tucked in; this is serious. He smiles at Nancy.

"So you don't want to go, Rebecca?" he asks, not looking my way.

"No, no thanks."

"Is that your dad, Tommy?" Nancy points to a picture of Tommy and Robert De Niro who he met once. I can't believe she doesn't know that. That's got to turn Tommy off, in spite of the skinny ass.

"No, it's Bobby D. He's an actor. So we'll see you later, Rebecca," Tommy says.

"See ya," I say.

"It was nice meeting you," Nancy says genuinely.

"You, too," I say, smiling as brightly as I can.

When they're gone, I stare up at Bobby D and Tommy. I took that picture of them. I can't believe Tommy is all right dating someone who doesn't even know who his favorite actor is. But what I really can't believe was how Tommy barely looked at me the entire time he was in the room. He wasn't intentionally ignoring me, but I guess in the past whenever we've been near each other, I have been certain that he was paying full attention to me. Now that he isn't doing it anymore I realize that is what he did.

I wait up for Tommy. I'm working on my concepts. They are still very rough, but it's starting to come together. Tommy comes in at a respectable eleven-thirty. I can tell that he is alone. I am going to quietly listen to see what he does and not approach him. I don't want to appear to care too much. I hear him humming as he walks toward my room.

He knocks. I use my most carefree voice and say, "Come in."

When he opens the door, I can see a change in him. He is glowing. I suck in my breath.

"Hey, are you all right?" he asks. He doesn't lose his smile. I think he is in love.

"Fine," I say, swallowing. "How was your date?"

"Great," he says. I think I see him close his eyes for a second.

"Great," I say.

"I think…" He looks away and decides not to say what he is going to say. "She has such a funny and cool way of looking at the world."

"Mmm," I say, nodding. I have to be happy for him. If this friendship is going to work like I want it to, I can't be selfish for no reason. "She seems really nice."

"She is. She thought you were great, too." He is even talking differently, like his whole persona has turned upside down. He wasn't supposed to find someone else first. He was supposed to wait patiently while I did.

"How's the stuff coming?" He gestures to my notebooks.

"It's going okay."

"I don't see any sketches."

"I'm just doing concepts," I say. I know he doesn't want to be talking about this, but he is trying not to harp on her for my sake. "I don't want to tie it down to animated or live action."

"That's a good idea."

"Thanks. When are you going to see her again?" I know he thinks he needs permission to talk about her to me. I can see the relief on his face.

"Well, I'll probably see her in the park tomorrow. I was actually thinking of making dinner for her tomorrow night. Do you mind?"

"No," I say really fast. "You know, Lauryn is coming in and we are going to Nobu."

"Oh, wow, you are going to love that." Now I think he is trying to establish how close we are, how well he knows me. It's my consolation prize.

"Yeah," I say. I feel my eyes narrow. No, I have to be positive. I have to help him through this whole dating thing in the way he helps me with everything. "Do you want me to help you? You know, think of something to make."

"Rebecca." He smiles and shakes his head. "I was going to ask. I totally want you to. Will you?"

"Sure," I reply, smiling. Tommy can cook some Portuguese specialties and that's about it. "We want to impress the girl."

"Thank you so much."

"No problem." I shrug. I glance back at my notebook just so I can make sure I won't have any tears in my eyes.

"I feel so happy that I can talk to you about this."

"You know you can," I say, smiling again. "You always can."

"Thanks. You know there is no one who knows me better than you."

"I know," I say, and look back at my notebook.

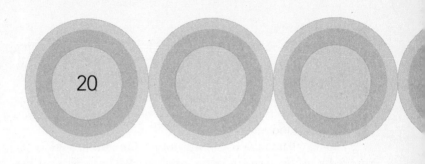

20

Good Fortune

I help Tommy prep all the food for his big dinner. We are making crab cakes and fresh tomato salad. I picked the tomatoes out myself this morning at the Union Square Market from the tomato guy.

A more immature woman would have baked a laxative brownie for her ex's new interest. Not me. I steer Tommy away from having beer and suggest blood-orange bellinis for cocktails. I got the recipe from Babbo and I know it's an impressive showstopper. You see how accepting and kind I can be?

Tommy is giddy about his dinner date. He gets up at like seven before going to man the children. He comes back during their soccer camp and that's when we whip up the feast.

Then he is back out to get the kids. I plan on leaving way before he gets home. I don't think I can stand to see him primping for someone else. And I certainly don't want to be here when Nanny Nancy comes over.

I shower and put on one of my new shirts. My old black capris actually fit. *I love running.* My cell phone rings and it's Janice. I glance at the clock—I don't have long to talk, but it's been a while.

"What's up?"

"Rebecca…" She starts giggling. "Oh, my God, I'm going to hell."

"What?"

"It's awful, really." I hear her trying to compose herself. "I mean, I shouldn't be happy about this, but I can't help it. And nobody's dead."

"Janice, what are you talking about? Are you drunk?"

"A little. We all went out for drinks. We're in Jersey. I just came outside to call you."

"Oh, I think Jen mentioned you guys had an off-site meeting."

"Yeah, like the fifth one we've had to keep morale up. God, in my next life I want to come back and work in Human Resources."

"Okay. So what happened?" So much for not being interested.

"Well, we were having all these trust exercises. And you know, how are we supposed to trust anyone when they just fired a bunch of people?"

"They did?"

"Yeah," she says matter-of-factly. "Promos. Completely gone. Of course they don't say fired, they say repurposed."

"Is that the new buzzword?"

"Yeah, so we have this exercise where we get up on this ladder and sort of fall back. And everyone in the team, there're like eight people per team, is supposed to catch the falling person. Oh, my God, this is awful, but at least no one is dead."

"Okay, who isn't dead?"

"Well, Rebecca, basically, no one caught Delores." Then she cracks up again.

"Wait, so what happened?" Janice can't seem to pull it together this time. She is cracking up and keeps taking little breaths and saying "hell." "What happened?" I ask again.

"I guess everyone expected that someone else would catch her, so it wouldn't be a big deal if they didn't."

"But no one did?"

"No."

"Oh, my God. I think I'm going to hell, too." We crack up for at least three minutes. Every time I start to compose myself, I imagine everyone just standing there with their arms at their sides and I can't stop laughing.

I get a beep on my phone, but I ignore it.

"Someone said they heard the paramedics saying full body cast…" Janice explains.

"Oh, no," I say. I stop laughing. "That is really too bad. I mean, that's awful."

"Yeah, but she's not dead," Janice reasons. "It could be a lot worse. She fell on grass. It could have been cement."

"You're right. No one's dead." We laugh again. "We are awful."

"Well, don't feel too bad for her. John thinks there is probably some way she could sue. Most likely there was supposed to be a height requirement that they overlooked."

"Oh, my God, because she's only four-four." We laugh for a while more. I know this is really an awful thing, but I also believe strongly in karma and fate and I feel like for the first time in a while the universe is on my side.

Janice and I promise to hang out soon. She jokes that we can go to visiting hours. I tell her how well I have been running and I will definitely do the Labor Day 10-K.

I want to be out of the house as soon as possible. I don't want to see the beginning of the date. I get a pedicure. Since it's a summer Friday, and most everyone has already gone to their summer places, there isn't much of a wait. I arrive at Nobu early. I tell the lovely hostess that I will be a party of four, but no one else is here, so I wait at the bar.

I get a message on my cell from Lauryn. She must have left it while I was on the phone with Janice, but it just comes up now. She missed the ferry she wanted to catch and now the one she is on will get her in a lot later than she anticipated. She says she's going to have to skip Nobu Next Door and she'll catch up with me tonight. I tell the hostess I'll only be three.

My phone beeps and I get another message from Kathy. For some lucky-for-her reason my phone didn't ring. What the hell is wrong with my phone? She is really sorry, but she can't make it and she hopes I'll understand. I guess I'm grateful that she doesn't offer a lame excuse and I'm sure she's psyched that she didn't have to talk to me. We are all getting so good at avoiding the obvious. I let the hostess know we'll only be two. It's my second change in eight minutes. She smiles politely at me and tells me to let her know when I'm ready to sit down.

So that leaves Beth. I decide to give her forty-five minutes. Of course Nobu Next Door isn't going to give me a table until my whole party is here. I order a Pellegrino at the bar. Any minute the hostess is going to come over and tell me I'm a friendless loser and I should just go home.

But I can't go home, because stupid Tommy is having a stupid date with Nanny Nancy. Forty-five minutes pass and another Pellegrino and a glass of expensive chardonnay because I'm worth it.

Beth isn't going to show.

I could just eat some rock shrimp tempura by myself. I've already spent what it would cost for the plate on drinks. I'm sure I won't enjoy it. I have been spending too much time alone lately to eat my favorite meal by myself.

Why do food and friendship have to be so complicated these days?

I settle my bill and leave. The hostess smiles warmly at me. Her life is simple, I'm sure. She eats tempura anytime she wants.

It's still light out. I decide to walk home. I'll walk slowly since these sandals are still killing my feet. Maybe by then, they will be in his room. Ugh! I don't think I can handle hearing it. I can't go home. I'll go to Rudy's or something. They've got cheap beers and free hot dogs. I'll drink and eat and it will all be great. But I'll probably have to dodge vomit and drunk boys. And what if Tommy wants to take the mommy substitute to one of his favorite bars and then they see me and it's "Oh, look, here's my ex-girlfriend who is going to be listening for squeaks in the bed—what is she doing out alone?"

I can't go anywhere in my neighborhood.

I see a sign for cheap beer, like some kind of scarecrow in the road. Ah, yes, I will shoot my film about solitude in black and white and color and it will be groundbreaking. But I hadn't expected cheap two-dollar pints in this part of town. I'm sure it's shit beer, but Tommy and Nancy will never come down here. It's safe.

I go inside. It's a pub that looks brand new. The metal of the stools glistens. The wooden bar and tables aren't scratched. It feels like winter in here, not hot and sticky like it is outside, but warm.

I sit at the bar. The cute bartender asks me what I want. I can't believe I can get a pint of Magic Hat #9 for two bucks, but I can. I do.

"Why is it so cheap?"

"We just opened."

"It's cool. What's the name of it?"

"We don't know yet, still deciding. It's a sore spot. What's your name?"

"Rebecca."

"Yeah, it could be anything." I could go for a little innocent—or not so innocent?—flirting. Bartenders always seem to work for Lauryn. This bartender is cute, but he is distracted by the guys at the other side of the bar.

There is a group of girls in a corner table, drinking bottles of beer. I'm guessing they're a couple of years younger than I am. They're at the stage when friends are still everything to them. I check to see if Beth's called. She hasn't.

"Something wrong?" I look up at a guy in a chef's jacket and plaid pants. He's come from the kitchen.

"No," I say, and try to smile. "I just…no."

"Wanna another beer?" I still have a couple more gulps left in my glass, but I shrug. He goes to the keg. "Magic Hat, right?"

"Yeah. Do you guys sell cigarettes?" I might as well smoke if I'm going to be drinking alone.

"No, we don't, but I'll give you one of mine."

"Oh, you don't have to." He reaches into his pocket and offers me his pack. "I couldn't, not in this city. It's just not cool."

"It's okay. I bought two cases in New Hampshire. Real cheap. I can give them away. Besides, I keep trying to quit." He lights my cigarette and one for him.

"Ben, fish and chips," the bartender yells from the other side of the bar.

"Well, duty calls. I'm the cook. See you in a bit?" I nod. He has smiling eyes. "We've got great fish and chips, I hear. I don't eat fish, but I know how to make it."

"Okay." He goes back behind the door again. He's left his cigarette burning in my ashtray. That means he'll come back. I go to the jukebox and put on some tunes. The girls are singing happy birthday to one of them. I smile and raise my drink.

"How old are you?" I say to the birthday girl.

"Thirty." So maybe there's hope for me and my friends. I go back to my stool. I stub out my cigarette. Ben's is one big ugly ash. He comes out and puts a piece of chocolate cake in front of me. He walks down to the other end of the bar and puts a place setting in front of one of the guys. Ben watches him take the first bite. So do I. The guy smiles and exchanges some words with Ben. I'm hungry and I want Ben to come back. I guess this cake is for me, but I'm not going to touch it until I get the okay.

"What, you don't like chocolate? It's on the house."

"Thank you. I haven't even had dinner yet."

"Nothing says you've got to play by the rules." He is so cute. There is something about him that feels familiar to me. "Do you want another beer?"

"I guess. If it goes with chocolate cake."

"C'mon," he says. "What doesn't go with beer and chocolate?"

"This is great," I say, chewing my cake. My spirits are rising. I don't want anyone else to order anything. I'm desperate for him to cook something for me, but I don't want him to leave.

"Ben," he says.

"Rebecca." I hold out my hand. He wipes his on his pants

and shakes. I have no idea what to say to him. I feel a bit over-whelmed. "This place is great."

"Oh, yeah. I love it."

"Do you own it?"

"No, I wish. The owner's a good friend."

"How is it doing?" I check out his hand for a wedding ring. He seems older than me.

"So far, so good. It's only the first week."

"It must be your fish and chips. So how come you don't like fish?"

"Ben, two shepherd's pies," the once-cute, now-evil bartender calls.

"This won't take long. I just got to heat it up." He holds my eye. "Rebecca, will you stay?"

"Okay." I like how he says my name. If I stay, he might say it again.

My songs come on. I sip my beer. For the first time in a long time I don't feel like going anywhere. I'm not anxious or sad or in a rush. What was in that chocolate cake?

He smiles when he comes back out, like he wasn't sure I would be here. He gives me a plate of fish and chips and brings the other food to the table the bartender points out. He comes back and smiles at his burned cigarette.

"We don't have a waitress yet. Know anyone who needs a job?"

"I do," I say, raising my hand. "But I think I'd be a shit waitress. I'm not very nice to strangers."

"I can't believe that," he teases. How is he so comfortable with me already?

"Thanks for this." I start to take a fry.

"Careful, it's hot."

"Okay. Besides, I don't think the food would ever make it to the table. I'd probably eat it on the way." We smile at each other. Damn! I'm starting to feel nervous about something. I don't know what to do, so I pick up a chip and eat it. It is hot, but crispy and perfect. I open my mouth to let some air in to cool off. "Issh delicioushh."

"Thank you. I'll get you some water and another beer." He does both. He is now my bartender, waiter and chef. What more can he be?

"So, you asked why I didn't eat fish?" Like a million minutes ago, but he was listening to me. "I'm a vegetarian."

"Really," I say, as if he just told me he had six toes. "It's funny that you make so much of the stuff you don't eat. I imagine the pub menu is full of meat."

"It is. I am almost a vegan, but every now and then I need a grilled cheese or some cheese on my pasta."

"Oh, God, I couldn't live without cheese," I say strongly. He laughs. I feel like a dork.

"I like your glasses." Maybe this is proof of how dorky I am.

"Thank you. I got them at a store nearby called Selima. My friend Kathy should work there." I tell him all about how Kathy wears glasses all the time and makes people get the right glasses for their face. He is looking at me the way I'm sure I'm looking at him, like everything is fascinating. The bartender calls him over for a shot.

"I'll be right back. It's this little tradition we have. Are you going to hang out?"

"Of course," I say before I can stop myself, but it makes him smile so it's worth it. I watch him do his shot. This is really strange. Is he just nice to all his customers? Maybe this is a ploy to drum up business.

"Whiskey will be the death of me. Or nicotine. You want another cigarette." I nod and take one out of his pack. "You ate all your fish and chips. Good girl."

"Oh, yeah. It was delicious. And I like to clean my plate." What the hell am I saying?

"Good, I'm glad you liked it." He stares at me.

"How old are you?" I ask.

He laughs. "Why?"

"Just wondering. How old?"

"Thirty-five. And you?"

"Twenty-seven."

"What did you do before you didn't have a job?"

"I used to write and produce a show called *Esme's Enlightenments.*" *Used to,* it still hurts to say.

"Really? I think I saw some of those. They were commercials, right? I used to watch Explore! all the time when I got off work when I lived in Santa Barbara."

"Yeah, they turned it into a show."

"That's really cool. Did the show get canceled?"

"No, I did."

"I'm sorry." He says it like he means it.

"Thank you." I want to lean over the bar and kiss his lips. I must be getting drunk.

"Ben, you got a turkey Reuben in your bag of tricks?" I have decided I hate the bartender.

"Yeah," Ben says, but he doesn't look at the bartender. He is still looking at me. I think he wants to kiss me, too. I hear the group of women get up behind me, it distracts me. The spell is broken. I look at them.

"Good night," the now-drunk birthday girl says to us.

"Happy birthday," I say.

"Have a good night," Ben says. I look back at him. "Another beer?"

"Okay, but you've got to get the turkey Reuben."

"I know, I just, I want you to stay."

"I will, I'll put some more songs on the jukebox."

"Okay."

This time when he comes back out he brings me French onion soup. I'm getting full, but I can't resist the melted cheese on top and a little of the broth and most of the soggy oniony bread.

"You see why it's so hard to give up cheese?" he says, smiling.

"You don't have to tell me." I try to scrape off some of the cheese from the side of the bowl. "So what were you doing up in New Hampshire?"

"My family's from there. I went to see them for the Fourth. Have you ever been?"

"Yeah, a couple of times. I went to school in Massachusetts."

"It's a nice drive up. A long drive, but I think you would like it." He stares at me again. "I'll be right back."

Every time he leaves I wonder what the hell is happening to me. I'm not the kind of person who picks people up in bars. Okay, I'm not that kind of person anymore. This seems like more than that, but how can it be? He's just nice, that's all. I just happened to pick the right seat. It's almost midnight. I should go. I should just leave. No, I have to say goodbye.

When he comes out again, I lose my cynicism and just accept the fact that I don't want to go, that I want to stay and talk to him. He has changed into a regular button-down shirt.

"What? No amuse bouche?" I ask, referring to the starter you get at the beginning of a meal at some restaurants. "Isn't this a reverse meal?"

"I get it, she's a foodie." He laughs.

"I prefer gourmand, thank you."

"You're welcome." Is he wearing contacts that make his eyes sparkle like that? "The kitchen is officially closed. I decided to just bring you me this time."

"That's the best," I say a bit brazenly.

"Do you want to do a shot with me?"

"Sure."

"Do you mind if I sit with you for a while?"

"Not at all." He gets two lemon-drop shots and sits next to me at the bar. We swivel in our stools to face each other. We clink glasses and do our shots.

"Another?" He raises an eyebrow. "I know the bartender."

"Maybe in a bit."

"Yeah, we don't even need alcohol. Okay, maybe I'll just get another beer, you've still got a lot of yours."

"I'm slowing down." We chat at the bar, keeping our stools turned toward each other. He approves of all the songs I play on the jukebox. He tells me all about some of the specials he makes and how he has other people taste them, if they eat meat. Every once in a while he touches my knee to emphasize certain points, but it's very light and not lecherous at all. I want him to keep making points.

"Do you want to go for a walk?"

"Oh." I look at my watch. It's almost one o'clock. "You know, I should go."

"Oh, no, just forget it, aah, let's stay." He looks crestfallen. "Forget I said anything."

"Well, where would we go?"

"We've got a whole city." Is he trying to get me to go home with him or something? I guess that would solve my Tommy/Nanny issue. No, I can't do that. He could be a crazy.

"I can't go walking with you, you could be a psycho."

"Hey, Will, am I a psycho?" he shouts to the bartender.

"Only sometimes." I laugh.

"You see, it backfires."

"No, really, I'm not, but forget it, we can stay. It's safe here. Just don't go home yet." I want to kiss him again, a lot.

"Okay, let's go for a walk."

"Cool."

We walk east over to Little Italy and Chinatown. He stops at a small restaurant and buys a fried veggie pocket. I'm full, but I take the bite he offers.

"That's delicious, but the oil is probably just as bad as the meat."

"Yeah, but nothing got killed." I nod, and then I'm sure that he is not a psycho. It's my gut feeling and I trust it.

We walk for a while. We talk about everything. It's been so long since I talked to anyone like this, since I listened to so many interesting stories. There are tons of people out, but it's a whole new vibe. Usually at this time I would be home or going home in a cab. Tonight, I suddenly have all this energy. I could stay up all night. I guess it doesn't hurt to sleep until noon every day.

"You okay?" he asks. "You think I'm a danger?"

"No, this is great." I don't mind letting him see how happy I am. "You know I've lived here for like five years and I've never done this, just walked late at night. It's like, you know, it's like it's our city. It's unreal."

"And you said you weren't nice to strangers." We stop and smile at each other. "Are you cold?"

"No." It is a little chillier than it has been because it's so late, but I don't notice.

"You have goose bumps," he says. He rubs my forearm with one of his knuckles.

And I think about Tommy, not because I'm comparing, but because of what he said about Nancy. I think I understand those feelings, sort of. Maybe I'm getting way ahead of myself, but something is happening here.

"It's you," I say. "It's like, weird."

"I know. It's weird for me, too."

"Are you married?" He laughs and shakes his head. "Girl-friend?"

"Nothing, no one. You?"

"No, no one." I can't seem to raise my voice above a whisper and then I remember Tommy again and I just want to be honest. "Actually, I live with my ex."

"Oh." He jerks his head back. "Did you break up recently?"

"No, about a year ago. I left, then I moved back in for financial reasons."

"Sounds complicated."

"It was, but I guess it isn't. Or it doesn't have to be."

"Nothing has to be. It's all what you make it."

"I know." I look up at the sky, expecting to see stars, but this is still New York—bright lights, no stars—no matter how unreal this seems. "I can't believe tonight. I was supposed to meet my girlfriends and they all dissed me."

"Well, lucky for me you are such a loser." He is still rubbing my forearm and then he wraps his hand around my elbow. He reaches his other hand up to push back my hair. Then he kisses me.

I haven't had a memorable first kiss in a long time, but this one is incredible. I put my hand up to the back of his neck and my own neck tingles. He smiles as he kisses me. It doesn't last very long. It doesn't have to.

"You smell like French fries," I say. "That's vegetarian just like you."

"You just smell amazing." He takes my hand and we start walking again. "I'll walk you home."

"Thank you." I know that we aren't going to sleep together tonight, but we will....

"Where do you live again?"

"Hell's Kitchen." We're still in Chinatown. It's going to be a long walk.

"Oh, good. I was afraid it would be the East Village and it would have to end."

"Where do you live?"

"Morningside Heights."

"Wow! I should walk you home. That's barely Manhattan it's so far north."

"I know, sometimes you can see stars there," he says, pointing our clasped hands to the sky. I'm not surprised he knew that I was looking for them.

"I hope I get to see that sometime."

"You will," he says, bringing my hand to his lips and kissing it. "You will...."

21

Full-Fledged Strangers

Lauryn is sleeping in my bed when I get into it. I forgot she was coming and that she has a key. It's almost five in the morning. We walked slowly. I'm glad she's there. It makes the bed cozier. I can't tell if Tommy is home from his date. I don't see any sign of him. I want to talk to him. I would tell him that everything is going to be okay between us, that no matter what we will still be there for each other. I feel so happy and almost high. I'm finally feeling summer. I hope I can hold on to this.

"What's up, sleepyhead?" Lauryn is awake and peering down at me. She looks like she has already been up for a while.

"Hey. Did you go for a run?"

"And took a shower and got bagels. You forget I get up at five most days on the Vineyard. I'll crash for a nap around three. Speaking of time, what time did you get in last night?"

"Almost five."

"Kathy stayed out that late?"

"No, she cancelled."

"You were out with Beth? Were you being bad?"

"No." I lie on my back on the bed. With a new day comes reality. "Is Tommy home?"

"I don't think so."

"I got in at midnight and watched TV until one-thirtyish. Nothing was here except dishes. He had that date, huh?" She sits on the bed and rubs my leg over the sheet. "Are you okay?"

"I am. I think. I met someone last night. Not that that has anything to do with it, but it might."

"Who?"

"Just some guy—Ben." I sigh and think about his eyes. "Ben."

"Where did you meet this Ben?"

"He works at a bar."

"Oh, I've had those." She rolls her eyes and gets up. I sit up in bed.

"It's different."

"You did it with him?"

"No, it isn't all about that. We kissed." I lie back in bed. Lauryn stops what she's doing and comes and stands over me.

"What the hell happened to you?"

"He smelled like French fries," I say, and curl into my pillow.

"You're a freak. How much did you talk to this guy?"

"We talked all night."

"Did you exchange numbers?"

"No."

"Jesus, Re, how are you going to see him again?"

"He told me to come see him tonight."

"We're supposed to go out with Kathy tonight." I sit up in bed.

"I was supposed to go out with her last night."

"It's our bachelorette night."

"Beth is going to cancel, why can't I?"

"Rebecca!"

"Honestly, I think this could be big."

"You've known him for a minute."

"Well, I talked to him like I've never talked to anyone. He walked me home from Chinatown."

"I can't believe you let some strange man see your apartment."

"You're not getting this. It was a big deal. It wasn't some stupid hookup with a random stranger in a bar I frequented but will never go to again." Now, why did I say that? If I were shooting this like a soap opera, that would be the last scene on a Friday, then the audience would have all weekend for the impact to dull. This is not a soap opera, but real life. And so I have to suffer the long, hurt look Lauryn gives me.

"I'm not going to listen to Kathy turn into a basket case again about this wedding. You need to go tonight. We planned this—*you* planned this! Now I have to go see my ex-husband." She slams the door.

We are twenty minutes late to the Royalton. There is no sign of Kathy or any of her family members on the swanky couches or lounge chairs. Lauryn claims there was a transit delay from her meeting with Jordan. I'm not sure if I believe her, but I had no time to question it because we needed to get here by eight. That's all she says about the meeting. I don't ask for details—I've learned not to—but Lauryn is a constant surprise.

"Look, Rebecca, I just want to apologize for my behavior this morning and for not being responsible enough to get home on time to get ready. Of course I couldn't have anticipated a subway delay, but I should have had the sense to leave earlier than I did."

"Okay," I say.

"To tell the truth, I was stressed out about Jordan and I am really feeling anxious about seeing Beth and Kathy."

"So am I," I say. I'm relieved that I'm not alone in that.

"I was hoping I would have last night to catch up with them because I don't see how we can do it all tonight." I understand that. I think I'm scared of my friends. I'm scared that it's all going to come out and we won't care about one another anymore. I'm scared that they are as annoyed with me as I have been getting with them. I'm slightly bitter that I feel obligated to put on a happy face for Kathy who dissed me last night. I'd rather go see Ben than pretend. I start to say this to Lauryn, but we are interrupted by two women who have been sitting with two other women at a table nearby.

"Are you two friends of Kathy's?" one of the women asks. She is here with Kathy's friends from work. She introduces herself but I forget her name as soon as she says it because I am feeling guilty that she might have heard what we were talking about.

We join them at one of the long glass tables full of candles and big-girl drinks. I order a metropolitan from the waiter; it's practically the cost of a plate of rock shrimp tempura. But I will celebrate the fact that my severance ends today. Yippee.

"How long have you known Kathy?" one of the women (Jessica?) asks us.

"For about five years," I say.

"Since I got to New York," Lauryn says.

"She's a hoot," one of the other older women says. I think her name is Brooke.

"Oh, my goodness, my kids love her. They always try to get her to come over," a woman whose name I'm certain is Hope says.

"She's going to be great with her own kids," the one whose name completely escapes me says.

I wonder what Kathy is like to all of her work friends. I'm not sure if she could be the same way she is to us. I'm jealous that they get to see her all the time. They aren't in her wedding party, but they probably have a better idea of all her day-to-day issues. They are more there for her than we are. I look over at Lauryn. She lights a cigarette and holds it out to me. I have a puff.

"Should we call her?" I ask. It's a quarter of nine. I don't know how long Blue Fin will hold our reservation if we're late.

"I'm sure she'll be here," says the one I'm pretty sure is Jill. "You know how it is when your family comes in for something. Everyone always runs late. I know she'll be here."

These women are a lot more like Kathy as far as career and ambitions than I could ever be. Lauryn elbows me, gesturing over to the door where Kathy has come in with an entourage of people who look like Kathy but are a lot chubbier, less blond and without glasses. Kathy is wearing a small wedding veil.

She comes over to our table, kissing the work friends before us. Their stools are closer to her. I have to stop being sensitive about this. Lauryn stubs out her cigarette. Her mouth is tense. Is it seeing all these people or being around wedding events that is stressing her out so much?

"Thank you, guys," Kathy says, taking us both into a big hug. She whispers. "Can you believe my sister is making me wear this awful veil?"

"Why don't you let me get you a drink," I ask, but Hope is already getting her one. One of her cousins has ordered a round of lemon-drop shots. I think of Ben's face when we clinked shot glasses last night.

I look at my watch. It's five after nine. I don't know why I made the reservations so early. I thought it would be too late for everyone, but now we need more time. There are also three less people than I was expecting. Each had family emergencies regarding children. Who put me in charge of this, anyway? And where the hell is Beth?

"Maybe you should call," Lauryn says, leaning into me.

"Beth?" I ask as I raise my glass and do the shot with the group.

"No," Lauryn says, making a face after her swig. "Ugh, that was strong. The restaurant."

"Right," I say. It seems like everyone at our table is screaming. I grab my cell and start to go outside.

"Where are you going?" Kathy asks, reaching both arms out to me. She pulls me into another hug. She must have been drinking all day. I'm sure I would, too, if my family was visiting.

"I'm just going to call the restaurant and tell them we might be a little late."

"Oh, is that okay?" Her eyes are big. I want this to go smoothly for her so bad.

"Don't worry," I say. I kiss her cheek. Another one of her cousins puts another drink in front of her. "Just enjoy your night."

I am briefly thwarted by Kathy's sister, Dina, who wants the scoop on the rest of the night. I tell her the plan. She wants to go to the top of the Marriott bar at the end of the night. She wants her cousins to see the view of the city.

"Okay, we can play it by ear," I say, trying to extricate myself to make the call. "Let's see what Kathy is up for."

The hostess tells me that because I have such a large party she will hold the reservation until ten. This buys us a little more time. I thank her profusely.

"You don't know how hard it is to get all these people to motivate." I hope that by befriending and appreciating her she will remember me fondly if we show up slightly after ten.

Next I call Beth. I'm shocked when she answers.

"I'm going to be late," she says as a greeting.

"You are already late," I say.

"Where are you? The restaurant?"

"No, we will be there at ten. You know where it is?" She grunts affirmatively, but without commitment. "Look, Beth, I need you to be there, and if you can't for whatever reason, I need you to tell me now. I want this to be a great night for Kathy. She deserves it. She would do this for you."

"I'll be there. Enough with the guilt." I sigh through my nose.

"Okay, I'll see you there."

I go back into the bar. Someone at another table ordered an appetizer of crab cakes. Ben could not eat that, because he doesn't eat fish. I can't stop thinking about him. If I can I will try to get to his bar before it closes, but already I doubt that is going to happen. It's impossible that I could have felt that way about someone I just met. I think I was just swept up in the moment. If I really liked him so much it wouldn't have bothered me that Tommy didn't come home at all today. It will go down as a great New York night that didn't amount to anything, but will be still wonderful in its blending of alcohol, sexual tension and food.

That can be enough for me, right? I wouldn't be surprised if he has a different girl every night. He's just friendly.

I slide into the stool next to Lauryn. She is halfway through her pack of smokes. I take one, hoping to relax a little.

"Is she coming?" Lauryn asks. I wonder what she knows about Beth or what she expects me to tell her.

"She says she is. The restaurant will hold our reservation until ten." Kathy is laughing loudly across the Royalton lobby bar.

"I got you a drink."

"Thanks."

At ten after ten we get to the restaurant. I am three drinks and fifty-five dollars down and ready to plead with the hostess if she won't seat us. I wasn't expecting Kathy's family and two of her work friends to primp for twelve minutes in the bathroom or for it to take fifteen minutes for a group of eleven to walk three blocks and an avenue.

"Hi," I say to the hostess. Dina is hovering dangerously close to me, waiting to tell me I fucked this whole thing up. "We had a nine-thirty reservation for fifteen. I spoke to someone who said she would hold it until ten."

The woman looks at her watch and shakes her head. Please, great god of food consumption, please let us still have our table.

"I know we're a little late, but you can't have already filled our table. Can you?"

"I have ten-fifteen."

"My cell has ten-ten. And that's world time." This makes Dina laugh, which I feel helps my cause. I can see the hostess fighting a smile.

"You're not all here," she says. "I count eleven."

"Actually we are going to be twelve. We have one person on her way." The hostess sighs. She is really milking this, but

I'm no stranger to the New York restaurant scene. I know how to stand firm, with just the right amount of give. I look her in the eye and raise my eyebrows, a classic cajole.

"Why don't you have a drink at the bar and someone will come get your party shortly." It's all such a money-making racket. They'll squeeze us for drinks at the bar, but I don't mind. I can compromise. "Would you like to check anything?"

"No, thanks." It's summer and none of us has anything to check. I wish Kathy would take off the veil, but perhaps it helps our cause. Bachelorettes spend money. At least they aren't making us wait until Beth gets here.

At ten-thirty, we are seated. I'm still anxious about Beth not being here, but the drinks are relaxing me a little bit. I have Lauryn on one side of me and Jill on the other side.

I am not the only anxious person. Dina is trying to get everyone to agree on appetizers and she is annoyed with me because of the empty seat.

"She's quite a handful, isn't she?" Jill whispers, referring to Dina. "Kathy's told me all about her."

"Yeah, I think she thinks it's her wedding."

"You're the one that works in TV, right?" I nod.

"Yeah, I used to work for Explore! Family. I'm currently unemployed."

"I love the Explore! Network. I loved that show on the science of sex. Oh, and I love that guy who runs around and teaches pets new tricks. You know him?"

"Yeah."

"Do you think I could get my kid an autograph?"

"Well, I don't work there anymore and all the adult stuff is produced in L.A." She looks upset. I can understand that, what's the point of having a connection in the industry if they can't help you? "But I'll see what I can do."

"I think we should order," Dina says to me.

"Why don't you see if Kathy is ready?" Lauryn says. I appreciate help. Kathy looks up at the sound of her name. I can see her trying to focus, unsure if she is reading tension.

"Isn't Beth coming?" Kathy asks.

"She'll be here," I say, not looking at Dina. "She's just running late."

"As usual," Lauryn says. Then she looks across the table to Kathy. "I can't believe they made her wear that thing on her head."

We order appetizers and dinner. I get shiso-scented tuna tartar and sautéed black bass. Moments after the server leaves, Beth arrives. She looks way more put together than any of us, including Kathy's cousins, who probably spent hours getting ready. She looks beautiful, but aloof. She circles the table, kissing the people she knows and being introduced to those she doesn't. There is a lot of air between her cheek and Lauryn's when they kiss. When she bends down to me I think I can feel her nervous energy. I can't bring myself to give her an attitude about being late. Things are weird between all of us; I just handle it differently.

"Are you okay?" I whisper into her hair. She nods at me and smiles a bit vacantly, then she circles back around the table. She sits in the empty seat between Dina and Hope. Dina looks her up and down. Dina had a baby three weeks ago and, according to Kathy, gained eighty pounds. She hasn't lost any of it and Beth's thinness seems to make her angrier.

"You're lucky they let us sit down," Dina says, narrowing her eyes. I can only imagine what kind of mother she is.

"Well, they did," Lauryn says loudly. I didn't even think she was paying attention, but tonight she is jumping to everyone's defense. I smile at her and she turns back to Jill.

None of the four of us is talking to one another. Even though Lauryn and I are sitting beside each other, we are each involved in other people. Kathy is drunk and talking loudly to everyone and Beth is just sitting straight against her chair back taking it all in.

Not since my almost-gone party have I hung out with so many people at once and I feel like I can't understand anyone. I feel pulled in different directions and buzzed. Now we are here and it's okay, but I am still tense. Without having a job, how am I ever going to connect with anyone again?

When the food comes, I feel better immediately. This is what I love about food—the moment when it is about to be set down in front of you. The server smiles like a loving parent. Still his work isn't done, you might want fresh pepper, you might want cheese. It would be the best meal or it could be the worst, you breathe in and you don't know what to expect, but your senses are ready. I take a bite of tuna, peppered and fragrant, and close my eyes. The food is decent, certainly not the best ever, but it distracts me and comforts me and relaxes me.

When I open my eyes everyone is finally quiet and eating their appetizers. Even Beth is picking at her salad. We are brought together in this simple ritual. This is why I love this city, these restaurants, this social activity.

The silence lasts until people start offering up bites. I look across the table at Beth, who holds up her fork to me.

"Go ahead," she says, and I hold out my bread plate for her to put a piece of beet with goat cheese. I offer her mine, but she shakes her head and smiles. The volume of the table rises again and then Jessica suggests we make a toast. She toasts Kathy for being the most stylish woman in the office and the person "who is able to deal with Stan's shit in the most efficient way." I have no idea who Stan is, but all the work people laugh, so I smile.

"But seriously, Kathy is a wonderful person. She makes work as fun as it can be. She is going to make Ron so happy. We are going to miss her on her honeymoon. We wish you the best. Congratulations." We clink glasses. Brandy (not Brooke) wipes a tear. These people are her friends in the same way Janice, John and Jen were mine. And I know I'm drunk then, because I miss those guys and how much fun work could be sometimes when we were together. It's a gift to like the people you work with. I can't imagine that where I work next will be as good.

The waiter clears the plates and brings everyone their dinner. I know we are all getting drunk. Every few minutes someone else offers a toast—someone besides the three of us. I don't feel stable enough to say anything.

I look at Lauryn. She is still talking to Jill. Beth hasn't said a word, she just keeps picking up her glass robotically and drinking more wine. It's just past twelve. I am sure we are going to get dessert and then there will be more drinking somewhere else. I can't not go to that. If Beth showed up, I can't just bail. That would make me the worst friend. I am not going to see Ben tonight. It's got to be for the best. I just keep thinking about how his eyes lit up in his teasing way.

"That's a big wedding," Jessica says to Kathy.

"How many?" Hope asks.

"Two hundred and fifty-seven invited," Kathy says, slurring. Her veil is starting to come off. I never knew how many people were going to her wedding.

"That's so many," Jill says. I have a feeling they have sat around their office ironing out all the details of Kathy's nuptials. All of us complained about dresses and happily let any talk of wedding favors drop whenever we could.

"My sister has to invite everyone," Dina says. The copious amounts of liquor haven't driven the bug from out of her ass.

"Who are you having?" Lauryn asks.

"I don't know, lots of people," Kathy says, her eyes almost rolling around her head. Then they settle on me. "Tommy."

"You're inviting Tommy to your wedding?" I ask, confused. "Or you're inviting me with guest?"

"Ron and Tommy are friends," Beth says, finally deciding to contribute to the conversation. I don't think it's the right place to bring up all the times I pleaded with Tommy to do stuff with Kathy and Ron when they first started dating. I don't see how *he* can be invited.

"Ron really likes Tommy," Kathy says. She is having trouble forming all her words. "You know how they like to talk about, I don't know, all that stuff."

"Who is Tommy?" Jill asks me.

"He is Beth's brother," Kathy says, drunkenly pointing to me and then to Beth. "And Rebecca's ex."

She lets the *ex* ring out for a while, playing with the sound in her mouth, and then she rests her head in her hands, almost slumping over her seared scallops.

"That's got to be a strain on a friendship," Brandy says jokingly. Brandy is a nice person and I'm sure she doesn't mean to start anything. But Beth gets up to go to the bathroom, placing her napkin in the plate she barely touched.

"It is," I say.

"There are worse things," Lauryn says loudly to Brandy, but really for Beth to hear. Beth ignores her and heads toward the bathroom.

"You're not mad, are you, Rebecca?" Kathy asks. Her mouth is almost a squiggle. She is too drunk to get a handle on her emotions.

"Of course not," I say. "It's your wedding."

Considering I just stood up the closest thing I've had to a wedding date prospect, I order another bottle of wine. I am going to drink until all of this is easier to deal with.

Lauryn sleeps through the first bus she planned on taking. We passed out together in my bed. When I wake up she is throwing her stuff in a bag, cursing under her breath.

"Hey," I say, rubbing my eyes. "What's up?"

"Sorry," she says. Her mascara is caked on her eyelashes and her teeth are gray from wine. "I think I'm going to miss this one, too."

"Are you feeling okay?" It's only a few blocks to the Port Authority. She could probably get there if she hustled.

"No, I feel hungover." She looks at the clock and shakes her head. She crawls back into bed. "Fuck it! I'm going to miss it."

It's close to two when finally we wake up. Lauryn checks the schedule and finds she has three more hours to the next possible bus. She flops back in the bed and rubs her head.

"Is there a hot guy to bring me water and coffee?" I get up and give her a big glass of water and the bottle of Aleve. We each take two.

I never met Ben, of course. We stayed out until 5:00 a.m.

After dessert two of the work friends and one of the cousins went home. We moved to the bar atop the Marriott where all the tourists *oohed* and *aahed* at the view of the city and Dina gloated as if the whole night had been her idea. I foolishly drank a warm liquored cocoa with whipped cream that bloated me. Beth took off after the first round, leaving Lauryn and I to count our exchanges with her on one hand. Kathy practically clung to Beth on the way out. She drunkenly told Beth how pretty she was and how much she loved her. Beth nodded and for a moment I thought she was going to cry.

"You're soooo special to me," Kathy whined. "I just miss my girlfriends."

It was a really weird scene. I had another round of something stronger that Brandy ordered for me. I think it was a mojito. All of the various liquors began to mix in my stomach. That didn't stop me from going to O'Flaherty's with Lauryn, Brandy, Jessica and one of Kathy's cousins after Dina threw up in the bathroom and Kathy passed out into her cosmopolitan.

We had a great time with the three women we didn't really know. I wished that Kathy could have seen us all hanging out and I wished that Beth hadn't acted so weird or that Brandy hadn't asked "what was up with that girl?" And I wished that Lauryn and I could have done something more than shrug.

When we got home, there was a message on my cell from Tommy saying that he and the nanny had taken a late-night jitney to the Hamptons on Friday and he would be staying until Sunday night.

"I can't wait to see them at the wedding," I said to Lauryn as my room spun behind her. I felt too drunk to be alone. I was lonely in spite of Lauryn, who passed out immediately. Then I called information to try to get the number to Ben's pub, but remembered it didn't have a name yet.

I calculated that I started the night with $260, but ended it with six. I think at some point I used my credit card to buy a round of drinks at O'Flaherty's. That's about twenty-nine plates of tempura. Sweet, sweet, severance, why are you forsaking me?

When I lay in bed, I imagined the room would stop spinning if I could just close my eyes.

Eventually, it did, but now the Aleves are doing little to help my hangover as I sit here with Lauryn and her luggage at the Edison Café. We called Dina's hotel room to try and see if Kathy was still around to join us, but they had checked out.

"Breakfast or lunch?" Lauryn asks. I was thinking eggs, but it is close to three.

"That's the question." When the waiter comes I order a BLT. Lauryn gets a bagel with cream cheese, fries and pancakes. I can tell the older Russian waiter is impressed that someone her size would eat this much.

"Wow!" I say when he leaves.

"Yes, did somebody say carbo load?"

"It's the perfect hangover treat." She sips more coffee and we quickly get refilled. "So, nice job planning last night."

"Thanks," I say. "I hope Dina was happy."

"Well," Lauryn says, laughing. "If it matters, I think Kathy was."

"Did you have a good time?"

"It was okay. I think I'm going to turn into a big reclusive bird woman. I feel very out of touch with people these days."

"We didn't really get to talk to anyone."

"Not anyone we considered a friend beforehand, no."

"What's happening?" Lauryn shrugs. I wasn't expecting her to have the answers, but there is relief in knowing I'm not the only one to feel this way. Maybe if I had the courage to bring it up to Beth and Kathy, I'd find that they felt the same way, too. "Is it a phase?"

"I don't know," Lauryn says. Then our food comes and we don't talk about it anymore.

Later that night, I fall asleep on the couch early and move into my bed by ten. I am sleeping when I hear Tommy come in. I can tell that he is alone, but once again he is whistling.

I jog over to the Union Square Market early Monday. I want to get to the fresh fish before it's all gone. I buy a two-pound whole trout from a bearded man who convinces me I'm getting the freshest fish in the city.

"I was cleaning it at eight o'clock last night."

"Sold," I say, and hand over my money. I head over to the tomato guy I like. Maybe I'll make some gazpacho.

"How you doing today?"

"I'm wonderful."

"Not too hot," he says. "How did that salad come?"

"It was terrific. Really fresh. Thanks for the recipe." He doesn't need to know that I passed it along to Tommy to wow his new girlfriend. I'm getting to know the vendors. I never want to have a job.

I buy a pound of potatoes. I go over to the herb people for some cilantro. Someone touches my shoulder as I'm smelling the purple basil. I turn around. It's Ben.

"Hey," I say.

"Hi." He smiles, and his eyes are smiling, too. I feel like a dick. "How's it going?"

"Good. I'm sorry I didn't come by."

"Yeah, I missed you," he says. "I missed you all day and then I missed you not coming by."

How can he be saying this? I don't even know him. I look down at the dirt on my hands from the basil.

"Are you getting stuff at the market?" I ask.

"No, I was just looking for you. I remember you said you came here and I wanted to find you."

"Oh." Are those a bunch of lines? Is he stalking me?

"Do you wish I hadn't? I just thought—"

"We don't even know each other," I say.

"I just thought that the other night was really fun."

"It was, but I mean, it seems unreal."

"But it wasn't." Even though I am wearing sunglasses, I look away. I must look like shit, still sweaty from the run. I probably smell.

"I don't even know your last name."

"It's Rosette, but what difference does it make?" Ben Rosette is a beautiful name.

"We don't know each other."

"You said that. You also said I felt familiar to you, but that was the other night after many beers. Maybe you didn't mean it."

"No, I did."

"But, now…"

"I just…" I don't know what to say. "I don't know. I mean, how do I even know who you are? I read *Kitchen Confidential*—I know that chefs have the life. Maybe the other night was just a fluke."

"A fluke? This doesn't seem like you at all." He feels confident about who I am, even though I am doubting him. He shakes his head. "Have you been talking to someone about me?"

"No, well, yes. I don't know that I'm in the right place," I say.

"What do you mean?" I look around Union Square. It's starting to get more crowded.

"I don't know. Lately I feel like I am not sure what I'm doing. You know my whole life." I sound like I'm pleading with him. And for what—to leave me alone? Is that what I want? I don't know. I just don't know if I'm ready to get close to someone, to be disappointed by them or to disappoint them, myself. It's all happening so fast.

"I see." He looks at me, like he can see through me.

"I know it sounds lame."

"Yeah, it kind of does." I wasn't expecting that.

"What are we going to do? Start dating?"

"Why not?"

"We met at a bar. It's weird."

"To who?"

"Me. Everyone."

"Not me and not you. Not the other night."

"I know, but the other night wasn't…" I really don't know what to say. His expression is weakening my resolve. He wants something from me that I'm not sure how to give.

"What?"

"It was unreal." He doesn't say anything. "I was just getting used to being alone."

"And that's what you want? Why are you so scared?" Why is he so persistent? I make what I'm certain is a very exasperated face. He reaches out and touches the inside of my arm with his knuckle, like he did on the street. I was sweating—now I have chills.

"I'm not a psycho and I'm not interested in anyone else," he says without removing his hand. "You know where I am. I won't try to bother you again. The ball is in your court, Rebecca."

"Okay."

"Can I know your last name? Now that you know mine. In case I find out that you were the psycho killer." I laugh, awkwardly.

"It's Cole."

"Rebecca Cole. That's a beautiful name."

"Thank you." He is able to say the things I can't. I sigh.

"Well, I hope I see you around, Rebecca Cole." Here is my chance to say something to save this, but I don't say anything special.

"Bye." And he walks away. Who can blame him? Now it's all up to me.

Great, I love it when the ball is in my court. Proactive is my middle name. Yep. Rebecca Proactive Cole. I wonder if he would think that was a beautiful name.

After meeting Ben, I no longer feel like running. I take the subway back up to Midtown. There is another ad for the Teaching Fellows. It says, "You made your dreams come true, how about someone else's?" I think of Ben.

How about nobody's?

There is a message from Meg, Hackett's assistant, on my cell phone. She wants to set up a meeting with Hackett and me. I don't get it. I've known Meg for a while and she had nothing to do with my layoff, so I call her.

"He didn't say why, just wanted you to meet him at the Red Cat." Yum. Talk about fresh fish…

"When?"

"Tomorrow at six."

"I can't make it until seven." I know this is a stupid game.

"I'm sure that will be fine. Hey, did you hear what happened to Delores?"

"Yeah, from several people."

"These things happen to people who don't know how to order their own office supplies." Ah-ha, assistant revenge. What a breath of fresh air.

Tommy calls me as I am rubbing the freshest fish in the city with salt and pepper.

"What's up?" he asks. I can tell right away that he is going to tell me something I don't want to hear or disappoint me somehow.

"I wasn't sure if you were making dinner tonight. I wasn't expecting you to, but if you were I wanted you to know that I wasn't going to be home. I'm, um—not going to be around." I appreciate the notification. It is unlike the Tommy I know. I failed to train him properly and now someone else is doing a better job. Perhaps Failure is a better middle name. Rebecca Failure Cole.

"Okay. Thanks for letting me know." Cordial, now that might be a good one.

"You weren't making dinner tonight, were you?"

"Of course not, don't worry about it."

"All right, see you tom—whenever."

"Okay, bye." I think about telling him to use a condom, but Martyr doesn't appeal to me.

The freshest fish in New York gets wrapped in foil and saved for another day when it won't taste as good. But then again, it might not taste very good tonight, alone.

I eat my usual summer meal of tomato, basil and fresh mozzarella. I take a few extra pieces of the fresh mozzarella. I jogged today and disappointed a boy. I could use a little cheese to cheer me up.

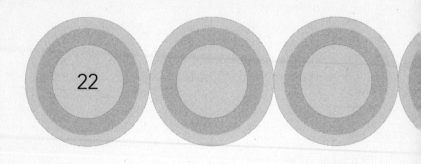

22

Snakes/Mna na hEireann

Hackett is already at the bar when I get there. He gives me a big smile and a kiss on the cheek. I am not sure how I want to be with him, but I let him get me a drink.

"I put our name down for a table."

"Oh, was this a dinner date?"

"Yes, I have a proposition for you."

"Really," I say. It's been a long time since I have been wined and dined by an expense account, but I must be strong. "Actually, I made other plans for dinner. I thought we were just having a drink."

I haven't prepared anything, but there is a low-fat burrito and day-old fish in the freezer and it's worth the missed gourmet meal for the look on his face.

"Okay. I hope you are open to what I have to say."

"Of course I am, shoot." I sip my drink through the straw. I used lipliner and I don't want to ruin it. I accept that I'm trying to make an impression although I'm not exactly sure why.

"You heard what happened to Delores." I nod. "I have to say people feel very loyal to you still."

"I wonder if it's me or just that they hate her."

"Regardless, we have a vacancy." He sips his drink and looks at me. "C'mon, Rebecca, you know what I'm suggesting."

"No, I really don't." He cocks his chin. "I cannot believe you are saying you want me to take her job. Remember, I got terminated for performance problems. According to my documents, I couldn't handle my job. Do you realize how shitty that is?"

"Look, Rebecca, we knew there was a problem and we tried to deal with it. It didn't help that you antagonized Jack Jones."

"I didn't antagonize anyone. I said what I thought. We were supposed to be a kids' channel, not a bunch of anorexic white supremacists."

Hackett laughs and shakes his head. "You're incredible."

"Thanks, I guess. What, is *she* fired now?"

"No."

"Because it wouldn't be cool to terminate someone in a body cast?"

"She's not in a body cast, but she is unable to work. Eventually she will be—" he hesitates "—repurposed."

"Oh, the new buzzword. Isn't everyone? Doesn't it ever get tiring to just keep replacing people with whoever puts a bug in your ear?"

"Rebecca, this is the industry."

"Well…" I don't know what to say. He is making me feel so naive. "It sucks."

"You would be doubling your salary. The assignment would be three months. If I'm not mistaken your severance ended last week. Also, when the three months are finished, I am more than sure we will have a place for you."

"What? Working side by side with the troll?"

"We all have to do things we don't want to do."

"You're right, we do. It's not that I don't want to pay off my credit card bills or get my own apartment, but under those circumstances I'd prefer being unemployed."

"You know the expression cutting off your nose to spite your face? I'm not the enemy." I shake my head, and he orders another round. "Oh, I guess it doesn't matter. You're young."

"I don't feel young anymore."

"I'm sure you don't, but you are, and that's why you can be like this. God, I wish I could bottle that. Are you sure you want me to take the offer off the table?" For a minute, he has dropped the businessman and become the sort of paternal character he was when I first started working for him. It's seductive. I could so easily say yes and get my old office back. I could have a door and a place to go again. "Are you sure?"

"Yes." I manage a smile. "I don't need to be tempted anymore."

"Okay, then can I be frank with you?"

"Does that mean you are going to insult me?"

"No, I'm going to give you a piece of advice and an observation."

"Okay, shoot." He takes another rather large sip of his drink.

"You are a likable person, Rebecca, but just remember that can piss some people off."

"So are you suggesting I be less likable?"

"No, I'm suggesting you don't take things personally and that you remember that sooner or later it all comes around. You will have to deal with some of the same people again, and in their own way, they will have to deal with their consciences."

"For as long as I can, I am going to avoid being in a position of managing other people to do things I don't believe in, or working with people I can't stand. Even if it means I never have an office or a show or money. Peace of mind is worth more than that."

"Nice, Rebecca. I would love to hear how that works."

"And I would love to keep being patronized." The nice thing about not working for him is that I have the balls to say what I want in whatever way I want. "What's your observation?"

"Well, why didn't you fight your termination?"

"What do you mean?"

"You just accepted it in the HR office. You barely batted an eye."

"What could I do? I was in Human Resources getting a severance package to sign. It seemed like the deal was done."

"I think you never believed you could do it."

"Do what?"

"I think all the while you kept expecting it to happen, expecting to get canned. Even before Delores. You felt, I don't know, unworthy or something. You were always waiting for someone to wake you up from the dream. You thought you were lucky—not talented. That's one thing, that lack of trust in yourself, maybe the only thing I'll never regret about not being young. Confidence comes hard."

I feel like I just got smacked in the head by a bunch of bricks. I can't believe it. I think Hackett is right.

"One day, I suspect we'll work together again in some capacity, and I hope, Rebecca, that you only have to grow up just a little." He hands his credit card to the bartender.

"Thank you," I say, grateful that I don't work for him anymore so that he can say whatever he wants to me. "I mean it."

"I know," he says, and signs the receipt. He gets off the stool and squeezes my shoulder. "Thank you. Enjoy your dinner plans."

I know where I can find a better dinner than the one in my freezer. I think it's time I start ruling my destiny. I can wait for karma, but it might never catch up with me. I consider going jogging, but instead I take a risk and take the subway to Ben's bar. Will, the bartender, waves to me and says I can go on back to the kitchen. When I push the swinging door open, he is bent over a pot of chili, stirring.

"Hey," I say. He smiles when he looks up and then when he sees that it's me, his smile grows wider.

"Hello there." He looks me up and down and points out my purple toes. "I like your toes."

"Thanks, I just did them myself. My severance ended. I can't afford pedicures anymore."

"What's up?"

"I was hungry and I thought you could make something to eat when you're finished working and then maybe if you still wanted to we could go up to your apartment and look for stars."

"Okay," he says, nodding and wiping his hands on his apron. "Does that mean you are going to give this a chance?"

"Yes," I say. "I'm in."

When it rains it pours. Don calls me after my meeting with Hackett. In his message, he is the usual slick Don that I am starting to like, and he says that he needs to "pick my brain" about some things.

We meet at Molyvos, a Greek restaurant in Midtown. I get there first and wait for him in a booth. He kisses me hello on both cheeks. He looks and smells good.

"How are you?"

"I'm fabulous. I got laid off."

"Oh, no! Because of Jordan?"

"Partially, they think I could have done a better job casting. Honestly, it was too confusing for kids to get to know Gus and then try to relate to his cousin. Also, it seemed too much like *Blues Clues.* Meanwhile, that's what they said they wanted. Anyway, the network's pretty broken. I've already got five offers."

"That's great, Don. I wish I had your connections. Where are you going to go?"

"That's the beauty of it. I'm not going anywhere. I'm taking this opportunity and using it to my advantage. I am following fate. I'm reading the signs." Not the follow-your-bliss crap again. Please.

"What are you doing, joining the seminary?"

"I think Sarah would have a problem with that." He winks at me, but keeps talking. "I'm starting my own production company."

"That's cool," I say.

"I figure I have worked on and developed enough shows in-house to know what I need to do. I'm not getting any younger. I'm thirty-two. It's now or never."

"I guess so," I say. I have never seen him this excited before. It's almost contagious.

"Anyway, I want to start pitching shows. It's us against them now."

"Us?" What is he trying to tell me?

"Yes, Rebecca. I need your tween-girl connection. You're like a big self-conscious tween, and I want that. It's big."

"Thanks, I guess. But what do you want me to do?"

"I want you to start writing spec characters and scripts. It's going to be different now. We're going to get the best deals and beaucoup cash. It will be a while before we see any of it, but I can promise you that even if something happens between us, you'll never get screwed on your shows again."

"What if they don't sell?"

"They'll sell. One thing I learned is that the networks listen to whoever charges the most. And we are going to be pricey, Rebecca. We are going to pillage them, we are going to bend them over a chair and—"

"I think I get it," I say. "When do you need these?"

"I just need paragraphs by next month. I brought a contract. It lays out what I will pay you for the ideas and what you'll get when the show gets picked up. It's time to start behaving like guerrillas."

I wonder if this is too good to be true or if Don has started taking drugs or what. When I look at the contract I'm speechless. He is going to pay me a decent sum for the specs and if the shows do get developed I will be getting more depending on whether I help develop and produce them. Either way, I should be able to support myself by just creating these characters. I can't believe someone is going to give me money to do something I love. With this kind of money I could eat a plate of rock shrimp tempura every night. How could I be so lucky? And like some kind of sick Jiminy Cricket, I remember what Hackett said about not believing in my own talent.

"You're crazy," I say. But, I'm worth it, right? I deserve this. "Okay. I'm down."

23

Strength, Courage & Wisdom

I work nonstop for two weeks on the ideas. Ben's schedule is such that we can sleep in together and then when he goes to work, I go for a run and spend the rest of the evening coming up with concepts. I get myself on kind of a weird schedule completely opposite from Tommy's. I leave to meet Ben at the bar before Tommy gets back.

Everything with Ben seems to have happened so easy and naturally. Yes, it happened fast, but sleeping with him was as familiar and natural as everything else about him. In short, really really good. Maybe I shouldn't be too into this, but when I catch myself holding back with someone like Ben, I wonder why I'm fighting it. So I think I'm just going to go with it and not question what my intuition tells me is right.

I sleep at Ben's when I can because Nancy stays over a lot. I don't see her very much, but I know she has dabbled in a few of my bathroom products. I think this is very uncool. But I don't make an issue of it.

When I first start brainstorming I can't shake the feeling that I am cheating on Esme. She lived inside me for so long and all of a sudden, there's a Kim and a Robin and a Kelly. Each girl has her own story and I have to move away from the way Esme spoke and thought. It takes me a while to get used to this, but then I decide I can't censor myself, and I jot down everything that comes to me—which is a lot. I write up paragraphs on about ten ideas, but full pages on those three.

With her wedding only a month away, Kathy constantly calls with new requests. Because I am not really employed I am the person she asks to do the most favors. I never dreamed I would be picking up her dyed shoes or helping her count invites, but somehow I get roped into it all.

Every time I try to bring up how upset she was the day before we went to the movies in the park, she changes the subject. I have a feeling that she wishes she'd never told me and wants me to forget her moment of weakness. I don't bother bringing it up anymore. If she chooses to be the bride who doesn't deal with her issues, who am I to stop her?

"Brides get self-centered as it gets closer to the wedding," Lauryn says. She has another couple of weeks before she moves to Boston and starts school. She has been having a lot of sex with the coed we met at the bar. It's more fulfilling now because he's looking her in the eye, she says.

"I just wish it would be more evenly dispensed," I say, about my status as a wedding slave.

"Well, Beth is MIA, and would you want to deal with Kathy's sister?"

"You've got a point."

"I object to having to dye my shoes, I have to admit," Lauryn says.

"We are never going to wear the dresses again, and now we have to ruin a perfectly good pair of shoes with a color that doesn't exist in nature."

"Did somebody say 'waste of time and money'?"

"I did," I say, laughing. "I also said nothing on the registry for under sixty bucks."

"Yeah, I snatched up the last thing under, which was fifty-dollar swizzle sticks. A set of six."

"You better make damn sure that they feed you mixed drinks when you go over there."

"I intend to."

Jordan was not invited to Kathy's wedding, but Lauryn told me that she agreed to have coffee with him again when she comes down for the wedding.

Tommy eventually asked me if I'd mind if he took Nancy to the wedding. It was one of the rare times we were alone in our apartment together. I was kind of surprised that he was around without Nancy and wondered if the only reason was to ask me this question. I know the answer he wanted to hear was no, but I was so surprised by the question that I just kind of shrugged.

"I won't if you don't want me to," he said. I know I have no legitimate reason to stop him. Why should he have a bad time? On the other hand, why does he have to bring her around our friends? "I just expected you were going to bring that guy."

"Ben," I said angrily. "Can you at least remember his name?"

"Yeah, Ben. Aren't you going to bring him?"

"I don't know yet." I really liked Ben and knew I should bring him, but I worried that he was going to be bored with me performing all my bridesmaid duties (and there were already a ton I had to do). I know it was wrong and selfish, but why was Tommy allowed to have fun with Nanny Nancy when I was going to be forced to prance around in uncomfortable dyed shoes catering to Kathy's weird belle-of-the-ball fantasies?

"Well, let me know when you decide," he said. He stared at me for a minute and then turned and left the apartment.

I knew I was acting foolish, but I couldn't help it. Once again, it seemed like I had no idea how to be broken up with Tommy. Even though I was so happy with Ben, I guess I couldn't help being upset that Tommy didn't care as much about me. It was scary to think that after all the drama and the back and forth, we were getting to a place where we were finally going to have to let go. This guy shaped so much of my adult life, and now he just wasn't going to be there. Don't get me wrong, I didn't want to get back with him, that's for sure. I just didn't know if I wanted *him* not to want to get back with me.

Tonight, after my talk with Tommy, I talked to Ben about it over a beer at the bar. They have finally decided on a name for the pub. It's to be called Knuckle Sandwich. The bar staff gets a huge kick out of this name and say it whenever possible.

I always hesitate about bringing up Tommy to Ben. I don't want to make Tommy out to be an asshole and I don't want to make Ben jealous. As usual, Ben listens to me very carefully before answering me.

"The way I see it, Rebecca, you just have to negotiate your new relationship with Tommy. I know that's not easy, but he's a big part of your life, it seems." He takes a sip of his beer and then leans over and kisses me. "I bet he feels the same way you do. Maybe you should address that. I think you want to keep him in your life. I certainly want to meet him."

"You're neat," I say. Every time I see Ben I like him more. "I think it's terrific that you can talk about this with me without being jealous."

"How can I be jealous," he says, leaning over and kissing me again, "when I know you're crazy about me?"

"Where do you come from?" I still can't believe it is this easy to be with someone I am so attracted to. I am almost certain that no other shoe is going to drop.

"New Hampshire."

"Right, so do you even want to come to this wedding?"

"Well, the chance to see you in the dress you describe with such graphic distaste is appealing, but it's not like I enjoy getting all dressed up in an uncomfortable suit."

"So, you don't want to go." He laughs and shakes his head. Will brings us two more beers.

"I didn't say that. Of course I want to meet all your friends and be there for you, if that's what you want. I think you have to make this decision, Rebecca."

I knew he was right, but I wished he would just tell me what to do.

★ ★ ★

Don and I meet to go over my concepts at Wild Lily Tea House. It's a funky little place that Ben took me to for our first official date. I think the tranquility will offset any tension I feel about having a business meeting. I make sure we get the table where we kneel beside the small fish pond at the front of the restaurant.

I busy myself maneuvering the green-tea-marinated slices of chicken with the dainty wooden chopsticks and try not to worry about what Don is thinking of all my ideas. He keeps making little "hmph" noises as he flips through the pages. I don't know if that means that he likes my ideas or he is wondering if there is any way for me to pay back the money he advanced me. Just when I think he's done reading, he flips back through the pages and starts making notes with a pen. He is completely neglecting his pretty little salad. I consider reaching over and snagging one of the sugared walnuts on top. He looks up at me and smiles.

"Well," I say, locking my jaw together afterward.

"I think it's interesting that you chose these three to highlight," he says, holding up the one-sheets I did.

"Why?"

"I don't know." Great. "I think this one is too much like Esme."

"Oh," I sigh, and shake my head.

"No, but that's really the only one I have an issue with. I think the space and underwater ideas are very promising. I feel like they would have to be animated, because the cost to do it live action would be sky-high. So work that out, think about scaling some ideas back for the space one in case we pitch it to a network that isn't comfortable with animation."

Don has lost the slick producer voice and is talking like he really wants to work on developing these. He looks back at the pile of papers and picks one of them up. He pats it a few times and looks up at me.

"This, this is really a good one. You're calling her Kim, but

I think you should switch the names with the Robin you are using in the underwater one. A kids' cooking show. How perfect! We'll pitch it to all those lifestyle channels and kids' TV. And we can skew the adult supervision you mention here, depending on who we are going for. You're brilliant!" He takes a giant bite of his salad.

"Thank you," I say. "Why do you want me to change the characters?"

"Well, I like how you've given your young cook braces. I see lots of funny eating shots, spaghetti getting stuck in braces, metal fork to metal brackets—" he is talking really fast now, like his juices are flowing and he can't stop shoveling greens into his mouth "—I think we need to call it *Robin's Recipes* or something."

"Well, do you think we have to do alliteration? Isn't that old?" It's not easy to say this to the man who developed *Gus and the Gopher, Bob in the Barn* and *Amy's Animal Adventures.* He cocks his head and smirks at me like he has never heard anything so ridiculous. I fear that this could be the deal breaker.

"Rebecca, we want to be cutting edge, but there are some rules we can't break. It's either alliteration or rhyme. I don't know, maybe you can play with kitchen—*Gretchen's Kitchen.*"

"I see," I say, and eat my last bite of chicken. I obviously still have a lot to learn about kids' TV.

I didn't get to go for a run this morning. It's probably for the best since the race is this weekend and I want to conserve my energy. I walk up along the river to get back home. When I turn down my block I see that Beth is sitting on our stoop smoking a cigarette. I haven't been alone with her in a while and I start to feel nervous. She doesn't look up at me as I head down the street, giving me a chance to study her. She looks thin, and even though she is dressed really well, her hair is kind of a mess. She looks like she hasn't changed since last night.

"Hey," I say, startling her when I get to the building. She jumps up a little and turns to me. She has sunglasses on and I wish I could see her eyes.

"Hi," she says. She looks as antsy as I feel. "I was looking for my brother. Do you know if he's home?"

"I don't think so," I say. I look at the door as if it knows the answer. "Did you try the bell?"

She nods. I know that there is something wrong with her, but I just don't think she will tell me. I try, anyway.

"Are you all right?" She nods.

"Do you want to come upstairs and wait for him?" She shakes her head. Above her glasses I see her eyebrows knit a little. She sighs.

"You're sure you're all right? You can talk to me." She doesn't do anything, but then she shakes her head and takes a big breath. I know she doesn't want to talk to me about whatever it is. I'm not even sure she would talk to Tommy.

"Do you want a hug?" I ask. It's a last resort. Instead of shaking or nodding her head, she stands there still until I put my arms around her.

"Thanks," she says, pulling away. "Sorry."

"No problem. Sometimes we all need a hug. Did you have a rough night?"

"No, I should go." She starts to get flustered.

"Wait, listen, let's go over to Film Center Café and get a drink."

I see her internally debate, and then she agrees and we walk over to Ninth Avenue to the café. She seems kind of shaky and nervous, but I'm happy to actually have her with me.

We order drinks and she barely touches hers. She doesn't remove her sunglasses. I keep the conversation light—I basically babble about nothing—but she doesn't seem to mind.

"I think I need to stop partying so much," she says finally. I wait to let her finish. I could lay it out on the table and lecture her on sleeping with people's exes and partying too much, but she looks defeated. "I think—I think I'm having trouble with all this."

Her lip shakes a little. I feel myself starting to get emotional, too. She is in some kind of pain I just don't get. More than knowing why and demanding an explanation, I just want to listen and be here.

"I, uh, don't know these days what's going on with me, you know. I can't make heads or tails of anything I do."

"I know how you feel," I say. "Things get pretty confusing these days."

"Yeah." She studies one of her nails.

"You know, I read about this," I say. "It's called the quarter-life crisis. It's not uncommon for women our age to feel this way."

When she smirks at me I realize that I sound like I'm giving a lecture. "Oh, really, Rebecca, where did you read about this?"

I'm already laughing when I say, "The *New York Times* Sunday Styles section." And she laughs, too. The kind of laugh you have when you are very close to crying, the kind of laugh you have when there is nothing else to do.

Nancy is over when I get up in the morning. She is wearing sneakers and running clothes. I was hoping to talk to Tommy about Beth. Nancy is bright and cheerful, as usual.

"What are you up to?" Her blond hair is pulled into a perfect ponytail. I push a strand of my unruly hair behind my ear.

"I was going to run in the Race for the Park. Are you?" I was certain Tommy had forgotten about the bet the night we went to Half King.

"Yeah, we are." Are human voices really this high and chirpy? Tommy comes out of the bathroom. He looks very fit in his T-shirt and shorts. "Tom, isn't it great? Rebecca is going to run the race, too."

"I know," he says, and smiles at me and points at Nancy. "She is totally forcing me to do it."

He *has* forgotten. He is just doing it for her.

"Tom, don't tease." Clearly this is someone who spends too much time with toddlers. "Now we can all go together."

"Actually, I have to leave now. I told Kathy and Janice I was going to meet up with them beforehand for a bagel." Nancy looks crushed and I feel bad, but running this race is going to be torturous enough. I just don't think I can stand to watch them coo over each other on the subway. I hastily make my exit.

"You need to carbo-load for energy," Kathy advises. We are waiting for Janice and John in the bagel store near the park. It is so brutally hot out that we need an air conditioner. Kathy has just finished complaining to me about the bridal shop where all of our hideous bridesmaid dresses have been held hostage for more money than was agreed to. Kathy managed to liberate them with the help of the contract and Jill, who works in the legal department of Kathy's office and knows enough of the language to intimidate. Now we are having our fitting somewhere in Chelsea. The final fitting is next week and I am expected to be there in spite of the plans I made to go to Block Island with Ben. Lauryn is also being summoned from the Vineyard, even though she was planning on moving to Boston.

I am in no mood to be trifled with today. Kathy talked me into running in this stupid race and I'm certain Nancy and Tommy are going to be waiting way before me at the finish line, holding hands. After six miles I am going to stink. I've gotten myself into all of this because I don't stand up to Kathy. Well, I am about to give her a piece of my mind. In fact, I am about to get a sausage, egg and cheese sandwich and say "fuck off" to this whole running thing. I was not meant to run for anything. Who was I kidding? The winter is coming—I need fat to insulate me.

Lucky for Kathy, Janice shows up at the very moment I am about to bring forth my rage. John is in tow and he looks even more miserable than I do.

"It's hotter than hell and she gets me up to run," he whispers to me.

"You'd be ready if you'd trained," Janice says. "Look at Rebecca. She trained. She's ready."

"Yeah," I say. "Real ready."

"Come on, Rebecca," Kathy says. "It's for your own good. Look how great you look. You're going to be beautiful at the wedding."

I want blood, but I must channel it into the race I am obviously helpless to get out of. I would rather not have Nanny Nancy learn that I chickened out.

"Way to go dissing Hackett," Janice says.

"You're everyone's hero," John says. If nothing else, that motivates me.

After chowing down our bagels we are waiting at the starting line for the signal. According to John you can't just have a race in the city for the hell of it. He thinks it has to be for something and there have to be a ton of speakers telling you how wonderful you are for giving your money and energy to whatever charity you are running for. In this case, I collected money from Ben and the people at the bar to help the parks, but I don't need to hear how thankful the city is. I am anxious to start.

"I would like to just get on with it," John whispers to me.

"Tell me about it."

"We could ditch and go to a bar," he says. I am ready to agree because through the crowd I spot Tommy's head and below it Nancy's ponytail.

"Shut up," Janice says to John. Then she kisses his hand.

"Hey, isn't that Tommy? You didn't tell me he was doing this," Kathy says. Before I can say anything, she starts to wave and yell. Jesus. "Tommy! Hey, Tommy!"

Of course, Tommy turns and waves. Nancy turns, too, and, seeing me, smiles and brings Tommy over. She is completely psyched to run into me.

"Hey, Rebecca," she says, her smile making me feel even more guilty. "I'm so glad we ran into you. Tommy was such a slowpoke this morning. I told him we should have picked a meeting place so we could start with you guys. Hi, I'm Nancy."

She shakes hands with all of my friends. How did Tommy find someone so flawless and so opposite to me?

"Now we can all run together," Nancy says.

"Actually, I'm a pretty slow runner," Janice says. "I don't want anyone to wait for me—not even John."

"Actually, I probably won't make it to the finish line," John says. Janice glares at him.

"Yes, you will," she says. And he will.

"Why don't we start together and see how it goes?" Tommy asks Nancy. He catches my eye, and I know that he's said that for my benefit.

We get the countdown, and the gun—or whatever it is they use—goes off. There are so many people starting out that we barely get to run until we are about a half mile in. Immediately, I start breathing heavier. We lose Janice and John pretty quickly. John wasn't kidding about not being prepared.

"It's okay, breathe in and out," Kathy says. She starts talking to me, trying to keep me breathing properly by talking. I am able to do this until about two miles. By then I am dripping with sweat. It's just too hot. Tommy and Nancy keep looking over at me. I wish they would stop.

We get to a hilly part of Central Park. It's not a big hill, but the course along the river or from my apartment to Union Square is very flat. I am not prepared for this. I wonder how John is handling it.

"You should lean over like this," Nancy says. "It will help your momentum."

"Thanks," I say. Normally I would try to convey what a nice, non-bitter ex-girlfriend I am in every word I say to her—but not this time. I am too hot and overexerted for pretense. I turn to Kathy. "I think I'm going to fall behind and take my walking break now."

"Just wait until we reach three miles. It's going to get better in a sec." Kathy has granted me one two-minute walking break. Well, she suggested that's all I take, but I have a feeling she is going to be disappointed.

"Let's run up ahead," Tommy says to Nancy. I'm so glad. "C'mon."

"I'll see you at the end," I grunt. I make sure to smile at

Nancy this time. A little pretense is palatable if it gets me away from the happy healthy couple.

They run ahead and I slow down. Kathy exaggerates her breathing as an example of what I should be doing.

"You don't have to wait with me," I say, trying to get the words out.

"I want to. Come on, you're doing great. Don't worry about talking. Just breathe."

We run along like this for a while. We run past the guy who announces the three-mile mark. I look at Kathy, who shakes her head and mutters words of encouragement. I run beside her, trying to imitate her breath. It works, but after a few minutes, I really need a walking break.

"Okay, I'm going to slow down. I'll see you at the finish line."

"Are you sure? I can slow down, too."

"I know you don't want to walk, so just go ahead. I'll see you there." Somehow Kathy manages to give me a running hug and cheer me on. Then she takes off and I know she's been holding out on me.

I slow, then stop and walk. Two minutes, it's going to help. I breathe heavily. People are passing me—I feel like a loser. I look behind me for Janice and John. They are nowhere in sight. Maybe he convinced her to go to the bar, after all. Ugh, if I had a beer right now I would throw up. A cheese plate might be perfect, though. I pass the four-mile mark. According to my watch I have been walking for one minute and thirty-four seconds, but everyone is going by me. Oh, what the fuck? I start to run again, ahead of schedule, for the record.

This time I relax. I think about how Kathy was breathing. I repeat it over and over, in and out. I will finish. I've got to finish. I remember the day I ran along the river. Go back to that feeling of peace, Rebecca! Okay, I'm there. I feel strong. I can do that. I have a decent pace as I go past the five-mile marker.

I am doing this. I am almost done. I am running. I am a runner. I am sweating and gasping, but I am a runner. That's like an athlete. That's what I am. When I'm done, I will be able to

eat whatever I want, because I have already burned the calories. That's what runners do—they (we!) eat and run.

But wait a second, I've passed the six-mile mark. Shit! Fuck!
The .2 miles! It's 6.2 miles. It's a 10-K. Why is this the only
place we really use the metric system? Why can't I just be done
with my exercise for the year? Why does running suck so
much? I can't breathe! I am floating in my sweat. I hate Kathy!
I hate Janice! All runners are assholes.

"Hey," says Tommy, jogging toward me. I won't be fooled.
He is some kind of mirage, like you get in the desert when you
are dehydrated. That's what it is. He is going to say that even
though I am falling for Ben, he has decided to live as a monk
and support me at all costs. After all, there are no other women
like me, so why try to accept alternatives?

"Rebecca, are you all right?" Tommy asks. He might be real.

"Well, I'm running. How all right could I be? What are you
doing?" He turns and starts running alongside me.

"Well, some people at the finish line are very upset with me,
because I turned around after I went through."

"Are you crazy? Why did you do that?"

"When I passed the six-mile mark, I knew you would probably be ready to give up. I thought I'd make sure you did it."

"Thank you," I say. It's better than a vow of chastity and a
constant candle held for me. It's what a friend would do.

"Kathy tried to turn around, too. She is really worried about
you. She turned around when they started yelling at her."

"She's a wimp," I say, smiling. Along the police barricade
people are cheering. This is fabulous. I've never been cheered
before. It's better than solid ratings. It's almost better than rock
shrimp tempura.

"Only another few yards," Tommy yells over the crowd.
Then he starts humming the theme from *Chariots of Fire,* so
I'm laughing when I go past the finish line.

Kathy throws her arms around me and hands me some
water. I even let Nancy hug me despite my river of sweat.

"You did it," Kathy keeps saying. "You did it."

24

Me

To celebrate our completion of the race, we decide to go to Peter McManus. It's an old Irish pub in Chelsea that Lauryn and I used to go to a lot when we lived in the Flatiron district. Janice and John are moving in with each other in Chelsea and have never hung out down there. I tell them about Peter Mc-Manus and spend a good twenty minutes singing the praises of Whole Foods and Chelsea Market.

"You're really into food, aren't you? Not that that's a bad thing," Nancy says. She is trying to be nice to me. She is not from New York—it's just her nature. It can't be easy to have your new boyfriend living with his ex-girlfriend.

"Yes," I say, smiling. This time I really will try to be mature.

"She actually helped me make your dinner," Tommy says.

"It was wonderful, thank you."

"Sure. Speaking of food…" I say, flagging the waitress over.

"We have a fish-and-chip special," she says.

"You love fish and chips," Kathy says.

"I do," I say. "But I'll have the turkey club."

I go to the little phone booth by the jukebox and call

Knuckle Sandwich. I know Ben was doing prep this morning
and working the lunch crowd.

"How was the race? Did you win?" He laughs.

"No, but I finished. We're at Peter McManus having some
drinks. I denied the fish and chips because I knew they would
pale in comparison to yours."

"That's my girl. I'm almost done here. Will wants to try out
this day chef, so maybe I will come up and meet you."

"You will?" This means he'll meet Tommy. This means that
we'll both be here with our significant others. This is big.
"Okay."

I get back to the table as the food does. "Ben's coming."

"Great, I can't wait to meet him," Janice says, then she
glances at Tommy. I notice Kathy is doing the same thing, only
less obviously.

"Who's Ben?" Nancy asks.

"It's Rebecca's new boyfriend," Tommy says to her. Then
he smiles at me. "And I can't wait to meet him."

I am desperate to finish my whole turkey club. It is an act
of defiance for actually finishing the race. I feel it is my duty
to consume as many calories as possible, as this is probably the
most calories I will ever burn at once. The problem with club
sandwiches is there is never enough bread to make all the sandwiches possible out of the ingredients. I can't even make it
through half. Everyone is eating big: Tommy got a Reuben,
which he offers both Nancy and me a bite of. Janice and John
went with fish and chips and Nancy got a cheeseburger. Nancy
isn't stingy offering me her fries. I find this quite endearing.

Only Kathy is watching what she eats. They were out of veggie burgers, so she got a plain turkey sandwich on white toast.
She looks great, but I feel like she is living in constant fear of
gaining an ounce. She eats about a quarter of it and orders a
white wine after her beer.

"We just ran 6.2 miles, Kathy—you could use a sandwich."

"Well, I wish they had whole wheat. I'll have a salad when I
get home." She looks at her watch. "And actually, I have to go.
I need to call a couple of the vendors and I shouldn't be out late."

"Why?"

"Because I'm getting married," she says condescendingly, as if there is any way I could forget.

"In two weeks," I say, equally as annoyed. She rolls her eyes at me. I don't want to make a scene in front of everyone, so I don't say anything else.

"I have to catch a cab to Grand Central," she says.

"Well, are you sure you can't just wait until Ben gets here?" I really want to introduce him to her. I've told him all about the issues we've all been having lately and I know he is excited about getting to know the Big Three—Kathy, Beth, Lauryn.

"Oh, Rebecca, I can't," she says, acting genuinely apologetic. "I don't want to miss this train."

On Saturdays the trains to Kathy's town run every half hour. Late nights the trains run even more sporadically, sometimes every hour. In the past missing a train meant we could hang out and drink and have more fun. Those days are over and I realize that. I am going to have to stop comparing our friendship now to what it was in the past.

"Okay, I'll walk you out," I say. Kathy says her goodbyes to everyone and even gives Nancy a "looking forward to seeing you at the wedding" comment.

We go outside the bar. I start to hail Kathy a cab.

"So, she seems really nice, right?" Kathy asks.

"Yeah, she's cool," I say. "I don't think it would be easy no matter who it was."

"But you're okay?" I am touched that Kathy cares so much about my feelings. I am almost feeling guilty about being annoyed that she isn't going to meet Ben, until she adds, "There is not going to be any drama at the wedding, is there?"

"No, there isn't going to be any drama." I am annoyed again. Where is the supportive, cheering friend who hugged me when I crossed the finish line? "Is the wedding all you care about?"

"Of course I care about you, Rebecca." She is growing exasperated with me. "I just want it to be a special day."

That's the same thing she said to Lauryn when Lauryn expressed concern about all of us wearing matching eighty-dollar costume jewelry necklaces.

"It's going to be special. I was just hoping you could meet Ben." She nods like I've reminded her of something.

"You know, I hope he realizes that you are going to be very very busy that day."

I shake my head. "Kathy, I haven't even decided if I'm bringing him, but if I do it won't prevent me from being at your beck and call." She tips her head at me like I'm being a mischievous child.

"Rebecca, don't be so dramatic. Look, here is my cab." Her cab comes at the perfect time for her to make her escape. She kisses me perfunctorily on the cheek.

"Hey." I turn to see Ben and back to where Kathy's cab has already turned. He is never going to meet any of the Big Three.

"Hi," I say. I kiss him, then I kiss him again because I can and it feels good. I always forget how attracted I am to him until the moment I see him.

"What are you doing out here?"

"I just got Kathy a cab and was reminded that she is getting married."

"Nice," he says. "Are you ready for your men to meet?"

"I guess so." Tommy happens to be in the bathroom when we get back to the table, delaying a possible release of my tension even longer.

I introduce him to Janice, John and Nancy. Janice winks at me when she thinks no one is looking, but John is. He shakes his head at her and then winks at me. Ben goes up to get a drink, since there isn't any server in the front of the bar unless you get food. So of course he is waiting for his drink at the bar when Tommy gets back to the table. It's like some sort of French farce. It's too much for this girl to take.

"I think I'm going to put some songs on," Tommy says, getting up to go to the jukebox.

"No!" I yell a little too loudly. The table looks at me inquisitively. Time to cover. "Just wait a sec, I think I saw a bunch of people putting songs on. Who knows how long it will take?"

"Okay, weirdo," he says. But he sits back down.

"Tom," Nancy says reproachfully. I am starting to like her, but I think she might be one of those people who is too nice to have a sense of humor. I find it strange that Tommy is into her, but who am I to question love.

Finally Ben comes back and time seems to stand still when he and Tommy shake hands and greet each other with a "hey, man." I'm certain I could tell you every piece of clothing Nancy had on when I met her and the color of her toenails. But neither Tommy nor Ben seem to be that interested in anything but their beer.

"They put the Bass keg on?" Tommy asks.

"Yeah, it's fresh. No Guinness on tap, unfortunately."

"Tell me about it. It's a real jones."

"Yeah," says Ben, shaking his head. That's it, no big bully pushing match? No "I think we should take this outside and settle it once and for all"? No "Stay away from my woman"? No "I love her like you never did"? No nodding in the joy of the shared knowledge of my expertise in the sack? Don't get me wrong, I wanted them to get along, but I wanted it to be more than a conclusion that each is a cool guy because they like to get their Guinness on.

Boys are nuts.

But we have a good time. It's like we're on a triple date. I miss hanging out with Janice and John. I think now we've crossed the line from just being work friends to actually being call-up-and-hang-out friends. Janice tells me that Jen is fed up with the whole kids' industry. She is planning on going to nursing school.

"That's too bad, she was so into kids."

"I know, but she wanted to do something that mattered."

"Yeah, I was supposed to be a stockbroker," Nancy says.

"Really?" Janice says, leaning into the table.

"Yeah. I interned for like two months and I knew that it wasn't for me. And I know it's not a real job, but I like nannying. I like that I can support myself and still play my cello whenever I want."

"It's so great that you have that," Janice says. I can see she is really impressed. "You may have to deal with kids, but I bet you can clear your mind and focus on your music."

"It's true, and they're great kids. I think, what's more important, helping raise two human beings or putting more money in someone's pocket?"

"That's awesome. Sometimes I just want to get back into painting again," Janice says. "I am just so tired at the end of the day."

"Well, you've got to force yourself to do it," Nancy says, "because in the end it's doing the things that you love that gives you the most peace."

"Yeah," I say, starting to understand the things Tommy likes about her. I think that lately, other than hanging out with Ben, the only thing I love doing is eating. No, wait, that's not true. I loved the idea that kids were seeing what I was creating and it was helping them somehow. That isn't really a tangible action, but it is something I love. Maybe one of these Don concepts will turn into something like that.

"What we do, what I did, is good," I say to both of them. "It's just that we get so far removed from the actual audience, we don't realize it."

"Yeah," Janice says, nodding. "We make things for kids, but when do we ever actually see them?"

"Kids are great," Nancy says. It's obvious, and it's the booze talking, but it's true.

The guys are getting along. They are practically creaming over the possibility of what the final installment of *Lord of the Rings* will offer them. I should have seen it coming. Tommy is clearly the bigger movie and comic buff, but Ben impressed everyone with little-known trivia and John is able to draw a really good Spider-Man on a ketchup-stained napkin.

All of this socializing is helped by copious amounts of alcohol. While the food at Peter McManus is nothing to scoff at, the real reason I love coming here is the consistency of their buy-back policy. For every two drinks you buy, the bar buys you one. If you can walk out of here you're lucky. Nancy is clearly feeling it when her laughter gets louder. Tommy suggests that they head home.

"Oh, yeah, we have a train to catch," she says. It takes me a second to realize she is making fun of Kathy. That's pretty ballsy, and even if it's only because she is drunk, I think it means she feels comfortable with me. Maybe she has a sense of humor, after all.

They say goodbye to the rest of us. Tommy makes sure to tell Ben that it was nice to meet him. When he bends to kiss me goodbye, I whisper that I won't be coming home tonight, if he wants Nancy to sleep over.

"Thank you," he says.

We hang out for another drink. The sun hasn't even gone down yet, but I am buzzed. Janice and John insist that we walk by their new apartment. They smile when they look up at the brownstone on tree-lined Twenty-first Street. Then they catch a cab downtown. We say goodbye and I remind Janice that sooner or later I might snag her away from Explore! to do some top-secret work for Don and me.

Ben and I are far enough west to walk over to the river. I'm glad to be outside walking with my hand in Ben's. The air has turned cooler and I'm still in my T-shirt from the race. He puts his arm around me and points up to the overpass west of Tenth Street. He tells me about all the ecology that is developing there and how someday it will make a great park.

He talks like we'll be together for a long time; this is something I have to stop second-guessing. I think he makes me live in the moment. I tell him that he and Lauryn would get along.

"She's the bird girl, right?" I can't believe that "bird girl" is how people now refer to Lauryn.

"Yeah, I wish you could meet her. Well you will, if you come to the wedding."

"I can still meet her, even if I don't come to the wedding."

"Does that mean you don't want to go?"

"Like I said, I want you to do what you want."

"They breed good men in New Hampshire."

"I think it's you who has good taste."

"Oh, right, now you love Tommy." I smile. Even though I would have enjoyed a little chivalrous drama, I think they are both adults for not trying to eclipse each other.

"I like Janice and John, also. I think you surround yourself with good people."

"Wait until you meet the Big Three. God, I wish you met them five years ago. They were so different."

"I'm sure you were also. Who knows if we would have liked each other then. You might only now have been ready for me." He has a point. "You know, I think you give what you get."

Esme is back. We are walking by the river the way Ben and I were. She isn't talking, but she keeps thinking the words "You have to decide, you have to decide." Is it because I want other people to make my decisions?

"What are you trying to say? Wait!" Esme laughs. Her laugh sounds like mine and the voice-over I picked and the new voice-over she has now. I know she isn't mine anymore and she never will be. I loved her and created her, but now she is out in the world and I have no control of her.

She climbs on the railing. She is going to jump into the Hudson River and I won't see her again after that. She is going to be fine without me, but will I be fine without her?

When I look at her waving goodbye before splashing into the river she actually speaks, "Goodbye, Ms. Cole."

Ms. Cole. I wake up to Ben spooning me. There are tears in my eyes. I think about waking Ben up, but her words stick with me. He sighs in his sleep and squeezes me.

I could be happy writing shows for Don, and I will be. For me, it's easy money. But my shows will always be changed and twisted. I will never be in control. I can deal with that. But I need something more real. I need a connection with people. I want a connection with kids. I don't want to see them behind glass at a focus group. I don't want to only deal with child actors. I'm going to keep writing, but I'm also going to teach.

I am a sucker for those ads on the subway. I'll apply to be a

teacher starting next year and if it doesn't work out, I will find something else. I just want to interact with real kids.

Ben moans. I turn around to face him and kiss him on the lips. He smiles and slowly, pleased with my decision, I start to wake him up.

I get my first check from Don and use it to pay off more than the bare minimum of my credit card. I won't miss the automated voice at Unemployment. I want to go to Nobu Next Door with my jackpot, but instead I take Ben to Other Foods, an amazing organic restaurant where I can get fish and he can get weird grain things that look funny and taste delicious.

I also get a haircut. It's not as young-urban-professional-looking as the one I got when I was promoted to executive producer, but it's shorter with a few layers and I had some red highlights put in that complement my glasses.

Kathy calls me in a panic every day for the entire week before the wedding. Each conversation ends with some kind of demand and a reminder that this has to be a special day.

She wants us all to meet in Westchester at 6:00 a.m to get our hair done in her salon. This isn't a gift, this is another eighty bucks. The majority of my current credit card bill is due to wedding-related costs. I tell her I won't be able to make it that early. I'll do my own hair. I'll be there in time for the pictures at two.

If I hadn't just spent sixty dollars (which was considered a steal) on dress alterations so that the dress is like a second skin, I would think I was out of the wedding.

"What are you doing about your hair?" I hear Kathy gasping. This stress cannot be good for her.

"Kathy, I just got it cut, it's too short to put up. It's going to look really cool."

"Oh, my God. I think I'm getting an ulcer. Your wedding hair is giving me an ulcer."

"Okay," I say. I am trying to adapt a new policy with my friends. "Take a Tums and I'll see you on Saturday at two."

★ ★ ★

"Jesus, what a dress," Ben says from my bed. I'm actually wearing it. "I've seen your breasts and they aren't that big."

I look down and hike up the neckline a little. It doesn't help much. I stare at myself in the full-length mirror. My stomach is definitely flatter than when we first tried the dresses on. Love may make you fat, but Ben being a vegetarian and my constant running has helped make me more toned.

My red glasses sort of match the red dress. The thin red jacket Dina picked out is trimmed in a white cotton faux fur. I can't believe she would pick this out for a wedding in late September. I think Dina's pregnancy made her delusional.

"Why are you smirking? You look pretty. Your date is going to be very impressed." I smile at him. He hasn't put a shirt on. I wish I wasn't already dressed. It's twelve-thirty and I better get going if I don't want to get chastised.

There is a knock at my door. I open it a crack. It's Tommy. I still don't exactly feel comfortable when the two men are in the apartment but Nancy's here, too, in Tommy's room. He smiles when he looks my dress up and down.

"Not a word," I say. "I mean it."

"This beats Lauryn's," he says. I was Lauryn's maid of honor eons ago.

"It's also about ten tempuras cheaper."

"Nice," he says. "Are you ready to go?"

"I'm just waiting for my date," I say.

"Well, your date is here." I open my door a little wider and Lauryn, my date, is standing there with the same dress and the same smirk. Her eyes are sparkling as she rubs the white cotton muff that Kathy paid for. I can't wait to get mine.

"Did somebody say Santa's little helper?"

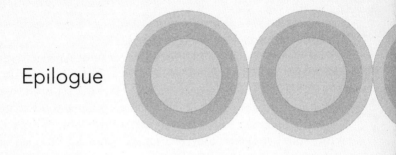

Epilogue

Landslide

We're over at Kathy's new house in Connecticut watching her wedding video for the third time. The last time I fell asleep. It's just the four of us—Kathy, Beth, Lauryn and me. Ron is working late. We are all drinking wine except Kathy. Kathy hasn't said why she isn't having any, but when she leaves the room Lauryn, Beth and I whisper "pregnant" to one another.

We've been talking about alternating these girls' nights since the wedding, but so far this is the first one. Lauryn is back for winter break, so it all worked.

My big news for the night is that I've decided to be a teacher—that I want to make a difference to kids on a more immediate level. As I expected, the girls had mixed responses.

Kathy said, "Oh, boy, we've got to get you some new 'hot for teacher' glasses."

Lauryn clapped and asked, "Did somebody say summer vacation—forever?"

Beth smiled and said, "I could see that, but you are going to have to get up really early."

I find out if I get through the first round of applications next month, then I have to come up with a lesson plan. I think I will focus on world history through foods of the world. I'm hoping I can bribe the judges with snacks.

I won't find out if I make the final cut until April and then my whole summer will be spent in teacher training for next September. That's less than a year away. But I don't want to get ahead of myself. In the meantime, my cooking show, *Brooke Cooks(!),* got picked up and I decided to executive-produce it with Don. I've never done live action before so I'm glad that Don is still around to help. We are casting next week and I'm going to choose the most positive girls out there, no matter what they look like.

I told Don that if I got picked to become a teacher he was on his own for producing season two if it got that far, but I would still write it for as long as he wanted me to. He said as long as I covered for his wedding (in June, to Programming Sarah) he accepted my terms.

I think my ass looks fat in the video, and I keep pointing it out. Beth thinks she looks four months pregnant in her brides-maid dress and we all kind of glance at Kathy to see how she reacts, but she doesn't. I suspect she's waiting until the first trimester is over to tell us.

The cameraman focuses on Nanny Nancy and Tommy ball-room dancing. Since then she's convinced him to take lessons, but even at the early stage I have to admit they make a nice pair.

"Do you want me to fast-forward?" Kathy asks, like she has the past two times.

"No, I wanna get a look at Fred and Ginger," Lauryn says.

"You're so much prettier than she is," Beth says.

"Yeah, she could do more with her hair," Kathy says.

"I'm surprised she can even walk in those heels," Lauryn says.

These girls aren't catty. And I'm being really adult about the whole Tommy thing—for real this time, no attempt at a rat-ings-grabbing reunion—but I still like hearing it. I liked hear-ing it the day of Kathy's wedding when I was wearing an ugly red dress and the straps broke, after I tossed the Santa jacket. I had to hunt for a safety pin and looked lopsided and Nanny Nancy (okay, just Nancy) looked hot in a tight DKNY dress.

I may be an adult, but I'm not that adult.

Although I think the videographer could learn a thing or two about how to frame a shot, the wedding video isn't bad. I've thought about talking to Kathy about the production quality, but she doesn't want to hear it, I'm sure. I like watching this video because the day went so fast. In my mind I only have snippets, pictures out in the cold, how bad Kathy's voice shook when she said her vows, taking my millions of hairpins out at the end of the night and, of course, all of the food.

The video reminds me of everything else. My favorite part is on right now. I look over to see if Lauryn is enjoying it as much as I am. She is. She winks at me and Beth pours us more wine.

All of us together in a circle dancing to a Nina Simone song. There is Beth pinning up Kathy's bustle when someone steps on it.

"God, we're white girls," Lauryn says, and she's right. We look like assholes, but we didn't care then and I don't care now.

"The camera is definitely adding ten pounds to you, Re," Lauryn says, and I swat her.

"And it's all in her ass," Beth hoots.

"Shut up, mommy-to-be," I say to Beth.

"It was all that fucking pasta at the cocktail hour."

My cell phone rings. I know it's Ben calling to tell me what time he's getting off work. I decide not to answer it. I think they are waiting to see if I will. I'll check it on the train back to Grand Central. We still don't live together (I'm still rooming with Tommy), although Ben has the key. I'm looking forward to crawling into bed with him later on tonight, but I'm also looking forward to eating the baked Brie Kathy's got in the oven and finding out about the new guy that Lauryn is dating.

I keep wondering if Lauryn's going to make some other amazing career change, like studying monkeys in Costa Rica or something. She's had coffee with Jordan this morning. She's happy, so I guess it went well.

Ben got Jordan a job as a bartender at Knuckle Sandwich

after Tommy, and then Lauryn, asked me to put in a good word. It seems to be working out.

"Have you used all your wedding presents yet?" Beth asks when the video is over. Kathy got a ton of shit.

"Everything except the crystal shot glasses you guys got me."

"Did somebody say shot glasses?" Lauryn asks, tossing her heavy cardigan off her shoulders. We laugh. The shot glasses cost way too much.

"I guess there's no hope of that, huh?" I ask.

"Why not? I'll get them." She gets up and goes into the kitchen. This will be telltale when she doesn't do the shot. We will be able to confront her about the bun in the oven. There will be no escape from our interrogation. We will know the exact moment the sperm hit the egg.

She comes back with a tray balancing the shot glasses, bread, the Brie and a bottle of Stoli Vanilla. There are four shot glasses. We each grab bread and Kathy pours out four shots. The rest of us are looking at one another, trying to figure it out. Maybe she's bluffing. We watch her, confused.

"Cheers," she says, and holds up her glass. Slowly, we clink, and then down our drinks, and so does Kathy.

"Kath," Beth says, horrified.

"Kathy," Lauryn squeaks.

"What?" Kathy asks.

"You're endangering the life of the child," I say.

"If we're pro-choice it's just a fetus," Beth says, suddenly politically correct. "But really, Kath, what gives?"

"Ever hear of fetal alcohol syndrome?" Lauryn asks.

"What are you guys talking about?"

"Aren't you preggers?" I ask. I can't take it.

"No!" She laughs.

"Why no wine?" Beth asks, still trying to trip her up.

"I wasn't in the mood."

"You're not knocked up?"

"No. I wouldn't be eating Brie, either, if I was." She shakes her head like it's the silliest thing she's ever heard. But I find it interesting that she knows what she can and can't eat. "Do you want another shot?"

"Did somebody say more Stoli?"

Sometimes I wonder how I ever became so tied to these people. What was it that we ever had in common? Was it all just coincidence? Was it just that Lauryn's last name starts with a *D* that made us sit near each other in first grade? What chance put Beth and I together as college roommates? What if Beth hadn't answered Kathy's introductory e-mail? What was it that kept us tied together? What still keeps us?

I don't know all my friends' secrets and they don't know mine. Maybe all the weirdness has just been a phase. But who knows? Maybe it's only just begun. Maybe we're getting to another phase.

My friends can always surprise me and I may not agree with everything they do. On nights like this, doing shots, eating cheese, I don't really care. I can just settle in and just enjoy being with all these women. Somewhere I know that if I need something serious like a hug or something shallow like hearing that I'm prettier than my ex's new girlfriend, I believe they'll be there. Whatever it is that keeps us together, we're here. And I think if we need each other, we'll be there, even if we can't always hang out like we used to. Our friendship is a constant cycle and it will evolve. If taking the bad means getting the good, I'm down. I'm in.

On sale January 2004

Lost & Found

From the author of *Name & Address Withheld,*
Jane Sigaloff

It's no secret that women keep diaries. And it's
no secret that we divulge our innermost thoughts and
feelings in our diaries—as well as life stories we could
never share with the outside world. Now imagine you
lose your diary halfway across the world. Unfortunately
this nightmare is a reality for high-flying London lawyer
Sam Washington. So when TV producer Ben Fisher
turns up on her doorstep, Sam has to wonder if he has
found her diary. And more important—has he read it?

Praise for *Name & Address Withheld*

"...without a doubt an engaging romantic comedy."
—*Booklist*

**RED
DRESS**
I N K
™

Another fabulous read by Ariella Papa

On the Verge

Twenty-three-year-old Jersey girl Eve Vitali is
on the verge of something…whether it be a
relationship, the fabulous life that she reads about
in the Styles section of the *New York Times,* or
a nervous breakdown. Despite her Jackie O suit,
Eve works as an unappreciated assistant for—of all
things—a *bicycle* magazine. Everyone keeps telling
her that she's got her foot in the door, but the rest of
her is surfing the Net and schlepping around with
Tabitha, an Amazonian sex goddess. Between glam
parties, obligatory visits home and myriad men,
Eve is realizing that it takes a lot of work to get
beyond the verge and on to the next big thing.…

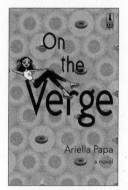